THE CROWN OF BLOOD

BOOK ONE

THE CROWN OF BLOOD

THE SARAVAT CHRONICLES

MANOJ SHITAL BHAVNANI

NU VOICE PRESS

First published by NU VOICE PRESS 2024
An imprint of Hubhawks Pvt. Ltd
www.nuvoicepress.com

This is a work of fiction and all characters and incidents described in this book are the product of the author's imagination. Any resemblance to actual persons, living or dead, is entirely coincidental.

ISBN: 978-81-970218-4-8

Typeset by Saanvi Graphics, Noida
Printed at Nutech Print Services - India
Published by Nu Voice Press

For my November girls.

Author's Note

As with every good fantasy, this book is a tale of discovery, of a world that does not exist, and characters who have never walked the earth.

The pages to come will allow you to journey into this world of my imagination. But I was its first explorer, and there are some truths that it taught me. About the world we do live in. About the humanity I have sought to project into my fantasy universe.

So, here they are:

The cause of almost every human conflict has been one ***man's*** ambition, and millions of lives have been sacrificed to assuage the egos of the few. (I have highlighted **man** here, for it is the exclusive guilt of one gender over the course of history).

The past will almost always dictate our present. For good or bad, is up to each and every person.

Honour is the ficklest commodity in times of strife, and deeds which were once unthinkable become commonplace.

Until women rise to their equal place in society, there can never be true peace on earth.

Peace is like a tree, and even the strongest roots can be uprooted when a greater force arrives.

The greatest heroes are the ones who lose the most, or the ones who are willing to lose the most.

The greatest villains are the ones who lose the most, or the ones who are willing to lose the most.

War begets peace begets war, just as life begets death begets life. The universe is a never-ending cycle, and what begins must end.

Welcome to Saravat.

THE CONTINENT OF
SARAVAT
URVARANYA
SISAMGARH
TRILOH
SAAKIVAN
SAPTAVENI
NAAVIPUR
VANAGARH
VYUSTANAG
HIMBAGAR
DAKSHINASAGARA

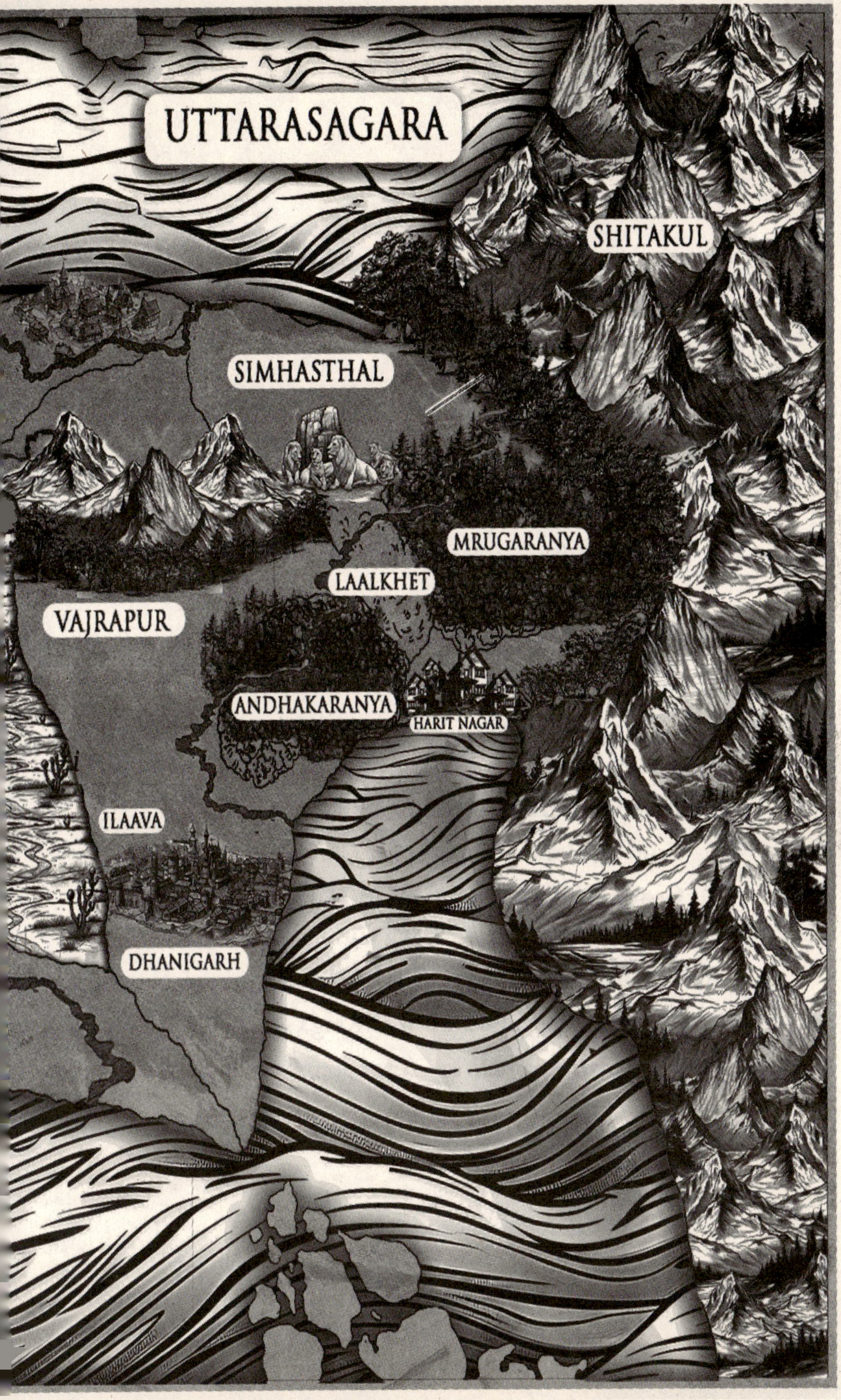
UTTARASAGARA
SHITAKUL
SIMHASTHAL
MRUGARANYA
LAALKHET
VAJRAPUR
ANDHAKARANYA
HARIT NAGAR
ILAAVA
DHANIGARH

List of characters

From Simhasthal:

1. **King Giridhar:** Ruler of Simhasthal
2. **Queen Nandini:** Wife of King Giridhar
3. **Crown Prince Vikrant:** Son of King Giridhar and heir to the throne of Simhasthal
4. **Princess Gayathri:** Firstborn child and only daughter of King Giridhar
5. **Lord Chandran:** Husband of Princess Gayathri
6. **Prince Indranuj:** Youngest child of King Giridhar
7. **General Kashyap:** Commander of the Simhasthali Army and younger brother of King Giridhar
8. **Colonel Gautam:** Husband of General Kashyap
9. **Lord Atulya:** Royal advisor to King Giridhar
10. **Lord Ayushmann:** Minister of Security

From Vajrapur:

1. **King Vijendra:** Ruler of Vajrapur
2. **Queen Indrani:** Daughter of Lord Satwik from Naavipur and wife of King Vijendra
3. **Princess Idhika:** Only child of King Vijendra
4. **Prince Biraj:** Younger half-brother of King Vijendra
5. **General Rannveer:** Commander of the Vajra Army
6. **Lord Jayendu:** Richest and the most influential man in Saravat
7. **Atishi:** Former whore, now in the service of Princess Idhika

From Triloha:

1. **King Theeran:** Ruler of Triloha
2. **Crown Prince Sreedharan:** Firstborn son of King Theeran and heir to the throne of Triloha
3. **Prince Meghnad:** Secondborn son of King Theeran
4. **Princess Jyothika:** Thirdborn child and only daughter of King Theeran, twin to Prince Kartik
5. **Prince Kartik:** Youngest son of King Theeran, twin to Princess Jyothika, also Minister of Security

NINETEEN YEARS AGO

For a month now, death has come knocking for the citizens of Dhaningarh.

And so it does this night, keeping a restless city awake. Lamps and torches burn bright in almost every house, and the rain pitters and patters against tiled roofs—a cold shower which draws out the sweet fragrance of the earth.

The scent does not reach Captain Rannveer, nor his wife Kruttika. A putrid stench overpowers their senses, churning the food in their stomach to mush.

It comes from their son, Sanket, whose wails fill their bedchambers, even as Kruttika rocks him in her arms. Outside, the babe's cry is echoed by dozens of others, rich and poor, young and old, who suffer as he does. *From the fever.*

Rannveer is familiar with the disease. He had seen it before, three years ago, when it burned through his father's body, crushing his bones to powder, before a pale grey sludge poured out of his bowels and ended his life.

That stench had been nauseating but it was nothing compared to the smell which hung over the city. The smell of burning bodies, over five thousand of them—family, friends, strangers, even royalty, like the two older princes who succumbed to the disease, soon to be followed by their families.

In those days, the pyres had burned day and night, and now they do so again. Hundreds have died already; thousands more wait on their deathbeds, among them Crown Prince Vijendra, his younger half-brother Prince Biraj, and Queen Susheela.

And my son, Sanket, Rannveer thinks, as he takes in every detail of his child. The brown of his eyes, the pink of his lips, the soft hairs on his head. He holds a hand up. Short arms. Short legs. *A short life?*

For now, hope remains. The *vaidyas* have learnt from past experience, and their efforts bear fruit. He has heard of three recoveries already. Who knows? His son might yet live.

His wife tugs at his sleeve. *Time for the medicine,* she mouths. He rolls out of bed and walks to the dresser to retrieve a vial of clear crystal glass, holding a white syrupy liquid, the only treatment for the fever.

He carries it back to bed. Kruttika unhooks her blouse and bares a breast, rubs the syrup on her nipple, then brings her child's head to nurse. He latches on greedily, and his throat bobs up and down as the medicine-laced milk flows through to his belly.

Dham! Dham! Dham!

Someone bangs on the front door. Kruttika turns to look at the nightcandle, a time-keeping device with grooves marked to indicate the hours. The candle burns past midnight. She looks questioningly at Rannveer, who shrugs his shoulders, then leaves to see who it is.

Outside, his commanding officer Colonel Prateek stands, soaked by the rain, but palpably excited, with a broad smile stretched across his face. He rushes into the house. "The Prince lives," he shouts. "The Prince lives."

Another survivor. Hope rises in Rannveer's heart. "Which Prince?"

"Both of them," Prateek replies. "Vijendra and Biraj." He grabs Rannveer by the shoulder. "Captain, do you understand what this means for our people? The Crown Prince lives. The plan continues."

Rannveer eyes turn dark as death. *Is this what he thinks is important?*

"Colonel, I am happy to hear of the Prince's recovery," he says, with a sharp edge to his voice. "At this moment, however, I do not care about the plan."

The smile vanishes from Prateek's face, and his mood sobers. "Your son. I had forgotten. Forgive me, my friend. How is he?"

Rannveer's anger dissipates. "His fever remains."

"Have you given him the medicine?" Prateek asks.

"We have," Rannveer says.

Prateek looks relieved. "Then you must stay hopeful, my dear Captain. I have been getting reports of survivors from across the city."

"I have heard the rumours," Rannveer says, "And hope to be one of them soon." He glances at the door. "Forgive me, Colonel, but I must return to my boy. Kruttika needs me."

"Of course, of course," Prateek mutters. He clasps Rannveer's shoulder. "It will be fine. You will see. Sanket will recover. And all we have dreamed for our children will come true."

He leaves, and Rannveer returns to his bedchamber to find his wife sleeping. Sanket lies beside her. His tiny chest heaves erratically, and the nauseating stench grows in the room.

Rannveer recognises the signs. He had seen them right before his father died. His heart catches in his throat as he gets into bed and rolls to his side, facing away from wife and child. Outside, the rain falls heavier, a thundering omen of doom.

A little while later, Kruttika screams.

Rannveer does not turn to face her. He feels her anguish in his heart, even as his mind turns to the future—the one his son will never see.

Crown Prince Vijendra survives, and their dream survives with him. One day, they will march across the continent, and elevate him to the greatest title in the land.

Emperor of Saravat.

SARAVAT

The peninsular continent is an ancient land, home to hundreds to tribes for over seven thousand years, who lived simply and fought violently, over land and food and water. Boundaries existed beyond the realm of their imagination, until fifteen hundred years ago, when the first kingdom was formed.

Triloha (the land of lead, iron and gold)
Capital: Sisamgarh

The Trilohans have always been a force to reckon with. Gold made them wealthy, lead and iron made them powerful, and they soon claimed almost a third of Saravat as their territory.

Vajrapur (the lords of lightning)
Capital: Dhaningarh

The Vajras arrived from a distant land to challenge the might of Triloha, and establish a kingdom that stretched from the western coast all the way to the Rodasi mountains. Over time, they set aside their warrior ways, turning to trade instead, an area in which they were soon outmatched by the Naaviks.

Naavipur (the seafarers)
Capital: Himbagarh

Originally, the Naaviks were underlings of the Vajras, who worked them hard and paid them little. However, with the assistance of the Trilohans, the Naaviks managed to throw off the yoke and stake claim over half of Vajrapur.

Saptaveni (the land of seven rivers)
Capital: Vanagarh

The Saptas are made up of peoples who renounced violence and moved to the western coast, where the dense forests offered them all the protection they would ever need. They remain a part of Saravat, but live separate and in secret, and their citizens are rarely seen outside the forest land.

Simhasthal (the roaring lions)
Capital: Kuragarh

Only five hundred years old, it is the youngest of the five kingdoms, named after its founder, the great King Simha, who led a tribe over the Rodasi mountains, fought bloody battles with Vajrapur, and laid claim to the eastern half of their kingdom.

CHAPTER ONE

So, this is what war looks like.

Vikrant had read many books, heard many stories—of the heroes' brave deeds and the villains' sinful crimes. But they never spoke of this, of the true horror of war, where thousands of scared men fight thousands of scared men to death.

The Simhasthalis and the Vajras battle, and the verdant grass of the Laalkhet lie crushed beneath them. The groans of the dying echo in the clearing, while the dead rot in the broiling sun, the air swelling with the stink of blood and shit and piss.

The smell stokes Vikrant's fear, yet he fights on. So does the Vajra soldier, a boy with wispy hair for a beard. The boy swings wildly, hoping, rather than aiming, to kill. Vikrant keeps his patience, and dances to the awkward strikes. He can afford to.

The boy wears ill-fitting armour, roughly painted crimson and made for a man twice his size. Vikrant, on the other hand, wears his armour like a second skin. The sturdy grey steel glints in the hot sun, and a ferocious white lion roars from his breastplate, once the scourge of his people, now the symbol of his kingdom.

The Vajra lunges. And misses. Vikrant does not. He swings his sword with deathly intent. Steel slices through flesh, and warm blood sprays his face.

The boy with the wispy beard falls to the ground. The adrenalin dulls, and Vikrant feels his fear return, gripping him as tight as the drenched clothes beneath his armour.

I remain the little rabbit, he whispers to himself, recalling his nickname, given to him by his people, for his nature being that of a scared boy, which is an unusual trait for the Crown Prince of Simhasthal.

Then again, he has always been an unusual Simhasthali.

Unlike his broad and muscular clansmen, he stands tall and slender, narrow-faced, with cheeks that blush with the pink of innocence. But his dark brown eyes speak of his intelligence, far above average for a boy of twenty.

Vikrant takes stock of the battle. The scouts had reported an enemy force twenty thousand strong, but he counts over forty. The Vajras have deceived the Simhasthalis into abandoning the safety of their fortress. Only one option remains now.

They must sound the retreat.

Vikrant searches for his father, his King, the only man who can give the command. But the crush of the battle is too thick, and the men are indistinguishable from one another.

He tries to spot the Parasu instead. The royal guards in their black armour should be easier to pick out. Moments later, he has them. Up the field, a few hundred metres to his right. Surprisingly, they stand with their swords by their sides. Even his chacha, General Kashyap, stands with his blade pointed at the ground.

Ahead of them, two men fight to the death.

The first is King Vijendra, ruler of Vajrapur, the man who set this battle in motion. Vikrant notices how he fights with a slight limp. The Vajra is wounded, but not as badly as his opponent, who staggers in front of him, barely able to keep his balance.

King Giridhar, ruler of Simhasthal.

Vikrant's eyes widen. *My father*.

CHAPTER TWO

Death is a sweet release.

The philosophers often claimed this, but Giridhar had never believed them. What do those quill pushers know of death, never having stared it in the face? Now, however, he hopes they were right, for the sake of his men.

Across the battlefield, they fall by the hundreds, slaughtered by the Vajras, by their hatred. Where the hate comes from, Giridhar cannot say. The two kingdoms have been at peace for over seventy years, a peace that now drowns in a river of red. *How did this come to pass,* he wonders. Only five months ago, he had travelled to Vajrapur to attend the coronation of the man he once called brother. Upon his return to Simhasthal, a missive had arrived.

From Vijendra.

Pledge your army and your fealty, he had said. Join him in his conquest of Saravat, and once he is crowned Emperor, he will name Vikrant his heir.

Giridhar could not believe it. As a child, Vijendra had spent many summers in Kuragarh, the capital of Simhasthal. They had played together, trained together.

And now, they stare each other down in a battle to death.

Two years separate the Kings, but in stature, they are as apples to oranges. Forty-five years of age, Giridhar stands six and a half feet tall, a bull among men, with his wide-barrel chest and tree-sized limbs. Streaks of grey run through his thick beard and long hair, and his broad face is fearsome, much like the roaring white lion emblazoned on his armour.

He towers over most men, as he does Vijendra, who stands half a foot shorter. A slender man, seemingly not much to look at in his crimson armour, with the gold lightning bolt emblem of the Vajras running across his chest.

But appearances are deceptive. Steel courses through the muscles of Vijendra's lithe frame, and what he lacks in stature and physique, he makes up for in agility and technique.

Their fight has taken its toll on Giridhar, and his blood oozes from a dozen cuts. He has inflicted a few on the Vajra, but the younger King has shrugged them off.

Vijendra casually grips his sword and prowls around his prey. "Give up, my friend. This bloodshed is needless. If only you had listened—"

"Listened?" Giridhar roars. "To your stupid plans? Your father's ashes lay warm on the ground, his crown new upon your head, and you sought to become Emperor of Saravat." He spits, and his blood stains the grass. "And now, you betray his memory and our friendship by declaring war on my kingdom."

Vijendra chuckles. "My father was a weak man, and a stupid one at that. He sat and twiddled his thumbs while his kingdom grew poorer. No, my friend, I cannot let that stand. There was a time when my ancestors ruled, from Naavipur all the way to the Rodasi. They were great men. But I will be greater. For I will rule all of Saravat."

"First, you must defeat Simhasthal," Giridhar says.

Vijendra smirks. "Simhasthal has already fallen. Look at my army. They were ready for this war years ago. Even when my father was King, they were loyal to me." His eyes shine with excitement. "As are many in the five kingdoms."

A shocked Giridhar lowers his blade. "You have spies? In my kingdom?"

Vijendra grins, broad and triumphant. "My friend, why do you think your scouts reported only half my army's strength?"

Giridhar struggles to contain his emotions. Loyalty is the bedrock upon which Simhasthal was built. It now crumbles to dust before his very eyes.

Is this to be my legacy, Giridhar wonders. *Stabbed in the back by my own?* He shoves the doubts aside. "My army may fall today, but your plan remains as foolish as before. You know you cannot succeed."

"I can," Vijendra says, "And I will. I beg you to see reason."

"You ask too much then," Giridhar says. "My ancestors signed a treaty to keep the peace. I will not forgo their honour or mine."

"Not even for your son?" Vijendra asks.

"Not even for Vikrant," Giridhar replies. "You claim you will name him your heir. But your promise means little." Anger blazes in his eyes. "I know what you seek. To make him your puppet, your slave. I will not allow that. Never."

Vijendra's smile turns sad. "Then you must die."

Giridhar roars as he raises his sword. "Come kill me. If you can."

He lunges forward. Vijendra blocks his thrust, then goes on the attack. Blood loss has weakened Giridhar, and a stronger

Vijendra forces him to defend. The Vajra's blade swings with thunderous strength, pummelling the Simha into submission.

Death appears certain, and Giridhar desperately searches for a new strategy. A risky move comes to mind. He had learnt it as a young man, when he was a student of the Parasu. Can it save him today?

He has no choice. He must try.

Giridhar pretends to stumble. His faltering feet offer Vijendra a sudden height advantage. The Vajra's strikes grow bolder and quicker, forcing him to hold up his sword in defence.

Once he has Vijendra focused on getting past his blade, he makes his move. A *kukri* lies concealed in his armour. With his free hand, he unsheathes it and grips it loosely, out of Vijendra's sight, waiting for the right moment to strike.

It arrives all too soon.

An exasperated Vijendra tires of the stalemate, and raises his sword high, driving his full force behind his strike. But before he can bring his blade down, Giridhar attacks.

The kukri flies through the air, its sharp edge destined for Vijendra's jugular. *You are mine*, he wants to scream, but the joy dies in his throat.

At the very last moment, Vijendra twists his head away, and the dagger slashes through empty air. Giridhar's eyes widen in shock, which soon turns to fear when he sees the triumphant grin on his enemy's face.

He was expecting the attack.

Vijendra spins his foe around and aims his sword at the new chink in Giridhar's armour. The gap, where the kukri had once been. But it isn't there now, and the Vajra blade sinks deep into the flesh, between the ribs, and stabs a lung.

Giridhar slumps to his knees. Blood froths through his lips as his eyes fall upon Kashyap. It pains him to see the sadness on his younger brother's face. Through thick and thin they have been together, and now death parts them.

He turns his gaze to the Parasu, but their feelings remain hidden behind their black masks. In his mind, Giridhar thanks them for their service, and regrets that he failed them in the end.

And then, he spots his son, a hundred feet away, battling hard in a desperate attempt to get to his father. A weak smile crosses Giridhar's face. It is too late now.

A gentle hand squeezes his shoulder. "I am impressed, my friend," Vijendra says. "The rabbit has some courage after all."

He detaches a horn from his belt, raises it to his lips and blows. Its wild screech deafens the ears.

Haarruuuuuppphhh!

The battle comes to a halt. All eyes turn to the sound. Vikrant turns as well, and Giridhar sees the horror writ across his face.

Vijendra calls out to him. "Tell me, little rabbit, what will you do now?"

CHAPTER THREE

On an unusually cool October afternoon, seven-year-old Vikrant rides with his father on the Laalkhet. The grasslands dance in the bright sunshine, as the Parasu march their horses across—*clip-clop, clip-clop*—in perfect step. They are no ordinary fighters. They are the protectors of the royal family of Simhasthal, whose oath is as famous as their bravery.

"Dead we are now, death to our enemy.
For Simha, for Simhasthal."

Vikrant finds them fearsome, armoured in black from head to toe, with alert eyes peering out through holes cut into their black masks. At full strength, they number a hundred. On this day, however, forty soldiers ride across the grasslands. Watchful. Silent.

His father, King Giridhar, rides ahead of them. Thirty-two years of age, he wears a blue kurta over a black shalwar. Simple attire for such a powerfully built man, whose wavy hair and thick beard mark him as a true descendant of the great King Simha.

The same cannot be said of Vikrant, however. The Crown Prince is dressed the same as his father, yet it only gives him the appearance of being scrawnier than he is.

His father raises his hand and barks out a command. "Parasu. On guard."

They spread out in groups of four, then turn to cover all sides, until the King and Prince are safe within their ring of protection. An unworried Giridhar surveys the fields, the way they ebb and flow, like waves in the ocean. He dismounts, and signals for Vikrant to do the same. The horses enjoy a grassy lunch as father and son walk together.

"Do you know where we are?" Giridhar asks.

"I don't, baba," Vikrant says.

"This is the Laalkhet," Giridhar informs him.

"*Laal?*" Vikrant rushes to correct his father. "Baba, it is green, not red."

Giridhar smiles at his childish innocence. "Gaze upon these fields through the eyes of history, my son. For centuries, this was the forgotten land, until King Simha fought King Suryakumar of Vajrapur. It has seen over a hundred battles since, and the blood of hundreds of thousands has nourished its soil." He bends and comes up with a fistful of mud, which he lets fall. "This is our sacred land."

Vikrant views the plains with renewed wonder. His childish mind conjures visions of the battles, men fighting and dying, blood streaming through the fields.

"Baba, have you ever fought here?" he asks.

"Once. Before you were born."

"Did you kill many men?"

"One."

Vikrant is surprised. "Only one?"

Giridhar raises his eyebrows. "You think that is too little? Perhaps now you think less of your father?"

Vikrant holds his tongue. He does not wish to give offence.

"Look at the men behind us," Giridhar commands. Vikrant turns to the alert Parasu. "A few of them fought with me that day," Giridhar says. "There was this foreign tribe. The Pathikals. They arrived here and claimed the Laalkhet for themselves."

A wistful look crosses his face. Vikrant cannot be sure, but he seems almost sad.

"They weren't many," Giridhar continues. "Maybe seven thousand. Mostly women, children, and elderly. But it was an affront to Simhasthal. And to your grandfather, King Hridhyanshu, who commanded me to deal with them. So, I rode out with fifteen hundred soldiers."

"Only fifteen hundred soldiers?" asks Vikrant, astonished. "Against seven thousand?"

"Fifteen hundred Simhas," Giridhar corrects his son, "Against twenty-five hundred of their warriors. They were untrained foot soldiers, and our men tore into them. Some of the Parasu killed five, some ten, some fifteen."

Vikrant glances at his guards, his fear of them now greater than ever.

"And I killed one," Giridhar continues his story. "But that man... he was the one worth killing. Dhanesh, chief of the nomads. A brave and skilled warrior. Our duel lasted almost an hour, and there were times when he could have killed me. But I had better armour." He draws his weapon, and sunrays dance along its blade. "And a better sword. In the end, his death was inevitable."

"What about his tribe, baba?" Vikrant asks. "Did you kill them all?"

Giridhar shakes his head. "We are not the lions of the jungle, my son. We are the lions of Simhasthal. We hunt the strong, but never prey on the weak. I let his tribe return to their war-torn lands across the Dakshinasagara, and bound them to an oath to never set foot on Saravati land again." He senses his son's nervousness. "Does war scare you?"

Vikrant nods his head.

"Do you know what they call you behind your back?" Giridhar asks.

"A rabbit," Vikrant replies.

"Do you know why?" Giridhar asks.

Vikrant does, but is ashamed to admit it. "No."

His father does not let him off easily. "It is because you are small. And because you flee at the first sign of danger." Giridhar squeezes his son's shoulder and speaks to him kindly. "One day, you will be King, and the duty to uphold justice will fall upon you." He rests his blade upon his palm. "Now, you can dispense justice by the edge of a sword. Or… you could dispense true justice."

Vikrant is confused. "True justice?"

"With the wisdom of your heart and mind," Giridhar says. "You are a clever child. Guru Vedant believes you will be the wisest king of us all. But a wise king knows he cannot be a coward. The days of innocence are at an end. You are the Crown Prince, and you have to be strong."

Giridhar taps his sword on his son's scabbard. Vikrant pulls out a blunt blade, barely a third as long as his father's.

Giridhar leans in and whispers. "Are you a rabbit or a lion?"

"A lion," Vikrant answers timidly.

"And do you know what makes a lion fearsome?" Giridhar asks.

Vikrant does not.

"His roar," Giridhar says. "Roar, and attack."

Vikrant screams, "Roaarrr," and swings his sword. His father defends the blow with ease. Steel rings against steel with a dull thunk.

"Again," Giridhar commands.

"Rooooaaaarrr," Vikrant shouts, and swings his sword. An easy defence, a dull thunk.

"Again," Giridhar shouts.

"Rooooaaaaaaaarrrrrrr," the boy Prince screams his lungs out, and swings his sword with all his might.

THUNK!

Steel meets steel, but the sound is no longer dull. A smile breaks across Giridhar's face, and for the first time in his young life, Vikrant believes his father is proud of him.

CHAPTER FOUR

The memory fades, lost to time.

Vikrant watches the man who taught him bravery, on his knees, with the enemy's sword at his neck. His father, his King, now at death's door. He wants to scream, but it dies in his throat. His feet turn to stone, and he can hear his heart, not in his chest, but in his ears, a throbbing beat which grows louder with each passing moment.

His gaze turns to Vijendra, who has brought war and death to their door. The Vajra King smiles as he swings his sword. The murderous steel slices through Giridhar, and takes his head off in one clean stroke. For a second, his body remains frozen. Then it slumps to the ground.

The severed head rolls to rest a few feet away. Grief grips Vikrant's heart; fear numbs his mind. His father is dead. The command is now his. He knows he must order the retreat, but he cannot find the strength.

Fortunately, Kashyap still keeps his wits. "Parasu, protect the Crown Prince."

The Parasu, those forty-three who yet survive, surround Vikrant in an impregnable ring of steel and flesh. Kashyap raises his sword above his head and swings it in a circle.

Once. Twice. Thrice.

At the edge of the Mrugaranya, many watchers sit on high branches, their sharp eyes following the battle and making reports. One watcher, however, has eyes only for the General.

He sees the signal, and brings a horn to his lips. Four times it sounds, before the call is repeated, over and over.

Huuuu! Huuuu! Huuuu! Huuuu!
Huuuu! Huuuu! Huuuu! Huuuu!
Huuuu! Huuuu! Huuuu! Huuuu!

The retreat begins. The Simhasthalis fall back, yet Vikrant refuses to move. Colonel Gautam, husband to his *chacha* General Kashyap, arrives by his side and grabs the Prince by the arm. "Please, Your Highness. We must go."

The words barely register. Vikrant's gaze remains fixed on his father's head lying in the mud. *How can I leave his body behind?*

A sixth sense makes him look up, and he sees the Vajra King watching him. Across the field, the two take stock of one another. Then, Vijendra laughs and waves his dismissal, before he turns and walks away.

Vikrant watches him go, and confusion clouds his mind. *I am right here. Why does he not strike?*

Gautam's grip tightens on his shoulder. "Please, Your Highness."

Vikrant stares at the departing figure of Vijendra one last time, then turns and joins the retreat.

CHAPTER FIVE

The candle burns at the midnight hour, as a tired Atulya gazes out the window.

Only fifty years of age, he already feels like an old man, thanks to his aching knees. There is a weakness in his bones, the vaidyas say, likely caused by the cold which blows from the mountains and bites at his shawl. He remains warm enough, though. The fireplace roars in the corner, and many torches are lit in his cosy office, making the weather tolerable.

He glances down at the city of Kuragarh, the capital of Simhasthal, which appears less bright than it was an hour ago. The citizens retire after another anxious day. But there will be no rest for Atulya.

Not yet.

Fifteen years ago, King Giridhar had shocked one and all when he appointed the soft-spoken schoolmaster as his royal advisor. Atulya had proved all the naysayers wrong. Over the years, his advice and cunning had staved off many problems, and even put a nobleman or two in their place.

But that cunning had deserted him a month ago, when Vijendra declared war on Simhasthal. An unexpected move. The Vajra was new to the throne, and a good friend of both

Giridhar and Kashyap. He had spent many childhood summers in Kuragarh, and was well-liked in the city.

Still, Atulya should have uncovered Vijendra's deceit before it was too late. The failure was his, and now others pay the price in blood.

The door opens, and his assistant, Shardul, walks in with a tired and bloodied infantryman. Atulya addresses the soldier. "Tell me you have good news."

The man bows his head and speaks in a pained voice. "My lord, King Giridhar fell in battle against King Vijendra."

Atulya's legs turn to jelly.

My friend is no more.

He recovers quickly. His grief can wait. Right now, he must remain strong.

"And the Prince?" he asks.

A sliver of relief creeps into the soldier's voice. "Prince Vikrant lives, my lord. He rides home with the survivors."

Atulya sighs, and holds the soldier by the arms. "I am grateful for your service," he says, before turning to Shardul. "Take him to the vaidyas. And bring him a hot meal from the kitchens."

Shardul nods his head and leaves with the soldier. The door closes behind them, and the veneer of calm deserts Atulya. A lonely tear rolls down his cheek as he shuffles across the room to the corner cabinet. From it, he retrieves a firewood chest, made from the sturdy tree found in the Mrugaranya, and polished so fine it glows as if ablaze.

Atulya touches his forehead to the box. "Farewell, my friend."

Cradling the chest under his arm, he leaves the room. The journey to the Queen's chambers is up a few levels and through a few corridors. The white lion roars at him from every corner, and old Kings sit within gilded frames, studying him as he walks past. They were fierce men, who lived long and hard lives.

And now, they will welcome another in their midst.

He enters the royal quarters. Surprised guards jump to attention. They notice the box, and whispers grow in his wake as he arrives at the Queen's chambers. A few handmaidens gossip and giggle outside, but fall silent when they see him.

"I wish to see the Queen," Atulya says.

None question the inappropriateness of the late hour. The kingdom is at war, and normal courtesies are forfeit. A handmaiden rushes to rouse her mistress. She returns a few minutes later and rejoins her group.

Queen Nandini follows soon after, dressed in a sober yellow sari. If she feels the chill, she does not show it. Her red eyes search Atulya's face for answers. "My lord, is there news from the battle?"

Atulya kneels. A painful struggle, considering the problems with his knees. He holds up the box and declares in a loud voice. "I pass this honour to you." His voice catches in his throat as he utters the last word. "Ranimaa." Queen Mother.

Nandini notices the box, and the colour drains from her face. Atulya feels sorry for her.

It is an old Simhasthali tradition. Before a King goes to battle, he must surrender his symbol of authority to his royal advisor. If he lives, it is returned to him. If he dies, it passes to his Queen, who holds it in trust for the Crown Prince.

Nandini's hands tremble as she opens the wooden chest. Inside, on a bed of black satin, rests the golden crown of the King of Simhasthal.

CHAPTER SIX

Jayendu tosses and turns in bed.

This summer has been hotter than most, but that is not why he loses sleep. His mind wanders to the Laalkhet, to thoughts of battle. The plan he had hatched decades ago is now set in motion, while he lies in bed, clueless of its outcome.

Patience. He must have plenty of it. He has waited decades for this news. He can wait a few days more.

A *myna*'s song travels across the chamber and sings in his ears. Jayendu can picture it in his mind, for he has heard its melody a thousand times. In the gardens. In the fields. In the forests. Back when he was a young man travelling the world.

He opens his eyes to see it perched upon the windowsill, gazing at his luxurious chambers. His late wife would regard the sighting as a favourable omen.

But Jayendu cares little for omens. If his seven and a half decades on this earth have taught him anything, it is that good fortune only favours the brave.

A sharp pain shoots through his body. A sad state of affairs. Lord Jayendu, the richest man in Saravat, richer than the Kings even, yet all the money in the world cannot soothe his aches, nor can it reverse the ravages of time.

Though he was never a handsome man, the years have made his features even more grotesque. His nose is crooked, his eyes clouded, and a large scar runs across his face, a permanent reminder of a teenage mishap. Most of his hair fell many moons ago, as did half his teeth, and his skin hangs wrinkled beneath his nightshirt.

He laughs. Old age has a sadistic sense of humour. It leaves you just enough to get by, and without warning, snatches even that away.

He pulls on the rope hanging by his bedside. A few seconds pass before his attendant, Datta, walks in with a cup of warm honey water.

Jayendu sips the drink and sighs, then notices the scroll in his servant's hand. "What is it?"

Datta offers him the paper. "My lord, this arrived an hour past midnight. It was hand delivered by an infantryman returning from the Laalkhet."

"Why wasn't I woken up?" asks Jayendu, annoyed.

Datta stares at his feet. His master's temper is legendary, and on an empty stomach, twice as deadly. "Apologies, my lord. I had visited your chambers. But I could not rouse you."

Jayendu glares at Datta. *Does he lie, or is his concern for my well-being genuine?*

His anger vanishes once he reads the message. A smile breaks across his face, and he leaps off the bed, startling Datta, who rushes to catch his master. But Jayendu does not fall. He feels like he has risen for the very first time.

"Giridhar is dead," he declares. "The gods be praised. Giridhar is dead."

This is excellent news indeed. The conquest of Simhasthal was only the first step in his plan to crown Vijendra as Emperor of Saravat. There is much more left to do.

"Quickly," he tells Datta. "Send a message to the palace. Ask for an audience with the Queen. No. Wait. Don't ask. Demand. We have plans to make."

In his excitement, he fails to notice the worried look on Datta's face. He shouts at him. "Why are you still standing here? Run. Go to the palace."

"My lord," Datta says, "The Queen is not at the palace."

"What do you mean?" asks Jayendu, confused.

"My son, Omkar, was at Dhaningarh," Datta says. "He goes every day to deliver milk. This morning, he spotted the Queen's convoy ride out the gates under the guard of Captain Sambhit."

Jayendu's joy turns to ash, and he grabs Datta by the shoulder. "Princess Idhika? Was the Princess with her?"

"Omkar spoke to one of the palace guards," Datta says. "Queen Indrani and Princess Idhika ride to join King Vijendra at the Laalkhet."

Jayendu loses his balance. Fortunately, Datta catches him before he falls and injures himself. He guides his master to the bed and sits him down. "My lord, are you okay?"

Jayendu stares at him, neither comprehending his words nor registering his presence. His thoughts lie with the King. His King. The King he had chosen.

Vijendra, you fool, he cries to himself, *what have you done?*

CHAPTER SEVEN

An hour after dawn, Prince Biraj emerges from his tent. The muggy air embraces him warmly, and within seconds, his kurta clings to his skin.

He surveys the Laalkhet, which looks different now. The Vajra camp stretches across the land as far as the eye can see, leaving few signs of the bloody battle which took place only fifteen days ago. The dead had been cremated, and the putrid smell of burning flesh had lingered for many days, a cloying stench Biraj hopes never to smell again.

The older soldiers, however, were not put off by it. Nor was his brother. They had lived through the great fever which ravaged their capital a generation ago, when the dead had burned for months.

Once the embers cooled, the ashes were collected and sent for immersion. Now, there is nothing to do but wait. The men keep themselves occupied with archery games, *kabaddi* tourneys, even festival sword fights, which do little to still their anxious minds.

Biraj empathises with their frustration. They had the enemy on the run. The Simhasthalis were wounded, and their retreat through the Mrugaranya would be slow.

Easy prey, for an energised and victorious army.

But the Vajra horn had blown mere seconds later. A call to stand down. The battle was over. He had stood with his battalion, watching the enemy vanish into the forest. The die had been cast. And now all wait for his brother to decide their next move.

As he makes his way across the field, men stop and bow. To an unsuspecting observer, their behaviour might appear born out of respect. It is, but not for his royal position. He carries a far weightier title.

The survivor.

Twenty-two years ago, a fever raged through the capital of Vajrapur, taking the old and the young, the rich and the poor. The royal family thought they had walled themselves off. A deadly mistake. The illness took hold of the older sons of King Dhirendra, and the fate of the continent shifted.

Though he had an heir in Vijendra, the King's advisors convinced him he needed a spare. Just in case. Vijendra's mother died trying to deliver a stillborn, and the King married again, far too soon for the Crown Prince's liking. Their relationship never recovered.

The new Queen, Susheela, was quick to conceive. A boy, whom she named Biraj.

The spare.

The kingdom rejoiced, but its joy was short-lived. The fever returned, and once again, took hold of the royal family. The heir. And the spare. Vijendra was to celebrate his twenty-third name day. Biraj was yet to see his first.

This time, however, forty-three survived, including Vijendra and Biraj.

The survivors.

That is what the forty-three came to be known as. Superstition soon decreed that fate was on their side, that their deeds would resonate across the centuries.

A false belief.

Only twenty-two of the survivors yet lived, and none had performed any deeds which could be considered great. None, except Vijendra, who sets out to become the first Emperor of Saravat.

Biraj enters the King's tent, and sees his future stand before him.

Twenty-two years separate them, yet the two are like twins, dark-skinned and handsome, square-faced, with stubby noses and high foreheads. And they are tall, not as tall as Simhasthalis, but taller than most Vajras.

Biraj finds his brother deep in discussion with General Rannveer. They turn when he walks in, and Vijendra greets him with a warm smile. "I feared you would sleep the morning away."

Biraj bows his head. "That would be an achievement, *dada*, given this sticky weather."

Vijendra chuckles. "True, true. Come, join us."

Biraj stands by his brother's side and smiles at Rannveer, who acknowledges his presence with a formal bow. Biraj likes the man, a trusted commander whose loyalty stretches back to the days when he was a young Captain, yet to make a name for himself.

He turns his attention to the map of Saravat spread across the table. Five kingdoms divide the bird-shaped continent. Saptaveni sits at its head, Triloha, Naavipur, and Vajrapur on its wings and belly, and at its tail, Simhasthal.

The last Kingdom is the topic of discussion. The location for the attack is marked out. A camp, spread across the valley of the Rodasi, encircling the fortress.

"So, it will be a siege?" Biraj asks.

"If it comes to that," Vijendra says. "But it won't."

Biraj looks confused, and Rannveer explains. "The Simhasthalis are a proud race, Your Highness. They built an impregnable fortress, but not once have they hidden behind its high walls."

"That is good news," Biraj says. "Their men are wounded and tired. The battle will be short."

Vijendra glares at Biraj. "Keep your confidence in check, brother. If it soars too high, the next battle might just see our heads rolling in the dirt."

Chastised, Biraj lowers his head in apology.

"Besides," Vijendra continues, "It will not come to war either."

Biraj is confused. "Forgive me, dada. I do not understand."

"You do not need to," Vijendra says. "I have another task for you."

Rannveer averts his eyes. Biraj catches his meaning. The General is aware of the battle plan, but Vijendra has deemed his brother unfit to be privy to the information.

Others might take offence, but Biraj does not. He cares little for politics, or power. A loyal soldier. That is all he aspires to be.

He wonders what the task is. The last one had been pretty distasteful. Vijendra had commanded him to have Giridhar's head stitched to his body and sent home.

"See to it personally," he had said.

And Biraj had obeyed. He had stood in the tent as the vaidyas expertly sewed the head back on. They had washed Giridhar clean, his armour as well, before they dressed him and laid him in a ceremonial chariot. Biraj had placed Giridhar's sword beside him, and said a quick prayer for the dead King. Then, he had sent the chariot on its way.

To Kuragarh.

And now, another task awaits. "What are your orders, dada?"

Vijendra points to a spot on the map, a few miles away from the fortress city. "The guides will bring you to a tunnel here, which leads to the rear entrance of the palace."

Biraj nods his head. "What must I do there?"

"I have a spy inside." The look of astonishment on Biraj's face brings a smile to Vijendra's. "You will meet with him and find out all you can. Their strategies, their strength. And most importantly, what they think of their new King."

"Vikrant," Biraj says.

"The little rabbit, yes," Vijendra says. "I wish to know what the boy has grown up to become."

Biraj remains unsure of the purpose of his task, but he does not question his brother. "As you command, Your Majesty." He hesitates a moment, then decides he must raise the issue which gnaws at his mind. "Forgive me, dada. This war could be over in a week's time. Why do we not press our advantage?"

"You are mistaken, my brother," Vijendra says. He holds Biraj by the shoulders, his grip strong and certain. "Our advantage has yet to arrive."

Though his confusion remains, Biraj does not press the issue. He bows and leaves the tent to prepare for his departure. A journey shrouded in darkness, as are his brother's plans for the battle of Simhasthal.

His mind returns to their conversation. Vijendra has always had a flair for the dramatic, and Biraj's mind cannot shake off its curiosity. *What advantage does my brother speak of?*

CHAPTER EIGHT

A familiar terror follows Captain Sambhit.

The unnatural silence of the Andhakaranya stands the hairs on his neck. He rides across the dimly lit forest, wary of predators and bandits who lurk in the shadows, waiting for the right moment to pounce.

Most travellers prefer to take the long road around the forest, bypassing its dangers. But Sambhit has his orders. A royal command from the King himself, to ferry the Queen and her daughter to the Laalkhet within the week.

Still, his caravan progresses at a leisurely pace, for he does not wish to cause the royals any discomfort. Two days have passed without incident, and he hopes the Queen is impressed. Who knows? Maybe she will whisper a few words of praise in the King's ear. But first, they must arrive at their destination. Unharmed, and in a good mood.

Sambhit turns his gaze skywards. He senses the dark deepening, marking the setting of the sun.

"Halt," he shouts.

The convoy comes to a stop. His second-in-command, Lieutenant Abhay, rides over.

"We will camp here tonight," Sambhit instructs his junior. "Clear a space for the royal tent. And set up a perimeter."

"As you command," says Abhay, and sets his men to work.

Minutes later, a soldier rides over. No, not a soldier. Sambhit does not know his name, but his green uniform marks him out as a Queen's guard.

"You have been summoned," the man says. He does not wait for a reply, and rides back the way he came.

Creases frown on Sambhit's forehead. What could the Queen want? He rides to the royal chariot, dismounts, and approaches the window. A thick mesh covers the opening, helping keep the insects out while letting the cool breeze in.

The honeyed voice of Princess Idhika calls out. "Captain Sambhit?"

Thank the gods. He had feared to hear the sharp tongue of the Queen, but the soft voice of the Princess is like music to his ears. He jumps to attention and bows. "Your command, my Princess."

"My mother wishes to know how much longer before we join my father."

"Seven days, Your Highness," Sambhit says. "Eight at the most."

"Eight days, is it?" Idhika's voice remains soft. "Hmm. My mother is convinced baba wanted us there in five."

"Her Majesty is correct, Your Highness," Sambhit says. "But there are many dangers on this road. And if the bandits learn of the presence of the royal family—"

"Oh, I understand, Captain" Idhika interrupts him. "I will inform my mother of your inability to protect us from forest bandits."

What is happening? "Forgive me, Your Highness, that was not my meaning. I only thought—"

"To disobey my father's command?" asks Idhika, with a sharp edge to her voice. Sambhit gulps nervously. A short pause, then her voice sweetens once more. "May I suggest we take shorter rests?"

"As you command, my Princess," Sambhit says. He bows, then jumps on his horse and gallops back to the front, where Lieutenant Abhay has men setting up the royal tent.

Sambhit calls out. "Lieutenant."

Abhay turns. "Yes, Captain?"

Sambhit pulls up alongside him. "There has been a change of plans. Pack it all up. We ride on."

Abhay is confused. "In the dark?"

Sambhit glances at the foreboding forest, and the hairs on his neck rise once more.

He nods his head. "In the dark. Give the orders."

CHAPTER NINE

A crisp breeze welcomes the soldiers as they stumble out of the forest onto the Kura Bazaar.

The marketplace lies deserted, robbed of the colour and chaos which once greeted visitors. Instead, a desolate land welcomes the twenty thousand Simhasthalis, those fortunate soldiers who stared death in the face and lived to tell the tale.

Some hobble on crutches roughly fashioned from branches, a few are carried by friends, and others are ferried on horseback, weary from their trudge across the Mrugaranya, 'the forest of the deer'.

Crown Prince Vikrant rides among his men, his narrow face drawn, his bloodshot eyes peering from behind droopy lids. He returns defeated, bloodied, absent of a father and a third of his army.

Worse, somewhere in the forest behind him, the enemy marches. The last he had seen of them was on the Laalkhet. A Vajra horn had blown after their retreat, and he had thought they would give chase.

But they had not. Quite the opposite. The ten-day march through the Mrugaranya had been uneventful. A few soldiers had died along the way, their wounds too deep, their blood loss too heavy. But of the enemy, there had been no sign.

Vikrant is not deceived. In a few days, the Vajra army will arrive to challenge him once more—a meeting he does not look forward to. He remembers the battle well, and still carries the bloody signs on his person. A little his, a lot spilled by others. Seven men, dead by his sword, whose faces he already forgets.

He does not forget his own dead, though. Above all, his father, now a head lying in the dirt, severed by the blade of the enemy.

By Vijendra, King of Vajrapur.

Vikrant remembers him as well. How could he forget? The smile on the Vajra's face, the taunt of his dismissal. The memory will haunt him the rest of his life.

He turns his gaze ahead, and his heart lightens at the sight.

Kuragarh.

In the orange shadow of the dusk sky, at the feet of the Rodasi, stands the capital of Simhasthal, a five-hundred-foot colossus of wood and stone. It was commissioned nearly three hundred years ago by King Navadeep, who gave the builders a simple task. Construct an impregnable fortress.

Their creation remains a marvel of engineering.

The fortress is made up of four levels, stacked one atop the other, like smaller and smaller boxes, with outer walls fifty feet high, patrolled by soldiers.

A single road, the Naagmarg, runs through the structure, coiling like a snake to tunnel through the mountain and emerge on the other side.

Round and round it goes, in and out the mountain, until it reaches the palace courtyard. Here, it is narrowest, and also the most easily defended. If the enemy manages to make it this far, they will have to walk six abreast up the narrow road, only to be cut down by archers, or lit up in flames with fire-oil.

The courtyard is flanked on the left by the Ranibagh, the Queen's garden, and on the right by the royal stables. And then, there is the palace—an imposing edifice constructed with stones cut from the Rodasi—that overlooks the kingdom, the Kura Bazaar, and the Mrugaranya.

It is a frighteningly beautiful fortress. On any other night, it would have been bathed in the fiery light of a thousand torches. But as the last rays of the sun retreat, the land is shrouded in darkness.

Save for one fire.

Behind the palace, dark blue flames blaze in the ceremonial tower, a feat achieved by a special mixture of powders tossed in with the wood. The fire rises to lick the mountain face, and its eerie glow spreads across the land with a clear message.

The King is dead.

It burns with a fierce intensity, and will continue to do so until a new ruler enters the kingdom. Vikrant's destiny awaits, and he rides to fulfil it.

His chacha, General Kashyap, rides on his left, his face a mask of suppressed anger. As it should be. Kashyap was closest to the King when he fell, and remains ashamed that he could not defend his brother.

Colonel Gautam, husband to Kashyap and the finest swordsman in Saravat, rides to Vikrant's right. Though he is not from Simhasthal, he fought hard for his adopted land, and is sad to return defeated.

The Parasu, those forty-three who survived, ride behind Vikrant. He is their ruler now, their King-in-waiting, and to protect his life is their duty.

A small tent flutters at the gates, where Guru Vedant, the royal priest, waits with his disciples. Vikrant dismounts and touches his feet.

"*Ayushman bhav*, young Prince," Vedant blesses him. He gestures to the tent. "Rise. And enter."

Vikrant walks in, followed by two disciples. They strip him of his armour, and he stands naked as they wash him clean of the blood and dirt. Then, they pat him dry and dress him in white silk, a tribute to the lion which once terrorised his ancestors, and now stands as a symbol of their power.

Vikrant steps outside, and his people fall on one knee, their fists clasped to their chests in the traditional Simhasthali salute. Only Guru Vedant remains standing, and an attendant leads a black stallion over.

"Crown Prince Vikrant," Guru Vedant says, "Your kingdom awaits."

Vikrant mounts his horse and spurs it to a slow trot, while the rest follow on foot. The gates to the city swing open, and inside, his subjects line the streets to pay their respects, their hands holding torches, which come alive one after another.

In their light, Vikrant makes his way up the winding road until he arrives at the palace steps, where his council of ministers wait.

As does his family.

Gayathri, his older sister, who has always been like a second mother to him, weeps openly, while her husband, Chandran, holds her in his arms. Prince Indranuj does not weep, but Vikrant recognises the rage which burns deep within him. He wants to go to them, to hold them, to grieve with them.

But he cannot. *I have a new responsibility now.*

He spots his mother, standing to the side, away from the gathering, the sorrow on her face greater than his own. Her arms cradle a firewood box, and within it lies his destiny.

The crown of Simhasthal.

Vikrant climbs the steps to his mother, who moves to the side. An odd thing to do. After all, it is her duty as Ranimaa to pass the crown to him. Instead, a frail old lady makes her way ahead, and he finds himself smiling for the first time in days.

He had forgotten about her. *The senior Ranimaa.*

Wife to the late King Hridhyanshu, mother to the late King Giridhar, matriarch of the royal family of Simhasthal, seventy-year-old Ranimaa Bhairavi is a force to reckon with. Her advanced years have dulled neither her wit nor intellect, and she has always been an exceptionally powerful woman.

But in this moment, she appears a broken soul, bereft of life, like any mother would be upon hearing the news of her son's death.

Vikrant touches her feet. "Your Highness. *Dadi.*"

She leans forward and kisses his forehead, then turns to her daughter-in-law, who holds open the firewood box. Inside, the crown rests. A ring of solid gold is at its base. Upon this, a curved plate is fixed, with asymmetrical jagged spikes, resembling the peaks of the rodasi. And at its centre, inlaid in silver, the great white lion roars.

Bhairavi retrieves the crown and raises it high for all to see. Her voice is surprisingly strong. "The King is dead!"

As she places the crown upon her grandson's head, the ceremonial fire dies. Loud and clear, she declares once more. "Long live the King!"

The ceremonial fire comes alive again, and this time it burns true to its nature. Orange and yellow flames rise to touch the sky, and their glow casts far and wide across the land.

Vikrant rises with the crown upon his head, and his people call out in one voice. "Long live the King! Long live the King! Long live the King!"

The citizens take up the chant, and very soon, Kuragarh pulsates to its reverberating beat. Vikrant touches his grandmother's feet once more, then his mother's, followed by Guru Vedant's, and Lord Atulya's.

As he turns to his chacha, a horn blows, silencing the chants.

Huu! Huu! Huu! Huu! Huu! Huu! Huu! Huu!

The short continuous burst can mean only one thing.

The enemy approaches.

The Parasu move into formation, ready to defend their King, while Kashyap, Gautam, and Indranuj race to the edge of the courtyard to determine the size of the enemy force.

Vikrant, however, stands rooted to the spot. His thoughts turn to Vijendra, and he wonders what fresh surprise the Vajra King has in store for them.

CHAPTER TEN

When the enemy arrives at the gates of Kuragarh, Vikrant cannot hide his surprise.

A lone ceremonial chariot, meant to ferry honoured dignitaries on important occasions, rolls into the city.

Achingly slow, it makes it way up the Naagmarg before arriving at the courtyard. As it rides across, the soldiers gasp and drop to one knee, even as their fists swing around and slam against their chests.

Whom do they salute, Vikrant wonders.

His sixth sense tingles as he makes his way to the chariot, which comes to a halt in the middle of the courtyard. His mother reaches a second before him. She sees who it is, and her legs give way. "Noooooooooooo!" she cries out, loud and screechy, the agonising wail of a woman whose soul has been ripped apart.

Vikrant runs forward and catches her before she hits the ground. "Fetch water," he shouts. "Now."

The handmaidens rush into the palace, and Gayathri and Indranuj appear by his side. He hands his heartbroken mother over to their care, then turns to the man inside the chariot.

On a soft white mattress, King Giridhar rests in peace. His head has been expertly sewed onto his neck, and shows little sign of its decapitation. He is dressed in his armour, which has been scrubbed clean and polished, and his sword lies by his side.

Vikrant reaches in and caresses his father's cheek. "You look at peace, baba," he wants to say, but the words refuse to cross his lips. The rage surges within him. Against the world. Against fate. Against the man who did this to his father. It rises and rises until he fears it will consume him.

A hand grasps his quivering shoulder, and he turns to face Atulya. "Your Highness," he says. "A letter. From King Vijendra."

He holds out a scroll. A lightning bolt strikes across its seal. The symbol of the King of Vajrapur. Vikrant breaks it and reads the message.

Little rabbit,

Our two kingdoms are at war. But I hope you realise I am not your enemy.

I deeply regret the avoidable loss of life. As a mark of respect, my men will perform the last rites for your dead.

Your father's body, however, I return to you. He was my friend in life. And someday far in the future, we will renew our friendship in death.

Cremate him with the honour he deserves. After his soul has walked through the gates of heaven, a month from this day, I will arrive at Simhasthal. And we will talk.

Your King,
Vijendra.

Before Vikrant can react, Kashyap appears by his side. His chacha holds out a hand, and he hands him the letter. A few seconds pass before the rage courses through the General as well.

"Your King?" Kashyap roars. "The man dares pronounce himself King of Simhasthal?" He flings the scroll to the wind, then turns to Gayathri. "Your Highness, please escort your mother inside and care for her health."

He turns to the royal priest. "Guruji, please attend to my brother. And make arrangements for his funeral as you see fit."

Finally, he looks at Atulya. "Summon the council. We have much to discuss."

Then he storms off into the palace.

All follow him, except Atulya, who glances at Vikrant for a brief moment. Seeing no reaction from the Prince, he too heads into the palace.

A lonely Vikrant remains in the courtyard, his gaze lost to the Mrugaranya, a faint shadow in the dark night. Somewhere within the forest, Vijendra camps with his army. In a few weeks, he will arrive.

And Vikrant will have to be ready.

CHAPTER ELEVEN

Three weeks after Giridhar's funeral, Atulya enters the late King's study for the first time. The room looks unfamiliar, though the furniture remains the same, the carpeting is as before, as are the paintings and the portraits.

It is not the room, his inner voice whispers. *It is Giridhar's absence.*

With each passing day, Atulya misses his friend more. They had sat together in this very room, tackling the issues of the kingdom, debating great philosophical conundrums, making plans for the future. Fifteen years of partnership. Four decades of friendship.

Gone, in an instant.

The door opens, and the Crown Prince walks in. Atulya bows to Vikrant, who waits for his advisor to rise, then touches his feet. Atulya blesses him with a long life.

Vikrant glances at the papers in his hand. "I hope you have not come to discuss the coronation."

Atulya offers him a wry smile. *I had to try.*

A week remains for the ceremony, yet Vikrant continues to avoid its preparations. His mind remains consumed by Vijendra, and his imminent arrival.

Atulya decides not to push the issue. "I just wanted to inform you that our messages to Triloha and Naavipur have been answered."

"That was quick," Vikrant says. "How do they reply?"

"Prince Kartik and Prince Dhairya will attend the coronation," Atulya says.

Vikrant is surprised. And hurt. "Not the Crown Princes?"

Atulya shakes his head. "No. Both Kings send their younger sons."

Vikrant's face turns grim. "Which means they do not intend to send their armies."

"They did not make mention of this," Atulya says. "However, I intend to bring up the topic with both Princes after the coronation."

"Spare yourself the trouble," Vikrant says. "Their answer is clear." He walks around the table and runs a hand over the King's chair. "I remember baba sitting here." His eyes glisten. "I miss him."

"So do I," Atulya says.

"I know you do." Vikrant's empathy is genuine. So is his bitterness. "Many believe he would still be alive, if only you had figured out Vijendra's intentions."

The accusation stings, as truth often does. Atulya accepts the blame. Giridhar's death is his fault. "Vijendra's trick was old," he says, "Stolen from our ancestors, the Kuras. Half his army hid in the Andhakaranya, emerging to join him only once we engaged."

"You offer excuses?" Vikrant asks.

"Not excuses, Your Highness," Atulya says. "I make none. The fault is mine, and the dead will haunt my conscience to the end of my days. I merely seek to offer an explanation." He takes a deep breath before continuing. "And my resignation."

Vikrant's reaction is measured. He gestures for Atulya to take a seat, then walks across the room and returns with a pitcher of *madeira*. A cup for Atulya, a cup for himself.

He takes his chair. "Where will you go?"

"Back home," Atulya replies. "To Harit Nagar and my family. I have not seen them in over a year, and I do miss my grandchildren."

"You would abandon me in my time of need?" Vikrant asks.

"Not abandon, Your Highness," Atulya replies. "I would prepare all that is necessary for your new advisor to guide you to victory."

"And whom do you see taking up the task?" Vikrant asks.

"There is only one name," Atulya says. "General Kashyap."

Many years ago, Kashyap had been second-in-line to the throne, a Prince, much respected and much admired. But after Vikrant's birth, the line of succession changed. The law was laid down in stone. Kashyap had to renounce his royal title and join the army.

Now, he commands it as General, and Atulya proposes a much bigger role. "Your uncle is widely respected, and you would be hard-pressed to find a more brilliant military strategist."

Vikrant remains silent. He sips his madeira and watches his royal advisor with thoughtful eyes. A wise move, one Atulya himself had taught him. *You will be King one day,* he had often told the young Prince. *Never rush to a decision. Let them wait, until your mind is made.*

A long while passes before Vikrant replies. "You will continue as royal advisor, until I am convinced you are no longer fit for the role."

"Your Highness—" Atulya protests.

Vikrant raises a hand. "A single mistake, regardless of its tragic consequences, does not wash away a lifetime of service. We will speak no more of this." The sadness in his eyes plead his case. "I need you, chacha. Your place is here."

Atulya does not reply, and Vikrant changes the topic. "What news of Vijendra?"

Atulya sighs. There is no new news, and he cannot say if that is a good thing or bad.

"He remains encamped on the Laalkhet," Atulya says. "His men occupy their time with games and gambling, and little else."

Vikrant remains unconvinced. "Another trick to deceive us."

"Perhaps," Atulya says. "I am not too concerned about Vijendra. If he marches on Kuragarh, all we have to do is let him lay siege, and watch him try to breach our high walls."

"You would have me hide like a coward?" asks Vikrant, unsure.

"It is the smart move," Atulya replies. "We have food. We have water. Avoid open war, and you will render him powerless."

"And myself as well," Vikrant retorts. "The people will hate me."

"Let them," says Atulya, determined to make him see reason. "Swallow their hate, and protect them. Too many have died." He breathes deeply, and speaks more kindly. "This is a distraction, Your Highness. The truth lies elsewhere, its seed sowed many decades ago, before Vijendra even came of age."

"By whom?" Vikrant demands to know.

"Lord Jayendu," Atulya declares.

Vikrant's eyebrows rise. All know the man, the richest in Saravat, friend to Kings and noblemen. Jayendu has visited Simhasthal many times, staying in the palace as a guest of both King Hridhyanshu and King Giridhar.

Atulya doubts Vikrant will show him the same courtesy.

Not now. Not ever.

"He was a good friend of my father's," Atulya says. "And after his death, he continued to visit the school to debate politics with me. One of his many outrageous ideas was to unite the kingdoms of Saravat under one ruler. An Emperor, who would defend the land against foreign invaders."

"And you never thought to mention this?" Vikrant asks.

Atulya admits his shame. "When Vijendra's missive arrived, I did not connect the dots. I have now, and seek to make amends."

"How?" Vikrant asks.

Atulya does not reply. Instead, he walks to the adjoining chamber, then returns with Lord Ayushmann.

Thirty-three years of age, the Minister of Security is an odd-looking man, with asymmetrical features and bushy eyebrows. His thin lips, however, are almost always curled in a smile, and make his face pleasant to look at.

Ayushmann bows. "Your Highness."

Though confused by his presence, Vikrant instinctively acknowledges him. "Lord Ayushmann."

Atulya offers an explanation. "The minister used to be my ward," he says. "I have raised him as one of my sons, and trust him with my life." He pauses before continuing. "I commanded him to glean what plans Jayendu has hatched with Vijendra, in the hope that it might prove useful to us."

Vikrant turns to his minister. "And what have you learnt?"

"Little as yet, your Highness," Ayushmann admits. A broad grin crosses his face, charming enough to distract from his broken nose. "A single question looms large, though, and warrants further investigation."

"And what question might that be?" Vikrant asks.

The minister's grin broadens. "Why Vijendra?"

Silence. The name hangs in the air. Five Kings rule Saravat, eleven princes their descendants. Why Vijendra, indeed?

Atulya breaks the silence. "I have pondered this question since the battle. As far as I can tell, the idea of an Emperor has been on Jayendu's mind for almost thirty years now. When did he decide Vijendra was the chosen one? And what conditions led to them setting the plan in motion now? The answers to these questions might help us devise our strategies."

Vikrant does not agree or disagree. He walks over to the cabinet and returns with a cup for Ayushmann. Once the madeira is poured, he takes his seat and sips his drink, lost in thought.

The minutes tick away as they wait for his decision. Ten, fifteen, twenty. Near the half hour mark, Vikrant stirs from his inner deliberations. "Very well," he says. "Lord Ayushmann will find out all he can. And track Vijendra's movements as well. I will not have him surprise us twice."

Ayushmann nods his head, the grin returning to his face in a flash. He drains his cup, bows to his King and leaves.

Vikrant turns to his advisor. "Are you sure about this?"

Atulya looks tired. "I cannot say, Your Highness. At the moment, the enemy holds all the cards. I simply mean to steal a few to help us achieve our goal."

"And what is our goal?" Vikrant asks.

"Vengeance, Your Highness," Atulya says, "For the death of your father." His eyes blaze with the spirit of a warrior, and his voice turns cold as ice. "Vengeance. For the death of my friend."

CHAPTER TWELVE

Biraj's foot slips once again, and he curses in frustration. The sound echoes off the smooth stone walls, mocking him as it races down the cave. He shakes his head. *Why did the King have to send me through here?*

After four nights of hard riding, he and his guides had arrived unseen at the Rodasi, a few miles east of Kuragarh. A short climb of a few hundred feet revealed the mouth of the cave, carved by hand at an angle to keep it invisible.

Torch in hand, he had entered the tunnel alone, wearing the uniform of a Simhasthali guard. The journey had been simple at first. The path was six feet wide and almost ten feet tall. A garden stroll. But the way soon turned perilous.

The tunnel began to shrink until, a good mile and a half away, it is only three feet wide and barely twice as tall. For the over six-foot tall Vajra, this proves to be an inconvenience. But not as inconvenient as the pebbles which lie scattered on the floor. Smooth as marbles, they turn every step into a dance with death.

He brings the torch ahead. Only a few hundred feet left to go. He will make it, if he does not slip on the stony marbles and break his foot. Or his neck.

One step at a time, with utmost caution, he shuffles across to emerge on the mountainside above the palace.

Here, he catches his breath. The path has been long and tough, but now he must find the way down. A few minutes later, he sees it, and is once again awed by the ingenuity of the Simhasthali builders.

Carved into the side of the mountain, the near-invisible staircase is just wide enough for two to walk abreast. Biraj now understands what the tunnel is. An escape route for the royal family, in case the impossible occurs, and their impregnable fortress is breached.

He makes his way down the steps, one hand gripping the mountainside. After surviving the cave, it would be foolish to break his neck here. There is time enough for his appointment. He counts them as he goes.

One... Two... Three...

Five hundred and one stairs later, he finds himself at its foot. Around the corner is the entrance, through which are a series of corridors that lead to the palace and the rest of the fortress. Biraj has his orders. He must wait for the signal, and a guard will let him in to meet the spy.

Vijendra's spy.

He must be a high-ranking official, if he can smuggle in the Prince of Vajrapur. The King gave no clue as to the identity of the man. It does not matter. Biraj will soon find out for himself.

An hour passes slowly, then another. Halfway through the third, he hears the creaking of hinges. Quiet as a mouse, he peeks around the corner.

Two guards engage in casual conversation in front of the open door. Then, one guard unhooks a thin rope from the back of his armour and hands it to his comrade, who attaches it to a hook sewn into the neck of his uniform. *So simple, yet so brilliant.*

No wonder only one guard protects the open courtyard. At the first sign of danger, he simply has to drop to the ground and the alarm bell will sound. If he is killed, his fall will ensure the same result.

After the first guard leaves, the other waits ten minutes before he bangs his spear on the ground.

Thump! Thump! Thump!

He waits three seconds, then repeats the action.

Thump! Thump! Thump!

Biraj's nerves stand on edge as he rounds the corner. *Could this be a trap?*

He breathes a sigh of relief when he arrives unharmed at the door. The guard nods his head, and lets him pass through. In the passageway inside, a man waits in the shadows. Not the spy, but a servant, who steps into the light and bows.

"Welcome, Your Highness," he says. "Please follow me."

The man leads him through a maze of corridors, turning this way and that, his step never faltering once. They pass few people, who glance at Biraj's uniform, and pay them no attention. In a matter of minutes, they arrive at their destination.

The man bows once more. "My lord awaits your presence inside."

Biraj opens the door, and for the first time that night, he is truly shocked.

CHAPTER THIRTEEN

Chandran almost laughs when he sees the Vajra Prince's reaction. Biraj was expecting a Colonel maybe, even a nobleman or a minister. *But not me.*

And why would he? Chandran is used to being underestimated and unappreciated, mostly due to his physical appearance. Flabby, not very handsome, and already balding before the age of thirty.

Despite these disadvantages, he still managed to snare the affections of Princess Gayathri, and now lives in the palace, at the heart of the action, one of the many advisors to his brother-in-law, Crown Prince Vikrant.

Chandran beams at Biraj. "Your Highness, you arrive at last. My poor man has been out there every night, thumping his spear with no reply."

The Vajra continues to gape open-mouthed.

Does the boy lack intelligence? Chandran wonders.

Surely, he must have pieced together the obvious. Chandran is the goodwill ambassador of Simhasthal, and has often led delegations to the other kingdoms, including Vajrapur.

"I beg your forgiveness, my lord," Biraj finally says. "I was not expecting a member of the royal family. It is an honour to meet you."

"The honour is mine, Prince Biraj." Chandran leads the Vajra into the room and closes the door. "Come. Sit. May I offer you something to drink? Some madeira, perhaps? Or some *arrack*?"

"Arrack?" Biraj looks surprised.

Chandran smiles. "A commoner's drink, yes. A dirty habit which I find hard to let go of."

Biraj does not comment. "Some madeira for me, please."

Chandran heads to a small table laden with pitchers and cups. He pours the Prince some madeira, then a cup of arrack for himself. His eye falls upon the portrait hanging above him. King Giridhar, lording over the room. Chandran raises his cup to him. What would the late King have said if he saw his son-in-law consort with the enemy?

Chandran shakes his head. *We will never know.*

He returns to Biraj and hands him the cup. "How was your journey through the tunnel?"

"Humbling," Biraj admits. "Somehow, you feel the weight of the mountain hanging over your head."

"Ready to crumble at any moment and crush your skull." Chandran sympathises. "I know the feeling. They took me there days after my wedding. I confess, it scared me out of my wits. But I dared not show it. My father-in-law was watching me like a hawk."

Biraj nods his head, then chuckles. "But after a while, I didn't care much about the mountain. If anything was going to kill me, it was those damn pebbles."

"Yes," says Chandran, a mischievous smile breaking across his face. "There is a trick to it. Quite simple, actually."

"And what might that trick be?" Biraj asks.

"Special footwear," Chandran says. The stunned look on the Prince's face makes him laugh. "I could not provide them for the journey here. But I will see that you get a pair for your return."

"I thank you," says Biraj, sarcastically. "Who knows? I might return to my brother with my neck intact."

"I hope so," Chandran chortles. "Or I will lose mine."

"Indeed." Biraj drains his glass and sets it aside. "Let us talk. The King requests some information."

As part of the council of ministers, Chandran is privy to everything. He begins with the military strength, and Biraj is pleased to note that the Simhasthal army has dwindled in number. The attack on the Laalkhet served its purpose.

Chandran then furnishes a map of the fortress. Biraj and he pore over it, but even a cursory glance is enough to realise attack is not an option. The map proves useful in other ways, though. Biraj notes the placement of the sentries, the hidden watchtowers, the archers' hideouts in the tunnels. Chandran provides him with a schedule of the guards, as well as the location of the food reserves.

Once all the information is in hand, the stark reality stares Biraj in the face. Lay siege to the fortress, and it will easily survive a year. Try to breach the walls, and the Vajra army will be slaughtered.

Frustrated, he pours himself another cup and gulps the madeira down. "This is impossible."

"It appears so," Chandran agrees. "But if there is a man alive who can find a way, it is your brother."

"Maybe," Biraj says. "And he will surely be grateful for the information you have provided." He switches track. "What about the mood of the people?"

"The mood?" Chandran looks amused as he pours himself some arrack. He offers madeira to Biraj, who declines. Chandran sips his drink. "The mood is angry, Your Highness. The people roar for revenge."

"So, it will be war?" asks Biraj, disappointed.

"It will be war," Chandran replies. "Do not pretend to be surprised. King Giridhar was well-loved by his people."

Biraj keeps his silence, and Chandran understands. In his heart, the Prince had always known his brother was sending him on a fool's errand. He wonders how the boy will receive the next piece of news.

"Lord Atulya, however, is against war," Chandran says.

Biraj was not expecting this. "The King's advisor? Why?"

Chandran shrugs. "Who knows? The old man holds his cards close to his chest, and has advised Vikrant not to face King Vijendra in battle."

"Surely, he must have given Vikrant a reason," Biraj says.

Chandran sips his drink. "If he has, Vikrant is yet to let us in on the secret."

Biraj lets this piece of information sink in. "What about Vikrant? Where does he stand in all this?"

Chandran smirks, his contempt evident. "The little rabbit? He is timid, indecisive. Brave on the battlefield, maybe. But the council room is a different sort of battlefield, isn't it? He will follow his council's lead. And make no mistake, they will declare war."

"But as King—" Biraj says.

"Yes," Chandran interjects, "As King, if he sues for peace, his ministers are honour-bound to accept his wishes. But he will not. He lacks the courage to defy anyone."

"Perhaps you could lend him that courage?" Biraj says.

Chandran shakes his head. "I could, if I were so inclined. But then my thoughts would be public, and this I cannot afford."

"Why?" Biraj presses the issue.

"Why?" Chandran chuckles. "My dear Prince, Lord Atulya faces open revolt for his stance. And he is the most respected man in the kingdom. What chance do I stand?"

"You are Princess Gayathri's husband," Biraj counters.

"And held in very poor esteem by all," says Chandran, his tone bitter. "I come from a simple spice trader's family, a lowborn who married above his station. This is a truth they never let me forget. Even my father-in-law, a man who welcomed me into his house, created the irrelevant post of goodwill ambassador only to provide me with the illusion of importance."

"So, you will not speak against war?" Biraj asks.

"I dare not," replies Chandran, adamant. "Still, it does not matter. I am certain King Vijendra will end this issue without bloodshed. He had failed to do so with King Giridhar, but Vikrant will prove easier." His keen eyes catch the momentary look of confusion on Biraj's face. "Surely, he must have spoken of this."

Biraj turns cautious. "My brother does not share his battle strategies with me."

Chandran chuckles to himself. *Even now, Vijendra keeps him in the dark.*

He pities the boy, and offers him a warm smile. "You are wary. That is good. You should be. For all you know, I might be a double agent. Alas, I do not have the wits for it. Fear not, my Prince. I will not betray your brother's confidence."

"He will be glad to hear it," Biraj says, and rises from his seat. "If there is nothing more, my lord, then I must take your leave. Our King will want to hear my report at once."

Chandran stands as well. "When will your army arrive?"

"In ten days," Biraj says. He heads to the door, but Chandran stops him.

"My Prince," he says, "If you would be so kind, I have a message for the King."

A curious Biraj turns to face him.

"Should it come to war," Chandran says, "Please ask King Vijendra not to forget his supporters in Simhasthal."

Biraj does not offer a reply. He bows, opens the door and leaves.

CHAPTER FOURTEEN

Do they see me as their King? Vikrant wonders, as he makes the long walk down the corridor to the royal room.

His people have gathered in the courtyard, following his every step, taking in his manner, his clothes, the sherman's coloured a deep indigo, the thick gold chain with a ruby at its heart, the ceremonial sword in its golden sheath.

Simple, yet regal, the way the King of Simhasthal should look. Still, his doubt persists, staying with him as he arrives at his destination. Quiet murmurs escape through the closed doors to whisper in his ears.

What kind of King will he be?

Will he avenge his father?

Will he fight, or submit?

For a moment, the years roll back, and he is a child once more, taunted by his peers, ridiculed by his people.

"Walked away from a fight," says one.

"Does not hit back," says another.

"Scared, like a rabbit!" they all declare.

"A rabbit! A rabbit! A rabbit!" they chant in unison.

A herald interrupts his thoughts. "Your Highness?"

Vikrant sees the man's expectant face. His appointed hour has arrived, and he must fulfil his destiny. He nods to the herald, who opens the doors and blows his trumpet.

Huuuuuuuuuuuuuuu!

The whispers die as the herald calls out in a loud, clear voice. "You are now in the presence of Crown Prince Vikrant, firstborn son of King Giridhar, descendant of the Kuras and the great King Simha."

Vikrant enters the throne room, which harks back to the simple ways of the Simhasthalis. The windows are wide, the thick curtains drawn to allow the sunlight to brighten the room. From the balcony above, huge portraits of his ancestors watch over the proceedings, while down below, sturdy redwood benches are laid out on either side, a plush red carpet between them that marks the aisle to the throne.

His people rise to their feet as he walks past, their eyes following him, watching, observing, analysing, even as the question grows silently in their minds.

Will he declare war?

Once the crown rests on his head, it will be his prerogative. Almost everyone—his family and ministers—are in favour. Only Atulya has spoken against. But his lone voice is not enough.

Vikrant spots the two foreign royals standing at the throne end of the hall. Prince Kartik of Triloha, thirdborn son of King Theeran, arrived a few nights ago with the best wishes of his father. Prince Dhairya of Naavipur, secondborn son of King Ranadutt, arrived yesterday with gifts and felicitations. The kingdom of Saptaveni, secretive as ever, sent no representative. However, the gift of a diamond-studded ceremonial sword was delivered to Lord Atulya.

The Princes bow, and Vikrant nods his acknowledgement, before he turns his gaze to the throne. Fifteen steps lead up to it, on which sit eight of the most important citizens in the kingdom.

On the left, the seats are taken by Chandran at the bottom, then Gautam, Kashyap and Atulya. And on the right, his family sits.

Vikrant climbs the first three steps and returns Gayathri's smile. *My sister is wiser and braver than me. If only she had been born a male. What a King she would have been.*

Three steps higher, his mother watches him with pride, though he is yet to achieve anything. *There is still time. I will make you proud, Maa.*

Three more steps, and he faces Ranimaa Bhairavi. The wise old woman stands tall, the way she had at his father's coronation. *I pray some of her intelligence and strength rubs off on me.*

And on the final three steps, just below the throne, is Indranuj. Sixteen years of age, he bears a striking resemblance to their late father. A smile breaks across Vikrant's face. *Sorry, brother. It's your turn to be the Crown Prince.*

He shifts his attention to the throne which watches over the room. Carved from a block of white marble, the unadorned seat of the King of Simhasthal reflects the simplicity and solidity of their way of life. Hanging above it is a massive bust of the roaring white lion, its fury symbolising the power of the King.

Here, Guru Vedant waits for the Prince to claim his destiny. Vikrant touches his feet.

"Ayushman bhava, son of Giridhar," Guru Vedant says. "Rise, and take your rightful place."

Vikrant sits on the throne, and the audience takes their seats. An attendant steps forward with the crown, and Guru Vedant holds it up for all to bear witness.

"Fifteen years ago, after the death of King Hridhyanshu, I crowned his son King of Simhasthal." His voice fills with sorrow. "King Giridhar was a strong King. A King of justice. Of truth. Of compassion."

He turns to face Vikrant. "And now, his son takes his place. Crown Prince Vikrant, will you abide by the laws and ideals laid down by your ancestor, the great King Simha?"

"I will," says Vikrant.

"Will you work for the good of your subjects and your kingdom?"

"I will."

"Will you lay down your life in the defence of this great kingdom?"

"I will."

"Do you swear your words to be true, in the eyes of the gods and all who have gathered?"

"I swear."

Guru Vedant smiles. "May your deeds be great. In the presence of the gods, the spirits of your ancestors and the citizens of Simhasthal, I crown you King Vikrant, firstborn son of King Giridhar, descendant of the Kuras and the great King Simha, ruler of Simhasthal."

With these words, he places the crown upon Vikrant's head. The heralds step forward and blow their trumpets out the windows. Their cry travels from the throne room down to the gates of the city.

Once their sound dies, an expectant silence fills the air. The question has been left hanging for far too long. Now, the people want an answer.

The crown rests heavy upon Vikrant's head. He faces his mother, who watches with joyful tears in her eyes. He faces his brother, who looks on with fervent hope. He faces the crowd, who wait with bated breath.

He whispers a silent prayer to his ancestor. *Simha, give me strength.*

He rises to his feet. "You have crowned me your King. This is the greatest honour of my life." His voice hardens. "But let us not forget how it came to be. Over a month ago, King Vijendra ended the life of my father, King Giridhar."

The mention of the late King stirs the crowd. He was loved by all, and each feels the anger rise within.

Vikrant continues. "My father did not fight to stoke his ego. He fought for us, for our kingdom. Vijendra means to subjugate and compel us to join his quest to become Emperor of Saravat."

The room erupts.

"No," screams one nobleman.

"Never," shouts a minister.

"Not while I live," General Kashyap thunders.

Vikrant raises his hand. The crowd falls silent. "Vijendra is on his way here," he says. "The scouts report his army is within the Mrugaranya, and they will arrive at our gates within a week."

Stoic silence greets this announcement. The news had spread unofficially through the kingdom many days ago.

Vikrant continues. "But I vow to you, as your King, as the son of Giridhar, as the descendant of the great King Simha..."

His voice drops to a whisper. A gentle breeze whistles through the room and carries his words to all corners. "I will not let him."

Vikrant draws his sword and holds it up. "I will fight him. Are you with me?"

The crowd roars its response. "Yes."

Vikrant shouts louder. "Are you with me?"

The crowd raises its voice. "Yes."

Vikrant screams. "Are you with me?"

The windows rattle as they cry out together. "Yes!"

Vikrant gestures for silence. "Rest well, my brothers and sisters. Eat. Drink. Hold your loved ones close. In a week, we go to war."

Unsmiling faces stare back at him, and he wonders if he has won them over.

Kashyap chacha is the first to react. He pounds his clenched fist against his chest. "War!" he chants over and over with each thump. "War! War! War!"

The gesture and chant are taken up by the others, until it echoes far beyond the room. In the courtyard outside and across the kingdom, the citizens join in, and within moments, the call to war reverberates across Kuragarh.

Vikrant breathes a sigh of relief as he thumps his fist against his chest and whispers the chant. They are on his side now. He wonders if his father is up in heaven, proudly looking down on him. The thought brings a smile to his face, as does the prospect of vengeance.

Soon, it will be his.

CHAPTER FIFTEEN

Atulya massages the ointment into his stiff, tired legs, trying to coax some life back into them. Of the hundreds of medicines he has tried, this is the only one he finds effective, and he sighs as it delivers the much-needed relief.

The day has taken its toll, especially after the declaration at the coronation. It had saddened him to see King Vikrant set aside his advice and embrace the looming spectre of war.

Almost all Simhasthalis prefer it this way. They have always been a warrior clan. But open war is risky, and Atulya must do all he can to avoid it.

What they need are allies, and those are proving hard to come by.

Seventy years ago, the five kingdoms signed a treaty, bringing an end to their petty wars. Saravat witnessed a prolonged peace for the first time in thousands of years. Boundaries were demarcated, trade alliances were set up, and disputes were resolved amicably through discussion.

They also swore to come to each other's aid in the event of an invasion.

Earlier tonight, Atulya discovered the strength of those promises. He met with Prince Dhairya a couple of hours ago. King Ranadutt of Naavipur sent his regrets, but not his army.

Summer was his excuse. Too hot to cross the Vikktabhumi desert, too stormy to ferry soldiers across the Dakshinasagara.

Saptaveni had replied as well, along expected lines. They would not send an army, for Vijendra's conquest sounded less like an invasion and more like a dispute, to be resolved among the two quarrelling kingdoms.

Now, Atulya will meet with young Prince Kartik. *Our best hope.*

No kingdom hates Vajrapur more than Triloha. They were once the dominant force in Saravat, ruling vast tracts of land, until the Vajras came across the sea and ended their hegemony. Over the years, the wars between the two had been vicious and bloody, and in the end, neither side could claim victory over the other.

Perhaps allying with Simhasthal could see that issue settled. But even if their answer disappoints, Atulya will not lose hope. If his sources are correct, another path might soon present itself. He prays he is not being deceived once more, for he cannot bear the loss of more life.

A knock drags him away from his thoughts. The door opens and Shardul walks in. "My lord, Prince Kartik is here."

At last.

"Show him in," he says.

Shardul leaves the room. Atulya gives his aching knees one last rub, then stands as his assistant returns with the Prince of Triloha.

Sixteen years of age, Kartik is traditionally handsome, with wheatish skin, a strong build and an innocent face. But Atulya is not deceived by his youth. The Prince has a burgeoning reputation as an accomplished negotiator, and cannot be taken lightly.

The gods must be thanked for Prince Kartik's presence at the coronation, instead of his older brother. Prince Sreedharan has little love for diplomatic niceties, and his temper has provoked many a bar-room brawl in their kingdom.

Atulya bows. "Your Highness, I thank you for meeting with me."

Kartik bows as well. "How could I not, my lord?" He grins. "After all, it has been such an interesting day."

Atulya smiles and gestures for the Prince to sit, then takes his own seat. "I understand your messenger has left for Triloha, carrying word of King Vikrant's decision."

"Yes," Kartik says. "And come dawn, I mean to follow him."

"I see," says Atulya, not surprised in the least. "As I am sure you are aware, our kingdoms have a pact to come to each other's defence. King Vikrant requests Triloha to fulfil its promise, and send its army to help us fight Vijendra's forces."

Kartik leans back in his chair. "Come now, Lord Atulya. I am sure you are aware that the pact only makes mention of assistance in the event of foreign invasion. Vijendra is a Saravati. Not a foreigner."

Atulya sighs. *Another promise, broken on a technicality.*

His tone hardens. "You will not come to our aid?"

A broad smile stretches across the Trilohan's face. The boy appears to be enjoying himself.

"Of course we will," Kartik says. "My father understands that if Vijendra wins, Triloha will bleed next. We do not wish for that to happen." His eyes shine bright, and he speaks with the authority of a man a few decades older. "The Vajras have bled our land in the past. Enough. No more. Our army will march for Kuragarh. And we will crush Vijendra between us."

Atulya cannot believe his ears. "That is good to hear, your Highness. Your assistance is greatly appreciated. I will inform King Vikrant of your decision, and I am certain he will want to thank your father personally."

Kartik's smile turns sly, and makes Atulya wary.

"I believe there is a way he can do that," the Prince says, "Before we march for Kuragarh."

Your hope rose too fast, Atulya's mind cautions him. This was too good to be true. "I assume your assistance comes at a price?"

Kartik chuckles. "Doesn't it always?"

"And what concessions does King Theeran expect from us?" Atulya asks.

"Only one," Kartik says. He leans forward. "King Vikrant is as yet unwed."

Realisation dawns at once. "Your twin sister—" Atulya starts to say.

"Princess Jyothika," Kartik completes for him. "King Theeran wishes for King Vikrant to accept her hand in marriage, and seal the bond between our two kingdoms."

Atulya is impressed. The young Prince hooked him with the military alliance, then reeled in his catch with a marriage proposal. He wonders how he will break the news to Vikrant. *My King has a decision to make.*

He stands and bows. "On behalf of King Vikrant, I thank King Theeran for his proposal. I will present it at our council meeting tomorrow, and our answer will follow soon."

Kartik stands as well. He turns to go, then stops. "Before I leave—" He pauses to give thought to his words. Then he speaks. "My lord, over seventy years have passed since the last time the five kingdoms went to war. Five hundred thousand men, women, and children died needlessly in those bloodbaths. Peace has reigned since; a peace Vijendra threatens to destroy." His voice rings with sincerity. "Please remind King Vikrant that this peace now rests in his hands."

He bows and leaves. Atulya watches him go.

A very wise boy indeed.

He makes a mental note to keep a close eye on this one.

CHAPTER SIXTEEN

Queen Indrani moans as her husband thrusts into her. They lust for one another with the passion of newlyweds, clawing and fighting for dominance, and Indrani climaxes many times before Vijendra reaches his own.

She rolls on her back, her eyes closed, her breath coming in short ragged gasps. She lies this way for a while, and when she opens her eyes, she finds Vijendra propped on an arm, watching her.

"What are you thinking?" he asks.

"Of how good this feels," she says, savouring the ecstasy which still races through her. "Like our first days of wedded bliss."

Vijendra laughs, and kisses her cheek. "Imagine how much better it will feel once we have conquered Saravat."

"Mmm," she moans. "I cannot wait."

"You will have to wait a little while longer, my love," says Vijendra, as he rolls off the bed and grabs his clothes. "For now, get dressed, and let us go break our fast."

He leaves her in bed, and heads to the adjoining tent. Indrani sighs, then rolls off, walks to the mirror and admires her reflection.

Short, delicate and fair-skinned, she is an elegant beauty, with proud cheekbones and full lips. But behind her light brown eyes stirs an iron will every bit as fierce as her husband's.

The only daughter of the wealthiest lord in Naavipur, none had cared much when she married the thirdborn son of King Dhirendra. Vijendra was not well liked, not until the fever took away his older brothers, and he became the Crown Prince.

But she had loved her husband much before that, for he had always treated her as his equal. For twenty-five years, they had shared every thought, every dream, every fear. *Two minds racing in the same direction*, he had once called them.

But now, for the very first time, Indrani feels doubt prick her courage. They embark upon a dangerous journey. Her heart weighs heavy, as she summons her handmaidens to help her dress.

A few minutes later, she walks out to join her husband at the breakfast table. A few deer pass her by, unworried by her presence. Humans do not hunt them here, and they strut about as if they own the place, with golden coats that shine in the morning sun.

Indrani does not take notice of them. She bites into a sliced apple, her mind still consumed by their plan for Simhasthal, a kingdom she had last visited almost a decade ago. In a few days, they will discover if all they have assumed about Vikrant is true or not.

She remembers the new Simhasthali King as an odd boy, always frightened and withdrawn, who never got into fights with the other boys. Her husband is convinced the man is the same.

For the sake of their family, and their dreams, she hopes he is right.

A voice cuts into her thoughts. "My King."

She turns to see Biraj approach and bow to Vijendra, then her. He seems surprised by her presence, as he should be, for it was kept a secret from all but General Rannveer.

"My Queen," says Biraj, his demeanour formal.

A smile breaks across her face. The boy will never change. Vijendra has been like a father to him, and after Queen Susheela died, Indrani happily took over the role of mother. Biraj had arrived months after the death of her second boy, and it had seemed like his birth would fill the void left in her life.

The vaidyas had doubted she would ever conceive again. But Idhika arrived, and survived, and two more pregnancies followed her birth. Sons, both of them, whose lives were cut short; one in six days, the other in a month.

Her heart brims with sadness at the thought of them, the five sons whom she had cradled in her arms, with only Biraj surviving to become a man. And though he never took after her, or Vijendra, she still loves him.

"Welcome back, Biraj," she greets him affectionately. "I am pleased to see you after so long."

"As am I, Your Majesty," he replies, returning her affection with a smile.

"How was the journey?" Vijendra asks.

"Treacherous, dada," Biraj says. "No army could ever attack from there."

"I do not intend to," Vijendra says. "Did Chandran have any information to pass on?"

"He did," Biraj replies. "The strength of their army, food reserves, watch towers. We have all the information we need. He also informed me that everyone clamours for war." A slight pause, then he continues. "However, Lord Atulya stands for peace."

"Atulya?" Vijendra is as surprised as Indrani. "Giridhar made the man who he is. I thought the schoolmaster would be the first to demand blood."

Biraj offers no comment.

"What about Vikrant?" Indrani asks.

"He is yet to reveal his intentions," Biraj informs her. "But Lord Chandran does not believe he will defy the popular mood."

"He will not," Vijendra declares. "The boy has a coward's heart. What about Chandran? Does he side with the warmongers?"

Biraj shakes his head. "He does not. I asked him to encourage Vikrant to sue for peace. But he refused. Too dangerous, he says."

Vijendra spits in anger. "Another coward."

"A clever man," Indrani corrects her husband. "Chandran values his skin. And he must. If he loses his position, he will be of no use to us. No, My King, this task falls upon you. You must change their minds."

Vijendra reaches across the table and takes her hands in his own. "You are wrong, My Queen. I only need to change Vikrant's mind." He smiles, and she shivers. "And believe me, it will change."

Indrani sees the fire in his eyes, feels his conviction flow through his hands, and all the doubts that plagued her earlier vanish in an instant. She need not worry about their future.

Not anymore.

Vijendra has never failed to keep his promise to her.

And he will not fail her now.

CHAPTER SEVENTEEN

Is this what my nephew has grown into? Kashyap wonders.

Giridhar and he had often debated the issue, for they had seen different sides to Vikrant's nature. On the one hand, he was the rabbit, whom everyone laughed at. But he was also the fearless adventurer, who had scaled the tallest peaks of the Rodasi.

For his part, Kashyap had tried to shape Vikrant's destiny. He had taught him to swim. To think. To wield a sword. And he has much more to teach, if only the King would listen.

But he does not, or they would not be standing side by side on the ramparts, gazing into the distance. A deserted valley stares back at them. The gates are barred, the steel barriers have been lowered in the tunnels, and archers man the road from the valley to the palace.

They stand in a stone cage, five hundred feet tall.

Kashyap cannot help but feel betrayed. His army prepares for a siege. He had spoken to Vikrant about it, who set aside his concerns. It will be war; the King had assured him. But the promise does not match reality.

He glances at Gautam, standing a few feet away, who had begged Kashyap to ignore his doubts. "Vikrant is your King now. Obey. That is all you need to do."

Kashyap shakes his head. Gautam may be his husband, the love of his life. Yet he comes from faraway Saptaveni, not Simhasthal. He does not understand our ways.

Or our history.

Many Kings have attempted to lay siege to Kuragarh. None succeeded, for they ended before they could even begin. The longest the fortress had been besieged was during the reign of King Treyaksh. A Vajra army, led by King Sumeet, had camped in the valley for a whole day before the restless Simhasthalis rode out to decimate them.

A warrior clan they were, a warrior clan they remain.

Kashyap glances at his nephew and wishes him luck. Confining three hundred and fifty thousand people inside the fortress will prove a stern test in the first week of his reign. Maybe if he accepts the Trilohan offer, a siege might be palatable. But the King refuses. For now, at least. Vikrant has decided to see what Vijendra is up to.

Or maybe he has been advised to do so.

Kashyap grits his teeth.

This is Atulya's doing. *The traitor.*

No words better describe the man. He was Giridhar's closest friend, and now he speaks against war.

Kashyap believes he knows something. If so, why not reveal it? Even Kashyap would admit to being curious of what Vijendra will throw at them. Yet, he knows the Vajra is not to be trusted. Or bargained with. The man killed his brother, and he will have his vengeance, come what may.

A Vajra horn sounds, faint and far away. Along the walls, the archers come to attention, ready to nock their arrows at a moment's notice.

But where is the enemy?

Vikrant turns to him, and he shrugs his shoulders. The watchers have not sounded the alarm, which means the enemy has not been spotted.

He wishes the Vajras would arrive soon. His watch creeps past four hours now, and his men have stood in the sun much longer. Surely, hunger rumbles within their bellies as much as it does in his. Still, they stand alert, ready for battle, and he knows he must stand with them.

At long last, the Simha horn sounds.

Huuu! Huuu! Huuu! Huuu! Huuu! Huuu!

He squints to spot the enemy. A tiny plume of dust rises in the distance.

A rider approaches.

Vikrant turns to him once again, and Kashyap shrugs as he did before. They must wait and see.

Soon, they get a clear view of the rider. The man is not much of a soldier. He wears no sword and carries no bow. His only weapon appears to be a spear, which lacks a sharp tip.

A gust of wind blows across the valley, and a tiny rectangular cloth flutters behind the spear. A flag, Kashyap realises at once. The blue cloth dances in the breeze, and ripples roll across the white rose painted on it.

The symbol for peace.

Hundreds of arrows take aim as the nervous rider comes to a halt fifty feet from the gates and holds the flag high.

"Your Majesty," he shouts, "King Vijendra demands a peace conference."

Kashyap turns to Vikrant, who appears lost in thought. "I do not like this, your Majesty. It feels like a trap."

His aide, Captain Dushyant, speaks up. "Your Majesty, I agree with the General. Give the command, and we will send his messenger back without a head."

"Captain," Gautam thunders. "He carries a peace flag. The law is clear. The King is duty bound to accept."

Dushyant scoffs. "Do you imagine Vijendra cares about the law?"

"Maybe not," Gautam admits. "But he is not a Simhasthali."

Neither are you, my love, Kashyap wants to say. But before he can, his junior continues.

"There is another way, Your Majesty," Dushyant says. "You could nominate an envoy to speak on your behalf."

Vikrant turns to face him. "And whom would you suggest, Captain?"

"General Kashyap," Dushyant says without hesitation.

Kashyap glares at him. The man should hold his tongue. If he were to take the King's place, it would hang like a sword over the rest of his reign.

Yet, as much as it pains him, Kashyap knows Dushyant speaks the truth. Vikrant does not possess the character to face Vijendra. The Vajra would walk all over him. He bows. "It would be my honour, Your Majesty."

Vikrant bears the look of a man who has been stabbed in the back. He shakes his head and speaks in a pained voice. "No, chacha. We will go together. Ask Lord Atulya to join us as well." He turns to Dushyant. "Accept the peace flag, Captain. And make the arrangements."

Dushyant does not hide his disappointment. Nevertheless, he leaves to execute his King's command. Vikrant heads back to the palace, and Gautam goes with him. Kashyap remains, his gaze fixed on the horizon. Though he cannot see Vijendra, he is certain the Vajra King is there. Waiting. Watching. Scheming.

This will be a battle of wills, and Kashyap hopes Vikrant is ready.

CHAPTER EIGHTEEN

At the heart of the Kura bazaar, midway between the fortress and the Mrugaranya, a peace tent is hurriedly set up, sparsely furnished, with two chairs for the Kings, a bench each for their advisors, and a table with refreshments.

An anxious Vikrant sits in his chair, drumming his fingers on his knee, while Kashyap and Atulya sit behind him with annoyed expressions of their own. Vijendra keeps them waiting. Mind games, which the young King struggles to ignore. But he must, if he is to hold his own in this meeting.

A Vajra herald enters the tent, and bows before making his announcement.

"All hail King Vijendra, thirdborn son of King Dhirendra, ruler and protector of the great kingdom of Vajrapur."

The tent flap parts, and Vijendra strides in, grinning from ear to ear, followed by a much more solemn General Rannveer and a very confused Prince Biraj. The two of them sit on the bench, while their King beams at the Simhasthalis.

He speaks to the General first. "Kashyap, my old friend, it is so good to see you." Then he turns to Atulya. "It is good to see you as well, Lord Atulya." And finally, he takes his seat and faces his equal. "And King Vikrant." He chuckles. "I admit it feels odd to say it out loud."

Vikrant keeps his emotions in check. "All of this feels odd, Your Majesty. Why are you here?"

"To talk to you, little rabbit," Vijendra says.

Vikrant swallows the insult. An easy task, one he has been doing his whole life. Kashyap, however, bristles at the taunt. "You will address our King by his proper title."

Vikrant glances at Atulya, gesturing for his advisor to keep the General in check. *Vijendra is baiting us. Do not rise to it.*

Vijendra scoffs. "I speak to the boy, Kashyap. His title holds no importance for me."

"No, Your Majesty," Atulya says. "I fear his title holds more importance than you care to admit. It is why you are here. King Vikrant is the lawful ruler of Simhasthal, just as you are the lawful ruler of Vajrapur." He speaks in an accusing tone. "Our kingdoms have lived in peace under the terms of a treaty signed seventy years ago. And now, your criminal acts have ended this friendship."

Vijendra ignores Atulya and addresses Vikrant. "Your advisor sounds wise, but even he knows what a treaty is. It is only words, scribbled upon paper by scared men who lack the capacity to dream beyond their pathetic reality. I say this to you, no treaty will stop me from fulfilling my destiny."

Vikrant remains silent. Better to let the man speak, with the hope that he may reveal his true intentions of asking for this meeting.

But as before, his uncle cannot hold himself back. "Is that why you killed my brother?" Kashyap demands to know. "To fulfil your destiny?"

A look of genuine sadness crosses Vijendra's face. Vikrant finds himself surprised. He did not believe the man capable of such emotion.

"Your brother—" Vijendra's voice croaks. He struggles to compose himself. "I admired Giridhar. He was a great man, whom I hoped to have by my side. Alas, I could not get him to see reason." He blinks, and the sorrow vanishes. "It does not matter, General. Not anymore. My friend Giridhar does not sit on the throne. His son does."

"And you think I will submit?" Vikrant asks.

"What choice do you have?" Biraj interrupts. "Your soldiers are tired, wounded, weak. They have been defeated once. Why let them suffer the same fate twice?"

"The same fate?" Kashyap roars. "I will admit, on the Laalkhet, we were ill-informed about your numbers. But now you face our true strength, Prince Biraj. Challenge us again, and you will meet your end."

The General does it again, and Vikrant feels his grip on this meeting slowly slipping away.

"My brother speaks out of turn," Vijendra says to Vikrant. "And so does your General. This is a meeting between Kings. The others may hold their tongues for a while." He glances sharply at Kashyap. "If they can."

Kashyap starts, but Vikrant silences him with a look, before turning to Vijendra. "Speak your mind, Your Majesty."

"You believe we are at war," Vijendra says. "I am here to assure you we are not. I do not wish to waste our soldiers' lives. Their deaths would defeat my purpose."

"Then why are you here?" Vikrant asks.

"Do you really not know?" Vijendra smirks and turns to Atulya. "Have you kept this a secret from your King?"

What secret? Vikrant glances at Atulya, who refuses to meet his gaze.

Vijendra laughs, loud and hearty. "I see the schoolmaster is a little tongue-tied. Let me spare him the embarrassment. I am here for you, my boy. I have come to change your destiny."

The day gets more and more perplexing. Vikrant glances at Rannveer and Biraj. Either they know what is going on, or they hide their confusion well.

"And you believe my destiny needs changing?" Vikrant asks.

Vijendra smiles. "Not just yours, my boy. Together, we will change the destiny of every man, woman, and child in Saravat."

"And how do you propose to do that?" Vikrant asks.

"By forging a new alliance between us," Vijendra says.

"A new alliance?" Kashyap scoffs. "I do not think that will be possible. Not anymore."

Vijendra appears unfazed. "It will not only be possible, my friend." His conviction is absolute. "It will be unbreakable."

He nods to the herald, who in turn gestures to someone standing outside. The tent flap parts once more, and a young woman walks in. She looks at each person in turn, before her eyes come to rest on Vikrant. Her lips curl into a teasing smile as she walks towards him, her anklets tinkling melodiously.

He wonders who she is. She must be seventeen or eighteen years of age. A short girl, short even for a Vajra. Her nose is a little stubby, her face a little plump.

But she is beautiful all the same. Doe-eyed, with soft features and a woman's figure, she walks with a dancer's grace, stepping to a beat only she can hear.

He stands, unable and unwilling to look away. Never has he sensed a spirit this fierce in so demure a woman.

She stops by Vijendra's side and bows to Vikrant. "Your Majesty, it is my honour and pleasure to meet you once more."

Vikrant searches for words. "I apologise for my rudeness, my lady," he finally manages to say. "But who are you?"

She giggles. A practiced laugh, but pleasing nevertheless. "How could you be rude, Your Majesty? You have seen me only once before. Ten years ago, when you last visited my home." Her smile is sweet, yet seductive. "As you can see, I have changed a lot since."

Vikrant remains tongue-tied, which pleases Vijendra. "Your Majesty," he declares, "Allow me to present my only child and heir to my throne, Princess Idhika."

Vikrant looks surprised, as do the other Simhasthalis. All except Atulya, whose face remains impassive.

"I offer you her hand in marriage," Vijendra continues. "All I ask in return is your fealty. Join your forces with mine in my conquest of Saravat. And I promise, after my death, you will ascend to the throne with my daughter as your empress."

He walks up to Vikrant and locks eyes with him. "I will expect your answer by noon tomorrow. Accept my offer, or prepare for war."

His ultimatum delivered, Vijendra leaves the room. Biraj and Rannveer bow and follow their King. But Princess Idhika remains, her eyes still on Vikrant, her smile continuing to tease him as she bows low. "I hope we shall meet again, Your Majesty."

I hope for the same, Vikrant thinks as he watches her leave.

CHAPTER NINETEEN

Chandran leans back in his chair and savours the chaos.

The council is locked in a fierce debate over Vijendra's offer. None are inclined to accept it, but all wish to understand why the Vajra King offers this proposal.

Chandran has been in the know for months now, but remains clueless about his feelings. Vikrant, heir to the throne of Saravat. A bold move, one which has certainly seeded confusion among the Simhasthalis.

But is it wise?

The boy poses no problems while Vijendra lives. But Emperor Vikrant might prove to be a disaster, if current events are any indication. The Simha King paces up and down the room, unwilling to meet anyone's eyes, or contribute to the debate.

Chandran pities the boy, who now has two marriage proposals and no idea which serves him better. Choose Triloha, and he will ally with the arrogant Theeran and his bloodthirsty son Sreedharan. Choose Vajrapur, and he will submit to Vijendra, his father's killer.

He shakes his head. *Poor, poor little rabbit.*

The door bursts open, and the two Ranimaas enter. Chandran's heart jumps with joy. The proceedings should liven up from here on. Sadly, for him, Bhairavi is a picture of calm as she walks slowly across the room and takes a seat.

Nandini, however, does not disappoint, breathing fire as she glares accusingly at Atulya. "You served my husband faithfully for fifteen years. And now, when my son sits on the throne, you hasten to betray him."

Chandran chuckles. *Well said, mother-in-law, very well said indeed.*

Atulya had been one of the most vocal opponents of his marriage to Princess Gayathri. To watch the royal advisor squirm in his chair brings some satisfaction.

"I did not deceive him, your Highness," says Atulya, a slight edge to his voice.

Nandini scoffs. "You did not?"

"I did not," Atulya says again. "I was commanded by King Giridhar to keep this information secret from everyone, including King Vikrant, were he to assume the throne. I only followed his orders."

Nandini's fury rages even more fiercely. "You invoke the memory of my late husband to save your skin?"

"I do not," says Atulya, still calm. "I merely obeyed his orders, and have done everything in my power to delay a decision until the King met with Vijendra."

"So, you confess to knowing Vijendra's plans?" asks Chandran, seeking to fan the flames.

"To an extent, my lord," Atulya confesses. "I needed to be certain his intentions would not change after King Giridhar's death. I was reliably informed that soon after the battle, Vijendra's wife and daughter set out to join him. There could be no reason for this, other than—"

"Other than to present her before me, hoping that I will be seduced." Vikrant stops pacing and glares at his advisor. "That still does not answer our question. Why keep this information from me?"

"What good would it have done, Your Majesty?" Atulya says. "You would have walked into the peace tent with everyone's voice in your ear."

He casts an accusing glance at the rest of the room, and sullen faces stare back at him. He ignores them and turns back to his King.

"Now, you know Vijendra's plan," he says. "You have met and spoken with the Princess. And you possess the knowledge necessary to make a decision. Triloha and Princess Jyothika. Or Vajrapur and Princess Idhika."

Ayushmann intercedes. "Forgive me, Lord Atulya. But that is not the choice before our King."

All eyes turn to the Minister of Security. Chandran likes Ayushmann. He has a cunning mind, and has always been friendly enough. Maybe because he is an outsider here, like Chandran. Ayushmann was not born to be a lord. He wasn't even born in Simhasthal, and only rose to the position thanks to Atulya's patronage.

Unlike Chandran, the other ministers regard him with hostility, as they always have. Ekaksh, Minister of Agriculture, speaks up. "Then pray tell us, Lord Ayushmann, what is his choice?"

Ayushmann smiles. "Should he remain King of Simhasthal, or should he become Emperor of Saravat."

The room reacts with surprise. They had not considered this.

Ayushmann continues before anyone can interrupt. "He will be Emperor, of that there is no doubt. If Simhasthal and Vajrapur join forces, the other three kingdoms do not stand a chance." He turns to Vikrant. "So, Your Majesty, you must decide. King. Or Emperor."

Chandran turns to Vikrant as well, curious as to what his answer will be. The boy does not offer one, and instead, resumes his nervous pacing.

General Kashyap jumps to his feet. "You speak without honour, Lord Ayushmann. I say we reject the proposals of both kingdoms. Who needs Triloha? Or its army? Not us. We are descendants of the great King Simha, and if tomorrow we decide Saravat needs an Emperor, we will march under King Vikrant's command." Angry tremors race through his body. "But to ally with Vijendra, the man who killed my brother—no, I cannot. I will not."

The ministers thump the table in agreement, and Kashyap's outburst is followed by his younger nephew.

"I agree," Prince Indranuj shouts. "Dada, you cannot marry the daughter of our father's killer."

Chandran notes the sadness in Vikrant's face as he stares at his younger brother, then at the rest of the room. The rabbit loses control of his very first war council. If he does not act soon, he may never regain it.

Bhairavi surprises everyone by reacting before her grandson. She slams the table—*bam!*—her cheeks quivering with rage.

"My son died honourably."

Stunned faces stare back at her. Few have ever heard her speak this way before.

"Giridhar was my son," she says, "My King, who died for the honour of his kingdom. That was his sworn duty. Vijendra did not employ any trickery. He did not ask his soldiers to fight for him. He did not stab my son in the back." She slams the table again—*bam!*—and emotion chokes her voice. "My son died honourably."

Her tone softens as she faces Indranuj. "Indu, my child, King Vijendra did not kill your father. He emerged victorious over him. And to the victor belong the spoils."

She looks at the General. "Kashyap, my son, Vikrant is your King now. Show him the same loyalty you once gave your brother."

Kashyap bows his head, but it is clear he does not agree.

She turns to Vikrant. "You are no longer the son of Giridhar. You are the King of Simhasthal. Be true to your vows, and act in the interests of your land, your people."

Wise words, old lady, Chandran agrees. *But which choice is in their interest?*

The same question occurs to Vikrant. "How do I decide?"

"I cannot answer that," Bhairavi says. "The decision must be yours. The future of this kingdom has always rested in the hands of its Kings." She changes the topic. "Is the girl beautiful?"

Vikrant nods his head. "She is."

"And her father promises to make you Emperor," Bhairavi says. "There's that as well."

"There's that as well," Vikrant repeats. He turns to his mother. "Maa, what do you say?"

"The ways of the world are strange," says Nandini, her voice filled with sadness. "A few weeks ago, I laid eyes on my husband's lifeless body. This morning, I faced the prospect of my son going to war. And now, you present two Princesses and ask which one should be my daughter-in-law. My heart is torn, my son, and has not yet recovered from its grief. Do not turn to me for advice."

Vikrant stares long and hard at his mother before he resumes his pacing. The minutes tick away, slowly, and the nightcandles shorten considerably before he finally takes his seat. Chandran hopes he will make the right choice.

Vikrant's words are meant for the room, but he addresses the royal advisor. "Lord Atulya, write to King Theeran."

A sinking pit forms deep within Chandran's stomach. He glances at his colleagues. Most smile, some nod their heads, and only Ayushmann remains without expression.

But their mood changes visibly with Vikrant's next declaration. "Inform him that I have accepted King Vijendra's proposal, and will soon be wed to Idhika, Princess of Vajrapur."

Their smiles vanish, but Chandran's returns. He does not know what Vijendra has in mind, but one thing is certain.

The Vajra King is winning.

CHAPTER TWENTY

"Faster, faster!" screams the boat captain.

The drummer picks up the tempo, and sixty-four muscled arms groan in protest as they row to match his beat. Kartik sits as an oarsman, the odd man out among the tall, heavyset sailors. Yet what he lacks in strength, he more than makes up with skill and determination.

The canoe, over a hundred feet long, scythes through the river. Four other boats compete with it, and the crowds along the bank cheer them on. Many have wagered on the kingdom's favourite sport, but even those who have not watch on anxiously.

"Row, you fools," the captain yells, and the tempo quickens once more.

Screaming and cursing, the oarsmen row harder. Kartik's boat pulls ahead. A centimetre. An inch. Three inches. Eleven. A foot. Soon, a narrow gap opens as his teammates push their endurance to the limit.

A horn blows as they cross the finish line, winning the race by a couple of feet. Kartik and his mates raise their oars above their heads and scream with joy, proud as warriors returning from battle. Now, a fat purse awaits them, soon to be lost to drink and women.

Kartik cares little about the money. Unlike his older brothers, he sees himself as a man of the people. He eats with them, drinks with them, and helps solve their everyday problems. In return, they shower him with love, and affectionately refer to him as the 'People's Prince'.

He steps onto land, and is at once surrounded by an adoring crowd. Women bat their lashes seductively, hoping to entice him into their arms. All they receive is a pleasant smile, as he rushes past.

A King's guard blocks his way and bows. "My Prince, His Majesty has requested your presence in his private office."

"And what matters does my father wish to discuss?" Kartik asks.

The guard looks up. "I do not know, your Highness. However, a messenger arrived from Simhasthal, and was taken straight to the palace."

Kartik smiles. "So, King Vikrant sends his reply. Very good. Fetch my horse. I will ride to the palace at once." He turns to his boat leader. "Captain, my father has summoned me. I must leave at once." He leans in and whispers. "Use my share to buy drinks for the men."

A wide grin breaks across the captain's face. Kartik's horse arrives, and he rides for the palace. On the way, his citizens bow to him, and their innocent faces stoke his conscience. He ponders the heavy price they will have to pay if it comes to war. Vijendra has proved to be cruel and cunning, a merciless man who would kill thousands to satiate his infinite ego.

The worry plays on his mind as he arrives at the palace, where he hands the reins to an attendant, then makes his way through the great hall, past the council chambers, and enters his father's private office to find King Theeran and Prince Meghnad already seated.

The anger in his father's eyes lets him know the message is not what they hoped. An unfortunate turn of events. He had placed a lot of faith in King Vikrant.

He takes his seat. "Aren't we missing the Crown Prince?"

Theeran's mood sours further. The King loves his oldest son, but is powerless to prevent him from causing mayhem. His voice is curt. "I have commanded Prince Sreedharan to deal with some bandits who raid our southern outposts."

Kartik turns to Meghnad. "Which means baba has once again banished our dear brother, who is now too drunk to find his way home."

Meghnad shifts in his chair. Neither brave nor intelligent, the secondborn son does not wish to upset his father or younger brother. He remains silent.

Theeran does not. "All the brains in the world, yet none of the wisdom."

"I apologise, baba," says Kartik, his tone reconciliatory. "I take it there is bad news from Simhasthal."

Theeran tosses the scroll across. "Read for yourself."

He reads the parchment and whistles softly. "So, King Vikrant is to marry Princess Idhika of Vajrapur. Looks like Vijendra stole a march on us."

"You mean he stole a march on you," Theeran says. "This was your idea, to offer that Simhasthali coward my sweet daughter's hand. A stupid plan from the very beginning. I should have known that boy would not stand up to Vijendra."

"I admit I failed," Kartik concedes. "But it was the smart move. Together, we would have defeated the Vajras and wrested their kingdom for ourselves."

Meghnad's voice betrays his fear. "But he has said no. And now, Vikrant and Vijendra will soon attack Triloha together."

"They will not," Kartik says.

"They won't?" Meghnad looks surprised.

Kartik shakes his head, and tries to lessen his brother's anxiety. "No, dada. They will conquer Naavipur before they arrive at our gates."

"That is the smart move," Theeran agrees. "The Naaviks aren't warriors, and their army is small. They will fall within a day."

"I doubt that," Kartik says.

Theeran regards his son suspiciously. "Why?"

"Because King Ranadutt has hired the Jahati Brigade from Sirukesh," Kartik informs him.

"The Jahati mercenaries?" Theeran is surprised. "Are you certain?"

"Yes, baba, I am," Kartik says. "Three hundred ships have departed to ferry over ten thousand warriors to Naavipur."

"That's almost a third of the Naavik army," Meghnad exclaims.

"Your love for numbers does you proud, dada." Kartik's words drip with sarcasm. "But it won't matter. They will fall in battle. King Vijendra is a master tactician, who now has close to a hundred thousand men at his command. The Naaviks and the Jahatis will lose."

He turns to his father. "In a few days, a letter will arrive from King Ranadutt. He will offer to marry his second son Prince

Dhairya to Jyothika if we ally with him. I urge you to refuse the alliance."

"Why should I?" Theeran asks. "If your information is correct, then a combined Trilohan and Naavik army will match the Vajras and the Simhas. Add the Jahatis, and victory is all but assured."

"Maybe," Kartik says, "But what purpose will that serve?"

"What purpose?" Meghnad is confused. "It will end the war."

"And we will have gained nothing in return," declares Kartik, his voice rising a notch. "I have made peace with the fact that blood will be shed. But if thousands of our men must die, let it be for a good reason. Here's what I propose. Let Vikrant and Vijendra attack Naavipur. Yes, they will prevail, but they will also lose many men in battle." Excitement sparkles in his eyes. "That is when we will strike. I have established contact with the commander of the Barabos Battalion. For a fair price, his fifteen thousand soldiers have agreed to fight with us."

A shocked Theeran slams his fist on the table. "The Barabosi? From Farisa? You hired those bloodthirsty mercenaries without my approval?"

"Father, I would never do such a thing without your permission," Kartik says. "I only enquired about their price and willingness, and now present the same to you for your consideration."

"You overstep your bounds, son," Theeran thunders.

"Then I will accept whatever punishment you see fit," Kartik says. "But I ask you to consider this. With the Barabosi on our side, we might be able to defeat the tired armies of Simhasthal and Vajrapur. Saptaveni will fall soon after. And with all the kingdoms defeated, you will become the first Emperor of Saravat."

Little love is lost between father and son, not since the King realised the people love their Prince more than their monarch. But Kartik is counting on the one thing Theeran loves more than anything in this world.

Power.

He is proven right when the King nods his assent.

"Make the arrangements," Theeran says, "And summon the ministers. We have plenty to discuss."

Kartik smiles in his chair. The world is about to get very interesting indeed.

CHAPTER TWENTY-ONE

Relax, Gautam's mind instructs his body. *Do not get distracted.*

He moves from one *asana* to the next, and the scars stretch across his bronzed skin. Reminders, of time spent in the fighting pits, down in the villages and outposts where lords and Kings never paid much attention.

Those days lie in his past. Now, he lives in a palace, loved by a husband who is both honourable and kind. What more could he ask for?

A softer bed, perhaps.

He glances at Kashyap, asleep on their rough coir mattress, the kind which all military men are used to. Good for the back, he says, but Gautam wishes for a featherbed instead.

Still, it is better than the ones he had slept on as a child. The cold wooden floor he had called home in Saptaveni. The mud in the wheat fields of Parvakesh, with rats for company. A gutter outside Himbagarh, in which he had fallen asleep after stealing a leg of lamb.

The old man's bed in Saakivan.

He had been an orphan then, alone, far from home and kingdom. Yet, fate had been kind to him. Kaushal had found him in Naavipur. A sword-smith, who had recognised Gautam's talent with a blade. He had given him a roof to sleep under, food to fill his belly, and training to become the finest swordsman in Saravat.

Where would I be without him, Gautam wonders. Probably still wandering from town to village, looking for food to steal or a warm place to rest his head.

He had saved me, even when he made me fight to the death in the arena. Gautam turns once more to Kashyap. *He led me to you, and for that, I will be forever grateful.*

As he moves from *veerbhadrasana* to *ardhachandrasana*, the silence is broken by a scream.

"No!" Kashyap jumps in bed, trembling. A dark anger clouds his eyes. Gautam rushes across the room and holds his husband.

"What were you dreaming of?" he asks.

"My brother," Kashyap says.

Two months have passed since Giridhar fell, yet he remains scarred by the memory.

Of a head, rolling in the dirt.

To make matters worse, his nephew, King Vikrant, has agreed to marry Vijendra's daughter, and ally with him in the conquest of Saravat.

Gautam does not judge the King. The lust for power brings out the worst in the best of men. But this decision has denied Kashyap his vengeance, and it has changed him.

This is not the man he once knew.

They first met fourteen years ago, at the festival games of Himbagarh, the capital of Naavipur. The smart money was on the General, a formidable swordsman and eleven-time champion.

The rules were simple. The first to strike the opponent's helm three times would be declared the winner. Gautam opened the tourney against Kashyap, who laughed when he laid eyes on his scrawny foe. He intended to win without breaking a sweat.

It ended up being a one-sided fight, but not the way the General was expecting. Gautam's hands moved as if possessed by spirits, and the whirl of his blades was too fast for Kashyap to see. The Simhasthali was harried into defending, while the Sapta was ruthless. Once. Twice. And finally, for the third time in as many minutes, his sword whacked against the hard helm covering Kashyap's skull.

Gautam went on to dazzle opponent after opponent, and won the games easily. Prize money in hand, he meant to leave the city, when the summons arrived.

From the General.

Gautam was scared at first. Wealthy nobles do not like to be beaten, especially not by a swordsman from the streets. Kashyap was not like them, though. He offered a position in his personal guard, which Gautam accepted at once, happy to earn a steady income.

The months flew past, and they spent much time together, bonding over their mutual respect for each other's swordsmanship. Slowly, the conversation steered to their lives. Their hopes. Their ambitions. And in the end, their love.

Once they were certain of their feelings, Kashyap sought Giridhar's permission to marry Gautam. His request caused a huge uproar, within the family and the kingdom.

But Kashyap remained steadfast, and his love was soon rewarded. Giridhar acquiesced to his request, and over time, the world came to accept their marriage.

When it happened, Gautam had believed they would be happy forever. *Yet now he lies in my arms, haunted by his memories.*

"What did Giridhar want?" Gautam asks.

Kashyap still shivers with rage. "He asked how I could sleep while his soul roams the spirit world, restless, waiting to be avenged."

"And what did you tell him?" Gautam asks.

"I told him I am helpless," says Kashyap, his pain evident. "Vikrant orders an alliance, and I must obey. But he laughed at me, and called me a coward. He said he would not have cared. He would have ridden off alone and challenged Vijendra."

"He did challenge Vijendra, my love. And he lost."

"I know that," Kashyap shouts. "Vijendra appeared then, sword in hand. He was laughing at me. And then—" His rage surges. "And then, he swung his sword and cut off my brother's head."

"Shhh," Gautam strokes his hair. "Put these thoughts of vengeance out of your mind. Our King has spoken."

"Yes." Bitterness sours Kashyap's words. "Our King has spoken. My nephew forgets his father's death, and puts his ambitions first. To think, the blood of my ancestors runs in his veins." He looks up at Gautam. "The wrong men advise him. Ayushmann whispers in his ears, and Atulya plots his actions."

"Atulya is a wise man," Gautam says.

"He is an old fool," Kashyap says, "A scared man who does not have the stomach for war. No, my love, I will do everything I can to have this marriage set aside. We will fight Vijendra. And I will kill him."

He jumps out of bed, grabs a robe, then turns to face his husband. "I will see you in the courtyard."

He storms out of the room. Gautam sighs as he watches him go. There is little he can do to help. Besides, he must prepare for practice.

There will soon be a wedding. But before that, there will be the games. And the 'First Fight'. Kashyap, Indranuj, and he will stand as champions for the groom against three champions of the bride.

He picks up his sword belt, one few Simhasthalis would wear. Two scabbards, two blades, one for each hand, the way he has always fought. As he wears it, he smiles.

Kashyap may or may not get his war, but he will certainly have to draw swords in Vajrapur.

CHAPTER TWENTY-TWO

Ayushmann rides down the road to the palace, unconcerned by the chaos which reigns all around him.

In mansion after mansion, servants dart from one corner to the other, dragging out chests and trunks, filled with clothes and gifts.

Saravati weddings are long, spread over six days. There's the 'Mother's Welcome', the 'Tribute to the Ancestors', the 'Father's Farewell', and the traditional games before the engagement. Then a day of rest will follow, before the wedding can finally take place.

The ladies have anticipated many changes of clothing, and have packed accordingly, for themselves and their families. Their carriages will run heavy. Not Ayushmann's though, for he has neither a wife nor children to add to his horses' burden.

The tale of his presence in Simhasthal is one known to all. He arrived one day in Harit Nagar, where Atulya took him under his wing. He has been with the schoolmaster ever since, even moving to Simhasthal when Atulya became the royal advisor.

A few years later, Giridhar appointed him as Minister of Security, which caused much heartburn among the nobles of Simhasthal. They tried their best to provoke him. Over his foreign antecedents, his dark skin, even his manner of speaking.

Ayushmann had never let it bother him. He had survived far worse.

He yawns as he turns onto the Naagmarg. The past few weeks have been exhausting. Sleep eludes him, as it had last night when his spy had returned with news from Vajrapur. He had tasked the man to investigate the relationship between Vijendra and Jayendu.

What he found wasn't encouraging.

Only two things seemed to connect them. Jayendu had been a dear friend of King Dhirendra, and often visited the palace to offer counsel and attend functions. And both had lost members of their family to the great fever twenty-two years ago.

Neither was important. Jayendu was a dear friend of all five Kings, and almost every family in Vajrapur had lost a loved one to the fever. Ayushmann ordered his man to dig deeper. *There must be something.*

He arrives at the palace courtyard to the sound of steel clashing against steel. Kashyap, Gautam, and Indranuj compete against three Parasu. A fair match, for the royal guards are well trained. Yet not as well as the three champions.

General Kashyap fights like a true descendant of the great Simha should. Sword in one hand, shield in the other, both used without fear.

His nephew, Prince Indranuj, looks like the younger version of his father, King Giridhar. But the boy fights like his teacher, Colonel Gautam, with two swords alternating between attack and defence.

The pupil is good, but nothing compared to his master. Gautam fights with guile and precision, his swords dancing through the air to dazzle his opponent. Ayushmann is impressed.

By his speed, his agility, his cunning, those very same traits which had defeated Kashyap all those years ago.

Even as the thought crosses his mind, Gautam's sword sneaks past the Parasu's defences and smacks against his helm. A short while later, Kashyap and Indranuj defeat their opponents as well. They stop for a rest, and Ayushmann joins them.

"Your Highness, my General, Colonel," he calls out.

They turn to face him. Indranuj smiles. "Lord Ayushmann, greetings."

Gautam greets him less enthusiastically. "A good morning to you, Lord Ayushmann."

Kashyap simply nods his head, then sheathes his sword and walks away.

Ayushmann watches him go. "The General appears to be in a foul mood."

"Rotten sleep," Gautam explains. "Fear not. He will get enough rest on our journey."

"Indeed, he will," Ayushmann remarks.

"Did you see me fight, my lord?" asks Indranuj, excited the way only a boy of sixteen can be.

"I did, Your Highness," Ayushmann says.

"What do you think?" Indranuj asks. "As good as my father?"

"No, my Prince," Ayushmann replies. The boy's dejected look makes him laugh. "You are far better than your father ever was. Believe me, if King Giridhar had to face you with a sword, he would have conceded defeat at once."

The smile returns to Indranuj's face. "Any idea who our opponents will be?"

"I can wager a guess," Ayushmann says. "Prince Biraj is a certainty. He is the bride's uncle, and a fine swordsman."

He pauses to think. "His second is most likely to be Captain Dhananjay. I have heard his name spoken often. A great swordsman, with an attitude to match. The third is anyone's guess. I would have assumed General Rannveer, but seeing as he will be the commander of Vijendra's new army, it would not be seemly."

"It does not matter," Indranuj declares. "They will fall to my sword."

Gautam looks disappointed. "Your highness, I have spoken to you about false pride. Win something first, before you believe yourself to be above us all."

The Prince bows his head in a gesture of mock humility, "As you command, chacha." But his eyes retain their arrogance. "Still, I cannot wait for the day I get to face a Vajra in the games, to humiliate them in front of their own citizens. Though, to be honest, I wish dada would order us to face them on the battlefield instead."

Gautam puts an arm around his student. "The King has not. And even if he does, you would not be able to fight. There must be an heir left behind. That is your duty, until King Vikrant produces a son."

"A stupid rule," Indranuj says. "I wish I had been born first. Then I could go to battle and my brother would have to stay behind."

"Why do you believe it is such a bad thing to be born last?" Ayushmann asks. "Did you know I am the last born in my family?"

Indranuj shakes his head. "I did not."

"I have three older brothers and a sister," Ayushmann says. The thought of his siblings does not bring him much joy. "They were always cared for, more than I ever was. But I still managed to make a name for myself, didn't I?" The grin on his face adds to the playfulness of his words. He bows. "Now, I must take your leave, my Prince, Colonel. I have to see to the King's travel preparations."

Gautam stops him. "Lord Ayushmann, before you leave. Your older brothers and sister. Since I have not met them, I assume they do not live in Simhasthal?"

"Your assumption is correct," Ayushmann replies. "My brothers live in Naavipur."

"And your sister?" Gautam asks.

For a brief moment, the smile vanishes from Ayushmann's face. It returns just as quickly, broader than ever. "My sister married a rich man in Vajrapur."

Indranuj is surprised. "Vajrapur? I did not know. I hope to meet her while we are there."

"I promise you will, my Prince," Ayushmann says. "My sister will be most pleased to make your acquaintance."

But how happy will she be to see me, Ayushmann wonders, as he walks to the palace.

CHAPTER TWENTY-THREE

The baarat departs from Kuragarh, two hundred carriages rolling through the valley, stretching almost a mile long, guarded by three thousand infantrymen, one thousand cavalry, and the Parasu.

The procession moves through the Mrugaranya, and the journey progresses pleasantly enough. Lunches under canopies of green, laden with fruit and flowers. Dinners by campfires, with stories to keep them company.

And then, nine days later, it comes to an end. Nandini gazes out the window as they cross the western border of Simhasthal and enter the Laalkhet.

Where her husband died.

She has tried not to think of it, and failed. As have her people. They may smile and laugh, but she knows their joy to be false. Few, if any, are in favour of this marriage, and the closer they get to their destination, the more their bitterness grows.

Indranuj is the worst of them all. She tried to speak with him, of his hatred towards the Vajras. Of his anger towards this marriage. Of his bitterness towards Vikrant for agreeing to it.

She tried to make him see reason. But why would he, when she herself refused to? She needs to understand Vikrant's decision. But she has not had the chance to speak to him yet.

Until today.

She had insisted on riding with him. But she had not expected him to be this reticent, sitting with brows furrowed, lips curled tight, watching an unknown spot in the distance. Her son, who had emerged from her womb crying his lungs out. The weak boy whom everyone had sniggered at.

Do they dare snigger now? He is a King and will one day be an Emperor. For now, though, he remains a boy, who chooses to avoid her, to avoid the conversation.

She cannot let him.

"My son," Nandini says, "I wanted to ask you something."

Vikrant looks at her. "You can ask me anything, maa."

She clenches her fists. "When you chose Idhika, did you think of how we would feel? Indranuj, Gayathri, Kashyap?" Her voice trembles. "Me?"

He blinks, and she senses his inner conflict. "I did," he says.

"And still you chose to marry her?" Nandini asks.

"I did," he says again.

"Why?" she demands to know.

"It was not much of a choice," he says.

"You could have chosen Jyothika," Nandini says. "After all, you spent many summers in Triloha, and have known her since you were children."

Vikrant smirks. "I know her brothers as well. Especially the oldest."

"Prince Sreedharan?" *What does he have to do with this,* Nandini wonders.

But Vikrant does not elaborate. "Yes. Under no circumstances do I want to be allied with him."

"You consider him worse than Vijendra, the man who murdered your father?"

Vikrant stares at his mother. "To quote my grandmother, Vijendra defeated my father in battle."

"An illegal battle," she retorts.

Vikrant shrugs. "It does not matter. In a few weeks, in the eyes of the gods and by our laws, I will call Vijendra father and he will call me son."

"The very thought sickens me," she says.

Vikrant does not seem to care. "Then you should have spoken your mind earlier."

"I was not in control of my senses then," Nandini protests. "But I have had time to think it over."

"The time for thought has passed," he states.

"My son, you are the King," she pleads with him. "I will always accept your decision. So will Indu and Gayathri. But you have to help us understand. Perhaps Gayathri does, but Indu does not. He is young, and you hardly spend any time with him as it is."

Vikrant opens a box and picks up some almonds. He tosses one in his mouth and crunches it loudly while he speaks. "Vijendra. Theeran. It makes no difference. Both only want to use me to propel themselves to a bigger throne."

"Then what swayed your mind?" she demands to know. "Was it Idhika?"

Vikrant remains silent.

"Is she truly so beautiful?" Nandini asks.

"Jyothika is beautiful as well," Vikrant says. "She is kind. And dignified. She would make a good Queen. But Idhika—" He smiles, with the wistful look of a boy in love. "She is beautiful, yes, but it's more than that. She has an inner strength that draws you in. You should have seen her that day. She was the smallest person there, yet she towered above us all."

"Careful, my child," Nandini warns her son. "Never forget, Idhika is Vijendra's daughter."

"I won't," Vikrant promises.

Nandini shakes her head. *Why do I get the feeling you already have?*

She decides to let the issue rest, and move to another. "Kashyap came to speak with me yesterday."

"And?" asks Vikrant, disinterested.

"The ministers and he feel you rely on Atulya's advice a little too much," she says. "As well as Ayushmann's."

"What of it?" Vikrant asks. "Atulya chacha is my advisor. And Ayushmann sits on the council of ministers. I trust them both."

How do I make him understand? "You can trust no one," Nandini says. "Only your family. Listen to me, please. It might be wise for you to relieve Atulya from his duties and choose a royal advisor of your own. Maybe your uncle."

"Atulya chacha suggested the same thing," Vikrant says.

Nandini cannot hide her surprise. This might be the best news she has received in weeks. "He did?"

"He offered his resignation," Vikrant says, "And proposed Kashyap chacha replace him."

"You should have accepted," Nandini says.

"I did not," Vikrant says.

Nandini turns crestfallen. "Why?"

"Because father trusted him above all," Vikrant replies, "And that is good enough for me."

His gaze returns beyond the window, to the outside world and his troubled thoughts. Nandini worries about him. He was always been this way, forever a thinker, never a doer. But there is little she can do about it.

They ride in silence. Late afternoon crosses to early evening, and the weather cools by the time the procession comes to a halt. Vikrant holds her hand as he leads her through the grass to the spot where Vijendra killed Giridhar.

Her heart grows heavy as she stands with her children and watches her people drop flowers where her husband's life ended.

Atulya arrives last, with the face of a man whose very soul is being tortured. Nandini does not doubt his sorrow, but his actions suggest he is playing a game of his own. *We cannot trust him anymore.*

Once he has moved on, the royal family pays their respects. Chandran and Gayathri go first with their children, then Kashyap and Gautam, followed by Indranuj. Tears flow freely down his face, and Vikrant steps forward to comfort his brother. Indranuj angrily pushes him away and storms off.

If Vikrant is hurt by his brother's actions, he does not show it. He touches his hand to the ground, then brings it to his heart. "Rest in peace, baba," he whispers, before he makes way for his mother.

Nandini steps forward. She lays a single flower upon the pile, then kneels in the grass. Her tears water the earth as she leans forward and kisses the ground.

"Goodbye, my love," she says, before she rises to her feet and heads back to their carriage.

With every step, her heart turns to stone. A single thought consumes her mind. Even if it takes the rest of her life, one way or another, she will make Vijendra pay for his sins.

CHAPTER TWENTY-FOUR

Decisions, decisions.

Indrani paces up and down the room, her gaze falling on the dozens of *saris* laid out for her approval. Many cloth merchants have come and gone, but not one has met the Queen's high standards.

Now another stands before her, shivering in his boots, praying his designs gain her favour. Indrani picks up a sari and runs her hand through the material. A new blend, softer than the usual silk, and light as air.

She beckons the merchant over. "What fabric is this?"

"Muslin, Your Majesty," the man replies. "A new kind of fabric, with which only I stitch."

She fixes him with a stare. "A big boast, merchant."

The man bows, nervous. "The truth, Your Majesty."

Does he lie? Indrani cannot say for certain. The cloth is fine, though. And there are many to choose from, in vivid colours. Midnight indigo, peacock green, sunset orange. The embroidery, too, is of the highest order, stunning in its creativity and intricacy.

Her handmaidens eagerly await her decision. So does the merchant, who wonders if the Queen will favour him for the royal wedding. The longer she takes, the more nervous he grows.

"I beg Your Majesty's forgiveness if my designs displease you," he says.

She breaks her silence at long last. "I am far from displeased." She graces him with a smile. "Your fame is well-earned. I will take them all. And after the celebrations, they will be my gifts to my handmaidens."

The girls squeal in delight and thank their Queen. She looks at them benevolently, though she grimaces on the inside, unable to bear their childish enthusiasm.

"Your Majesty," a man's breathless voice calls out. She turns to see a guard run across the room, gasping as he approaches.

"Catch your breath," she commands.

The guard breathes heavily, then bows. "My apologies for the intrusion, Your Majesty."

"Never mind that," she says. "Speak. Why are you here?"

The guard tells her, "Lord Jayendu requests an audience with Your Majesty."

A smile breaks across her face. "He does, does he? Let his messenger know the Queen is busy planning the royal wedding."

The guard shuffles his feet. "There is no messenger, My Queen. Lord Jayendu himself waits on the terrace."

Her anger awakens. "On the terrace?"

"Yes, Your Majesty," the guard replies. "He says he likes to look at the gardens."

"And you let him enter without my permission?" Indrani thunders.

The guard swallows hard. If looks could kill, the Queen would have dropped him dead where he stood. "Your Majesty, it is Lord Jayendu—" he starts to say.

"Yes," she says. "Lord Jayendu. A powerful man indeed. More powerful than your Queen, perhaps?"

The guard remains silent, awaiting his Queen's punishment. Fortunately for him, she is in a good mood this morning. "You may return to your post," she says. "I will deal with Lord Jayendu."

The guard bows and races away, grateful to have escaped with his head. Indrani sighs. Jayendu had tried to meet Vijendra and her since their return from Simhasthal. They had put him off on one pretext or another. But now, the time has come to face their problems.

She heads to the terrace. The long balcony overlooks the gardens, where flowers bloom and the trees grow pregnant with fruit. Jayendu sits on a comfortable chair, dressed in a loose kurta and dhoti, holding a lemon sherbet in his hand as he watches the birds and butterflies flutter in the greenery.

Indrani greets him warmly. "Lord Jayendu, it is a pleasure to see you."

Jayendu turns to face her, the smile broad on his face. "I very much doubt that, Your Majesty. But it is kind of you to say so."

Indrani ignores the jibe. If anything, his toothless smile bothers her more. On the inside, her stomach churns at the sight. But on the outside, she wears a pleasant expression and takes a seat.

"What troubles steal you away from your bed?" she asks.

"Your husband," Jayendu replies, "And his stupid decisions."

Indrani bristles, but keeps her composure. "And what decisions might those be?"

"This marriage of Princess Idhika," says Jayendu, his annoyance rising. "We had agreed, the three of us, to offer her hand to Prince Sreedharan. Not King Vikrant." Jayendu's lips quiver with suppressed rage. "I thought I had dissuaded your husband from this folly, after he sent that letter to Giridhar without my knowledge. I had considered the matter ended when the Simha King said no. But now, Vijendra repeats the mistake. Vikrant, heir to Saravat. Hah! From all I have heard, the boy has no sense, and even less courage."

"Idhika has both," Indrani retorts.

"Courage, yes. Sense? No." Jayendu sighs. "She lacks vision, she lacks the capability to be ruthless. If she had both, I would not have to spend my last few years on earth with all these worries." He shakes his head in frustration, and slaps his palm on the armrest. "No, My Queen, you and your husband have erred in this matter. I did not expect you to make such a common mistake."

"And what mistake would that be, my lord?" asks Indrani, her irritation starting to show.

"Loving your family more than your kingdom," Jayendu says. He raises a hand to cut off the Queen's protest. "Vijendra was like the son I never had. Yet I did not task him with that which he is incapable of achieving. The plan was simple. Conquer Simhasthal and end their royal line. Then offer Princess Idhika to Triloha. Sreedharan would have made a strong Emperor after Vijendra. But now, I fear for Saravat."

So do we, Indrani thinks as she takes his wrinkled hand in hers. "My lord, your worries are unfounded."

Jayendu looks at her with bleak eyes. "When your husband was only ten years old... even then, I saw something in him. Greatness. Someone who could inspire this land to greatness. I have done everything in my power to ensure he fulfils his destiny. But now—" He chuckles. "My Queen, I am an old man. In a few years, I will be gone from this world. So, I cannot say whether Vijendra and you will be proven right. But the die is cast. Vikrant is the chosen one now. And with him rest the fortunes of Saravat."

With great effort, he rises to his feet and bows.

"I pray those fortunes are good," Jayendu says. "For all our sakes."

He takes his leave. Indrani watches him go, hobbling on aged legs, seemingly a tired, defeated man.

Others may be fooled, but she knows better. Jayendu is an old ally, one who is unlikely to sit by and let events unfold as they may. Vijendra and she owe him everything, but perhaps the time has come to keep a closer eye on him, and all whom he meets.

She returns to her chambers, reminding herself to speak to Vijendra of their meeting.

CHAPTER TWENTY-FIVE

Am I the only one happy to be on this journey, Gayathri wonders.

Twelve days have passed since they departed Kuragarh. And now, they enter the gloominess of the Andhakaranya, which only serves to sour the mood further.

It does not matter, she tells herself. Soon, she will resume her past life, the one she had when she used to visit the other kingdoms with Chandran. She wonders if it will be the same. Laughing, drinking, being the life of the party, with men fighting to gain her attention.

And why wouldn't they?

At twenty-five years of age, and after three children, her figure remains as desirable as ever, slim waisted, heavy breasted. But it is her face which draws the most attention, its features delicate yet fierce—plump lips painted a deep red, soft eyes lined with kohl, and cheekbones chiselled to perfection. Her hair, too, is set in a modern fashion, braided down the sides and left loose at the back, giving her the appearance of frivolity and elegance all at once.

Their carriage hits a bump on the road, and she hears Chandran curse. "Damn these roads."

Gayathri turns to her husband. *The gods blessed me with so much beauty, still I married this chubby oaf.* Out of choice, no less.

"Language," she admonishes him.

"Sorry," he apologises, "But look at me."

Red sherbet clouds his cream-coloured tunic. She quickly uses her kerchief to gently dab the stain.

Chandran smiles gratefully. "Thank you, my love."

"You're welcome," she says.

"How much longer till we reach Dhaningarh?" a boy's voice asks.

She turns to Abhimanyu. Six years of age, he looks just like her, with a strong jaw and soft brown eyes. Too bad he is dim-witted like his father. Her four-year-old twins, Nivedita and Dhanush, sit beside their older brother.

They look like their father, but take after me. Gayathri shakes her head. Mysterious are the ways of nature.

"We have entered the Andhakaranya," she tells Abhimanyu.

He jumps in his seat, scared. "The forest of the ghosts?"

Nivedita giggles at her older brother's fear. "Dada, it's not the forest of the ghosts."

Abhimanyu glares at her. "What do you know? You're only a baby. Besides, nanimaa told me the Andhakaranya is full of ghosts."

"There are no ghosts here," Gayathri says. "That's just a story grandmothers tell their grandchildren to scare them."

Nivedita sticks her tongue out at Abhimanyu. "See? I told you."

Dhanush joins his twin sister in mocking their older brother. Abhimanyu's face reddens with anger.

"Enough of that," Gayathri scolds them. The twins subside, but Abhimanyu continues to seethe.

"Baba, we are bored," Nivedita says. "Tell us a story."

Chandran seems reluctant, until her brothers add their voices. "Please baba, please, please."

Their father gives in. "Okay, okay. Has anyone ever told you the story of how Simhasthal was founded?"

The children shake their heads.

"No?" Chandran is astonished. "I cannot believe it. Are you even my children? How can you not know the history of your kingdom?"

"We don't know, baba," Dhanush says. "But you can tell us."

"Please, please," his siblings chime in.

Gayathri sides with her children. "Stop teasing them and tell them the story."

"As you command, Your Highness," Chandran bows his head to his wife, then turns to his children and begins the story. "Five hundred years ago, Saravat had only four kingdoms—Naavipur, Saptaveni, Triloha, and Vajrapur. The borders of Vajrapur extended to the Rodasi, a barren, rocky land hardly worth the effort to tame."

He leans in closer, and his voice drops to a whisper. "Little did they know a secret land lay beyond the mountains. A frozen hell called Shitakul, where a cold and miserable tribe lived."

"The Kuras," Gayathri says.

"The Kuras," Chandran nods his head. "Their chieftain was a man named Simha. And his wife was named Gayathri."

The children turn to their mother. "Maa, just like you," Dhanush exclaims.

Gayathri nods her head. “Yes. She was the first Queen of Simhasthal, whom I am named after.”

Chandran continues the story. “Simha was tired of their existence, of fighting death every day. Fighting the bears, the wolves, and if you survived, fighting the great white lion and its great big claws”

He curls his fingers into claws, and swipes his hand across their bellies, imitating the fearsome killing strike of the lion. The children jump in fright.

“And then there was the cold,” he whispers. “A cold so sinister it could turn blood to ice in your veins.”

Both boys look at one another and shiver, while Nivedita watches her father with wide eyes.

“Yes, a horrible way to die,” Chandran agrees. “Simha decided to lead his tribe over the mountains. Thirteen thousand men, women and children, who crossed the snowy peaks to see what lay on the other side.”

“They found a barren land, but in the distance, they could see greenery. The Mrugaranya, teeming with fruit and meat and other wonders. Even better, they were no people. Simha ordered his men to set up camp. This is where they would build their new kingdom.”

“The valley was cold, but for those who had weathered the snows of Shitakul, it felt as good as summer. For a few months, they were content to live off the land. But Simha soon began to tire of this life as well. He knew there must be more.”

“No,” Gayathri interrupts. “My dear husband, if you must tell the story, tell it right. It wasn’t Simha who knew. It was Gayathri.”

Chandran smiles at his wife. The children turn to their mother, who takes over the story.

She says, "It was Gayathri who urged her people to explore the forest. They moved in small bands, scouting larger and larger areas. And all the land they crossed unchallenged, Gayathri claimed in the name of Simha. A year passed without incident. And then, one fine day, the King of Vajrapur learned of their presence."

"What did he do, maa?" Nivedita asks.

"King Anjuman did what Kings have always done," she says. "He underestimated his enemy. He despatched a platoon of five hundred soldiers to deal with these barbarians. Good warriors, but no match for the Kuras, who had faced death every day and survived."

"And they had Simha," Abhimanyu shouts. "The greatest warrior who ever lived."

His mother shakes her head. "Simha was but a warrior. It was Gayathri's intelligence which won them the battle. You see, their weapons were fashioned from the forests, arrows and spears made from wood. Deadly, no doubt, but no match for steel. So, she used the forest to their advantage, hiding her men in trees, ready to swoop down on the enemy. For days, they waited in the branches, until finally, the Vajras arrived."

"Maa?"

Gayathri turns to Nivedita, who looks sad.

"Did all the Vajras die?" Nivedita asks.

"Yes, my child," Gayathri answers her daughter. "As they walked through the forest, the Kuras caught them off guard. They killed all but one, whom Gayathri sent back with a message. The forest and the Rodasi valley now belong to the Kuras, a kingdom which shall henceforth be known as Simhasthal. The land of Simha."

"Maa, what did King Anjuman do?" Dhanush asks.

"He was furious," she says. "These barbarians? Killing his men? He flew into a rage, and in his anger, he forgot the first rule of battle." She looks at her children. "Which is?"

Nivedita throws up her hand. "Knowledge is power."

"Correct," she says to her daughter, who beams with pride. "The only Vajra survivor told his King that there were not more than a thousand tribals in the forest, for those were all he had seen. In his rage, King Anjuman rushed out with five thousand men, not knowing that in the Mrugaranya, over four thousand Kuras lay hidden and waiting, now armed with steel swords and spears, stolen from the corpses of the Vajras."

"This time, they dug traps and filled them with spikes fashioned from wood. More and more Vajras died as they marched deeper into the forest. Then, the Kuras launched guerrilla attacks, picking off stragglers. More Vajras fell, and more weapons were collected, and soon enough they were armed as well as their rivals."

"The Vajras began to give up hope. Then, the thousand Kuras appeared. They taunted the Vajras, before running towards the mountains. An angry King Anjuman ordered his men to give chase. Meanwhile, the remaining Kuras ran a wide arc around the enemy to arrive behind them. Once they had them trapped in between, they faced them in open battle. And this time, they killed them all, down to the last man."

"Did many Kuras die?" Dhanush asks.

"Close to a thousand died in that battle," Gayathri says. "But they took five thousand Vajras with them, along with their King. The enemy was scared now. Who were these tribals? What magical powers did they possess that they cannot be defeated?"

"Anjuman's son, Suryakumar, ascended to the throne. He had to avenge his father's death, or his people would never respect him. But he was scared. So, he raised a large army, twelve thousand strong, a force he believed none could stand against."

"Twelve thousand?" Abhimanyu shouts, his childish mind quickly comparing the numbers. "But maa, there were only four thousand Kuras."

"Minus the thousand who died," she says. "But it did not matter. The Kuras had Gayathri with them, who played her most powerful weapon." She pauses, then whispers the word. "Fear."

"Fear?" the children ask, confused.

"Fear is the deadliest weapon of them all," she says. "When King Suryakumar and his twelve thousand Vajras arrived on the Laalkhet, they saw only three thousand Kuras facing them. This would be an easy battle, they thought, and laughed at their enemy. Their laughter grew to a thunderous roar, until a Kura stepped forward."

"The man's name was Bighu. To the Vajras, he looked strong and fierce. But they did not know that Bighu had been grievously wounded in the last battle, and was not long for this life. Which is why he had volunteered for the task."

"What task?" Abhimanyu asks.

His mother replies, "The task Gayathri had thought up. Bighu stood halfway between the two armies and called out to the enemy. *May the gods accept my sacrifice,* he screamed to the heavens, *and bless my people*. Then he spoke the words we all know so well. The oath of the Parasu. *Dead I am now, death to our enemy. For Simha, for Simhasthal*. Finally, he lit himself on fire, laughing all the while."

The children do not believe her.

"He lit himself on fire?" Nivedita asks.

"Yes," says Gayathri, aware of how incredible and unbelievable this must all sound to their innocent minds. She continues, "And while he died, the other Kuras cheered."

The children look even more shocked.

"They cheered?" Dhanush asks.

"They did," she says. "At the top of their voices. And it worked. The Vajras were scared of these powerful barbarians who could light themselves on fire and laugh as they died. When the Kuras advanced, the Vajras stepped back, until their lines broke and their men fled." She smiles. "It was a very short battle. Eleven thousand Vajras died that day. Their army was completely decimated, and their King barely escaped with his life."

"From that day on, the border of the Mrugaranya became the border of Simhasthal. Gayathri set up outposts and devised a warning system. If the enemy was ever spotted, the Kuras would be ready."

"I like Gayathri," Dhanush says. "Maa, why did she not become the ruler of Simhasthal?"

Abhimanyu scoffs. "How can she become the ruler? She was a woman."

Nivedita runs quick to anger. "So? She sounds more intelligent than all the men."

"She was, my child," Gayathri agrees. "She was the most intelligent Kura ever. But it did not matter. She was a woman, and a woman can never rule."

Abhimanyu smirks, but Nivedita is not satisfied. "Why?"

She sighs. "Because we live in a man's world. And men are too foolish to realise that a woman could do everything they do, only better."

"Listen well to your mother," Chandran says, "Because she speaks the truth."

"But baba," Dhanush protests, "You are the head of our house."

"Only the face of it, my son," Chandran tells him. "Everything I do, everything we are, is guided by your mother's wisdom."

The boys look at their mother with awe. Gayathri holds her husband's hand, and looks at him with loving eyes. This is why she chose him all those years ago. Not for his wealth, not for his looks, not for his intelligence.

She chose him for his obedience.

In their marriage, she pulled the strings. And though the world may never know her worth, like her namesake five centuries ago, they will feel the force of her actions.

CHAPTER TWENTY-SIX

The two girls race across the fields. Farmers and villagers watch them run past, but none move to stop them. They do not dare. It would mean the loss of an arm if they laid a hand on the Princess of Vajrapur.

Idhika runs with carefree abandon. She is a precocious nine-year-old, always turning things to her advantage. Which is what she does right now, convincing her obedient friend to help her skip class and accompany her to the Andhakaranya.

"Run faster, Aparna," she screams, "Or we will be caught."

Aparna follows the Princess, terrified. Of being caught, and of the Andhakaranya. Her mother has often told her stories of children disappearing in the dark forest, never to be seen again.

Idhika laughs at her fears. She is not a child. She is a Princess. And a Princess fears nothing. People have tried to remind her that she is a girl, and there are limits to what she can do. She ignores them all. Her view of life is much simpler. If you can do something well, you should be allowed to do it.

It saddens her that her parents do not believe as she does. They lost their sons, and their daughter survived. Maybe it would have been better if she were born a boy. But boys are ugly and yucky, and unlike girls, they do not get to experience the finer things in life.

The girls halt at the edge of the Andhakaranya and look at one another. Neither has been inside, and from where they stand, it looks like it could swallow them whole.

"Your Highness, please," Aparna says, "Do not make me go in."

Idhika holds her hand. "Why are you scared? I am with you."

She drags her trembling friend into the forest, into the gloom, which envelops them until they are lost.

"Which way do we go?" Aparna asks.

Idhika looks around her. "Masterji said their flowers bloom white. They should be easy to spot."

Aparna nods her head and follows the Princess, who is determined to find the trees which flower with her favourite fruit. Her geography teacher said they grow in the Andhakaranya, where girls are forbidden to go.

Stupid masterji. She vowed to prove him wrong. So she goes, further and further in, until she finds what she is looking for.

The Sitarabaug.

A thousand white flowers glow above her, a shimmering oasis. To her childish mind, the sight appears so much like the starry night sky which she has often gazed at from the window of her chambers. Her excitement reaches its peak.

"Are you ready?" she asks Aparna.

Her friend shakes her head, and Idhika laughs at her fear. She hugs the trunk and searches for a finger-hold. Once she finds it, she carefully climbs the tree. Halfway up, she sees her friend still standing on the ground.

"Aparna," she scolds her. "Follow me. Now."

A reluctant Aparna begins to climb. It takes a while, but eventually the girls make their way to a thick branch laden with sour-sweet nectarines. Idhika plucks one and bites into it. The juicy pulp bursts into her mouth, and some dribbles down her chin. She giggles as she plucks another fruit and hands it to her friend.

She is proud of herself. She entered the forest, found the fruit, and nothing happened. She will tell masterji he was wrong. She grabs another nectarine and bites into it happily.

That's when she hears them. Horses neighing in the distance, and dogs barking. Aparna hears them too, and grabs Idhika by her sleeve. They know what this means. Vajra soldiers approach, searching for the Princess.

The dogs have the scent and lead the men right to their tree. They bark and claw against the trunk, trying to scare their targets into coming down.

"Princess Idhika," the leader of the guards calls out. "I beg you, Your Highness. Please come down. Your mother has commanded us to return you safely to the palace."

"Who speaks?" she asks.

"My name is Lieutenant Aditya, Your Highness," the man says. "I serve in Princess Indrani's guard."

Idhika looks at Aparna and grins. *Game's up.*

She stuffs a few nectarines into her skirt's pockets, then makes her way down, followed by her friend. Lieutenant Aditya lifts her onto his horse, while one of his men takes Aparna.

The run to the forest had taken the girls a good forty-five minutes. The horse ride back is made in ten. The guards take them straight to her mother's quarters, which worries her. Her mother is one of only two people in the kingdom whom she cannot manipulate.

She is brought before a fuming Indrani. Twenty-nine-years-old, and easily the most beautiful woman in Vajrapur, she has a famous temper. Up until this day, she has only ever been strict with her daughter. But, for the very first time, she vents her fury.

"Idhika, what is the meaning of this?"

Idhika smiles innocently at her mother, then removes the nectarines from her pocket and holds them out. "I wanted to fetch you some fruit, maa."

Indrani is not appeased. "If I need fruit, I can send servants to fetch them."

"But maa—" Idhika protests.

"Enough," Indrani shouts. "Your teachers tell me you are intelligent, but all I see is a stupid little girl. Tell me, do you know what you are?"

"A Princess," Idhika replies.

"*The* Princess," Indrani declares. "The heir of Crown Prince Vijendra. And one day, gods save us all, you will be its Queen."

Idhika is pleasantly surprised. "You mean I will rule Vajrapur?"

Indrani laughs. "Rule? Hah. Your husband will rule. But you will advise him, if you have the brains for it. Stupid, stupid girl. Running off to the Andhakaranya. What if a predator attacked you? Or worse, bandits kidnapped you? What would you rule then?"

Idhika looks at her feet. "I am sorry, maa. I promise, I will never do it again."

"Oh, you won't," Indrani says. "I will make sure of that." The confidence in her voice scares Idhika. Indrani turns her attention to Aparna. "Who is this girl?"

A handmaiden steps forward, trembling. "Forgive me, Your Highness. This is my daughter, Aparna."

"Your daughter?" Indrani smirks. "What is she doing with the Princess?"

"Her Highness likes her company," the handmaiden says. "She asked me to bring her to the palace every day."

"I see," Indrani says. She shouts a command. "Guard."

A guard runs in and bows. Indrani looks at her daughter. "You are a Princess. So, I cannot punish you the way I would an ordinary citizen. Your little friend will have to take your punishment instead." She turns back to the guard. "Five lashes for helping the Princess enter the Andhakaranya. And five lashes for not knowing her place."

Idhika is stunned by this harsh punishment. She cries and hugs her mother. "Maa, please. Don't. It isn't Aparna's fault. She did not want to go. I forced her. It was my fault. Please, please don't hurt her."

Indrani gently raises her daughter's chin and smiles cruelly. "And henceforth, you will know better."

She nods to the guard, who unfurls his whip. Aparna looks at her mother, who falls to her knees and begs for mercy. Idhika cannot bear to look. She buries her head in her mother's sari, but Indrani turns her face around.

"Watch," she commands.

She watches.

The whip flies through the air and cracks against her friend's back.

Once, twice, thrice.

Each lash of the whip is accompanied by Aparna's anguished wails, her mother's tearful cries and Idhika's silent whimpers.

The tears flow down her cheek as freely as the blood streams down Aparna's back.

Ten.

The guard rolls his whip and bows again. Aparna's mother rushes to her daughter's still body. Idhika fears her friend has died. But then she sees Aparna's stomach rise and fall ever so slightly, and she is relieved.

The handmaiden lifts her daughter and bows to Indrani, who dismisses her with a wave of her hand. The woman leaves with Aparna.

Indrani turns to face her daughter. "Never again."

Idhika nods her head. *Never again.*

CHAPTER TWENTY-SEVEN

Chhan, chhan, chhan-na-na-na.
Chhan, chhan, chhan-na-na-na.

The anklets tinkle to the beat, as Idhika's feet tap against the stage, her mind at peace, her heart content. Ever since she was a child, dance has been her escape from the world, and few had believed she would grow to be so good at it.

At the age of five, even the kindest souls considered her chicken-legged and awkward. But Lord Jayendu had seen her dancing in the gardens and was impressed by her raw talent. He had whispered in her father's ear, who then hired the most respected dance master in Saravat to tutor his only child.

At first, Idhika had hated Master Urijit. He was tough, and came with rules. So many rules. For him, dance was a science. For her, an expression. And a battle of wills had ensued.

In the end, his way won. She had found rhythm in his method, and those rigorous exercises she so hated had moulded her body to her art. By the age of ten, she had lost her awkward gait, and bloomed into a graceful young woman. At fifteen, her handmaidens were left in awe of her beauty and talent. The role was irrelevant. From the lonely housewife to the seductive nymphet, she was born to play them all.

And now, she will settle into a new role.

As wife to a stranger.

Her only interaction with her intended had left her unimpressed. She had met King Giridhar before, and expected Vikrant to be of the same mould. Imagine her disappointment to find a slender man with fair rosy cheeks, who takes more after his elegant mother than his mountain of a father.

If she was given a choice, the marriage would not be taking place. But no choice had been offered, and soon she will be a wife, compelled to further the line of the great Simha.

Maybe this was the role she was born to play. Her parents certainly believe so, for it is all they have ever expected of her. As her father would often tell her, "One day you will marry a Prince or a King, and it will be up to you to control him with your wits and your wiles."

A cruel childhood was her training, one which had robbed her of friends and companionship.

It had taken away Aparna.

All she had left was her dance, and the roles she played through them. She performs the final step and holds the pose as the music fades away. Her masterji applauds. Then she hears another man clap, and she turns around.

How long has he been standing there, she wonders.

King Vijendra enthusiastically applauds his daughter's performance. "Bravo, my child, bravo. Your talent grows by leaps and bounds."

A talent few will ever see, Idhika mutters silently to herself, then smiles and bows.

"Master Urijit," her father continues, "My heartiest congratulations. You are truly the greatest dance master in the land."

Urijit bows. "You are too kind, Your Majesty. But I must humbly decline your compliments. The Princess has worked hard, and deserves all the credit."

"I could not agree more," Vijendra says. "Come, my child. Sit with me."

Master Urijit and his assistants discreetly make their way out of the room. Idhika sits by her father's side. "I have heard King Vikrant's *baarat* is only two days away."

He nods his head. "Yes. I will receive him tomorrow at the palace."

"Not at the gates?" she asks.

"No," he says. "It is important for your betrothed to know who his superior is."

"I see," she says, not in the least surprised.

Her father has always loved playing mind games, and there are none better at it than him. Not even her mother, who can be a monster on any given day, but lacks the subtlety required to torture a mind.

"You disapprove?" Vijendra asks.

Idhika shakes her head. "I trust you, baba. I know you will have thought every decision through."

"Including the choice of your husband?" asks Vijendra, his keen eyes searching her face for any sign of disapproval. "Come now, you have met the man. What do you think?"

Now he seeks my opinion, and believes me foolish enough to speak the truth. Idhika protests. "I met him only for a few minutes."

Her father smiles. "And yet, you are intelligent enough to form an opinion."

She knows he will ask the same question a million ways until she answers. She decides to save them both some time. "He is not what I expected."

"You mean he looks like a weakling," Vijendra says. "He is. When he was growing up, his own people called him a rabbit."

"And you would have me marry this man?" Idhika asks.

"None better, my child," Vijendra says. "You are unlike any other Princess in our land. Maybe the world. They are all raised to be coy and kind, and take care of their husbands' every need. Not you. You were raised to conquer your husband's heart and mind. And his body as well." His voice softens. "I know you can do it. It's what we have trained you for, ever since you were a child."

Idhika wants to laugh. *You did not train me. A whore did.*

"What do you expect of me?" she asks.

"To seize the opportunity," her father says. "Vikrant is only a tool. Marry him and bring him under your control. Bear his children, and watch them take over once he is gone. That is all that is required." He smiles at her. "This is the future we have planned for you. And for your children. They will rule Saravat, and one day take armies and conquer lands beyond the seas. That is what you should always think about."

Idhika would laugh if it was not so painful. *My future is planned, without my consent.*

Not once did her parents ask her what she might want from life. She is not sure if she knows. Since the age of four, only one thought has been drilled into her head.

Obey.

Which is what she does even now. "I understand, baba," she says. "I will not fail you."

"Good," her father says. "Keep your wits about you, and everything will work out."

He kisses her forehead and leaves the room. Alone, Idhika feels the rage boil within her. Against her father. Against her mother. Against this cold, cruel world.

Everything will work out, she promises herself. It will be hard to do it on her own terms, but maybe she won't have to. Soon, King Vikrant will arrive, and she will find out if he will be the partner she needs to make her dreams come true.

CHAPTER TWENTY-EIGHT

A little over four thousand men, women, and children live in Krasheerpur, twenty miles west of Dhaningarh. It is an idyllic village, where cattle graze in the pastures and produce the best milk and cream in the kingdom. And though they live so close to the capital, they are a simple people, far removed from its politics and stress.

All, except one.

Lord Jayendu.

The village has been home to his family for generations. Most of the people are in his employ, and know through experience the value of keeping his secrets.

Which is why not a single soul stirs when General Rannveer rides through the gates an hour past midnight. He stifles a yawn as his horse trots down the main avenue. Jayendu's mansion lies on the outskirts of the village, a secluded house with high walls, which he prefers over the cramped accommodations in the city.

The guards do not question Rannveer at the gate. He has been a guest here for many years, from back in the days when he was a humble captain, with three sons and a daughter.

He hands his horse over to an attendant. Another holds the door open, and he makes his way to the foyer, where he is surprised to find Captain Dhananjay walking the other way. The two face each other in the middle of the room, and Rannveer finds himself looking up at his junior.

Dhananjay is as wide as he is tall, with a wrestler's build, stocky shoulders leading to bulging muscles. He has a well-earned reputation as a swordsman, a terror in the arena, where he has struck down countless opponents.

Dhananjay bows to his superior. "General."

Rannveer nods his head. "Captain Dhananjay. I did not expect to find you here."

The Captain smiles. A charming smile, not the kind you would expect from a man of his size and reputation. "Lord Jayendu wanted to give me the good news. King Vijendra has chosen me to stand as Princess Idhika's champion in the 'First Fight'."

His smile might work on the ladies. On Rannveer, it has little effect. "I see. Then congratulations appear to be in order."

Dhananjay bows. "I thank you, General."

He walks past Rannveer and leaves the house. Once he is gone, the General grimaces. This is Jayendu's doing, and only the gods know why. Dhananjay and his big mouth are likely to ruin the day. He sighs and sets the thought aside. He has his own summons to answer.

Datta waits for him in the living room, and leads the way to their master's study. Rannveer follows at a leisurely pace, taking his time to admire the beautiful artworks which hang in the corridors. If he could, he would spend days here, soaking in the portraits of famous warriors, landscapes of astonishing natural beauty, vivid renditions of the starry sky and the setting sun. And then there are the books, shelves upon shelves filled with voluminous manuscripts, the pages of which contain all the knowledge and strategies one would need to win, be it on the battlefield or in the council chambers.

He enters the study to find Lord Jayendu already seated. He bows low, lower than he would to the King. He owes the old man his position, and if he were to ever forget, it is not beneath Jayendu to remind him.

"My dear General," Jayendu beams. "Come, come. Make yourself comfortable."

Rannveer takes his seat, and a handmaiden places a cup of madeira in front of him. He grunts his gratitude, and she leaves the room with Datta.

Once they are alone, he speaks. "I see you have chosen the good Captain to stand as the Princess' champion."

"I have," Jayendu says. "Do you not approve?"

Rannveer's tone makes it amply clear he does not. "The man has a temper," he says, "And a mouth disconnected from his brain. The alliance with the Simhasthalis is shaky enough. A rash action or ill-spoken word might just ruin it all."

"And would that be such a bad thing?" asks Jayendu, his eyes twinkling.

Rannveer cannot believe his ears. "You seek to end the alliance?"

Jayendu's eyes darken. "The King is a fool. He made this alliance against my advice. Princess Idhika is the prized jewel of Vajrapur. To give her hand to the unfit Vikrant will prove disastrous for Saravat." He takes a deep breath, and his tone softens. "The hour grows late, so I will come to the business at hand. The time has come to choose sides."

Rannveer's senses go on alert. "I do not understand, my lord."

Jayendu leans forward. "Are you with Vijendra, or with me?"

A strong statement, Rannveer thinks, *coming from the King's biggest supporter.*

They have been thicker than thieves for close to three decades, sowing chaos, sacrificing innocents. For this? To fall out, at the very end?

"I am with you both," he replies. "Surely, my loyalty is unquestionable."

"It is," Jayendu says. "Still, I sit before you, asking you to choose a side."

"Isn't it one and the same?" Rannveer asks. "Vijendra? You?"

Jayendu chuckles. "No, my dear General. My loyalty is not to Vijendra. It is to Saravat." He leans back in his chair. "I have long foreseen danger. In the faraway kingdom of Dhritri, King Advait rules. A ruthless man, with many sons who take after him. Then there is King Karunesh in the island kingdom of Shavadweep. Strong, merciless, determined. What if one of them were to turn their strength against Saravat? Who would fight them?"

"King Vijendra," Rannveer replies.

"And after him?" Jayendu asks. "We waited all these years for Idhika to come of age, and for the right Prince to present himself as the heir. I had chosen Prince Sreedharan for the task. Strong, ruthless, a mirror of Vijendra. Now, I would support their cause against my own people, against this Simhasthali King whom Vijendra seeks to force down my throat." He leans forward. "I ask you again, whom do you stand with?"

Rannveer gulps hard. *Right now, I stand upon treasonous ground.*

The answer will seal his fate, and not for the better. Jayendu is powerful and ruthless, as is Vijendra. Allied, they are a force to reckon with. Divided, they will tear down all who stand in the middle.

There might be a third option.

"My lord, have you met King Vikrant?"

Jayendu shakes his head. "I have not. Nor do I need to. His own people think him a coward. And Vijendra proved them right. Hah. What kind of King capitulates to the man who killed his father?" He looks at the General, curious. "You have seen the boy. What do you make of him?"

Rannveer hesitates. *How do I put this?* He composes his thoughts. "A lion's cub is a wonderful pet to have. It will play with you and eat out of your hand. But it is a fool who believes that it will not grow up to be a lion. And an even bigger fool who believes he can treat the lion as indulgently as he did the cub."

"You believe Vijendra has made a mistake?" Jayendu asks.

Rannveer refuses to commit. "All I can say is the King believes the boy and the man to be one and the same."

"And he will be proven right," Jayendu says. "In all the time I have known him, his judgement of people has been unerring."

I know, Rannveer thinks, *he chose me.*

"Then trust his judgement once more," he pleads.

"How can I?" Jayendu thunders. "He makes this decision not out of a sense of duty, but to protect himself. He prefers a grovelling Vikrant to an assertive Sreedharan. I will not condone such stupidity."

"I do not ask you to," Rannveer says. "Still, I beg you to wait. Vikrant will arrive in two days. See him with your own eyes and judge his worth for yourself."

A long silence follows. Rannveer shifts in his chair, uncomfortable under Jayendu's piercing gaze. He has nothing to fear though. He has spoken the truth, and it can bring him no harm.

His thoughts are confirmed when Jayendu speaks. "Thank you, General. You have given me something to think about."

Jayendu turns and stares at the wall. Rannveer takes the gesture for what it is.

Dismissal.

He bows and leaves the room. A restless mind accompanies him as he walks back the way he came.

In a couple of days, Vikrant will arrive at Dhaningarh. King of Simhasthal. Betrothed to Princess Idhika. Heir to Saravat. All eyes will be on the poor boy. Rannveer wonders what they will make of him.

Most importantly, what will Jayendu make of him?

CHAPTER TWENTY-NINE

After seven miserable days and nights in the Andhakaranya, the sun appears at last.

A grateful Vikrant basks in its warmth, letting it reinvigorate his mind and reenergise his body. Strength, which will prove useful in the coming days.

The baarat passes through Ilaava, a tiny farming village bordering the forest. Smiling faces greet the kingdom's future son-in-law, and as they near the capital, the crowd thickens. Thousands throng the fields, and chants ring out—'Hail Vikrant', 'Hail Vijendra'—choreographed by unseen prompters who move among the people.

They arrive within sight of the gates, and the baarat comes to a halt. Vikrant descends from his carriage, and the crowd roars with joy, but not for him. He follows their gaze, which leads to Indranuj. Unsurprisingly, they believe him to be the King. Most of these people have only ever seen Giridhar, and the young Prince is the spitting image of his father.

Prince Biraj, however, knows who the true King is. He approaches Vikrant and bows. "Welcome, Your Majesty. Vajrapur is honoured by your presence."

Vikrant glances around. There is no sign of Vijendra, nor his council of ministers. *He does not wish to bestow me with a King's welcome.*

Vikrant shakes off the insult and smiles. "I am honoured to be here."

Biraj gestures to the dozens of tents which have been erected in the fields. "If you will follow me, Your Majesty, arrangements have been made for your baarat to wash away the dust of the journey."

Vajra attendants step forward to ferry the baaratis to their changing areas, while Biraj leads Vikrant to the largest tent. Inside, some attendants draw a bath, while others organise refreshments, and a few swing a large fan, a welcome relief in this sticky weather.

"My men will see to your every need, Your Majesty," Biraj says.

Vikrant thanks the Prince, who leaves. His own attendants enter and get to work. An hour passes, as they scrub him clean, then dress him in fresh clothes and perfume him liberally.

He steps outside, and all their efforts come to nought. The weather is too hot, his Simhasthali clothes too thick, and his dark green sherwani clings to his sweaty body. He sighs.

Too late to change now.

A ceremonial chariot has been readied for him, gold lightning bolts streaking down its sides. He climbs on, and an attendant hands him his crown, with the lion roaring at its centre. He places it on his head and the charioteer leads him to where Biraj waits.

"Shall we proceed, Your Majesty?"

Vikrant nods his head. Biraj glances at the heralds, who blow their trumpets loudly.

Haruph! Haruph! Harrruuupphh!

The chariot rolls down the road, and the large iron gates swing open. The citizens of Vajrapur line the road, dressed in their finest clothes and shiniest jewels, shouting his name with joy, blowing horns and beating drums. Flowers are tossed in the air, and the sweet-scented petals of rose and marigold rain down on him and his baarat.

King Vijendra puts on a fine show. But to what end? The Vajras were victorious on the Laalkhet. It is Vikrant who arrives, vanquished and humbled.

Perhaps Vijendra seeks to make amends, to prove that they are partners—equals embarking on a new journey together.

Vikrant doubts that very much, or the King would have greeted him at the gates. No, a farce is playing out, designed to fool the naïve, which he is not. He keeps his guard up, and rides on.

He had visited the capital once, with his father, ten years ago, and it has changed little, almost as if it stands frozen in time, its age hidden behind several coats of fresh paint. The kingdom has seen better days, and dreams of seeing them again, once Vijendra rules the continent.

He remembers his time spent here. His father had certainly enjoyed it. They were old friends, Giridhar and Vijendra, and the two had been inseparable. For the young Prince, however, it had been the dullest week of his life. Biraj had been away at his school, and Princess Idhika had been seen only once, as part of their welcoming party.

He remembered what he had called her then. *The invisible Princess*, rarely seen within the palace, and outside of it, never at all. Glimpses of her were caught at official functions, always from afar, leading to many rumours, from the believable to the absurd.

Some said she was disfigured in an accident. Some believed she was possessed by spirits. And others held to the notion that an ancient curse had turned her into a beast who roamed the palace at night.

Nandini had come closest with her answer. When Vikrant had questioned her, his mother had surmised that Indrani was keeping her child safe from danger. Her caution was understandable, considering she had lost all her sons, and Idhika was all that was left to her.

Pawoooooooooo!

The beastly trumpeting yanks him back to the present. The baarat enters the palace grounds, where gigantic grey elephants guard the entrance, their trunks raised in a cacophonous salute which causes the trees to tremble. As he passes through, they fall silent, as does the kingdom.

On either side of the courtyard, drummers step forward, and their sticks pound a slow, rhythmic beat on their dhols.

Boom! Boom! Boom! Boom!

A troupe of dancers takes over the head of the procession. As the baarat nears the palace, the beat quickens, and the dancers' steps match the new pace, their energy coursing through the courtyard and the Simhasthalis.

Vikrant watches them for a while, then turns to the palace, a solid stone edifice five storeys tall, that stretches a hundred metres from end to end. If his memory serves, the gardens lie right behind, on the edge of a small forest, which is home to a large number of exotic birds. A place he might consider exploring, if he can find the time.

His eyes come upon Vijendra, who stands at the top of the palace steps. Alone. There is no sign of his council, nor his Queen. And sadly, no sign of the Princess.

Vikrant's gaze wanders the corridors, the gardens, the balconies, and returns disappointed.

Why did I get my hopes up? He had known she was never going to be here. The Vajras follow the same Saravati tradition as the Simhasthalis, a superstition that denies the bride and groom the chance to see each other for a week before the engagement.

As he approaches the palace, the dholis pick up the tempo. Faster and faster they beat, as do the dancers' steps, until they reach a fever pitch. Horns blow, and the elephants trumpet once more, lifting the music to a crescendo that pounds within everyone's chest.

And then, all at once, they fall silent. The *dhols*, the horns, the elephants. The dancers hold their pose, gasping. Vikrant sympathises. Though he sits comfortable in a chariot, watching them has made even him turn breathless.

He jumps out and climbs the steps, followed by his family. Once he reaches the top, he kneels.

Vijendra steps forward to hug him. "No, no, Your majesty, there is no need for that. Such formalities are for strangers, and we will soon be family."

Vikrant smiles. "Thank you, Your Majesty. And thank you for this grand welcome."

"It is as grand as it should be," Vijendra says. "After all, Saravat will soon have an Emperor for the first time. All my people have done is mark our historic alliance the right way."

His gaze moves beyond Vikrant, who turns to see his mother approach.

"Where are my manners?" Vijendra scolds himself. "Ranimaa Nandini, welcome. It has been years since I last laid eyes on you. I must say, time has only made you more beautiful."

"It is kind of you to say so, Your Majesty," Nandini says. She gestures for Indranuj to step forward. "May I present my youngest son, Crown Prince Indranuj?"

Vijendra grasps Indranuj by the shoulder and admires his face. "It is as if time has rolled back and I gaze upon my old friend Giridhar once more."

"Many have felt the same," says Indranuj, speaking through gritted teeth.

Vikrant wonders if Vijendra has noticed his brother's angst. Apparently not, for the Vajra King has already moved on. He spots Kashyap and embraces him warmly. "My friend, it is so good to see you again."

Kashyap nods his head. "And in better circumstances."

Vijendra ignores the sarcasm and embraces the General's husband. "Colonel Gautam, welcome to Vajrapur."

Gautam bows. "I thank you, Your Majesty."

Vijendra smiles at Atulya and Chandran. "Lord Atulya. Lord Chandran." And then he sees Gayathri. "And Princess Gayathri. The last time we met, you were a mother of one, and I hear you are now a mother of three. Tell me, what are their names?"

Gayathri brings her children forward, who bow politely. "This is my oldest, Abhimanyu. And my twins Dhanush and Nivedita."

"Beautiful children," says Vijendra, bending down to pat Dhanush on his cheek. "Very beautiful."

He gestures to an attendant, who runs into the palace. A few moments later, Queen Indrani emerges holding an *aarti thali*. She thumbs the vermillion on Vikrant's forehead, then circles the diya before him. Once the welcome ritual is done with, a handmaiden takes the thali away.

"A joyous welcome to you, King Vikrant," Indrani says, "To you, Ranimaa Nandini. And to your people as well. I hope your journey was not too tiring."

"It was not, Your Majesty," he says.

Indrani smiles. "That is good to hear. You will need your energy for all the functions before the wedding." She winks at him. "And a few after."

Vikrant blushes, and Vijendra laughs. "My dear, do not embarrass the King. I have watched him search for our daughter from the moment he arrived in the courtyard."

"I had hoped to see her again," Vikrant admits.

"And you will," Vijendra says, "In four days, at your engagement." He addresses the baarat. "Ladies and lords of Simhasthal, I welcome you all. Arrangements have been made to make your stay comfortable. If you require anything, do not hesitate to ask. My kingdom is at your service."

He waves his hand, and attendants rush forward to help unload the carriages. The Simhasthalis are led to their quarters, and Vikrant finds himself arm in arm with Vijendra as he leads him into the palace.

"Come," Vijendra says, "Let us go inside."

The opulence takes Vikrant by surprise. He remembered it differently. Tastefully furnished, elegantly decorated. However, gold seems to be the dominant colour now, and the lightning bolt emblem glitters large and proud across every column and wall.

Indrani beckons the attendants over. "The royal family will reside within the palace itself. Our people will see you to your chambers and attend to your every need. If you wish to explore the kingdom, please inform the palace guard, and suitable arrangements will be made."

Vijendra smiles. "I bid you all to rest well. Come the morning, the ceremonies will begin."

The attendants step forward, ready to lead the royal family away. But Vikrant stops them. "A word, Your Majesty."

"Yes, my boy?" Vijendra says.

"We may not find time after tomorrow," Vikrant says. "I was hoping we could sit to discuss strategy."

"What strategy?" asks Vijendra, confused.

"After the wedding, we will begin the conquest of Saravat," Vikrant says. "I wish to know your plans for the same."

Vijendra laughs. "My boy, the conquest of Saravat began on the Laalkhet. Do not trouble yourself over that. You need to focus on your wedding, and the nights that follow."

"I see," says Vikrant, his palms curling into fists. "Is that all you expect of me?"

"Of course, my boy," Vijendra says. "You have only one duty, a duty expected of all Kings." He leans forward and whispers in Vikrant's ear. "Produce an heir."

Vijendra affectionately pats him on the back, before walking away. An attendant steps forward. "Your Majesty, may I escort you to your chambers?"

Vikrant stares at the departing Vijendra. Not yet my father-in-law, and already he shows me my place. He nods to the attendant, who heads down a corridor. Vikrant follows, his mind burning with the knowledge of what he is soon to become.

A puppet King.

CHAPTER THIRTY

So, this is what prison feels like.

Kashyap walks down the corridor, watched by the Vajra guards, who bow their heads in respect, yet not once do they take their eyes off him.

He stops a passing attendant. "My good man, could you please direct me to Prince Indranuj's room?"

The man bows. "It would be my honour, General. Please, follow me."

The attendant leads him down the corridor, through a small meeting room and into another corridor, where he stops at the third door and bows again.

"Prince Indranuj," he says, then leaves.

Kashyap opens the door. Unopened chests fill the room, with no attendants anywhere in sight, while Indranuj sits alone by the window, a cup of madeira in his hand, looking angry, hurt, ashamed, the way Kashyap feels as well.

He walks over. "You made me proud today, my boy. I know it was not easy."

Indranuj's lips tremble with rage. "I wanted to strangle that bastard with my bare hands."

"As did I," Kashyap confesses. "A day will come… and I pray it comes soon… a day will come when Vijendra will pay for his sins. But as long as Vikrant is determined to marry his daughter, we cannot touch him."

"I know it is a sin, chacha," Indranuj continues to fume, "But it is a sin I am willing to commit. Surely, the gods will not hold me accountable for killing my father's murderer."

Kashyap's eyes are kind, yet his voice is stern. "Do not speak for the gods. To give us justice is their privilege, and your brother's."

"My brother? Give me justice?" Indranuj laughs. "People used to call dada a rabbit behind his back. And I used to hate them for it. Now, I know better. I was wrong, and they were right."

"Yet he remains your older brother, and your King." Kashyap pours himself a cup of madeira, then speaks. "Even if it seems wrong now, history will be the true judge of Vikrant's actions, for their consequences may be felt decades from now."

Indranuj does not reply. He refills his drink and sips it slowly, his mind lost in thought. Once he finishes, he sets the glass aside.

"What would you have me do, chacha?" Indranuj asks. "Bow and scrape before Vijendra?"

"No," Kashyap says. He sips his madeira. "I would have you grow up. Start putting your anger to good use, instead of letting it eat you up inside."

"And how should I do that?" Indranuj asks.

Kashyap smiles. "Do you know how many festival games I have competed in?"

The answer is known to every Simhasthali. Kashyap was a giant in the games, and the mere appearance of his name in the lists would see the odds swing against his opponents.

"A thousand," Indranuj jokes.

Kashyap laughs, and his belly jiggles. "I am not that old yet, my boy. The number is closer to twenty-five. I started when I was your age. At first, I lost a few matches, but with experience came skill. Thirteen times I was crowned champion, until Gautam put me in my place."

"He is a great swordsman," Indranuj says.

"The best in the land," Kashyap admits, with some measure of pride in his husband's accomplishments. "However, we both agree. One day, you will be better."

Despite his anger, Indranuj cannot hide his happiness. "You truly believe that?"

Kashyap nods his head. "I do. But only if you can focus your rage."

"You do not tell me to get rid of it?" Indranuj asks.

Kashyap scoffs. "How can I? The same rage burns within me."

"Yet you ride to this wedding with a smile on your face?" asks Indranuj, confused.

"I do," Kashyap says. "The King commands it, and the soldier obeys."

"I am not a soldier," Indranuj declares.

Kashyap laughs again, and his belly jiggles some more. "All Simhasthalis are soldiers. You were a soldier the day you emerged from your mother's womb. And a soldier you will remain, until the day you die."

Indranuj glares at his chacha. "So, you ask me to obey?"

Kashyap shakes his head. "No, my boy. I ask you to focus."

Frustration builds in Indranuj's mind. "This conversation is going in circles."

Kashyap smiles. "Twenty-five games I have competed in. Do you know what I have seen? Swords sometimes miss their mark, cut between helm and shoulder guard, nick a neck. Not grievously, but enough to sting. Other times, they slice a jugular, and the man falls, bleeding to death."

"I have heard of this happening," Indranuj says. "I am not afraid."

"I know you are not," Kashyap says. His eyes turn cold and cruel. "But what about those who face you?"

Indranuj appears confused for a few seconds, then understanding dawns, and he looks at his chacha through excited eyes. "You mean—"

"Prince Biraj will be one of our opponents," Kashyap continues. "The King's brother. The bride's uncle."

He sips his madeira. Silence. The two are lost in the same thought, and the implications of its execution. Treason. Against their King, for certain. But against their kingdom? Here, the line blurs.

"What about dada?" Indranuj asks.

"I meant what I said earlier," Kashyap says after a long while. "Future generations will judge his actions. And they will judge ours as well."

Indranuj's eyes meet his chacha's, and the same determination stares back at him. "So be it," he says.

Kashyap sets his cup aside. "Good. That is all I wanted to hear." He pats Indranuj on the back. "Now, rest well, and meet me early in the morning, before Gautam joins us. We will train together, and I will teach you some new tricks."

Indranuj nods his head. Kashyap leaves him and walks out into the corridor. As he heads back to his room, peace settles within his mind and heart.

Soon, the long-sought vengeance will be within his grasp.

CHAPTER THIRTY-ONE

Chhan, chhan, chhan, chhan.

The anklets tinkle melodiously as Atishi walks down the corridor, cream dhoti wrapped around her curvaceous hips, red blouse pulled tight and cut low, *angavastram* slung lazily over her shoulders.

The guards' eyes wander her body. Like all men, they are only interested in her flesh, which she uses to her advantage. Her hips sway a little more than necessary, and there is a bounce in her step, which causes her breasts to jiggle seductively, an action which makes the guards uncomfortable.

Good, she thinks. *Let them suffer.*

The Parasu, however, are not so easily distracted, and they view her suspiciously as she approaches their King's door.

Will my charm work on them? She smiles sweetly. "King Vijendra sends a gift for His Majesty."

One of them nods, then opens the door and steps inside. He returns moments later. "The King will see you."

Atishi steps past the guards and enters the room. Inside, King Vikrant sits at the study table, a voluminous book open in front of him. He turns to look at her, and she can see the surprise in his eyes. He wasn't expecting a woman, at least not one as desirable as her.

She bows. "Good evening, Your Majesty."

Vikrant looks her over from head to toe before responding. "My guard said you bring a gift from your King."

"Yes, Your Majesty," she says.

"I do not see a gift," he says.

A sly smile breaks across her face. "She stands before you."

Vikrant's eyes narrow with suspicion. He walks over and towers above her. "And who are you?"

Who am I? Born in a small village in Farisa, Atishi was sold to flesh markets at the age of nine, where she spent her pre-pubescent days learning the art of pleasuring men and women.

She soon became a mistress of her trade, losing her innocence at the age of twelve. By seventeen, hundreds had been between her legs. She had welcomed them all, not just for their money, but also for their stories.

Late in the night, alone in bed, she dreamt of the places and people they spoke of, and imagined a life far away from her bedchambers. Then one day, that life arrived.

A Queen from a distant land bought her for the princely sum of a thousand gold coins. She travelled to Vajrapur, thinking a frigid old hag had purchased her to provide company to her husband.

But Queen Indrani desired something else, and even the sexually experienced Atishi was surprised by her command. "Train my daughter to rule in the bedchamber, so that one day she may use her charms to keep her husband in check."

Atishi did as commanded. Whenever an important dignitary visited, he would be brought to her cottage in the forest, while a young Idhika watched them from a hidden room. Later, the Princess would ask questions, and she would try her best to answer.

As the years passed, they spoke about more than just sex. She shared her stories of the world, which delighted Idhika, who had not stepped outside the palace in years. A sisterly bond developed between the two, and Atishi knew she would do anything to keep the Princess safe.

Now, that responsibility will lie with Vikrant, the King who will make Idhika a Queen.

Atishi smiles. "King Vijendra fears you might find rest hard to come by in these strange surroundings. He has commanded me to keep you company, and help you find a good night's sleep."

She senses his hesitation, and the desire in his eyes. He is attracted to her. *Who wouldn't be?* Her allure is undeniable. But it pleases her to see him give only a cursory glance to her body before he turns to her face.

"I thank King Vijendra," he says with a stiff demeanour. "But I have not had trouble sleeping since I was a child."

Atishi steps closer, letting her perfume fill the space between them, a fragrance designed to stimulate the senses and weaken a man's resolve. Vikrant breathes deeply, and Atishi is pleased.

"Are you certain, Your Majesty?" she teases. "It would be nice if you are well-rested."

His caution battles his lust, and wins in the end. "For that, I do not need your help. You may leave now."

But she does not. Instead, she removes a scroll from the folds of her dhoti and hands it over.

"If that is your answer, Princess Idhika has commanded me to give you this."

He looks puzzled as he takes the scroll. *He won't be for long.* She knows the message it contains, written in the Princess' own hand.

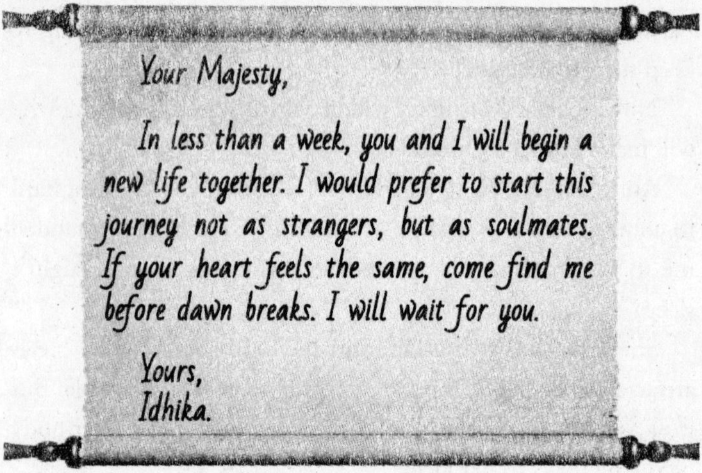

Your Majesty,

In less than a week, you and I will begin a new life together. I would prefer to start this journey not as strangers, but as soulmates. If your heart feels the same, come find me before dawn breaks. I will wait for you.

Yours,
Idhika.

The Simha King glances at her, then reads the message once more before he finally breaks his silence.

"The Princess sends this message?" he asks.

"Yes, Your Majesty," she replies. "I will wake you up at the appointed time and bring you to her."

"I see," Vikrant says. He takes a moment before he continues. "I would very much like to meet your Princess."

Atishi smiles. *I succeeded.* The Princess will be happy.

"In that case, Your Majesty," she says, "Perhaps you would inform your guards that you should not be disturbed until the morning."

Vikrant walks to the door, opens it and whispers a command to the Parasu. He then closes the door and returns to her.

She takes his hand and leads him to bed. "I suggest we sleep early. We will need to leave a couple of hours before dawn."

Vikrant lies down and lets her cover him with a blanket, before looking at her questioningly.

Atishi reads his mind and shakes her head. "King Vijendra expects me to be with you tonight. But that does not mean we have to share a bed."

She douses the lamp by the bedside, then does the same with the other lamps in the room, until she is little more than a silhouette in the moonlight. She makes her way to the plush divan at the far end of the room, drops a pillow at its head and gets comfortable before addressing Vikrant again.

"Good night, Your Majesty," she says. "May your dreams be sweet."

Then, she closes her eyes and sleeps.

CHAPTER THIRTY-TWO

Why am I here?

Vikrant finds himself in his bedchambers, alone. The place is in ruins, bereft of the furnishings, bereft of the paintings. A window creaks as it swings, its pane broken, allowing the cold air to rush in, and the snow to fall, like a blanket on the floor.

He glances around, and spies his crown. It gleams in the desolate place, resting calmly on a bed of satin, a few flakes of snow upon it. He walks over and picks it up, wipes it clean, then places it on his head.

Just then, a familiar voice whispers from behind him. "So, you finally took my crown?"

Vikrant turns to see his father enter the room. Not his father, no. He stumbles a few steps behind, away from this grotesque distortion of his worst memory.

Giridhar's head lies cradled in his arms, cartilage and bone sticking out from where his neck was severed. He roars his anger. "That is my crown. Mine. How dare you steal it from me?"

Vikrant stammers. "Baba, no... please... I did not mean to..."

"It is not your crown," Vijendra calls out.

The Vajra King walks in and puts his arm around Giridhar. Like brothers they stand, like brothers they speak.

"I took it away from you, remember?" Vijendra speaks in a gentle voice.

Giridhar tries to remember. "On the Laalkhet," he finally says.

"Yes," Vijendra replies. He turns to Vikrant. "And soon, I will take it from your son as well."

A fresh rage boils within Vikrant. "Never," he screams, as he draws his sword and chops off Vijendra's head. It rolls on the floor and continues to laugh at him.

"Is that all you can do?" the severed head asks.

It laughs, and Giridhar joins in.

"Little rabbit," he calls his son. "You never stopped being one."

Tears stream down Vikrant's cheeks. He turns away from the two Kings. Their mockery stays with him, reaching far beyond his mind and twisting a knife into his very soul.

A voice drags him away from them. He tries to resist, but the voice is insistent, calling out to him from the great beyond.

"Your Majesty."

He opens his eyes to find Atishi standing by his bedside. In his sleep-addled state, he does not recognise her, and leaps away in fright.

"Stay calm, Your Majesty," she says. "It is I. Atishi. We are in your chambers. In Dhaningarh."

He stares at her, uncomprehending. Slowly, the pieces come together.

I am in Dhaningarh. In the palace. Atishi was sent by Vijendra, but is here to take me to Idhika.

"Atishi," he says.

She nods her head. "Yes, Your Majesty. Come. Dawn is a couple of hours away. Time enough to meet the Princess and return without anyone being the wiser."

He dresses quickly. Once he is ready, Atishi walks to the cupboard, moves aside the clothes, and pushes the back panel. To Vikrant's surprise, it slides open to reveal a hidden passage, at the end of which lies a staircase.

"What is this?" he demands to know.

"A secret passage," she says. "It leads to a tunnel, which ends in the forest. That's where my home is, and this allows me to come and go from the palace without anyone the wiser."

"Then why did you visit my chambers from outside?" Vikrant asks.

The reply does not please him. "King Vijendra wanted everyone to know I kept you company through the night."

Vikrant understands at once. The Vajra wants the Simhasthalis to believe their King is under his thumb, accepting his favours as and when presented.

"However, the King did not choose this room for you," Atishi continues.

"Then who did?" he asks.

"Lord Jayendu," she replies.

Vikrant does not know how to react. Lord Jayendu. The man who planned the conquest of Saravat, and whose actions led to the death of his father.

"Why?" he asks.

Atishi smiles. "That is not for me to say. Come, Your Majesty. The Princess waits."

They go through the cupboard and down the hidden staircase. It leads to a dark tunnel, which runs for a mile before emerging in the woods. Soon, they arrive at a cottage, where three handmaidens gossip on the verandah. Three sisters, from the similar looks of them. They rise and bow as he approaches.

"Your Majesty," they chime together.

He acknowledges their greeting with a nod of his head, then turns to Atishi. She reads the question on his mind. "The Princess awaits your presence at the pond."

He thanks her and heads in the direction she indicates. In a hundred metres or so, he comes upon a small pond in a clearing. Torches are lit along its periphery, and in their light, once again, he is spellbound by Idhika's beauty.

She sits at the far end, her body hidden beneath the water. Her hair is wet, pressed tight against her scalp, and tiny droplets drip down her dimpled chin to rejoin the pond.

"Good morning, Your Majesty," she says, her voice sweet and lilting. "I hope I have not deprived you of your sleep."

"Not at all, Your Highness," he says. "And even if you have, it is worth it."

Idhika giggles like a girl half her age, and he finds it hard to tear his eyes away. In the light of the peace tent, she had looked beautiful. But in these surroundings, with the reflections of the torches dancing in the waters around her, her beauty is ethereal.

"It is kind of you to meet with me," Idhika says. "I thought you might refuse, since even Simhasthalis do not allow the bride and groom to meet before the engagement."

"They do not," he admits. "But as you pointed out, our future is better served if we do not remain strangers. Let us make a start. Here. Now. Call me Vikrant."

"As you command, Vikrant."

He smiles. “Tell me, Idhika, what would your father say if he were to see me here?”

“I only follow his command,” Idhika says.

Vikrant finds that hard to believe. “Your father sent you here?”

Idhika giggles. “No. But he did command me to bind you under my spell.”

Vikrant pretends to be upset. “Is that what you seek to accomplish? To cast a spell on me?”

Idhika giggles some more. “Would that be so bad?” She pauses for a second, then shakes her head. “That is not what I wish. I guess my curiosity brought me here.” Her light brown eyes stare into his. “You agreed to this marriage, even though my father killed yours. Why?”

Vikrant finds a rock to sit on and makes himself comfortable before he replies. “As my grandmother said, your father emerged victorious over mine in battle. His offer to make me his heir was also generous. My gut told me it was wise to accept.”

Idhika’s eyes twinkle with mischief. “What about your heart? Did it not sway you even a little?”

“More than a little,” he admits. “To be honest, if I had not laid eyes upon you that day, I might not have accepted. I believe your father knew that. Certainly, that is why he sent for you in the midst of war. And it worked. He got what he wanted. Our two kingdoms, allied for his cause.”

Idhika laughs again, almost mockingly. “Is that what you believe, Vikrant? My father is your ally?”

“You believe otherwise?” he asks.

“I know my father,” she says, and her voice takes on a sharp edge. “He has no allies, other than my mother. To them, everyone else is just a means to an end.”

Vikrant turns curious. "Including their daughter?"

"Especially their daughter," she sighs. "I do not blame my father. I suppose when you are King, your children's happiness matters little, and they are told to do their duty. If King Giridhar were alive and a fortuitous match had presented itself, he would have made it for you, regardless of your feelings."

"Maybe," Vikrant says. "But my father would do it for the good of his kingdom, not himself. I suspect your father's intentions are more self-serving."

"Oh Vikrant," Idhika teases him, "Such a bad thing to say about your future father-in-law."

He mockingly bows, and replies in an equally teasing tone. "I apologise, Idhika. I meant no disrespect."

She laughs, and Vikrant believes he could grow to like it very much.

"You may mean no disrespect," she says, "But in this kingdom, disrespect is all you will get."

His body stiffens. "What makes you say that?"

"Words I have heard," she says, "Words whispered by people who believe it safe to speak them." She grins, and he senses a hint of triumph in her voice. "Little do they know I can hear their whispers, even from afar."

"And what have you heard?" Vikrant asks.

"Would you really like to know?" asks Idhika, the mischief returning to her voice. "Very well then." She wades towards him, her body gliding effortlessly through the pond. Once she reaches the shallow end, she walks out, and the water drips down her naked body.

Unashamed, she steps up to him, and Vikrant finds himself rooted to the spot. His eyes take in her every curve and every blemish, and his heart pounds within his chest as his mind loses sense of time.

An eternity passes before her voice drags him back to reality. "Some of my people are suspicious of you, and your acceptance of my father's proposal."

"And what do you believe?" he asks.

"Me?" She teases him once more. "How could I ever think such awful thoughts about my betrothed?" She rubs her thumb against his rough stubble. "But if I were you, I would keep an eye on your people."

Her words only deepen his confusion. "My people?"

"Yes," she says, before barking out a command beyond the trees. "Ladies." In the distance, they hear the sound of anklets tinkling. The handmaidens will be here soon.

Idhika turns to face him. "Don't you know? It is always our own who hurt us the most."

Before he can ask what she means, the handmaidens and Atishi arrive. If they are surprised to see their Princess stand naked before him, they do not show it. One drapes a towel around her, while the other two ready her clothes.

"Atishi will bring you to me each morning," Idhika informs him, "And we will talk of our future. Let us see if together we can build a little corner of our own in my father's new world."

Vikrant remembers the first time he saw her in the tent. He feared his mind had conjured the vision of a strong-willed woman who could hold her own against any man. Now, he knows his visions were true.

With a smile on his face, he bows. "As you command, my Princess," he says, before following Atishi back to the palace.

CHAPTER THIRTY-THREE

The gods are cruel, Jayendu mutters under his breath, as he takes the first step. Fifteen still remain, each as large as a mountain, and he must conquer them all, if he is to make it to the throne room.

His aged body begs him to return to his bedchambers. But he cannot. Not today. The Simhasthalis will be presented at court, and all those who matter will be present. How could he be absent, when he matters more than all of them combined?

More important reasons bring him here today, though. He wishes to lay eyes on this King Vikrant, hear him speak with his own ears, and determine his worth for himself.

He gains the final step and sighs with relief. Now, the journey will be long, but the way will be easy. A festive look decorates the palace. Ornate flower arrangements distract from all the gold in the corridors, and colourful bands of satin dance along the ceilings. His late wife would have loved this. The pomp and the splendour, the clothes and the newcomers. Shalini would have loved it all. But she no longer lives, and now each day seems less bright than the one before.

He enters the throne room, pleased to find it empty. Good. The ingrate nobles will be denied the sadistic pleasure of watching him hobble to his seat.

Old age has robbed him of much of his powers, but he prays some remain to make this journey worthwhile. The Simhasthalis are not a subtle clan, and it should be easy for him to determine their true feelings towards this alliance.

And maybe, towards their King as well.

Soon, the Vajra nobility stream into the room. They are surprised to see him already seated, and walk over to pay their respects. Most owe their wealth or position to his generosity, and he is not one to let them forget.

The ministers arrive soon after, followed by Prince Biraj and General Rannveer. Now, they must wait for the King and Queen. A quarter of an hour later, a herald bangs his staff on the floor.

Thump! Thump! Thump! Thump!

The room falls silent as he calls out. "All hail King Vijendra, husband to Queen Indrani, thirdborn son of King Dhirendra, ruler and protector of the great kingdom of Vajrapur."

The King struts in, his *sherwani* a mesmerising melange of greens and blues, which reminds Jayendu of a peacock strutting in the gardens. No peacock was ever so powerful, though, and Vijendra looks every bit the Emperor he was born to be.

The herald booms again. "All hail Queen Indrani, wife to King Vijendra, firstborn daughter of Lord Satwik, benevolent mother to the great kingdom of Vajrapur."

The audience's roar is deafening. Queen Indrani gracefully makes her way to the throne, a vision of beauty in her turquoise silk sari. Today is all about her, as she opens her home for a new son. The 'Mother's Welcome', a tradition that dates back over a thousand years.

Once she is seated, she nods her head to the herald. The man calls out. "Ladies and lords, Queen Indrani is pleased to welcome King Vikrant, firstborn son of King Giridhar, ruler of Simhasthal."

Silence descends upon the room, and Jayendu turns his eyes to the entrance. This is the moment he has been waiting for. Alas, his cataracted eyes make him wait until Vikrant is almost at the throne before he sees him clearly.

He cannot help but be disappointed. Here stands a stick of a man, unworthy of being called a Simhasthali. He is handsome, yes, but that does not interest Jayendu. Is the boy intelligent? And does he possess the strength to rule as Emperor? These are the questions Jayendu needs answered.

Vikrant bows to the throne. "Queen Indrani, I thank you for your welcome."

Sniggers echo in the room, but he pretends not to hear it. At least the boy retains his dignity.

"It is my honour, King Vikrant," says Indrani, ignoring her people's laughter. "I trust your night was restful."

"It was, Your Majesty," Vikrant says.

"Good, good," Indrani says. A smile breaks across her face. "A Vajra wedding has many ceremonies, and you will need your strength if you are to survive them all."

A weak joke, in Jayendu's opinion, but the audience laughs wholeheartedly. Vijendra gestures to the empty chair on his left, and a smiling Vikrant climbs the steps and takes his seat.

The herald calls out again. "Ladies and lords, Queen Indrani is pleased to welcome Indranuj, secondborn son of King Giridhar, Prince of Simhasthal."

The Prince enters the room, and the mood of the audience changes. Many feel as if a ghost has walked in, so stark is the resemblance to King Giridhar. Jayendu notes Indranuj's stiff demeanour, haughty walk and proud eyes. Yes, this Simhasthali will be quick to take offence.

The boy walks up to the throne and bows curtly.

"I welcome you, Prince Indranuj," Indrani says, "And ask for your forgiveness."

Indranuj looks confused, as does everyone else. "Forgiveness, Your Majesty?" he asks.

"Yes," Indrani says. "My herald should have introduced you with your correct title. Crown Prince of Simhasthal. A heavy burden, but one you will not bear for long." She smiles mischievously. "I promise you; my daughter will produce an heir soon enough."

The audience laughs once more, but Indranuj is not pleased. If possible, the boy looks more upset than when he first walked in. Somehow, he keeps his temper in check.

"If you say so, Your Majesty," he mutters, and proceeds to take his seat in the front row.

He is followed by the rest of the royal family. Ranimaa Nandini arrives first, then Princess Gayathri with her children and husband. Jayendu smiles when he sees Chandran. Vijendra's spy, hiding in plain sight and bowing to his true master. Indrani welcomes them all with her customary greeting and witty comments.

Kashyap walks in next with Colonel Gautam. The excitement in the room is palpable, for their reputations precede them. The General is widely regarded as a master of war strategy. And Gautam is considered to be the finest swordsman in Saravat.

But it is their love story which enchants most. The first men to be wedded to one another, an unusual romance that many a poet has put to song, and has served as an inspiration for others to follow.

The herald announces their names. "Ladies and lords, Queen Indrani is pleased to welcome General Kashyap, secondborn son of King Hridhyanshu, commander of the Simhasthal forces. And his husband, Colonel Gautam, thirdborn son of Uday of Saptaveni."

The couple bows to the throne. Before Indrani can speak, Vijendra rises to his feet. "Forgive me, My Queen, but I beg your indulgence."

Indrani nods her head, and Jayendu wonders what they are up to.

The King addresses Gautam and Kashyap with genuine warmth. "It is our honour to welcome you both." He turns to the audience. "Most of you may not know this, but the General and I were good friends as children. I have many fond memories of my summer holidays in Simhasthal."

"Those were simpler times, Your Majesty," Kashyap says.

"Indeed, they were," Vijendra agrees. "But even as children playing childish war games, one fact was indisputable. There has never been a military commander to match you. And you will get a chance to prove it to all of Saravat."

Confusion reigns in the room, and no one is more perplexed than the General. "Your Majesty—" he begins to say.

Vijendra cuts him off. "For my first command of this new alliance, I name you, General Kashyap, commander of the joint forces of Vajrapur and Simhasthal. *You* will lead my army in the conquest of Saravat."

A stunned silence greets the announcement. In the front row, Rannveer shifts uncomfortably in his seat. Jayendu pities the man, and his loyalty which now goes unrewarded. Vikrant looks distinctly annoyed as well. It appears Vijendra did not share this news with him. A smattering of uncertain applause ripples around the room, as a surprised—and slightly pleased—Kashyap bows to his new King before heading with his husband to their seats.

The presentation resumes, and continues for the better part of fifteen minutes. There is Lord Atulya and his wife Lady Akanksha. Lord Ekaksh and Lady Dhamyanti. Lord Karunesh and Lady Samruddhi. Lord Abhishek and Lady Ambica. Lord Parth and Lady Janki. Lord Jaiwant and Lady Mayuri. Each arrives at the throne as the herald recites their names, their ancestry and their titles.

The last to make his way down the aisle is a dark-skinned, affable lord who seems very pleased to find himself here.

"Ladies and lords," the herald announces, "Queen Indrani is pleased to welcome Lord Ayushmann, Minister of Security of Simhasthal."

The man bows lower than any before him, yet something about his demeanour sets alarm bells ringing in Jayendu's mind.

"Your majesties," Ayushmann says, "It is a great honour to stand in your presence."

Despite his fawning words, the Queen looks quite displeased. She glares at the herald. "What is the meaning of this? A lord should be introduced properly. With his father's name."

The herald shivers in his boots, but is quickly saved by Ayushmann. "I beg your forgiveness, Your Majesty," he calls out. "Your herald is not at fault in this. It is I who declined to provide him with the information."

Indrani regards him suspiciously. "And why would you do that?"

Ayushmann's grin remains. "My reasons are many, Your Majesty, but the simplest one is I never had a father. He was barely around when I was growing up. And after I ran away from home, I never laid eyes on him again."

Jayendu's eyes race around the room. Most of the Simhasthalis, including Vikrant, seem confused by their minister's bizarre introduction. Only Atulya sits unperturbed and calm.

The old schoolmaster is up to some mischief.

"This is most inappropriate, Lord Ayushmann," Indrani thunders.

Vijendra sides with his wife. "I agree. Lord Ayushmann, I must insist you reveal your father's name at once."

"As you command, Your Majesty." Ayushmann bows again, only this time, he appears to mock the throne. "My name is Lord Ayushmann," he says, "Minister of Security of Simhasthal. But before that I was named Vidyut, natural born son of Lord Satwik of Naavipur, and firstborn son of his maid Sarita."

Confusion reigns in the room once more, as the import of his declaration dawns on all. Lord Satwik is the Queen's father. Which means—

The Queen has a bastard brother? And he is a minister in Simhasthal?

The gossipmongers will have a field day, but the true impact of the revelation is felt by those seated on the throne.

Indrani's face is a picture of fury, ready to unleash hell itself on Ayushmann for this highly public insult. Jayendu chuckles to himself.

She had believed him dead, and did not worry about ever having to acknowledge his existence.

The King is furious as well. This grand event was meant to showcase the servility of the Simhasthalis and his magnanimous acceptance of his former enemy. But now, he has been robbed of the pleasure by an upstart young lord who—by the laws of man and god—is his brother-in-law.

The man at the heart of the matter seems nonplussed by the chaos. Ayushmann bows once again before taking his assigned seat, the smile still intact upon his face.

Jayendu chortles happily. Seeing Indrani put in her place brings him immense pleasure. He pities Vijendra, though. The King has committed himself to this course of action, and now cannot afford to step back. Idhika will have to marry Vikrant, even if Indrani's bastard brother serves the Simha King.

Five days to the wedding. What more could go wrong?

CHAPTER THIRTY-FOUR

The porcelain vase flies across the chamber and smashes against the wall. It was a gift from the Queen's brother, a lord in Naavipur, given on her thirty-fifth name day. Its value lay in its sentiment, which now shatters into a thousand shards.

Indrani fumes in the centre of the room. Like the vase, her afternoon lies in ruins. Ayushmann was all anyone could speak of, in whispers so loud they could not help but reach her ears.

The Queen's bastard brother.

That's what they call him, and the man revels in the shame of his new title. Her detractors must be rejoicing. Let them. Indrani has suffered many insults in her life, and all those who once laughed at her now bow at her feet, or have long since departed from this world.

She was a young bride of fifteen when she arrived in Vajrapur, excited to be a Princess, who would live in a palace. But she was soon divorced from her delusions. Her husband was the last-born of three sons, and his older brothers had wives of their own, who did not take kindly to this newly titled upstart. Not a day went by without them excluding her from royal events, or preventing her from hosting social functions, even for her family.

Vijendra suffered the same humiliations, for his older brothers were thick as thieves, and did not show affection for their much younger brother.

Anger had simmered in their hearts, yet Jayendu had urged them to be patient.

You are the future of Saravat, he would say often, *and the day will soon come when they will all bow at your feet.*

Many months later, fate conspired to fulfil his prophecy. The fever took away the families of Anshuman and Hemchandra, leaving Vijendra as Crown Prince. And when the fever returned to claim his life, fate saw fit to rescue him once more.

She laughs as she remembers her old family, her fellow sisters who had made her life a living hell. Maybe they are up above watching her. How would they feel now, watching her on the cusp of becoming Empress of Saravat?

The thought causes her laughter to double, and that's how Vijendra finds her, laughing hysterically. Worried, he takes her in his arms.

"Are you alright, my love?" he asks.

Her laughter subsides as she turns to face him. "Of course I am."

Rannveer and Biraj arrive as well. Biraj fumes as he takes the knee before her. "My Queen, command me, and I will bring you that vile man's head."

"You will not," Vijendra says. "What cause do we have?"

General Rannveer interjects. "He insulted Her Majesty, My King. This cannot be allowed to stand."

"And pray tell, how did he insult her?" Vijendra asks. "All he claims to be is her long-forgotten brother, a fact the Queen did not deny." He turns to her. "Tell me, is his claim false?"

Indrani shakes her head. "I do not know. It is true my father sired a bastard son named Vidyut. But the boy and his mother ran away from Naavipur when he was nine, never to be seen again. We all took him for dead."

"So, he could be your brother," Biraj says.

Her anger returns. "Do not call that bastard my brother."

Biraj bows his head in apology. They are yet to come to terms with the news, but it is Vijendra who understands the consequences.

"Jayendu will try to use this to his advantage," he says.

Rannveer shuffles his feet, but Indrani does not notice, nor does anyone else. She continues to fume. "The Simhasthalis are plotting something. Vikrant knew of this; I am certain of it. They want to get back at us for killing Giridhar."

Biraj nods his head, and so does Rannveer. "I agree, Your Majesty," he says. "King Vikrant did pretend to look surprised. But Lord Atulya was not."

"No," Vijendra declares. "If this was indeed Vikrant's secret weapon to anger us, it is a weak one. All he has managed to do is cause us some humiliation, that is all. I would consider that a fool's play. And while the boy may be a coward, he is no fool."

"Then who is the fool we seek?" Biraj asks. "Did Lord Ayushmann act of his own accord, or is there someone else pulling the strings?"

"That is what we have to find out, dear brother," Vijendra says. He turns to Rannveer. "General, I need you to make contact with Chandran, and get all the information you can about the Queen's brother."

She erupts once more. "For the last time, do not call that bastard my brother. I will cut out the tongue of the next man who calls him that. He was not born to my mother. Then how can he be my—"

As soon as the words escape her lips, she turns to look at Biraj.

Too late.

"Biraj," she says, "I did not mean—"

If the boy's feelings are hurt, he hides it well. "No apologies necessary, Your Majesty," Biraj interrupts her. "The day's events have us all on edge."

She nods her head and says no more. Vijendra turns to Rannveer, gesturing for him to leave with Biraj. Once the doors close behind them, he glares at Indrani, and his voice quivers with rage.

"I have never known you to be this foolish, my love. I beg you. Regain your composure. We must remain in control, even if all around us seems lost."

She collapses on a divan. "I have always hated Vidyut. His very birth was an insult. To my mother. To my family. I prayed for years that he would die a horrible death, or succumb to a painful disease. And then, one day, they were gone. Him, and his whore of a mother. Vanished without a trace. I convinced myself one of my brothers had killed them." Her expression hardens. "To see him today, standing in our great hall with his evil smile... I wanted to kill him then and there."

Vijendra sits by her side and holds her close. "I understand. I truly do. But I beg you again, be patient. Jayendu already attempts to steal Rannveer away. Do not give him further ammunition. We will deal with this bro—" He corrects himself in time. "This bastard. I promise you. I will find a way to end him once and for all."

She squeezes his hand. “Promise me this. When you find a way, it will be me who gets to kill him.”

Vijendra looks surprised. “My love?”

“Promise me,” she says again.

Vijendra sighs and relents. “I promise.”

Indrani kisses him passionately. Her husband has never failed to keep his promises to her. Soon, she will have the revenge she had dreamt of all those years ago. And the bastard name of Vidyut will never be mentioned in her presence ever again.

CHAPTER THIRTY-FIVE

How harsh will my punishment be?

Ayushmann takes his seat in the King's chambers, a big smile stretched across his face. As always, Lord Atulya sits by his side, a pillar of support for his embattled ward.

The faces that glare back at them look distinctly unhappy. General Kashyap and Lord Chandran seethe, as does Ranimaa Nandini, though she seems to take some solace in Indrani being humiliated in her own court. Even Prince Indranuj appears somewhat happy.

But King Vikrant is not.

He is the most upset, and so he should be. His minister acted without his knowledge, a fact that will lower his esteem in the eyes of the Vajras.

"That was ill-advised," Vikrant fumes.

"I disagree, Your Majesty," Ayushmann says. "I could not have timed it better."

"Explain yourself," Vikrant commands.

Ayushmann obeys. "King Vijendra and Queen Indrani are a team who function together. One heart, one brain. A potent force, not easily broken. Now, my sister will be thrown off balance, and half of that formidable team will be distracted."

"Be that as it may," Kashyap says, "It was your duty to inform the King of your plans."

The General seems upset. Could it be because Ayushmann's revelations have ruined his big day? Commander of the joint army. A huge honour, indeed.

Ayushmann's voice remains calm. "The King has only ever asked me for reports on my actions, General. I have taken action, and am now providing a report."

"What nonsense is this?" Kashyap bellows. "Do you hope to escape punishment on a technicality? You are Indrani's half-brother. When were you planning to let us in on your secret?"

"I should take the blame for that," Atulya interjects. "King Giridhar knew, of course. But I had not yet found time to speak to King Vikrant."

Chandran seems to find this amusing. "Of course, Lord Atulya knows. After all, it was at his house that Lord Ayushmann arrived as a little boy, and through his patronage that the boy rose to become a minister. Tell us, my lord, was it your idea to change his name?"

"That was for his own safety," Atulya protests. "None could have foreseen this is how it would come to pass. Queen Indrani was only a child then, and when she married Prince Vijendra, he was third in line to the throne."

"Lord Atulya speaks the truth," says Nandini, though her support is given reluctantly. "In this matter at least, he is blameless. My own husband did not think it wise to share this information with me."

"Be that as it may," Kashyap says, "This is the second time in as many months that Lord Atulya has withheld information from the King. What game are you playing?"

"I play no games, General," Atulya says. "And to be honest, I fear you are the pawn in Vijendra's games."

His words only add to the confusion.

"What is that supposed to mean?" Kashyap demands to know.

Ayushmann speaks up. "Well, now that you have been named commander of the joint forces, your loyalty to our King… how can I put this…" He takes a moment before continuing. "Let's just say your loyalty might be questioned. Not by us, of course. But others might feel—"

He leaves the words unsaid, angering Kashyap further. "You question my loyalty? You believe I will betray my own blood?"

Ayushmann shakes his head. "You mistake my meaning, General. I only speak of King Vijendra's intentions. His declaration means you now report to him. In the eyes of everyone, *he* is your King."

A stunned Kashyap falls silent. Apparently, the thought had not occurred to him. A great military strategist he may be, but not so great with the intricacies of politics.

"Why would he do that?" asks Vikrant, the strain in his voice evident. "Why would he pass over General Rannveer?"

"Why indeed?" Ayushmann muses.

"There can be only one reason," Atulya says. "He aims to divide the royal family. If General Kashyap is seen following his commands, and you are absent in all strategy discussions, the word will quickly spread that you have no authority."

"It will not come to that," Kashyap shouts. "I will refuse the command. I do not wish to be a pawn for that man."

"Forgive me, General," says Ayushmann, his voice kind. "You cannot refuse. The announcement was made in the presence of our King, and for all intents and purposes, it signifies that he has blessed the decision. To refuse would mean to disobey your own monarch."

"I agree," Vikrant says. "Chacha, you cannot refuse." He smiles ruefully. "This also means you will have to stand down as my champion in the 'First Fight'."

Kashyap and Indranuj exchange worried glances. A fleeting interaction, which does not escape Ayushmann's alert eyes.

"Why would chacha need to stand down?" Indranuj asks.

Atulya provides the reply. "It would be unseemly for the commander of the joint forces to draw swords in the arena."

"But not illegal," Kashyap protests.

"Not illegal, no," Vikrant agrees. "Nevertheless, I forbid it."

Kashyap starts to speak, then checks himself. "As you command, Your Majesty. May I suggest Captain Dushyant take my place?"

Vikrant shakes his head, even as he glares at Ayushmann. "We are in this position thanks to the minister. Which is why he will take your place." Kashyap jumps to protest, but Vikrant raises a hand. "Thanks to Lord Ayushmann's little stunt, there is chaos in the other camp as well. Let us see if his presence in the arena can achieve the same result."

Ayushmann cannot help but smile. The day has gone better than he could have hoped for. Instead of being punished, he is being rewarded.

"I thank you for the honour, Your Majesty," he says.

"An honour you do not deserve," says Kashyap, his bitterness quite clear. "Not after your actions today."

Vikrant sighs. "Chacha, what's done is done. We shall let things play out, and see where it lands us."

His words signal the end of the meeting. Ayushmann walks to the door and holds it open for Atulya, when Indranuj calls out. "Lord Ayushmann."

He turns to face the Prince. "Yes, Your Highness?"

"Do you remember our conversation in the palace courtyard?" Indranuj asks.

"I remember it well, Your Highness," Ayushmann says.

"You promised I would meet your sister." Indranuj smiles. "I met her today."

Ayushmann grins. "Then I will consider my promise kept."

He closes the door and heads to his room without a care in the world.

CHAPTER THIRTY-SIX

Pia had never imagined the work would be *this* hard.

For the umpteenth time, she heads to the smoky kitchen, dodges past wandering hands to arrive unmolested at the cellar, where she refills her pitcher before racing back to work the tables.

The madeira flows freely, yet the feast for the 'Mother's Welcome' is a sombre affair. Not surprising, after the events of the day. Mistrust runs high among the ladies and lords of the two kingdoms, who sit apart and stare at one another. The royals do sit together, yet the mood at their table is no better.

Even the musicians fail to liven up the proceedings. The entertainers before them were more fortunate. There was the tiger tamer and his ferocious beast. The fire-eaters and flame-throwers. And a dull magician, whose show-stopping trick was to make himself disappear, an act which received the loudest applause of the night.

The second loudest, actually.

The most magnificent performers were the dancers. Dressed in diaphanous wisps of silk, the girls seemed to glide across the stage, mesmerising their audience.

Towards the end of their performance, their master laid out three small boxes, filled with hot coals and thick nails and sharp knives. She refused to believe what he intended. Surely, their feet would bleed if they dared step on these.

But step they did, and bleed they did not. The girls twirled in circles as they danced, their toes skipping from nail to nail, coal to coal, knife to knife, barely touching the dreaded objects. Faster and faster they twirled, and the music rose to a crescendo as they leapt high and landed perfectly on their feet.

The applause was thunderous. Even Pia set aside her pitcher and clapped enthusiastically. When the cheers died down, Queen Indrani presented the dancers with a bag of gold, then commanded the feast to begin.

Now, politics and gossip rule, as people discuss the unusual events of the day. She moves about the tables, and spots a lord beckoning her over. She refills the cups of everyone at the table, then returns to her earlier task.

Observing the crowd.

She is most curious about the Simhasthalis. An odd bunch, they stick together for the most part. But one seems friendly enough to mix with the Vajras. Lord Chandran, who is quite drunk. And pleased, which he has good cause to be. After all, this feast is in honour of his brother-in-law, the King who will soon wed the Princess.

Still, his behaviour is odd. Lord Chandran seems jovial enough with everyone, downright familiar even. But then he comes across Prince Biraj, and his body stiffens. Their interaction is awkward, formal, and far too uncomfortable for both men. Pia wonders what it is all about.

She sees a lord's hand in the air, waving his cup. She hurries towards him, when she finds her path barred by the one man she had hoped not to come across.

King Vikrant.

He should be at the royal table. Yet here he is, walking towards her, smiling at guests at the tables. Her legs turn to stone as he approaches, and she stands frozen in the middle of the pathway. Vikrant stops, waiting for her to step aside. When he sees that she will not, he mutters an apology and walks around her without so much as a second glance.

"Girl," the lord calls out angrily, still waving his cup. Pia jumps out of her stupor and rushes to him. Once his cup is filled, her pitcher runs empty. Cursing her luck, she heads back to the kitchen, only to be accosted on the way by another Simhasthali.

Lord Ayushmann.

She knows who he is, for she had stood with the other handmaidens in the throne room and watched as he plunged this morning's event into chaos.

The Queen's bastard brother smiles amiably as he takes her hand and leads her away from prying eyes. "You appear quite taken in by my King," he says.

"Forgive me, my lord," she says, "I meant no disrespect."

"Disrespect?" Ayushmann looks at her with mock astonishment. "Any man should feel lucky to receive the attentions of a girl as pretty as you."

"I am only a serving girl, my lord," she says.

"Are you now?" Mischief dances in his eyes. "What is your name?"

"Pia, my lord," she says.

"Pia." He repeats the name softly. "A fine name you have chosen. Well, Pia, my dear girl. I can assure you King Vikrant took no offence. But I suppose Queen Indrani might. Or maybe

King Vijendra. How would they feel if I stood you before them and revealed your desire for their future son-in-law?"

Pia is scared now. "Please, My Lord, I was not—"

Ayushmann laughs. "You act well, my dear. I am impressed. If my eyes were not so well-trained, I would surely have been deceived."

"My Lord, I do not understand—" she starts to say.

Ayushmann pulls her close and whispers in her ears. "Do you truly think a wig and some make up can hide who you are?"

Pia gasps and jumps back. She glares at him, furious at her deception being caught out. She expects Ayushmann to call for the guards, but the man simply stands there, grinning from ear to ear.

"Fear not," he says, "Your secret is safe with me. But I suggest you leave now. They may all be drunk, but it only takes one set of alert eyes to get you in trouble." *Is he letting me go?* Pia does not know what to make of this, nor does she wish to stick around and find out.

She turns and makes for the kitchens. There, she ditches the pitcher and heads to the woods instead. She walks for a good fifteen minutes, until she sees the glow of the torch, which illuminates the verandah in the cottage, where Atishi and the handmaidens sit and gossip.

They jump to their feet when they see her. "We weren't expecting you for a while," Atishi says.

Pia ignores her. She removes her wig and claws out the clay stuck on her face. One of the handmaidens brings her a bowl of water, and she wipes away the makeup. She pulls out the fillers in her cheeks, and now resembles her true self.

Idhika, Princess of Vajrapur.

"I had to leave unexpectedly," she says.

"Were you recognised?" Atishi asks.

"I was," Idhika says. "By a Simhasthali, no less."

Atishi is stunned. "That is impossible. Only King Vikrant has seen you."

"I do not know how," Idhika says, "But he did recognise me. Atishi, I need you to do something for me."

"Anything, My Princess," Atishi says.

"Keep an eye on this Lord Ayushmann," says Idhika, her voice raging with anger. "He is up to something. And I need to know what it is."

CHAPTER THIRTY-SEVEN

On the southern coast of Simhasthal lies Harit Nagar, a simple seaport, where people come to trade goods from all over the world.

There, on a hot summer's day, twenty-four years before King Vikrant will arrive in Vajrapur to marry Princess Idhika, a young boy and his mother sneak out of a ship.

Stowaways, who do not wish to be caught.

They have been running for a month now, weakened by loss of food and water. And it shows, in the sunken pits where the boy's rosy cheeks should be, in his broken nose, in his skin, which hangs loose and pallid on the bony arm which holds his mother.

She looks worse, and her every step is a struggle. Once, she may have been beautiful, but lack of nourishment has stripped it away, and a tremor races through her body as she makes the long, inevitable march to death's door.

Heads bowed, they cross the port, praying not to catch the attention of the guards. Luck walks with them, and they soon leave the town behind. Ahead, green fields beckon. Another long walk, another town, another day of fearful wondering if they will be caught.

The sun shines bright and strong, a blessed relief, after a week in the dank, dark confines of the ship's hold. It strengthens the boy's mind, and he resolves to put distance between them and the town.

Unfortunately for his mother, the sun's warmth is a death sentence. She pushes her son's arm away and lies down on the soft grass. Her eyes close, and the millimetric rise of her chest is the only indication that life remains within her.

The boy tries to shake her from her stupor, but she does not wake. He stares back at the large gates. He is afraid of being caught, but what choice does he have? If his mother does not eat or drink, she will surely die.

He makes his way into town, trying his best to blend in. A silly attempt, doomed to fail. The townsfolk are heavy-built, well-fed, and his dishevelled skinny appearance is an odd sight. None move to stop him, though, and he manages to arrive at the market without incident.

There, he comes upon a sight he has not seen in weeks.

Food.

The market square is lined with stalls, where meats grill on skewers and fish swim in curry, along with *naans*, rotis, rice, fruits and vegetables of different shapes and colours. The boy's mouth overflows, and his stomach growls louder. A couple of bites and a glass of water. It may be enough to save his mother.

He makes his way stealthily through the stalls. A skewer of *kebabs*, a naan, an apple. One by one, they make their way into his ragged kerchief.

A shadow crosses his face, and he looks up to find a thick-bearded man staring down at him. The grey uniform marks him out as a city guard, which reminds the boy of the guards in his hometown, who used to curse and whip him.

Terrified, he tries to run. But the uniformed man is surprisingly quick for his size. The man grabs him by his collar and turns him around. "Where do you think you're going?"

"Please sir, please," he sobs. "Let me go. I did not do anything."

"And with what money did you pay for those?" asks the man, gesturing at the food. The boy does not reply, and the man grunts. "I thought so. Hmph. Come with me."

The guard leads him away easily enough, for the boy is weak, and does not put up a fight. He knows what lies ahead. A small cell behind thick steel bars, and many restless nights with the rats. He thinks of his mother. *Should I tell them about her, or should I leave her to die in the fields?*

It might be a kindness to leave her to the gods. These men might return them to his father, who will exact terrible retribution from his mother and him. No, he cannot face that. They may both die here, but under no circumstances will he return home.

As he expected, the man leads him to a jail-room, where another guard sharpens his sword. This man looks kinder, with a big jovial smile to go with his large potbelly.

"Who do you have there, Bhadra?" the jovial man asks.

"A thief," Bhadra says. "I caught him in the market stealing some food."

He tosses the boy into a corner, who immediately curls up against the wall and stares at the two large men.

"Bhadra." The jovial man glares at his companion. "He is a child. Look at him. He has probably not eaten in days."

"Weeks," the boy says.

"The thief finds his voice," Bhadra says. "Rotten little bastard."

"Bhadra," the jovial man shouts again. "If you were in his condition, starving to death, surrounded by all that food, what would you do?"

"I would not steal," says Bhadra, his chest swelling with arrogant pride.

"Hah," the jovial man scoffs, and rubs his colleague's ample belly. "Easily said, when you have never known hunger. Run to the market and fetch some food for the boy. Now."

A sullen Bhadra thinks to protest, but contents himself with glaring at the boy, before he leaves. The jovial man pats the empty chair beside him. "Come here, child. Sit with me."

The boy does not move. The man sighs, picks up the chair and walks over to the corner. He sets it down and sits. "My name is Rishikesh. What is yours?"

The boy does not answer.

"Come, child," Rishikesh says. "How can I help you if you do not reply?" Silence continues to greet his pleas, and he gives up. "Okay, okay. Then answer me this. What is your father's name?"

The boy's eyes widen in fear, and he shivers uncontrollably. Rishikesh nods his head in understanding. "I see. You run from an abusive father. Do not be afraid. We will bring him to justice."

"Which kingdom are we in?" the boy asks.

"Simhasthal."

Then you can do nothing. "He is not from Simhasthal."

"Ah," Rishikesh exclaims. "That is sad, for now I cannot make him suffer. What about your mother? Is she still with your father?"

She might not even be alive, he wonders. The boy wants to tell the kind man about his mother, dying in the grass a few hundred feet from the gates. But the kindness could be a trick, and he keeps his mouth shut. The angry Bhadra returns with a small parcel. He hands it to Rishikesh, who unwraps the cloth to reveal a few skewers of meat and some freshly baked naans.

Rishikesh places the food and a glass of water in front of the boy, who wonders if it is real. The aroma of the charred meat and warm bread remind him of his mother, starving and dying.

His resolve breaks.

"My name is Vidyut," he says, and the tears flow freely down his cheeks. "I am the bastard son of Lord Satwik of Naavipur. And my mother Sarita lies dying in the fields east of your gates."

He buries his face in his hands, and does not see the stunned faces of the two guards. Rishikesh turns to his colleague. "Quickly now, Bhadra. Ride as fast as you can and bring that woman to the *ayuralay*."

Bhadra runs out the room, and a few seconds pass before they hear the sound of hoofbeats racing away. Vidyut leaves the food untouched, unwilling to eat until he hears from his mother.

The hours pass slowly, and many guards come and go. Rishikesh keeps the boy's secret, and invents a story of an abandoned child and mother, causing heads to shake in sympathy before they leave. It is nearly evening before Bhadra returns to them.

"Vidyut," he calls out, his voice kinder than this morning. "Come. I will take you to your mother."

They ride to the ayuralay, where the guard hands him over to a nurse. She leads him to the recovery area, where his mother sleeps. He runs to her and holds her tight in his arms. *Is she alive? Is she dead?*

A weak hand runs through his hair, and he looks up to see his mother smile at him. "Vidyut, my child, I knew you would save me."

He hugs his mother. His bones ache, but he does not care, for he is happier than he has ever been in his life. Mother and son remain this way for a while, before the nurse gently separates them.

"Come with me now," she tells him. "Your mother needs her rest." She rubs his shrivelled belly. "And you need to eat. You can see her in the morning. Come."

Vidyut looks at his mother, who smiles through her tears. "Go with her, *beta*. Eat and sleep well. I promise, I will see you in the morning."

He kisses his mother's cheek and leaves with the nurse. That night, he eats better than ever, and sleeps in peace for the first time in years. In the morning, some of the colour has returned to his face, and when he meets his mother, he finds she is recovering as well.

Their days pass this way, eating, sleeping, talking, and regaining their strength. Bhadra and Rishikesh come to see them every day, as does the kind nurse, Devika. Vidyut is surprised to learn she is Bhadra's wife, and they introduce him to their children, Aditya and Naina.

After a month, when they have fully recovered, Sarita determines that the time has come for them to travel to Kuragarh, and put more distance between them and Naavipur. When she shares this thought with Bhadra, he asks her and Vidyut to accompany him to the outskirts of the town.

There, they arrive at a school. Bhadra asks them to wait, so they make themselves comfortable on the steps. A half hour later, the school gong sounds, and a screaming horde of boys and girls run out to the courtyard to play. Vidyut is surprised. *How can they be so happy?* In Naavipur, children hate school, and do not dare play, not unless they desire a meeting with the headmaster's stick.

As he watches these carefree children, a friendly-looking man approaches. Bhadra greets him with a formal namaste.

"Sarita," he says, "This is the schoolmaster, Atulya. I have spoken to him about your situation."

Sarita pulls Vidyut close to her, concerned and afraid. She turns to look at Bhadra, furious with him for revealing her secret to this stranger without her permission. But Vidyut is unafraid. The man looks kind enough.

Atulya senses his mother's fear. "Do not worry," he says. "Your secret is safe with me. In fact, I have an offer for you."

Sarita is confused. "An offer, my lord?"

The schoolmaster smiles. "I fear I am not a lord. Atulya, or masterji. That's what everyone calls me. My offer is simple. Your son and you are welcome to stay in my home. Bhadra tells me you are a cook, which is fortunate, for my wife has been known to burn water."

Vidyut laughs, and his mother smacks him on the head. Atulya smiles at him before addressing Sarita. "You would be saving my life, and the lives of my children, if you agree to take over the task."

Sarita smiles, unable to hide her happiness. "Thank you, my lord." She bites her tongue. "Sorry, masterji."

"And as for you, young man," Atulya turns to Vidyut, "You will join my school. I sense you are an intelligent boy, destined for great things. I hope you will work hard and prove me right."

Vidyut nods his head. "I will do my best, masterji."

"Then we are in agreement," Atulya beams happily. "Now, if we are to keep your identities secret, you will need new names." He looks at the mother. "I suggest you change yours to Vaidehi, if you find it suitable."

"I do, masterji," Sarita says.

Then he looks at the boy. "As for you, I think Ayushmann is a good name."

Vidyut grins happily. *Ayushmann, one blessed with a long life.* He silently thanks the masterji, and hopes his words prove prophetic.

CHAPTER THIRTY-EIGHT

Atishi stifles a yawn as she enters the shaded forest. The day grows warm already, but she does not care. She is in her happy place, her own little castle, hidden away from the sadness and chaos that reigns within the stone city.

How times change.

She was shown to the cottage as soon as she arrived in Vajrapur. This was to be her home, where she could entertain important guests away from prying eyes, while Princess Idhika discreetly observed from a secret chamber.

Tears had welled in her eyes then. For a city girl, it was torture to be so close to the hustle and bustle of the capital, yet so far removed. She would miss the food and the shops, the people and the gossip. Above all, she would miss the stories, of the travellers who pass through for trade and rest.

But the months rolled by, and she felt her soul lighten. The smell of the flowers, the songs of the birds, the dance of the leaves in the wind. She slowly fell in love, and now this new world would be the only place for her.

Her ears perk up as birdsongs flutter among the branches. A melody without lyrics, there is a rhythm to their tune, and even the slightest change is a message for those who know to listen.

Their songs keep her company all the way home. She enters the cottage and heads to the kitchen to brew a pot of tea. As the water boils, she sets the tray. Tea leaves in a kettle, two cups, some warm milk, and sugar. Once the water is hot enough, she fills the kettle, then carries the tray to her verandah.

She takes a seat at the table and waits, content to simply stare into the woods. Then, she lifts the lid off the kettle and sniffs the tea. *Perfect.*

She pours the brew into two cups, then turns to the woods and calls out. "The tea is ready, My Lord."

Silence greets her call, followed by footsteps a few seconds later. A man emerges from the bushes, dressed like a gardener, with mud still on his hands and clothes. He climbs onto the wooden deck and takes a seat.

"I am impressed, my lady," the man says.

"Atishi, my lord," she says, as she hands him a cup. "I confess I did not know you were following me. But the birds did, and they sang out their warning." She taps her ears. "I have trained myself to listen."

The man smiles. "Still, I am embarrassed. No man has ever caught me before."

She happily accepts the compliment. "A woman's senses are far sharper."

"Indeed, they are," he acknowledges, and she is pleased to note he does so without reluctance. "I believe introductions are in order. My name is—"

"Lord Ayushmann," she interrupts him.

The look of admiration grows on his face. The poor man. His disguise is almost perfect, but his smile gives him away. Ordinary men and women would not be able to recognise him, but Atishi is a mistress of disguise, and it would take more than subtle alterations to deceive her.

Besides, he had ruined Princess Idhika's night, and she takes some pleasure in extracting a measure of revenge.

"A fellow expert," says Ayushmann, while adding some sugar to his tea and stirring it. He takes a sip, savours the taste and sets the cup down. "A far better expert than me. I presume it was you who disguised Princess Idhika last night."

"And you saw through it," Atishi says.

"It wasn't the disguise, my lady," Ayushmann informs her. "The Princess played the part of servant girl well enough. She was attentive, ran around, filled every cup. But there was no bowing of the head, no averting of the eyes. She could not hide her pride, and that was her downfall."

"I will inform the Princess of her errors," she says. "But in the meantime, how may I be of service?"

Ayushmann takes another sip. "You could tell me what you have been doing in my King's room these past two nights."

"I see you have kept a close eye on us," she says. "Very well. King Vijendra commanded me to help King Vikrant sleep well at night."

"And does he?" Ayushmann asks.

"Better than ever," Atishi says.

"How about in the morning?" Ayushmann persists. "How does my King feel then?"

Atishi shrugs her shoulders. "Perhaps King Vikrant would like to answer that question himself."

"Oh, I dare not ask him," he says, "For then I would have to answer for my actions."

"You mean you will have to answer for spying on him," she says, and sips her tea.

"I have not spied," he protests weakly. "Rather, I have kept an eye on him. After all, we are in Vajrapur, guests of the King who cut off his father's head."

"A King who will soon be his father by law," she retorts.

"And when that day arrives, I will cease my activities," he says. "I promise you, lovely Atishi, Queen Idhika will never have to suffer her privacy being intruded by bad, bad Ayushmann."

The man has an easy charm, which suggests there is little in the world which fazes him. Atishi wonders what kind of life he must have led to be this way. *Maybe I will find out someday.* She smiles at him. "I have met bad, bad men, My Lord. And you are most certainly not one of them."

He looks at her with genuine astonishment, then drains his cup. "I thank you for your kind words, and apologise for the trouble I have caused. You must be tired, so I will leave you to your rest."

He makes to leave, and Atishi grabs his arm. "On the contrary my lord, you have saved me some trouble." A puzzled Ayushmann takes his seat again, and she continues. "I was asked to deliver a message to you, which I had planned on doing later this morning. At the market."

"The market?" Ayushmann asks.

"A visit has been arranged," she says, "To keep the Simhasthalis entertained. They have planned another activity as well. A far more interesting one, if you are up to it."

"I am always up for interesting activities," he says.

"You should opt for it then," Atishi says. "I promise you will find it very informative."

"If you insist," Ayushmann says, and she can hear the wheels race in his mind, trying to decipher what clues hide within her words. "You said you had a message for me?"

She nods her head. "Twenty miles west of here, there is a town called Krasheerpur. On its outskirts, there is a house. If you arrive there after midnight, there is a man who would be very happy to make your acquaintance."

His eyes widen for a fraction of a second, before he regains his composure.

Too late.

Ayushmann knows who the man in Krasheerpur is. Atishi is not surprised. There is only one man of importance who lives there, and every person in Saravat knows who he is.

She feels his eyes search hers, trying to guess the thoughts that run through her mind. Many men have gazed into them before, but never has she felt her heart quiver the way it does now. This man is different. He admires her for her intelligence and her talent, which is far more than anyone has ever done.

"So, Lord Jayendu wants to meet. I wonder why?" The smile returns to Ayushmann's face once more. "For you, lovely Atishi, I will meet with him. I will hear what he has to say, and if it serves my purpose, I will be forever in your debt."

He stands and bows, then disappears into the woods. Once he is out of sight, her heartbeat slows, and her breath returns to normal. It took all her strength to keep her composure during that interaction, and she does not know if she can do it again.

Still, one of her tasks is complete. One more to go, but that will not be for a few hours more. She yawns as the tiredness claws at her mind. She needs sleep, desperately. And after the events of the morning, she has more than earned it.

CHAPTER THIRTY-NINE

This is what hell must feel like.

Chandran awakens in the morning, a hammer pounding at the walls of his head. His mouth feels dry, his nose stuffy, and his body aches from head to toe. He curses himself. *Why did I have to drink so much?*

The feast at the 'Mother's Welcome' had put him in a good mood. But it was more than that. He is comfortable in Vajrapur. They respect him here, not for his title or proximity to the throne, but for the man he is. And his King respects him as well, for he has always been a loyal servant.

He opens his eyes, and wishes the wedding were done with already. The need for so many functions has always baffled him. All a couple should be expected to do is stand in front of their families and vow to be true to one another.

His own wedding had been a week-long affair, each day more tedious and tiresome than the previous. By the time their wedding night arrived, Gayathri and he were so exhausted that they failed to consummate their marriage, and instead, surrendered to a blissful night's sleep.

Gayathri. Chandran jumps up in bed and looks around the room. She is nowhere to be found. She must be in the assembly hall, with the others, cursing him. He leaps out of bed and rushes to get dressed.

Fifteen minutes later, the astonished guards watch Chandran jog down the corridor to the assembly hall. A Vajra bars his way as he skips down the stairs. He tries to run past, but the man jumps in front of him.

"How dare you?" Chandran shouts. "Do you know who I am?"

"Apologies, my lord," the man says. He holds out a tiny scroll. "A message. From General Rannveer."

The man leaves a bewildered Chandran to read the message.

Do not go to the market.

He reads the line once more, and remains confused. The message speaks of where he should not go, but makes no mention of where he should. He does not have time for these silly riddles. He stuffs the paper in his pocket and hurries to the assembly hall.

The Vajra envoy bows his head when Chandran enters. As feared, he is the last to arrive, and he rushes to take his seat next to Gayathri, whispering his apologies. His wife turns just long enough to glare at him, before returning to her conversation with her mother.

Chandran glances around the room. Angry faces stare back at him, and the only man smiling at him is Ayushmann. He nods at the minister, not wishing to appear too friendly.

After all, he is the Queen's bastard brother.

As always, Ayushmann sits beside Atulya, and the two whisper as they wait for the King to arrive. Chandran wonders what important matters they discuss. Whatever it is, he is sure King Vijendra would love to hear of it.

His thoughts are interrupted by Vikrant's arrival. All rise to their feet and bow to their King. Once he is seated, the envoy addresses the room.

"Your Majesty, Your Highnesses, General, my ladies and lords. As you know, tonight there will be 'A Tribute to Vajrapur'. The festivities will feature a parade, followed by a dance performance and a historical play."

The envoy takes a breath before continuing. "But we will start the celebrations at noon, with a tour of the markets, where you will be able to explore the traditional handicrafts of our kingdom. The silks are wonderful, as are the wooden artefacts. This will be followed by a lunch in the gardens. The cook has only recently arrived from faraway Farisa, and vows to reinvent Vajra cuisine with herbs from that exotic land."

He pauses once more for breath. "Also, for the more adventurous, General Rannveer invites you to explore the Andhakaranya with him. He is the only man alive to have survived three years alone in the dark forest. I am certain he will lead you to many interesting places which you might never see otherwise."

Chandran's heart skips a beat.

Do not go to the market.

The meaning is clear now. So, King Vijendra has found a way to make contact. He prays and hopes not too many of his countrymen will accompany him to the forest, a prospect which brightens when Ranimaa Nandini speaks up.

"A tour of the markets does sound lovely," she says. "The ladies will get a chance to see more of the city."

"Indeed," Vikrant agrees. "As will the men. We will all head to the markets and see what delights Vajrapur has to offer."

The envoy bows, pleased by the King's words. "As you wish, Your Majesty."

The Simhasthalis look at one another and nod. Their King has commanded, and they will obey. Chandran could not be happier. He now has the opportunity to head to the Andhakaranya by himself.

"Your Majesty," he calls out. All eyes turn to him. "With your permission, I would like to tour the Andhakaranya."

Vikrant regards him curiously. "You wish to see the dark forest again?"

"I do not," says Chandran, trying not to sound too eager. "But it would be rude for none of us to take up General Rannveer's invitation."

The ministers look at one another. Why should any of them care about hurting the General's feelings? While Vikrant weighs his brother-in-law's words, Ayushmann weighs in.

"Your Majesty, I fear Lord Chandran is correct," he says. "In fact, I will accompany you to the Andhakaranya, my lord. To keep you company."

The man is a menace. Chandran sets his irritation aside and forces a smile. "Your company is much appreciated, Lord Ayushmann."

Vikrant does not seem to care much. "As you both wish," he says, and rises from his seat. He leaves the hall, and his people follow. As Ayushmann walks past, Chandran silently curses him once more. He does not yet know how he will rid himself of this annoyance so he can meet with Rannveer in private.

He has no choice.

Somehow, he has to find a way.

CHAPTER FORTY

The heat is stifling, as it usually is at this time of the year. For the Simhasthalis, long accustomed to the cool climate of the Rodasi, it is a torture to be outside. Some choose to suffer; others purchase colourful paper fans to cool themselves.

Gayathri is among the smarter ones, fanning herself as she makes her way from shop to shop. The bazaar is all the envoy promised it would be, though it cannot compare to the Simhasthali markets she is used to, which are much larger.

But there, the shops offer only the most essential of goods and a few items of comfort. Here, luxury is the main commodity; less about what you need, more about what you desire.

And Gayathri desires a lot.

Her handmaidens wait outside every shop, their arms already heavy with parcels. There are dresses made of silk and chiffon, vessels of brass and silver, necklaces with rubies and emeralds.

A doll-maker's shop catches her fancy. She walks in, and that's when she feels it again. That tingling sensation, a sixth sense that lets her know she is being watched. A casual glance around the marketplace fails to reveal the spy's identity. Whoever it is, he is well trained. She decides to linger among the dolls a little longer.

Though she is distracted by her attempt to find the spy, she cannot help but admire the dolls. There's the wooden soldier with the cleverly jointed arm, which allows him to swing his sword in attack and defence. There's the cotton-stuffed Princess with the big, red smile, and even an elephant who rolls along on four wheels. Her children would love these.

"Perhaps this one for your daughter, Your Highness?" a woman's voice interrupts her thoughts.

Gayathri whips around and comes face to face with an unassuming Vajra woman wearing a plain cotton sari, who holds out a wooden doll, much like the soldier she had seen earlier. To her surprise, this one has been carved to show off long flowing hair, and if Gayathri is not mistaken, the hint of a bosom as well.

The woman smiles as she presents it to the Princess. "I believe we are the only shop in Saravat who make dolls of women warriors."

"You must be," says Gayathri, as she takes the doll and inspects it closely. "I have never seen such a doll before. Then again, not many think we should be warriors."

"That is sad," the woman says. "But I believe it is more out of fear, for what warriors we would be. Take you, for example. I sense a fire in you, Your Highness. Put a sword in your hand, and all these men will quake in their boots."

Gayathri laughs, pleased by the compliment. "What is your name?"

"Atishi, Your Highness," the woman says.

"And how do you know so much about me, Atishi?" Gayathri asks.

Atishi smiles, and her face is no longer ordinary. She looks shrewd, sly, dangerous. "Because I have been watching you from the moment you arrived in our kingdom."

Gayathri looks at her disbelievingly, and curses herself. *I should have noticed you before.* She nods her head in admiration. "So, you are the spy. I have felt your presence, but not once have I been able to lay eyes on you."

Atishi acknowledges her compliment with a bow of her head. "I am not a spy, Your Highness. A watcher, perhaps. An admirer. A humble servant, who does as commanded by her mistress. It is she who asked me to follow you and learn all I could."

"And why would your mistress be so interested in me?" Gayathri asks.

"For you will soon be her sister by law," Atishi replies.

Gayathri's eyes widen. "Princess Idhika is your mistress?"

"She is, Your Highness," Atishi says. "She hopes to meet with you, so you can get to know each other better."

"Her wish will soon be granted," Gayathri says. "The engagement is the day after tomorrow. You may tell the Princess I look forward to welcoming her into our family."

Atishi appears unsure. "If I may be so bold, Your Highness? Engagements are such formal affairs. I believe my mistress would like to spend a bit more personal time with you."

"And how would that be possible?" Gayathri asks.

Atishi smiles. "You could feign an illness this evening and ask your brother's leave to miss the event. Once everyone is at the grounds, I will escort you to the Princess."

Gayathri collects her thoughts, trying to figure out her best course of action. She does not know this woman, and even if she works for Idhika, what possible reason could the Princess have to meet with her?

There is only one way to find out. "Are you certain we won't be caught?"

"It is my job to be certain, Your Highness," Atishi replies confidently. She bows her head. "Please accept the doll as a gift. From Princess Idhika to your daughter."

Atishi leaves, and within seconds, is lost in the crowd. Gayathri is intrigued by their strange encounter, with a stranger one yet to come this evening.

A hand grabs her shoulder. She jumps in fright. Then she sees who it is and calms down. "Maa, you frightened me."

"Sorry, my child," Nandini says. She notices the doll in Gayathri's hand. Its appearance confuses her, and she leans in to examine it closely. Once she realises what it is, she laughs. "A woman soldier. I cannot believe it. Reminds me of you as a child. How you used to love taking a practice sword and challenging all the guards to a duel. Honestly, I can almost imagine this doll is you."

"I do not see a resemblance," Gayathri remarks sarcastically. She holds up the doll's arm. "See? No kitchen knife."

Nandini laughs even louder. "Come," she says. "Your brother needs your opinion. There's some gift he intends to buy for his bride."

She links her daughter's arm with hers and leads her away from the doll shop. As they make their way to Vikrant, Gayathri scans the crowd for any sign of Atishi. She finds none, nor was she expecting to. There is nothing left to do but wait for tonight, when Atishi will return to steal her away for her secret meeting.

With Princess Idhika.

CHAPTER FORTY-ONE

General Rannveer curses his luck.

He had been certain none of the Simhasthalis would accept an invitation from him. Yet, here he sits on horseback, at the edge of the Andhakaranya, awaiting the arrival of the two Simhasthali lords.

One whom he wants to meet.

The other whom he doesn't.

That pesky Ayushmann has ruined Rannveer's plans. But it does not matter. If not here, he will rendezvous with Chandran elsewhere. Maybe at the celebration tonight. And if he fails, he will be only too happy for the King to assign the task to someone else. This is beneath him, as is the Simhasthali he must deal with.

It must have been so easy for King Vijendra to prey on Chandran's insecurities. *Spy on the Simhasthalis,* he must have said, *and report back to me.*

An easy task, with little to no risk. And in return, Chandran would be rewarded with the governorship of a kingdom, or maybe a plum ministry in the new empire, positions of importance he could never have dreamed of.

His thoughts are interrupted by his soldier's arrival. The two lords ride close behind. Ayushmann appears comfortable on his horse, but Chandran seems ill at ease, trying hard to gain control of the beast. It reluctantly comes to a halt, snorting furiously and shaking its head from side to side.

They bow their heads and greet him by name. Rannveer returns the courtesy. "Welcome, Lord Chandran, Lord Ayushmann. I am honoured you accepted my invitation."

"The honour is ours, General," Ayushmann replies with a pleasant smile. "To have such a distinguished commander guide us through the Andhakaranya… I imagine few have had the privilege."

The man's tongue drips with honey. Rannveer tries to smile, but ends up with an awkward half-smile, half-grimace. "The two of you will be my first guests from outside Vajrapur."

Ayushmann bows his head, humbled. "Then the honour is greater than I imagined. We are in your hands, General."

Rannveer glances at Chandran, who continues to struggle with his horse. The man is no rider, but there is nothing to be done about it now. He turns his horse around and leads the way into the forest.

Over the next few hours, he regales them with stories of his time in the Andhakaranya. They visit the small hut he used to live in, snack on the berries and fruits he ate, as well as the animals he hunted. Squirrels with sharp teeth, snakes with skin that turns red when endangered, and the indigenous boar with large spikes on its back.

They even come across the elusive panther which rules this forest. The black beast watches them warily from his high branch, wondering if he should attack these pesky humans or leave them alone. He ponders the question for a few seconds, then drops his head between his paws and closes his eyes.

When they arrive at the Sitarabaug, Rannveer finds himself riding alongside Ayushmann. Behind them, Chandran's fight with his steed continues, and a Vajra soldier unsuccessfully tries to assist him. Ayushmann shows little concern for his fellow Simhasthali. Instead, he gazes at the glowing white flowers overhead, which twinkle like stars in the darkness of the forest.

"This grove is called a Sitarabaug," Rannveer informs him.

Ayushmann nods his head. "We stopped under one on the way to Dhaningarh. A beautiful place, especially in a forest such as this."

Rannveer smiles. "There are many such groves, some far closer to the capital. And the fruit?" His eyes twinkle as he remembers their taste. "Sweet and sour nectarines, which you cannot find anywhere else in this world."

Ayushmann looks impressed. "You certainly know the forest well. If my asking does not offend you, why did you spend three years in the Andhakaranya?"

Rannveer's smile disappears. "It was a long time ago."

"A little after the fever took hold in Dhaningarh?" Ayushmann asks.

A devil with a smile. Rannveer regards him with studied silence for a long while. Then he replies. "A couple of months after the last of the dead were cremated."

"Did you lose someone?" Ayushmann asks.

The man does not give up. "My father, the first time. The second attack got my son."

"My sincere condolences," Ayushmann says.

"I thank you, my lord," Rannveer says.

"Was your father old?" Ayushmann asks.

Rannveer shakes his head. “Baba was close to fifty. Not too old, with much life yet to live. His death came as a shock. But it could not even compare to how I felt when my son died. A babe, barely three months of age.” His voice fills with sorrow. “I needed time for my soul to heal.”

“In the darkness, you sought the light,” Ayushmann intones.

Rannveer smiles wistfully. “You could say that.” He chuckles. “I did not take you for a poet, my lord. Perhaps you should consider a new vocation.”

Ayushmann laughs. “I fear not, General. I like my job a little too much.”

Their conversation is interrupted by Chandran’s yelp of exasperation, as his horse continues to refuse his commands.

Ayushmann takes pity on him. “My lord, you fight a losing battle.”

“I believe you are right,” Chandran agrees. “General, how much further do we have to go?”

Rannveer points beyond the trees. “A couple of miles. We will soon come to the last highlight of our tour. The Luptasheel.”

“The land of the lost?” Ayushmann asks.

Rannveer nods his head. “That is correct, my lord. There are dangerous marshlands there, which will swallow you whole if you do not know the way.” A smile breaks across his face. “Fortunately for us, my men and I know the way.”

Ayushmann smiles as well. “In that case, lead on.”

Chandran appears uneasy. “General Rannveer, my Lord Ayushmann, I am afraid you will have to continue without me. Riding this horse for so long has made me a little queasy.”

“I am sorry to hear that, Lord Chandran,” says Rannveer, his concern genuine. For the horse, not the Simhasthali. “Perhaps we should return to the palace.”

"No, no," Chandran says. "I suggest you carry on with Lord Ayushmann. I will wait here for you."

"I have a better idea," Ayushmann says. "General, I do not wish to impose on your hospitality. Since your men know the way, perhaps they can lead me to these dangerous bogs, and try their best not to lose me in one. The two of you can rest here for a while, and return to the palace once Lord Chandran feels better."

Rannveer cannot believe his luck. Still, he tries not to appear too eager. "Are you certain, my lord?"

Ayushmann glances at the forest, then back at the General. He chuckles. "We shall find out."

Rannveer smiles. "As you wish, Lord Ayushmann."

He turns to his men and gives them their orders. Three stay behind, while the rest lead Ayushmann into the forest. A blanket is laid out, refreshments are unpacked, and Rannveer sits down with Chandran for a light meal.

Once his men are out of earshot, he speaks. "I had hoped you would arrive alone."

"I almost did," Chandran replies. "Vikrant commanded everyone to the market, but Ayushmann decided to spoil my plans."

Rannveer glances at the forest. "Does he suspect something?"

"The man suspects everyone and everything," Chandran says. "Do not be fooled by his smile. He is little more than a snake in the grass."

"Yes," Rannveer agrees, "But whose hand will he bite?"

"That is yet to be determined," Chandran says.

"The King wants a question answered. Who else was privy to his particular secret?"

Chandran sighs. "I know for certain Vikrant was clueless, as was the rest of the royal family. However, Lord Atulya knew. He has always known. After all, Ayushmann was raised under his roof."

"But did he know about the stunt in the throne room?" Ranveer asks.

"I think so," Chandran says. "The minister and the schoolmaster have gone rogue, and not even Vikrant knows what to make of them."

"Hmm." Rannveer ponders the reply. "Queen Indrani wants him dead."

"As is her right," Chandran says. "Ayushmann insulted her in front of the entire kingdom. Do the deed, General. The world will be better for it."

"I have no cause to," Rannveer says.

"You do not need cause," Chandran informs him. His face brightens. "I have news. General Kashyap no longer stands as champion for Vikrant. Ayushmann has been chosen to take his place."

Rannveer finds that hard to believe. "Are you certain? Kashyap is the King's uncle."

"He is also the commander of the joint forces," says Chandran, oblivious to look of annoyance which crosses Rannveer's face. "I was present in the room when Vikrant issued the command."

"But is Ayushmann a good swordsman?" Rannveer asks.

"I have never seen him wield one," Chandran replies. "I do not believe he is, and it should be easy for you to make it look like an accident."

Rannveer mulls over this new information. "It is possible. Accidents do happen in the arena." He makes up his mind. "But it will be considered an ill omen, on the eve of the Princess' marriage. No. I will stick to His Majesty's task, and find out Ayushmann's intentions."

"If that is the King's wish," Chandran says, "I will do my best to seek him out."

The man's servility annoys Rannveer. "No, you will not," he shouts, then checks himself. "You are too important, my lord. None should suspect your loyalty to the Simhas. Hopefully, he will make a mistake, and give us an excuse."

Chandran shakes his head. "I fear your plan will fail. Ayushmann has lived with this secret for far too long, and even the best of us could not discern his true identity. He will not be easy to catch."

A smile breaks across Rannveer's face. "Whatever his intentions, they will not matter once the wedding is done with. The alliance will be sealed, and war will follow."

Chandran stares at him for a few seconds, then nods his head. The Simhasthali helps himself to some food, while Rannveer turns his thoughts towards the report he will have to make later in the evening.

First to King Vijendra.

And then to Lord Jayendu.

CHAPTER FORTY-TWO

The kingdom wears a festive look, as the citizens throng the streets to pay tribute to Vajrapur's glorious history. Colourful lanterns dangle from every window, and in the marketplace, the children are entertained by puppets, or win prizes at the game stalls.

But the crowd is thickest in the main square, for this is where the show is grandest. They watch the tableaux—chariots modified to pull stages—as they ride past the royal enclosure, re-enacting scenes from Vajra history, paying homage to its art, or offering tribute to its Kings, past and present.

Oohs and aahs ring out, sometimes soft, sometimes loud. In the royal enclosure, however, King Vikrant looks distinctly uninterested as he sits to the left of King Vijendra, along with Indranuj and Kashyap, while his mother and Chandran are seated to Queen Indrani's right. His sister is absent. She was not keeping well, and had begged his leave to skip the show.

So far, little of note has taken place, and he feels the minutes drag longer than they should, slowed down by the prospect of meeting Idhika in the morning. The thought of her gladdens his heart, and a faint smile crosses his lips.

"You seem to be enjoying yourself," Vijendra says.

Vikrant turns to face him. "The tableaux are quite wonderful."

Vijendra looks amused. "Save the diplomacy for others, my boy. If I had my way, I would forbid such nonsense from ever taking place. But alas, the people are fond of them."

"I did not think you cared much for what the people want," Vikrant says.

"Oh, but I have to," Vijendra says. "There are only two ways to keep the people on your side. Give them an enemy to fear, or keep them distracted enough to forget their lives are meaningless."

Spoken like a true tyrant, Vikrant thinks.

Vijendra isn't the first one in the history of Saravat to make this claim. There have been many Kings like him before, who inspired the bloodlust among their people on flimsy grounds. Vikrant has studied their lives, sometimes in school with his teachers, other times at the feet of his father, or Atulya chacha.

And now, the lesson is learnt from the source.

"Is that what you think of them?" Vikrant asks.

Vijendra nods his head. "They are born, they obey another man's commands, they die."

"They live, they laugh, they love," counters Vikrant, unwilling to cede the argument. "There is another way to look at their lives."

"You may be right," Vijendra concedes. "Alas, such a life is impossible for you and I. It was to be my destiny once, while my brothers yet lived. But destiny has a fickle mind."

"Indeed," Vikrant says.

He applauds politely as the final tableau makes its way past the dais. It features a marble likeness of the great conqueror

Vijendra, standing with sword held aloft, like a victor on a battlefield, and the crowd welcomes it with rapturous applause.

Once it is out of sight, stagehands rush to erect a square wooden platform. The dancers arrive soon after, and the audience cheers once more. Vikrant does not register their presence. His mind remains caught up with other thoughts.

"Do you miss your brothers?" he asks.

For a fleeting moment, anger burns in Vijendra's eyes. Just as quickly, it is gone, replaced by sadness. "Sometimes I do. It has been so many years since they passed. Still, I remember their faces well, and their affection towards me."

"Their death made you King, though," Vikrant says.

"As your father's death made you," Vijendra retorts.

"At your hands," says Vikrant, his voice rising a notch.

"Then a little more gratitude would be nice, my boy," says Vijendra, with a hint of irritation in his voice. "By killing your father and starting this war, I offer you more than you ever knew to expect."

"And what might that be?" Vikrant asks.

"Saravat," Vijendra declares. *A great honour, drunk from a poisoned cup.*

The Vajra King has certainly made promises, but Vikrant wonders if he will keep it. History does not offer hope, yet he knows he has no choice. This alliance must remain strong, even if his pride takes a fall.

"But did you ever consider the cost?" he persists with his argument. "Thousands have died. Thousands will die. Is it worth it?"

The conviction in Vijendra's voice surprises him. "The cost is borne by the present. The benefits are reaped by the future."

A smile breaks across his face. "There is always a price to pay for greatness. If you are willing."

Vikrant smiles as well. "Words are easily spoken, Your Majesty, when soldiers and innocents must shed the blood."

Vijendra cannot hold back his laughter. The others turn to look at him as he leans forward and whispers in Vikrant's ear. "My boy, of all the people in the world, you should know better. *The battle is never over until the King is dead.*"

Indrani taps his shoulder, and Vijendra turns his attention to her. Vikrant stares at the Vajra King for a while, then looks away. Though he hates to admit it, Vijendra's words ring true. The price must be paid. In blood.

Only one question remains.

Is he willing to pay it?

CHAPTER FORTY-THREE

Idhika sits on the verandah and waits for her guest.

The first time she visited the cottage in the woods, she had not known it would change her life forever. She was a child then, twelve years of age, when her mother brought her to meet Atishi, the whore from Farisa. In no uncertain terms, Idhika was told what was expected of her.

"Learn the art of seduction, my child," Queen Indrani said. "It will be as valuable to you in the future as your intelligence."

The Queen left her daughter in the care of the whore, who was just a few years older than her. At first, Idhika had pitied the weak and timid girl.

She shouldn't have.

Atishi proved to be a master performer, skilled in the art of deception, and as the years rolled by, Idhika saw her convince lover after lover into believing they pleasure her.

She still remembers the first. A middle-aged man, with a drooping belly and many chins. She watched, shocked, as Atishi disrobed the man, then shed her own clothes, before proceeding to pleasure him with her hands, her mouth, and finally her sex.

Later, Atishi taught her the trick. *Do not be desirable*, she said, *for that is easy enough.* What's much harder is to become what a lover desires; vulnerable if commanded, strong if required.

She could not bring herself to consider any act of desire as evil. Rather, its was the imposition of one's desire on another soul which caused real harm.

Once Idhika mastered the secrets of the bedchamber, Atishi revealed her other talents. She could transform herself in a matter of minutes, and blend into any setting. Idhika had tested her once, commanding her to dress as a noblewoman and mingle with the ladies and lords at a feast. That night, she watched the proceedings from the balcony, yet she could not pick out her friend in the crowd, not until Atishi returned to her chambers later that night.

Their friendship is unbreakable now. They may not have the same blood, or the same upbringing. But they share the same desire, and there is no stronger bond in the world.

Her thoughts are broken by the sudden chirping of the birds. Her guest is here.

Atishi arrives first, followed by a woman dressed as a handmaiden. Idhika rises to receive her with the proper respect. After all, they are equals.

For now.

"Welcome, Princess Gayathri," she says. "It is a pleasure to meet you."

"The honour is mine, Your Highness," Gayathri says. "I have desired to meet you since the day I learned we will be sisters."

Idhika smiles and leads her to a chair. "Come. May I offer you some madeira?"

"That would be wonderful," says Gayathri, as she makes herself comfortable.

Idhika pours her a cup, then one for herself. Gayathri sips her madeira before speaking. "I was pleasantly surprised when

Atishi delivered your message. I did not know you were this eager to meet me."

"May I call you Gayathri?" asks Idhika, her tone deferential. "I quite despise formal titles."

Gayathri seems pleased to hear this. "Of course, Idhika. After all, we will be family soon."

"Yes, we will," Idhika says, and the deference vanishes. "Therefore, I will speak honestly, as one should with family. The reason I was so eager to meet you is because you are the wife of Lord Chandran."

Gayathri pauses, mid-sip, her eyes wide, her lips parted.

Idhika smiles. *Good. I caught her off-guard.*

For a few moments, the Simhasthali Princess regards Idhika with suspicion. Then she regains her composure and sips her drink. "I fail to grasp your meaning."

You understand well enough. Idhika giggles. "Do not be afraid. I am aware your husband is a loyal ally of my father."

"I see," says Gayathri, trying to remain calm. "I was unaware King Vijendra shared such information with his daughter."

"He does not," Idhika confesses. "But I have my spies as well, and they whisper in my ears, just as your husband whispers in my father's." She places a hand on Gayathri's. "Your secret is safe with me. But if I may ask, what has my father promised your husband after the war?"

Gayathri regards her for a long while, and Idhika sees her struggle to reach a decision. She sips her madeira, which only serves to make Gayathri more uncomfortable.

"Naavipur," she says finally. "He has offered to make my husband Governor of Naavipur."

"Interesting," Idhika says, "I would have thought Triloha would be a much more valuable prize."

"In terms of wealth, yes," Gayathri admits. "But only for the moment. Naavipur is the largest trading post in Saravat, with lots more potential, and it suits my husband's capabilities better. He is a trader by heart, really, not meant to manage mines, nor forge steel and gold. Cloth and spices, that's where he is most comfortable."

"A man who knows his limits is a wise man," Idhika declares. She smiles sweetly. "Which is another reason I was so desperate to meet you. After I am wed, our two kingdoms will go to war against the other three. And at the end of that war, my father will be Emperor."

"Yes," says Gayathri, a smile on her face as well. "He will."

"And after my father, my husband will rule," Idhika says.

"That is what has been decided," Gayathri agrees.

"Vikrant will need trusted Governors in the other kingdoms," Idhika says. She takes a moment before continuing. "I do not wish to say it, but what is to stop Lord Chandran from betraying mine?"

"He will not," says Gayathri, her confidence absolute. "Because I will not let him."

"Do you really believe you can control your husband?" Idhika asks her.

Gayathri smiles slyly. "Oh, that part is easy."

"I wish I could believe you," says Idhika, unconvinced. "From all I have heard, you are strong-willed and intelligent, not one to suffer fools. And yet you took one for a husband, for love no less."

Gayathri stares at her for a long moment, and Idhika fears she may have taken offence. But then the Simhasthali Princess bursts into laughter. Her cheeks redden, as mirthful tears roll down them, and a long while passes before she finally subsides.

Still chuckling, Gayathri drains her glass and smiles at Idhika. "My sweet innocent girl, what makes you think I married my husband for love?"

Idhika regards her curiously. "You did not?"

"No, my dear Princess," says Gayathri, wiping her tears. "I was a girl of sixteen, and my father spoke to me of marriage to Crown Prince Shourya of Naavipur. I would have been Queen of that kingdom someday, an exciting prospect to most women."

"But not to you?" Idhika asks.

Gayathri shrugs. "Queen, lady, commoner. These are mere titles, which offer us power, yes. But that power is an illusion. The real power lies with our husbands, and while they live, they set the rules. Where we live, what we do, how we behave. Then they die, and we are cast aside to let our son's wife take our place, and lead the same miserable life we once did."

Idhika understands her emotions. "But that still does not explain your marriage to Chandran."

Gayathri smiles. "But it explains everything, my dear girl. I first met him when I was exploring the market and walked into his shop. He was nineteen then, and could not tear his eyes away from me. He fumbled and slipped every time I asked a question, and gave me more spices than I had ordered. You have to understand. Until then, I had only met Princes and lords, cocky men who dismissed my thoughts without consideration. But here was this man, pleasant enough to look at, who considered my thoughts to be more important than his own. I liked having him around, if only to boost my ego."

She drinks deep from her cup before continuing. "It didn't take me long to realise he would be the ideal husband. One I could control, one who would help me rule my own destiny. Before my father could make an alliance, I informed him of my decision to marry Chandran. My family was furious, but none could change my mind, for it is hard to change."

"So Chandran was a marriage of convenience?" Idhika asks. "As mine is?"

Gayathri nods her head. "Our lives are more similar that you think. I am the firstborn child of Giridhar; you are the only heir of Vijendra. Yet our fathers never saw us as rulers. No. To them, we are merely vessels to further some man's lineage. I refused to walk that path. But now you do, and with a man far weaker than my husband."

Finally, our discussion turns to Vikrant. In their two meetings, Idhika has yet not managed to gauge his weaknesses, nor guess as to his strengths. The man remains an enigma — servile to her father, considerate to her opinions, strong in his beliefs. Still, she is determined to figure out who he truly is, hopefully before they are wed, for afterwards it will not matter anymore.

"Is he truly as weak as everyone says?" she asks.

Gayathri smiles. "May I be honest now?" Idhika remains silent, and she continues. "I love my brother, but he is a weakling. He always has been. So, you will have to take control and guide him." She squeezes Idhika's hand. "Now that we have met, I see a lot of myself in you. The same spirit, the same desire. Do what I did. Take control of your destiny, and let others believe they hold the reins."

Idhika smiles. “When I do, I will need allies who are loyal to me, not to my father or my husband.”

“And you shall have them,” Gayathri says, “As long as you can prove your worth. Nothing would please me more than serving a capable woman. But I must ask, do you have it in you to be the power behind the throne?”

A smile breaks across Idhika’s face, and the ambition surges through her. For the first time in her life, she considers the possibility of fulfilling her one and only desire. Taking control of her destiny. She leans forward, and is surprised by the strength of her own voice.

“I do,” she says. “And I will.”

CHAPTER FORTY-FOUR

Midnight comes and goes, and the citizens of Krasheerpur sleep, blissfully unaware of the stranger in the Vajra Corporal's uniform who rides to the far end of the village, then turns his horse into an alley, where he dismounts and looks around.

Once he is satisfied that he is alone, he removes a bag handing from his saddle and retrieves clothing more fitting for a nobleman. He changes quickly. Off go the eyebrows, the fake nose, the moustache and the wig, and Lord Ayushmann emerges. He gathers his uniform and disguise, and places them in the bag, where they will remain until he journeys back to the city.

Then, he rides to the mansion of Lord Jayendu.

At the gate, the guards jump to attention and lower their spears. He brings his horse to a halt an inch from their sharp tips and smiles.

"I am Ayushmann of Simhasthal," he says to them. "I believe Lord Jayendu is expecting me."

The guards relax. They pull open the tall iron gates, and Ayushmann rides through to the house, where an attendant takes his horse and Datta holds the door open for him.

"Greetings, my lord," he says. "Lord Jayendu awaits your presence in his study."

Ayushmann nods his head, and the man leads him to his host. Jayendu makes the effort to stand. "Welcome, my dear Lord Ayushmann," he says. "I was afraid you had declined my invitation."

Ayushmann feigns shock. "Me, turn down an invitation from the most influential man in Saravat? Impossible." He bows low. "My Lord Jayendu, it is indeed an honour to make your acquaintance."

"Come, come," says Jayendu, with a toothless smile. "I fear morning will arrive if I allow you to continue." He ushers his guest to a chair. "Let us sit and talk."

Ayushmann takes the proffered chair, and a handmaiden offers him a glass of madeira. As he sips his drink, Jayendu sinks into his heavily cushioned chair with a sigh of relief.

"The perils of old age," he says, as he massages his legs. "I pray you never know them."

"I pray for the same, my lord," Ayushmann says. "But you did not invite me here to discuss the misfortunes of growing old."

Jayendu chuckles. "No, I did not. I have known your father for many years now, and his three sons as well. I did not spend much time getting to know his bastards, though. The man has way too many."

"He has a daughter as well," Ayushmann says, "Whom you forget to mention."

"Yes, yes." Jayendu's mood sours. "Your sister. Queen Indrani. How can I forget, when I was the one to arrange her match with Vijendra."

"She must owe you a great debt for that, my lord," Ayushmann says.

"One would assume so," Jayendu says, "But the Queen seems not to care. Not these days, anyway."

"It saddens me to hear that," Ayushmann says.

Jayendu leans forward, and his clouded eyes fix on the Simhasthali. "Maybe it does. Maybe not. I do not forget her, for she is the reason I have asked you here. If I may be direct, my lord, what are you up to?"

"Up to?" Ayushmann sounds deeply hurt. "My lord, I am up to nothing."

Jayendu chokes violently on his own laughter. He sips his madeira and calms himself. "My dear Ayushmann, it pains me to admit I do not know much about you. And I pride myself in knowing important people. That tells me one of two things. Either there is little to know about you, or what is worth knowing is so important you have gone to great lengths to hide it from the world. Like your identity."

Ayushmann smiles, unworried. "I confess I hid my identity, for reasons you surely understand. But now my only secret is out in the open. There is little else worth knowing."

"Oh, I doubt that very much," Jayendu says. "Do you know how old I am?"

"I do not, my lord," Ayushmann admits.

"Seventy-five years of age," Jayendu declares. "I might be the oldest man alive in Saravat. Hah. Like that is an achievement. My life is though. It has been truly glorious. I have travelled the world. Not just Saravat, my boy, but far beyond. To Sirukesh, to Farisa, Shavadweep, Dhritri. I have lived among their people, traded with them, studied their languages and customs. And do you know what I learned?"

"What, my lord?" Ayushmann asks.

"They are very different from us," Jayendu says. "They are, one and all, ruthless people whose desire to conquer lands and grow their kingdoms is never satiated." He slaps his armrest. "Powerful enemies, who will one day turn their eye towards Saravat."

Ayushmann sips his drink and watches Jayendu over the rim of his glass. He nods his understanding. "So, you decided to take action?"

"I decided to take action," Jayendu admits. "This land needs a strong leader, one who can unite the five kingdoms under a single banner."

"I agree wholeheartedly," Ayushmann says. He sees the surprise on Jayendu's face and smiles. "My lord, the day is not far when a powerful foreign invader arrives on our land. If he finds us divided, Saravat will fall."

"Precisely," says Jayendu, pleased to see the Simhasthali understand. "And the leader I have chosen is Vijendra."

"May I ask why?"

"He has no equal," Jayendu says. "He is dedicated, focused, and utterly ruthless—perfect traits for the first Emperor of Saravat. I have known this to be true since he was a child."

Ayushmann's ears perk up. A thought races through his mind. *Could it be?* He sets it aside for later.

"True," he says in agreement. "But is Vijendra wise?"

Jayendu cocks his head to one side. "What do you mean?"

Ayushmann does not reply. He walks over to where the madeira is kept, pours himself a drink and sips it as he returns to his seat.

"This marriage of Princess Idhika and King Vikrant," he says. "I would have advised against it."

"Why?" Jayendu asks.

"King Vikrant is an intelligent man," Ayushmann says. "The world may think him a coward, but I believe there is more to the man than that."

"The boy forgoes the vengeance of his father's death," says Jayendu, his disgust evident in his voice. "What would you call that, if not cowardice?"

Ayushmann shrugs. "He forgoes, but he does not forget. He is not your normal Simhasthali. General Kashyap is, as is Prince Indranuj. Maybe all of them are. They will not rest until they have avenged King Giridhar's death."

"And what about you?" Jayendu asks.

"Me?" Ayushmann manages to look mildly astonished. "I am not a Simhasthali, my lord. I merely live in their kingdom, for reasons you are now aware of. They gave me a job, which I perform to the best of my ability. And if tomorrow King Vijendra commands our two kingdoms, I will serve him just the same."

"My boy, these are merely words," Jayendu says. "Easily spoken, easily forgotten. I find it hard to trust you."

"Trust is a two-way street, my lord," Ayushmann says. "You claim King Vijendra is your ally. Yet here you sit, with the man whom his wife despises above all else. Do you not trust him anymore?"

There it is. A slight tremor in his lips betrays Jayendu. There is little love left between Vijendra and him.

"It is true," the old man says. "King Vijendra does not heed my advice the way he once did. But he is still the best hope for Saravat."

"Is he?" asks Ayushmann, his disagreement clear.

"You believe otherwise?" Jayendu asks.

Ayushmann leans forward in his chair. "I judge a man's worth by his deeds, not by people's perceptions of them. Vijendra chose the easy way out when he named King Vikrant his successor. Far easier to control than the temperamental Prince Sreedharan."

There it is again. That nervous quivering of the lips. Ayushmann knows his words have hit their mark.

He pretends not to have noticed, and continues. "I can only assume these were the two options before him. However, King Vikrant had two choices as well. Princess Jyothika and Princess Idhika. He chose the harder option, one which he knew would make him many enemies, even among his own people. So, it begs the question. King Vijendra may be more cunning, more ruthless and more determined. But is he wiser?"

Ayushmann leans back in his chair and leaves Jayendu to ponder his words. The old man will not be easily convinced, nor does Ayushmann intend to change his mind.

No, he is here to see which way the wind blows.

"You are the second man to speak such words to me," Jayendu says.

"Who is my kindred soul?" Ayushmann asks. "I would be honoured to meet him."

"Oh, you have," Jayendu chuckles. "Not that you know it. Still, the two of you have given me a lot to think about."

"It is only right that we do not rush to hasty decisions," Ayushmann says.

"I agree," Jayendu says. "I invited you here in the hope that you would assist me in ridding our kingdoms of this alliance. But now—"

He pauses, trying to frame his thoughts correctly. Ayushmann waits patiently.

"We will come to an agreement," Jayendu speaks at last. "The alliance will continue as is, and if I am convinced of Vikrant's worth, the boy will get my full support." He leans forward in his chair. "But if I am not, you will join my side, and help me steer Saravat to its true destiny."

Ayushmann cannot believe it. This is far more than he had hoped for. He rises to his feet and bows before Jayendu. "My lord, we are in agreement."

He takes his leave. Outside, his horse is brought around, and a few minutes later, he returns to the alley to disguise himself once more.

Dressed as a Corporal once more, he rides back to Dhaningarh, blissfully unaware of the man standing on a terrace, making a note of his departure.

For Queen Indrani.

CHAPTER FORTY-FIVE

The night is muggy and warm, more so than usual, and Idhika sighs with relief as the cool water laps her chest. Only three days more, and she will be a bride, a wife, a Queen, married to the man her parents have chosen. The fact should please them. But it doesn't, for even now they consider her unworthy.

She is not surprised. They have been this way since the day she emerged from her mother's womb, missing a knob of meat between her legs, and their resentment has only grown over the years. They miss her brothers, two older, two younger; the ones who did not survive to take this burden away. She laughs silently to herself. They seek a replacement, and hope to find it through her marriage.

She banishes the thought. Vikrant should be here soon, unless he has finally succumbed to Atishi's charms, and lies naked and happy in her arms at this very moment.

She doubts it.

Despite her father's impression of him, she'd wager her life that there is more to the man than common gossip.

They had a good conversation the previous morning. He spoke of his childhood, and she was surprised to learn that he is an accomplished mountaineer, who has scaled six of the Rodasi peaks, and even visited Shitakul, the land of his ancestors.

Idhika has heard of this desolate land, where great white lions and other gigantic beasts wander in the snow. She thinks of all that has been spoken about Vikrant, and then remembers the pleasant manner in which he spoke about the dreaded frozen plains. One or the other must be false, though she cannot say which.

"Sometimes I wonder if you were a fish in another life," his voice calls out.

Idhika did not hear him approach. He stands at the edge of the pond and smiles at her. A nice smile, not haughty or condescending like most men. *I could get used to it.*

Idhika giggles. "Maybe I was. Growing up, I loved playing in the river, and I could hold my breath underwater for almost three minutes."

"That is most impressive," Vikrant says.

"Do you like the water?" Idhika asks.

"Very much," he replies.

"Then why do you not join me?" her eyes flutter seductively.

Vikrant hesitates. "I do not think that would be appropriate."

"But there is no one to see us," Idhika insists. "Besides, we will be wed in a few days."

Vikrant stares at her for a long while, lost in thought, before he gives in. He takes off his clothes, folds them, and lays them neatly on the grass. Naked, he steps into the pond, conscious of her eyes on his body. His cheeks redden, and he hurries to find a rock to sit on a few feet away from her.

"Isn't this better?" Idhika says.

"Much better," Vikrant agrees, though his body remains tense.

"So, tell me, husband-to-be, how was the feast?"

Vikrant makes a bored face and rolls his eyes. "Dull. Long." He pauses. "Educative."

The last word piques her curiosity. "Educative?"

"An interesting conversation with your father," Vikrant informs her, "About the price one has to pay for greatness."

"Blood," Idhika says.

"Blood," Vikrant echoes.

"He has spoken of it many times," Idhika sighs.

Vikrant locks eyes with hers. "Do you disagree?"

Does she?

Even though girls were not taught much of history, Idhika is well-versed with the lives of the Kings of Saravat, and the greatest among them had pages dripping with blood. Her father is no different. Only the scale of his ambition sets him apart.

"Do you consider King Simha to be great?" she asks.

Vikrant smiles, but does not answer. He does not need to. Instead, he changes the topic. "I have been trying to guess your true nature and mind."

"And have you come to a conclusion?" Idhika asks.

"I have," Vikrant says.

Idhika cocks her head to one side, waiting for his answer.

"You are stronger than you let on," he says. "Your coy smiles do not deceive me. If your father had fallen on the Laalkhet instead of mine, you would have proven a far more formidable foe than your uncle."

"Prince Biraj is a very strong warrior," Idhika counters.

"I mean him no offence," Vikrant says. "I have faced strong warriors before. And strength does not always win a fight." He taps his head with his finger. "This counts for a lot. Biraj is intelligent yes, but like my brother, he allows his emotions to rule."

"And what about you?" her smile teases him.

"We shall find out," Vikrant says.

"Maybe we will," Idhika says. "But let us not speak of such things now."

"What shall we speak of?" Vikrant asks.

"Happier things," Idhika says.

They speak of happier things. The games they played as children, the books they read, the foods they love. She tells him about her dreams and aspirations; he reveals his fears and worries.

In her mind, Idhika comes to understand that, scared as he may be, Vikrant is no fool, nor is he one to make a decision without thought.

Which leads her to the most important question. *Why did he agree to marry her?*

The answer will have to wait for another night. She hears anklets tinkle, and her handmaidens and Atishi arrive.

"What is it?" she asks, annoyed by the interruption.

"Your Highness, dawn is almost here," Atishi replies. "The King must return to his chambers."

"It comes too soon," Idhika grumbles. "But very well."

She swims across to Vikrant and takes his hand. The feel of her skin shocks him, and his fingers go stiff. His reaction pleases her, and she tightens her grip as she leads him out of the water.

They stand facing one another, naked, as the handmaidens dry their bodies.

Once they are dressed, Idhika takes his hand in hers again. "There is something you need to know. About your minister, Ayushmann."

"What of him?" Vikrant asks.

"He met with Jayendu last night," Idhika says.

Vikrant does not look surprised. "And you know of this how?"

"Forgive me, Your Majesty," Atishi interrupts. "I delivered the message to Lord Ayushmann. At the command of Lord Jayendu."

Vikrant is confused. "You work for Jayendu?"

"That's what he believes," says Atishi, her lips curling into a sly grin.

Idhika turns his face back to her, and she does not smile. "Vikrant, do not take Jayendu lightly. He has spent most of his life planning this war." She squeezes his hand. "If he believes you to be an obstacle, he will not hesitate to have an assassin remove you from his path."

Vikrant considers her words, then smiles. "If his assassin succeeds, I fear another Prince might have to endure all these ceremonies." He turns to Atishi. "At least, the next time, Atishi will not have to work so hard."

He bows, and leaves a puzzled Idhika staring after him.

CHAPTER FORTY-SIX

Thok! Thok! Thok! Thok!

The heeled sandals of Queen Indrani pound the marble as she storms through the hallways, a scroll grasped tight in her fist. An innocent roll of paper, delivered to her room only a few minutes ago, is to blame for her anger. It contains a report of Lord Jayendu's nocturnal activities, and once she read the name of his visitor, she lost her mind.

Ayushmann.

She hates the man almost as much as she hated the boy. A walking, talking reminder of her family's shame. Her father sired many bastards, but at least the other women had the decency to accept money and skip town before giving birth. Not Vidyut's mother, though. No, the woman continued to live and raise her child in front of their eyes.

Indrani was fifteen when she woke one morning to the news of their disappearance. A good omen, and so it had proved.

Lord Jayendu visited their house a few months later, with a proposal of marriage.

To the Prince of Vajrapur.

Indrani was overcome with joy that day. She would be a Princess, and live in a palace. Lady Luck continued to intervene in the years that followed. The fever took away her brothers-in-law and their families, and her husband rose to become the Crown Prince. The fever came for him as well, only to be denied.

Now, he is King, she is Queen, and all their dreams were about to come true.

Until the bastard showed up again, with a new name, but the same effect. *To steal her happiness.*

She storms into the dining hall. At the table, her husband sits with Biraj and bites into a *ghee*-laden *paratha*. She walks up to them and tosses the scroll at Vijendra.

Thick lines crease his forehead when he reads the report. He shakes his head and passes the scroll to Biraj, who reads it as well. He jumps in anger, and his chair topples to the ground.

"Your Majesty," he says to Indrani, "Command me, and I will have him behind bars within the hour."

"For what crime?" She waves him to pick up his chair and take his seat, then sits by her husband's side. "The Simhasthalis are our allies. Meeting with them is not against the law."

Vijendra nods his agreement. "The man schemes, that is all. But to what end?"

"Control of the throne," Indrani declares.

She locks eyes with her husband, and watches realisation dawn. This is what it is all about.

Control of the future ruler of Saravat.

This is why Sreedharan was never an option. They would never have been able to rein in his bloodlust. And who is to say he would not desire the throne of Emperor far sooner than they were willing to concede?

No, it had to be Vikrant, a more docile option, but one with a large and powerful army. The boy could be kept in check, in the shadows, away from power and command, until he produced sons who could be trained for the job. It was a clever plan, far too clever for the likes of Jayendu, who was too proud to listen to anyone's voice but his own.

And now, he makes his move.

"I fear you are right, My Queen," Vijendra says. "But do not let your hatred for the bastard cloud your judgement. This is Atulya's doing. The schoolmaster knows the alliance and marriage cannot be broken. So, he seeks to gain power for his King."

"But what do we do now?" Biraj asks.

"There is nothing we can do," Indrani replies. "At least, not openly."

After all, Jayendu is their oldest ally, and a powerful one at that. To cross swords with him might mean driving him into the enemy's arms, and all his wealth along with him. Indrani fumes with impotent rage, unable to believe he would lose faith so close to the end. Emperor of Saravat. This was the dream he sold to them. And now he sits and plots its failure.

He won't succeed. Not if she has something to say about it.

Her eyes stare unblinking at a point on the wall, as an idea takes root in her mind. A simple plan, yet strong enough to solve all their problems.

Vijendra sees her thoughtful expression. "What is it, my love?"

"Tradition," she declares.

"What of it?" Vijendra asks.

"It will solve our problems," she replies.

Vijendra waits for her to elaborate, but Biraj cannot contain his impatience.

"How?" he asks.

A mischievous smile breaks across Indrani's face. She does not answer her brother-in-law. Not yet. For now, she savours the thought of seeing Jayendu's face when he discovers he has been checkmated once more.

Good. The time has come for the old man to realise whom he is up against.

CHAPTER FORTY-SEVEN

I cannot wait to leave this place, Gautam thinks, as he rides his horse through Dhaningarh.

Last night, Kashyap and he had tried to make love, but his husband could not perform. His conscience weighs heavy, desperately trying to reconcile itself to his new command under King Vijendra, the man who killed his brother.

This morning, they had tried again, with the same luck. A furious Kashyap had stormed out of the room, and did not return.

Now, a heartbroken Gautam rides to practice with Indranuj and Ayushmann. Tonight, there will be the 'Father's Farewell'. And tomorrow, thousands will be in attendance as they face the bride's champions in the 'First Fight', with the honour of King Vikrant resting in their hands.

It will be tough to win, tougher than it was before Kashyap was withdrawn as champion and Ayushmann cast in his role. The minister had practiced with them yesterday, and though he seemed comfortable with a sword, the man was clearly no warrior. But the King insisted on his participation, and Gautam will have to do the best he can.

So far, they have only trained in the shaded confines of the palace gardens. Today, they move to the arena, dressed in battle armour, with the sun threatening to cook them in their steel. They need to get a feel of the environment; the firmness of the earth beneath their feet, the burn of the sun upon their backs, the daunting spectre of the stands boxing them in.

They arrive at the stadium, and attendants rush to lead their horses away. Inside, steel rings against steel, their sound echoing the strength and fury of the warriors who wield them.

Ayushmann smiles at his companions. "It appears we won't be alone this morning."

An anxious Gautam leads them into the arena, which is as it was ages ago, when he fought here as a young man. And though he knows what to expect, it still manages to take his breath away.

It measures four hundred feet from end to end, with stands that rise a hundred feet high, and can easily fit over thirty thousand people. Two stone towers divide the stands. One for the bride's family, the other for the groom's, facing off on either side of the arena as their champions do the same on the grass below.

On the far side of the ground, the Vajras practice. Biraj, Rannveer and Dhananjay. Gautam watches them train, trying hard to spot a weakness. There isn't one, but they do have a strength.

The Captain.

Dhananjay fights unlike any Vajra Gautam has seen before. Where Biraj and Rannveer play it safe and defend, he launches into every attack, putting his size and brute strength behind his shield, and turning it into an offensive weapon.

"He fights like a Simhasthali," whispers Ayushmann, impressed. "Bold and fearless."

"Maybe he does," says Indranuj, swinging his swords in the air. "But he remains a Vajra, and will fall to my blade."

Gautam turns angrily to his student. "Careful, Your Highness, or their skill with a sword might not be what defeats you."

"Then what will?" Indranuj asks.

"Your hubris," Gautam replies. "Keep it in check. You are not yet a champion. Learn to respect your opponents, and earn their respect in turn." Before Indranuj can argue, he turns to Ayushmann. "My lord, we can assume they know of my skill with a sword. And they are smart enough to be wary of Indranuj's strength and size. So, they will first come after you. With Dhananjay."

Ayushmann laughs. "I see my hubris is of little concern to you, Colonel. But I do believe you are right. Even in armour, it is plainly evident I am the weak link."

Gautam is grateful for the minister's deprecating humour, which helps break the tension. "Now, here's how we can beat them."

The plan is simple. Ayushmann is to keep the Vajra captain engaged long enough for Gautam or Indranuj to overpower their opponents and come to the minister's aid.

"Do not assume everything will go our way," Gautam cautions them. "We must prepare for every eventuality."

He beckons three Parasu over to stand as their opponents. Gautam draws his swords, as does Indranuj.

Ayushmann draws his sword, but holds his shield ahead, assuming a defensive stance. "If I am to keep the big one at bay, I will need my shield more than my sword."

Gautam agrees, then commands their fight to begin.

It is a long and weary contest. The Parasu hold nothing back, and Ayushmann does his best to hold off his opponent. Some rounds he succeeds, in others he does not. Indranuj and Gautam, however, fare much better. Their moves are quick and precise, and they manage to win each round easily. Even in a battle of two against three, they perform remarkably well.

After an hour of solid practice, Gautam calls for a halt. Ayushmann collapses to the ground, and is still gasping for breath when Biraj and his companions join them.

"It appears we will have a good contest tomorrow," the Vajra Prince says.

"For the sake of our audience, I hope so," Gautam says.

"Forgive me, Colonel," Dhananjay interrupts them. "I do not remember seeing Lord Ayushmann and Prince Indranuj on the Laalkhet."

Biraj and Rannveer throw sharp looks at Dhananjay, but he ignores them, and keeps his eyes fixed on the Simhasthali Prince.

Indranuj's face reddens. "You fought in the battle?"

Dhananjay nods his head. "We all did, Your Highness. A good fight it was. Far too short, though. I only managed to kill eleven men before the battle ended."

Indranuj grits his teeth. "Those were my men."

"They were your father's men, Your Highness," Dhananjay smirks. "King Giridhar is dead. Now, I believe we are all King Vijendra's men."

Indranuj takes a step forward, and Gautam places a hand on his shoulder. He casts a pleading look at the young Prince. *Do not give him the satisfaction.*

Gautam turns to Dhananjay. "My dear Captain, I believe we are King Vijendra's allies. And yours as well. But only until we enter the arena. Then, friendship will be forgotten, and we will put your sword to the test."

Dhananjay laughs. *A deep-throated rumble.* "Colonel, you can certainly try."

He bows and walks away. Prince Biraj smiles apologetically. "The heat of the contest gets the better of the Captain. I hope you will forgive and dismiss his bravado."

"Of course we will, Your Highness," says Ayushmann, a beaming smile on his face. "They are only words, easily forgotten."

Biraj gives him a curt nod. Rannveer bows, and together they leave the arena. Once they are out of sight, Indranuj seethes. "I will not forget, Lord Ayushmann. And I will not forgive."

"You will keep your focus," Gautam scolds his pupil. "Or you will see yourself defeated."

Indranuj glares at his teacher. "We shall see who is defeated tomorrow."

He tosses his swords to the ground, then storms off in a huff. Gautam makes to go after him, then thinks better of it. Indranuj has always had a temper, easily awakened. And if he does not stay focussed, it will destroy him.

Worse, it will destroy everyone and everything he loves.

CHAPTER FORTY-EIGHT

"*Didi*, do you hate me?" Vikrant asks.

What prompts this question, Gayathri wonders.

She was surprised to receive his invite to join him for a mid-morning walk. When was the last time they spoke this way, just the two of them? Vikrant had not sought her out, not even after their father's death, and if she were being honest, that tragedy had only deepened the silence between the two.

They stroll through the gardens, which they have to themselves, except for the Parasu and the palace guards, who watch from a distance. The day is hot, and she holds a parasol over her head. Her brother, however, basks in the sun, seeming to like its warmth.

Gayathri answer his question with one of her own. "Why do you ask?"

Vikrant smiles at his older sister, and she is reminded of their childhood. Whenever she walked into a room, he would run over and hold her close. She had been like a second mother to him, always at hand to banish his fears, to bring a smile to his face. *How she loved him then. How she loves him now.*

"A simple no would suffice," says Vikrant, smiling.

"No," says Gayathri. "I do not hate you. But my curiosity remains."

His sadness ruins his smile. "I believe Indu and Kashyap chacha have both turned against me."

"That cannot be," Gayathri says.

"It is," Vikrant declares. "They hate this marriage, this place, Vijendra. Him, they hate above all. They will do as commanded, but only out of a sense of duty, not love." He turns to face her. "Do you feel the same?"

Gayathri pities him. *A childhood wasted in doubt and fear, and he still hasn't grown up.*

"You are my King," she says, "And I must obey. But that is not why I do. I trust you. Do I agree with your decision to marry Idhika? No, I do not. But you had a tough choice to make. And only time can tell if it was the right one."

A grateful smile breaks across his face. They walk in silence for a while, enjoying their surroundings. The gardens are quite lovely this time of the year. Birds sing in every tree, butterflies and bees dance among the flowers. Gayathri considers it a relief to step away from the stress and the intrigue, if only for an hour.

"Do you hate being King?" she asks.

"I don't know," Vikrant replies. "Sometimes I think the crown came to me too early."

"Maybe," Gayathri says. "I remember this one time. You were nine, and Baba had taken you to the Laalkhet. Someone told you there were ghosts on the Laalkhet, who can possess your body. You came running into my arms that night. I tried to tell you there are no such things as ghosts. But you already knew that."

Vikrant nods his head. "It wasn't the ghosts which scared me. It was baba. He told me I would be King after him, who would have to deliver justice and fight to defend our land."

"Yes," Gayathri says. "And the thought scared you then. You begged me to be King instead."

"You would have made a better King than me," Vikrant says.

Gayathri shrugs. "Maybe. Who can say? But it was always your fate, little brother. Never mine."

He looks at her, his expression serious. "When I am Emperor, we shall see if we can change that."

Gayathri is surprised to hear him speak this way. Her brother has always been different, but never a rebel against tradition. Still, how does it matter? He would not succeed even if he tried. To put a woman in a position of power? The noblemen would be up in arms from Saptaveni to Shitakul.

"What does Chandran think of all this?" Vikrant asks.

Gayathri hesitates. Vikrant never asks after Chandran. He does not like him, just like the others. Has her husband given them cause to suspect his loyalty?

She chooses her words carefully. "My husband is a simple man. He does not concern himself much with these matters."

"Hmm." Vikrant walks a few metres before he continues. "He seems to be the only Simhasthali happy to be here."

"And what if he is?" says Gayathri, a little too defensively. "After all, he has visited here many times, and many Vajras are his friends."

"So, he still retains his old relationships?" Vikrant asks.

"I am certain he does," Gayathri says. "We may not care much for Vijendra, but his people are blameless, even if they support his cause. They follow their King, good or bad, the same as us."

"True," Vikrant says. His smile returns. "I want to thank you—the both of you—for your support." He turns around.

"We better get changed for lunch. Or the rest will starve waiting for us."

A cheeky smile breaks across Gayathri's face. Vikrant spots it at once. "What?"

"I instructed the cooks to prepare a special dish for you," Gayathri says.

"Which dish?" Vikrant asks.

"Fish in coconut curry," Gayathri says.

His favourite meal, one commonly found in the coastal regions of Simhasthal. While studying in Harit Nagar, Vikrant had eaten it everyday, and misses it very much.

His lips curl into a childlike grin. "Do not joke with me, didi."

Gayathri shakes her head. "I do not." She laughs and lifts her skirts. "Race you to the palace?"

She takes off with surprising speed, causing the guards to jump. They were not expecting this. Vikrant shouts and runs after her.

She laughs even louder. *Too late, little brother. This race is mine.*

CHAPTER FORTY-NINE

Atishi awakens to the sound of vessels clanging.

She calmly walks to her dresser and retrieves a small knife. Holding it behind her back, she tiptoes to the sound, only to find a man standing over the stove, trying to light the wood.

Atishi relaxes when she sees who it, and calls out to the intruder. "You may be good at many things, my lord. But not at this."

Ayushmann turns and grins. He throws his hands up in mock defeat and offers her the flint. She uses it to spark the wood, which catches flame at once.

Smiling, Atishi turns to the intruder. "I wasn't expecting you to bring lunch."

"I wasn't going to," Ayushmann admits. "But you looked tired this morning, when you left my King's chambers. I thought the least I could do was bring you some food. And some company."

Atishi gestures to the table in the corner. Ayushmann makes himself comfortable, as she busies herself heating the food. Ten minutes later, she joins him. Parathas, rice, fish curry and some vegetables are laid out before them. They eat in silence. Once they are done, Ayushmann makes her sit while he clears the table. The leftovers are neatly packed and covered, and the banana leaf plates are tossed into the basket outside.

Ayushmann grabs a pitcher of madeira and two cups, then takes her hand and leads her to the verandah. They sip their drinks at the table, letting the serenity of the woods fill their minds.

After a long while, the Simhasthali breaks the silence. "How long have you lived here?"

"Six years," Atishi replies.

"An odd place to live," he says, "For a girl from Farisa."

Atishi is surprised. "I thought I had lost the accent."

"You have," Ayushmann admits. "But your inflections on certain words. And the colour of your eyes—" He leans forward, and looks into her light, grey eyes. "It was easy to guess where you came from. But I remain clueless as to why you came."

Atishi smiles. "According to popular gossip, I am the King's mistress."

Ayushmann does not look convinced. "Vijendra is far too devoted to my sister to want another woman. No, you are here for some other purpose."

If only you knew. Atishi admires his style of questioning, like a cat toying with a mouse. Playful, yet deadly.

"The Princess seems fond of you," Ayushmann says.

There it is. "And how would you know that?"

"She trusts you to spend the night with her betrothed. And to disguise her, so she may secretly attend social events in her kingdom."

So this was his intention to wake her up in the middle of my sleep. To keep her tired, drowsy, so she does not guess what information he truly seeks.

"You are correct, my lord," Atishi says, "Queen Indrani purchased me, and commanded me to train Princess Idhika in the art of seduction."

Ayushmann seems unfazed. "And has she been trained?"

"Surely, that question should be put to King Vikrant," Atishi replies. She grins. "After their marriage, of course."

Ayushmann smiles. Full, from the heart. Hardly the smile one would expect from a man who keeps so many secrets.

"I will keep my head," he says, "And not ask my King such questions."

"A wise choice, my lord," Atishi says.

"But you see my confusion?" he persists. "Surely, you would not stay so many years if all that was required of you was to teach the Princess a sensual trick or two."

Atishi sighs, as if the answer does not merit importance. "On occasion, the King and Queen ask me to entertain a trusted ally. A captain, a minister, a friendly diplomat. I have even kept Lord Jayendu company."

The name catches Ayushmann by surprise. "I cannot imagine the old man still possessed such desires."

Atishi shakes her head. "He did not want my body. Only my company."

Ayushmann nods his head in understanding. "Old age can be lonely without the company of a loved one."

"And how would you know, my lord?" asks Atishi, teasing him once more.

"Through experience," Ayushmann says. His eyes tear up, though the drops refuse to escape. "A few years ago, my mother died alone in Harit Nagar, while I remained in Simhasthal. I know her end was peaceful, surrounded by kind friends, who had helped us escape a miserable life. Yet, I was not with her. Her only son, whom she had protected all her life."

Atishi feels his ache in her heart. She cannot say what it is like to lose the only person you have ever loved. The closest she has come to family is the Princess, and she remains pragmatic enough to know their relationship is only an illusion.

"I am sorry, my lord," she offers her sympathy. "And you are right. It is loneliness. Lord Jayendu likes to speak of his youth, of his travels around the world, and the people he has met. I like spending time with him, for it allows me an escape as well."

"Does he ever speak of his late wife?" asks Ayushmann, regaining his composure.

"He speaks of her often," Atishi says. "Almost as often as he speaks of King Vijendra. Son, he calls him. The son he never had. The old man likes to say he has trained the boy for greatness since he was only a child."

"Does he now?" Ayushmann remarks. The sadness in his eyes disappears, and they look as sharp and intelligent as before.

Atishi does not know what to make of his reaction. "He does, my lord. Other than his wife and the King, I do not think I have heard him speak a kind word for anyone else."

"I see," Ayushmann says.

"There was one other thing," Atishi says. "Lord Jayendu would often mutter in his sleep. 'She died, she died'. He would repeat the words over and over in the middle of the night. Too often for my liking."

The Simhasthali ponders this information. Atishi cannot speak of its importance, but she had always found it sweet. Lord Jayendu mourning his late wife, whom he must have loved very much to let her death haunt his sleep.

"These other men Vijendra sent over," Ayushmann says.

"What of them?" Atishi asks.

"Any of them Simhasthali?" he asks.

The man misses nothing. Atishi knows many secrets, words uttered in the heat of passion, or its aftermath. She has never found cause to repeat them, nor sought to disclose their identities, to anyone other than her Princess.

"Would you be jealous if they were?" she teases.

"I might be," Ayushmann says, "If he were someone important."

"He wasn't as important as you," Atishi says, "I can assure you that."

His eyes flicker. The corners of his mouth twitch. And Atishi wonders if she has said too much.

"An unimportant man," Ayushmann muses, "Yet important enough for King Vijendra to see him entertained."

I have said too much. Atishi finds herself in an uncomfortable position. Usually, it is she who coaxes the information out of her unwitting lovers. Now, she understands what it feels like to be at the other end of the stick. The only difference is, her fools did not possess the wits to know they were being tricked.

"I thought you came here to feed me," she pouts.

"And to keep you company," Ayushmann says.

"It feels more like an interrogation," she retorts.

He takes her hand in his, tenderly, like a lover, and her heart shivers. For a woman who has spent most of her life being owned by men, it is a strange experience.

"I apologise, my lady," Ayushmann says. "To be honest, I have always viewed people with suspicion. Sometimes because of my job. Sometimes because of my past."

"Which causes you to treat me this way?"

"Loyalty," he says without hesitation. "To my King, and my adopted kingdom."

"Then I cannot fault you," says Atishi, holding his hand in hers. "We both serve others, and do the best we can to further their interests. But does that mean we must lose sight of our own in the bargain?"

"Maybe not," he agrees, and the smile returns to his face. "One day, we might even find time to speak of it."

"But not today?" Atishi asks.

"Not today," Ayushmann says. "You must return to your sleep, and I to my duties."

"Very well, my lord," says Atishi, disappointed.

He kisses her on the cheek, then gazes into her eyes. "Until we meet again."

She watches him go, and is surprised by the sadness she feels. Such childish behaviour, which brings a smile to her face. It remains with her, on the walk back to her bedchamber, as she gets under the covers, and long after she has fallen asleep.

CHAPTER FIFTY

Indrani watches the riot of colour descend upon her gardens, as the ladies and lords of Vajrapur arrive, dressed in shimmering shades of blue and green and yellow.

The Simhasthalis follow soon after, and she is glad to see they have abandoned their thick clothes, and now dress like their hosts, though their colours are muted. Simple and plain, as is the Simhasthali way.

Her wandering eyes catch Jayendu's, who offers her a toothless smile, which she happily returns. The old man was likely the first to arrive, as he always does, and with all they have planned for tonight, Indrani wonders if he will be the first to leave as well.

The guests are shown to their seats, and cups are filled as they await the arrival of the Kings. Indrani wishes they would get here already. She cannot wait for the farewell to begin.

Thankfully, only a couple of minutes pass before the trumpets blow and the herald makes the announcement. Surprisingly, Vijendra and Vikrant walk in together, which is unfortunate, for the difference in attire is stark.

The Vajra King wears a light cream sherwani flecked with gold, contrasting the vivid red of his wife's sari. Vikrant, on the other hand, wears a midnight blue sherwani, dark and sombre. A bitter look for a man soon to be wed.

Vijendra takes his seat in the centre, with Indrani and Vikrant on either side. Once they are seated, a group of musicians take to the stage. Their music is slow, brooding, perfect for the occasion.

The song they sing is ancient. 'The Sad Goodbye', it is called, and tells the tale of a daughter who will soon leave for her husband's house, to bear his name and his children.

The words express the emotions of her father, who rejoices in his grief, for the daughter he once held in his arms, whom he will soon give away.

"Halt those tears, dear father
Still your aching heart
A wife, a lover, a mother
She goes to play her part."

Hearts are touched, tears are shed. None by Vijendra though, nor by Indrani. She sits as a statue, letting the words fly past her, never once feeling its mournful touch.

A serving girl fills her cup, and she sips the madeira, impatience growing within her. *Finish quickly*, her mind barks at the musicians, *there are more important matters to address.*

But the song continues for a good fifteen minutes, through the life of the daughter, as she becomes a wife and a mother. Once her father is old, death arrives, and the tale comes to an end.

A haunted silence greets the musicians. Indrani watches Vijendra force a tear out his eye.

"Beautiful," he exclaims, "Simply beautiful. One of the most touching renditions of our ancient song."

He claps, and the nobles cheer as well. A herald steps forward with a purse of gold. The musicians accept it gratefully, bow to the King and exit the stage.

Vijendra holds up his hand for silence. "Ladies and lords." He turns to the dais. "And my fellow royals, I welcome you all to the 'Father's Farewell'."

Polite applause ripples through the crowd. Vijendra waits for it to die down. "This should be a sad day for me. But it is not." He turns to Vikrant. "After all, I gain such a fine son."

Vikrant acknowledges his praise with a nod and a smile. Vijendra nods his head as well, then returns to the audience.

"Tomorrow, my only daughter, Princess Idhika, will declare her intention to marry King Vikrant." A mischievous look crosses his face. "But before she does, they will have their 'First Fight'."

Cheers ring out, and Vijendra beckons Vikrant to join him. "Come, let us declare the champions."

The Simha King walks over. Vijendra makes the announcement. "The first champion to stand for Princess Idhika will be… Prince Biraj."

Biraj steps forward to loud applause and bows to the Kings.

"The second champion," Vijendra calls out, "Is General Rannveer."

Rannveer strides forward and bows to his King and Queen, then smiles at the cheering audience as he stands beside Biraj.

"And the last champion is…" Vijendra stretches out the moment, before declaring the final name. "Captain Dhananjay."

Thunderous applause greets Captain Dhananjay as he walks in. Indrani smiles as well. He is a crowd favourite, a beast in the arena, and a brilliant swordsman. Also, a master showman, she is pleased to note, chuckling as the man bows slow and low to her husband, before turning to wave at the crowd.

Once the applause dies down, Vikrant steps forward and announces his champions. The mood of the audience sours. Vijendra had them energised and excited, but the Simhasthali King manages to suck away all the joy.

His voice is achingly monotonous as he calls out the name of his brother, Prince Indranuj. The boy is greeted with warm applause. Vikrant proceeds to name Colonel Gautam as his second champion, and the crowd grows more enthusiastic. All have heard of his exploits in the arena, and respect the man for his achievements.

Vikrant pauses before declaring his last champion. "Lord Ayushmann."

A hush descends upon the grounds. Ayushmann steps forward and joins his fellow champions. None know how to react, for they were anticipating General Kashyap as champion. Instead, Vikrant has chosen the Queen's bastard brother. Does he mean to offer insult to his future in-laws?

Indrani feels their eyes upon her. *The poor souls. They believe I will be furious.*

Instead, she claps, and Vijendra joins her applause. The smile on Ayushmann's face turns to a frown for a brief second, before returning to its original brilliance. Seeing their King and Queen applaud, the others half-heartedly join in.

Vijendra calls for silence. "My ladies, my lords, the champions stand before you. Come the morning, they will fight for my daughter's honour. Or my son's." He grips Vikrant's shoulder. "And now, I will present my gifts."

Indrani savours the moment as her husband speaks. "As you all know, it is customary for the father of the bride to present her betrothed with two gifts at the farewell. One which the son-in-law will treasure, and one which will help him remind my daughter of home." He holds up his hands for the audience. "But as you can see, I have no gifts to give."

Confused faces stare back at him, none more than Vikrant's.

Vijendra continues. "I intend to give my daughter and King Vikrant the same two gifts. The first I have already presented, Your Majesty. I have named you my heir, and my daughter along with you."

His smile turns cruel, as does Indrani's, and she mouths the words along with him, for they had written it together.

"In a few days," he says, "Once the wedding is over, we will march to war. In accordance with Saravati tradition, as my heir, you must remain behind."

Nothing brings more joy to Indrani's heart than the shocked look on Vikrant's face. He was expecting to be Vijendra's right hand, discussing strategies, giving commands, avoiding the dangers of war, but basking in the glow of victory.

Now, his plans are shattered.

Vijendra ignores the murmurs in the audience, and continues. "Which brings me to my second gift. I gift my daughter and you my kingdom, my Vajrapur, and ask that you keep it safe, until I return from my conquest."

All eyes now turn to Vikrant. The audience waits for his response, and the seconds drag interminably long.

Does he dare refuse, Indrani wonders.

A smile breaks across Vikrant's face, and he bows low. "I thank you… *father*. If I may call you that. Your gift is happily received."

Stunned silence greets his acceptance, and neither the Simhasthalis nor the Vajras know what to make of his enduring servility. Vijendra beams, and walks across to embrace Vikrant.

Indrani's eyes turn away from then and to the audience, her gaze cutting through the people to find Jayendu. The old lord looks annoyed at being upstaged.

Good. She has achieved what she wanted. Jayendu has been shown his place. The dream he had promised them will be realised. Saravat will have an Emperor. But it will not be on his terms.

Not anymore.

CHAPTER FIFTY-ONE

A furious Idhika storms across the palace. Only a few minutes have passed since Atishi arrived in her chambers to inform the Princess of all that had occurred at the farewell.

This cannot be, she had screamed. *This will not be.*

The guards outside the King's chambers watch her approach. Confusion clouds their faces. The Princess means to enter. *Do they stop her? How?*

Before their feeble minds can come to a decision, she races past them and bursts into the room. The nervous guards glance at one another, then quickly move to close the door behind her.

Inside, her parents celebrate the events of the evening, with cups of madeira in their hands and big smiles on their faces. They have achieved a small victory by caging their son-in-law, and for all intents and purposes, the Simhasthalis as well, for while their King remains in Vajrapur, guarded by Vajras, they will not dare betray Vijendra.

"How could you do this?" Idhika demands of her parents.

They look annoyed, especially her mother, who jumps to her feet. "What do you mean?"

"Vikrant and I are to live in Vajrapur?" She shakes her head. "No. You will say you have changed your mind. I will not live here after my marriage."

"You will do as you are told," Indrani says. "You are our daughter."

I was your daughter. "For years, I have done as you asked. You locked me away in a palace, denied me a childhood, promised me that one day I will marry and rule my own life. Not once did I complain. I took your word to be true, and dreamt of a day when I would be free." Her eyes blaze with anger. "Now, it is here, close enough to become reality, and you conspire to deny me once more."

"We do not conspire, my child." Vijendra's tone is gentle. "We only plan our future. And yours."

"My future?" asks Idhika, disbelievingly.

"Yes," he replies. "We are all pawns in the larger game. Your mother and I have played our parts. And we have no regrets. For our dream of ruling Saravat is so close."

"It is not my dream," Idhika says.

"Oh, foolish girl," Indrani chuckles, "It should be. One day, you will be empress, and your son will be its Emperor."

"My son?" Idhika laughs. "That's what this is all about, isn't it? You name Vikrant your heir, but he is not. Not really. You think I do not see it, maa, but I do. You only mean for me to produce heirs, and once they arrive, you will have no need for me, or Vikrant, or anyone else. They will be the sons you could never have, replacements for my dead brothers." She screams. "For your dead sons."

She never saw it coming, the open palm flying through the air and smacking into her cheek. Vijendra shakes his head, sad, while Indrani quivers with uncontrollable rage, directed at her daughter.

"Stupid girl," she thunders. "After all we have sacrificed for you, this is how you repay us?"

"What of my sacrifices then?" shouts Idhika, her cheek reddening. "My childhood. My innocence. A normal life? I never had any friends, save one. And even her, you almost had whipped to death."

Indrani appears confused for a moment, then remembers Aparna. She laughs. "The servant's daughter? I had forgotten about her."

"I haven't," Idhika says.

"Apparently not," Indrani says. "Your father keeps reminding me you are intelligent. And he has yet to be proven right. You are a Princess; she was a servant. I only reminded her of the fact."

"Aparna was kind," Idhika says, "And sweet, and gentle. Things you can never be."

"Good," Indrani says. "I will be an empress. And cannot afford such peasant sentiments. Mark my words, one day you will learn what it means to be a ruler. Courage, wisdom, yes. But above all, you need an iron heart."

"Yes, maa," Idhika seethes. "I will never forget your lessons. Mark my words, one day, I will use them all. And then, you can tell me if your sacrifices were worth it."

She turns and storms away. Her mother's footsteps follow, then stop when her father call out. "No, Indrani. Let her go."

Idhika's mind roils as she returns to her chambers. All she had ever desired was to live a life of her own, far away from this palace. And now, that has been denied to her once again.

Her parents have their plans. Let them. She will find a way to plot her own path. And come what may, she will make her dreams come true.

CHAPTER FIFTY-TWO

Idhika does not look pleased.

Vikrant expected to find her swimming naked in the pond. Instead, she sits on a rock, dressed from head to toe, glaring in his direction.

"Is something the matter?" he asks, as he walks over.

"You are a coward," she says.

The barb cuts deep, and from her point of view, true as well. But he does not react. Instead, he finds a rock to sit on. "And what makes you say that?"

"You surrendered to my father," Idhika accuses him.

He left me no choice. "I did."

Idhika smirks. "Opportunities keep arriving at your doorstep, Your Majesty, and you constantly ignore their knock." She sighs. "You should have rejected my father's proposal in that peace tent itself, and accepted King Theeran's offer. Why didn't you?"

A sad smile breaks across Vikrant's face. "Have you heard of Prince Sreedharan?"

Idhika nods her head. "He is the Crown Prince of Triloha."

"Is that all you have heard about him?" Vikrant asks. She does not answer, and he continues. "Then you are most fortunate. He is a cruel, bloodthirsty man, who makes your father appear an angel. Not the kind of man I would want as my brother-in-law." He pauses, before adding. "Nor wish him as a husband for you."

Idhika's eyes narrow. "I do not understand."

Vikrant does not let her off easily. "Come now, Your Highness, you are more intelligent than that. There were only two unmarried Crown Princes in the land, with large and powerful armies. Prince Sreedharan. And I. If I had refused, your father would have laid siege to Simhasthal, and offered your hand to Prince Sreedharan instead. He was going to win one of us as his ally. Be happy it is me. A far worse fate awaited you if it had gone the other way."

She weighs his words with careful thought. Vikrant waits patiently. He does not wish to rush her, for he empathises with her confusion. After all, he had felt this way, just a couple of months ago, when the burden of kingship suddenly fell upon his shoulders, and many decisions were made in the heat of the moment.

Idhika breaks the silence. "Let us assume what you say is true. What now? Are we to live in Vajrapur, caged like birds, surrounded by people loyal to my parents?"

"I say again, I did not have a choice." Vikrant holds her hand. "The heir stays behind. This has always been the tradition. And the offer to rule his kingdom was not one which could be politely refused. He gets what he has always desired. The credit, the glory, and the loyalty of my men, for their King remains hostage in Vajrapur."

"So, what do we do now?" Idhika asks again.

"We do what we have been commanded to," Vikrant says. "We live in Vajrapur and produce heirs. We have time on our side, and maybe the element of luck. Strange things can always occur on the battlefield. An arrow is misdirected, and hits a target it never intended. A soldier's sword gets lucky, and cuts off the head of a King. We count on luck and wait our turn."

Idhika's anger returns, fiercer than before.

And can I blame her? Vikrant wishes he could tell her things will be otherwise, but he cannot. Not yet. Events remain in motion, ever changing, and until he is certain which way the wind blows, it is best to remain silent.

"Maybe everyone is right. You do not have it in you." Idhika rises to her feet. "I have spent a lifetime as a caged bird, Your Majesty, but know this. I do not intend to do so after my marriage."

She storms off, her sari swishing in the still air. Vikrant remains seated alone for a while, until Atishi arrives. "Your Majesty, shall we return to the palace?"

Vikrant does not heed her words. Many minutes pass before he pats the rock beside him. Atishi walks over and takes the seat.

"Your mistress is not pleased with me," Vikrant says.

"No, she is not," Atishi agrees.

"Yet I need her by my side," Vikrant says.

"You do," she agrees again, then adds, "More than you know."

Vikrant raises an eyebrow, curious. *What does she mean by that?*

Atishi reads his expression. "May I speak freely, Your Majesty?" Vikrant nods his head, and she continues. "You have enemies everywhere. Even in your own kingdom."

"I know," Vikrant says. "My brother-in-law, Lord Chandran."

He sees the surprise on her face. She should not be, for she was the final confirmation to turn their doubts into certainty.

It was Ayushmann who first suspected Chandran, during the feast at the 'Mother's Welcome'. Seeing him so friendly with the Vajras, even after the death of his father-in-law, struck a nerve. But the eagerness to take up General Rannveer's offer, and Atishi's mention of an unimportant-yet-important Simhasthali, clinched the evidence in his mind. He had shared his suspicions with Vikrant, and now, Atishi confirms it to be the truth.

She continues to stare at him, shock writ across her face, before her lips curl into a smile. "Lord Ayushmann is cleverer than I thought."

"He is," Vikrant agrees. "And a loyal man." He watches her intently. "How long has Chandran worked for Vijendra?"

"I first met him four years ago," Atishi recalls. "The King asked me to keep him company for the night. He returned the next night as well, and every night until the day he departed."

"Was my sister with him?" Vikrant asks.

"No," Atishi replies.

Vikrant hesitates a moment, then asks, "She does not know about about you?"

"She does not," Atishi says with absolute certainty. She hesitates a moment, as if making up her mind. Finally, she speaks. "But I do know that it was her idea to ally with Vijendra."

The news comes as a shock to Vikrant. "Are you certain?"

"As certain as I can be," Atishi replies. "Once his lust is quenched, Lord Chandran is quite a talkative man. I guess he never learnt the virtues of silence."

How many times must I be stabbed in the back? Vikrant cannot believe his older sister would betray him this way. Only this afternoon, she had and pledged her support.

Still, her involvement makes sense. She has always been the smartest of them all, far smarter than Chandran, who would never have been able to hide this deception all by himself.

A bitter smile crosses his face. "I am surrounded by enemies on all sides. And even my wife-to-be keeps secrets from me."

"She must," Atishi defends the Princess, "For you have yet to give her reason to trust you." Her voice is gentle. "The Princess is fond of you. I know it in my heart. When she speaks of you, it is with genuine hope for your future together. But to make it true, you must become the man she needs you to be."

It is all Vikrant has been trying to do since the day his father died. *Prove himself worthy.* The path he has chosen is risky, but it was the only one worth taking. Ayushmann and Atulya are with him.

Do I dare involve Atishi as well? He arrives at a decision. "I need allies."

"Whom should we approach?" she asks.

"Everyone," he declares.

Atishi stares at him. "Your Majesty, you ask for the world."

"And I intend to get it," Vikrant says with a steely resolve.

"How?" Atishi asks.

"Do not concern yourself with that," Vikrant tells her. "But you can help me make a beginning."

"Command me, Your Majesty," she says, "And I will do my best."

Vikrant lays out the task for her. Her eyes widen, for she cannot believe what he asks. It is a bold plan; one she will be honoured to carry out.

He rises to his feet. “Princess Idhika cannot know.”

“She will not,” Atishi assures him.

They head to the palace together, each lost in their own thoughts. Vikrant knows he takes a risk, but he has been left with no choice. He has lost the love of his mother, his brother, his uncle, his betrothed. Even his sister plots against him.

He smiles ruefully. *I do not have anything left to lose.*

CHAPTER FIFTY-THREE

Atulya arrives at the arena a couple of hours before the games begin. And the mindless hysteria that accompanies it.

He is not a fan, never has been, though he does understand the attraction of it, from a psychological point of view. Men compete against one another in feats of skill and strength, to allow people lesser than themselves an escape from the mundane aspects of their lives.

He thanks the gods the games have grown less barbaric. In the olden days, the sword-fights were to the death, and mostly took place between poor men who fought for a rich purse and the promise of food for their family. Then it all changed, a hundred and twenty years ago, when Crown Prince Ashwini of Triloha decided to compete.

Fearing for his oldest son's life, his father, King Jayant, decreed that the swordsmen would all wear armour, and the fights would no longer be to the death. Instead, three strikes to an opponent's helm were enough to be declared the victor.

Across Saravat, noblemen and royalty soon seized upon this rule, and their ranks swelled among the competitors. The poor were cast aside, condemned to compete in illegal competitions in remote villages and towns, or in foreign lands where their lives still fetched coin.

A sad state of affairs, Atulya believes, and hopes it will soon come to an end.

An hour passes with these thoughts before Jayendu arrives, hobbling across the ground, supported by the ever-present Datta. When he sees Atulya, his eyes narrow, before his lips curl into a smile. Though they are now adversaries, they were once friends, and still respect one another.

Atulya rises to his feet as Jayendu approaches. "I was given to understand you like to reach early and save your seat."

Jayendu smiles. "It is not the seat, dear Atulya. It is my dignity which I wish to save."

He sinks into his chair and sighs with relief. Datta moves a discreet distance away, far enough not to overhear the conversation, close enough to rush in if help is needed. Jayendu massages his legs.

"I have the same problem," Atulya says. "By nightfall, I can hardly bear the pain."

"Wait till you reach my age, young man," Jayendu says. "I live with this pain, day and night, and will do so until my last day."

"A most unwanted companion," Atulya says. "There is an ointment I find helpful. I will have some sent over."

"Save your ointment. I have tried them all." Jayendu chuckles. "Come, my friend. We have known each other long enough to dispense with the small talk. Speak your mind."

Atulya smiles. He hates to admit it, but he remains fond of the old man. He thinks back to the day twenty-five years ago, when Jayendu had sought him out in his humble home in Harit

Nagar, a few months after the death of his father. They had spoken of many things, and Atulya had been impressed. Jayendu possessed a keen understanding of man's true nature, and was adept at manipulating it.

Late into the night, they had debated the one true danger which faced Saravat.

"A divided land," Atulya had declared.

"A divided land," Jayendu had agreed. "You are correct, of course. So what must be Saravat's greatest strength?"

Atulya had answered immediately. "A united land."

Jayendu's voice had hardened. "Precisely. But do you truly understand what that means?" Atulya had not, and Jayendu had explained. "At present, we have peace. But peace does not breed unity. It is brittle, like glass, easily shattered by a single blow."

"I do not agree, my lord," Atulya had said. "Peace and friendship promote unity. Coming to one another's aid in times of crisis, that is all that is needed."

Jayendu had shaken his head. "The Kings who brought us peace were wise men. All five of them. A rare occurrence, unlikely to be repeated in our lifetimes. Our Kings are petty, foolish. There will come a time when this peace is tested. Their greed will take over then, and they will haggle like fishmongers in the market. No. The only way to be certain that Saravat remains strong is for the land to be ruled by one man."

"An Emperor?" Atulya had asked.

"An Emperor," Jayendu had declared. "Who that man will be, I cannot say. But I will ready his army for the future." He had leaned forward and looked the schoolmaster in the eye. "Will you join me?"

Atulya had been mesmerised. There he sat, a nobody, and one of the most powerful men in the land sought to recruit him for a higher purpose. He had been tempted, certainly. Yet a gnawing thought had held him back.

What Jayendu demanded was treason.

Atulya might have to serve a foreigner, and work against his own King, his own country. Besides, innocent blood will be spilled, for the cause of every noble purpose demands black deeds.

And so, he had refused the offer. Jayendu had never held it against him. Quite the opposite. The man had continued to visit and debate the merits of an Emperor versus five Kings many times.

That was many years ago, and the time for debate has long since passed.

"I was wrong," Atulya admits. "And you were right."

"About what?" Jayendu asks.

"About the fragility of our peace," Atulya says. "Vijendra shattered it in a second. And when help was needed, our friends in Triloha put a price on it."

"Yes," Jayendu says. "Marriage to Princess Jyothika, no doubt."

Atulya does not bother to deny it. Instead, he says, "I must commend you on your choice for Emperor. Vijendra has proved himself worthy."

Jayendu seems pleased to hear this. "You truly believe so?"

"I do," Atulya says. "But if I may ask, did you ever consider anyone else?"

"I did," Jayendu admits. "I weighed them all, even his older brothers. And King Giridhar. But none came close to the resoluteness of Vijendra. The man is focused."

"He is brave as well," Atulya adds, "And intelligent. He has outwitted some of the most brilliant minds in the continent. The two of us included."

Jayendu reacts sharply. "What do you mean?"

You know exactly what I mean. "My dear friend, surely this marriage is not part of your plan. You assumed the strings were in your hands, yet Vijendra shows he will not share power. Not with you. Not with anyone."

Jayendu regards him with barely concealed anger. "The King still listens to me."

"Does he?" asks Atulya, his disbelief evident. "Then this plan to keep King Vikrant here in Vajrapur must have your blessings?"

"It does," Jayendu says.

Atulya laughs. "Come now, my lord. We know one another better than that."

Jayendu leans forward in his chair. "Why are you here?"

"I come with a message from my King," Atulya says. "He requests a meeting."

"Why would I meet with him?" Jayendu scoffs. "Vikrant is little more than Vijendra's prisoner. And if you are right, My King no longer listens to me. So what purpose will it serve?"

"If he is a prisoner, so are you," retorts Atulya, his voice rising. "This is *your* dream. To unify this land under an Emperor. But now, your King usurps the dream." He takes a deep breath, composes himself and speaks kindly. "King Vikrant asks for your assistance, so you may both extricate yourselves from Vijendra's influence."

Atulya lets Jayendu consider his words, and turns his gaze to the arena. Soon, cheering crowds will fill the stadium, and armoured men will compete for glory and money, before the champions fight for the bride and groom's honour.

I am a champion as well, he thinks. *For my King's future.*

"We will meet," Jayendu speaks at last. "I will make the arrangements and have word sent to you."

I emerge victorious. Atulya rises to his feet and bows. "On behalf of King Vikrant, I thank you."

"Do not thank me yet," Jayendu warns. "If I do not like what your King has to say, what little support he retains might soon vanish."

Atulya smiles. "It will not come to that. I promise you."

Mission accomplished, he returns to the palace, where his King waits for an answer.

CHAPTER FIFTY-FOUR

The games commence a couple of hours before noon.

Indranuj views the stadium from his tent, set up on the periphery of the grounds, where he stands with his chacha and Lord Ayushmann. Across the field, a similar tent is erected, where Princess Idhika's champions sit. And in the stands, the nobles and common-folk gather, thirty thousand men, women and children, who cheer loudly as the games progress.

Indranuj ignores them, turning his gaze to his brother, who sits in an enclosure with Vijendra and the other members of the royal families. King Vikrant appears relaxed and happy, far from the way Indranuj feels.

Soon, he whispers to himself. *Soon, I will have a chance to put an end to this.*

But first, he has to sit through the archery and wrestling competitions, to which he pays scant attention. His spirits only perk up when the kabaddi games are announced.

It is a favourite of the young Prince, who often plays the game when he gets a chance. Seven men stand guard, while an opposing team member crosses the boundary, chanting the mantra 'kabaddi, kabaddi, kabaddi'. He must touch an opponent and cross the boundary to his side. But if the other team catches him and pins him down, his team loses a point.

A harmless game, on the face of it.

But it is not.

The players can be vicious. A pinned opponent might receive many blows to his body, and if he is truly disliked, a punch or two to his head. Indranuj chuckles. Surely, there is no love lost between these teams, and the games will be bitter and bloody.

He is soon proven right. The players claw and scratch and pummel one another, and few if any are left unbloodied. The competition continues for over an hour before the winner is declared. A Simhasthali team once again, which pleases Indranuj.

After the winners' purse is presented, they take a short break for lunch. The food looks more delicious than ever, the aroma wafting through the tent and setting his taste buds tingling. But Indranuj resists the temptation, as do his fellow champions.

It was his chacha who warned them against eating. "It's an old trick," Gautam said, "The food might be laced with a sedative. Not strong enough to put you to sleep, nor weak enough to fight off drowsiness. But your reflexes will slow, and that is all our opponents need to prevail over us."

So they avoid the thick curries and the ghee-laden naans, and instead, choose some meat, plainly roasted in front of them, followed by slices of fruit.

The games resume soon after, with the traditional sword fight. The pickings are slim this year. Most games see fighters from all five kingdoms, and from far off lands as well. Indranuj wonders what keeps them away—the suddenness of the marriage, or the knowledge of Vijendra's impending conquest of Saravat. The only foreigner he sees is a swordsman from Farisa.

A mercenary, he concludes.

His chacha confirms his suspicions. "A soldier of the Barabos Battalion."

Lord Ayushmann agrees. "A small bet, Colonel Gautam? A hundred gold coins on the Barabosi."

Gautam shakes his head. "I think not. Let us keep our minds on the games. We will soon be called to fight."

Indranuj laughs. "Come on, chacha. A little betting might lighten the mood. Lord Ayushmann, I will happily take your bet."

The minister smiles, but Gautam does not. The games begin, and it is soon evident the Barabosi possesses the two traits that mark out all great swordsmen. A dancer's grace, and a *rakshasa's* strength. The others do not stand a chance. One after another, his sword finds his opponents' helm, and he soon stands before Vijendra, victorious in under an hour.

Indranuj turns to Lord Ayushmann. "Well won, my lord. But now the real contest begins."

The minister laughs. "Just remember, I am on your side."

Indranuj chuckles as the attendant prepares his armour. Once the three are ready, they await the herald's call. The crowd grows restless. This is the main event. The 'First Fight', which will determine who will be the dominant partner in the marriage.

The herald steps into the middle of the arena. "Ladies and lords, King Vijendra is pleased to present 'The First Fight of Princess Idhika and King Vikrant'."

The applause is deafening. Once it dies down, the herald continues. "Fighting for King Vikrant, from Simhasthal, Lord Ayushmann, Colonel Gautam and Prince Indranuj."

The three emerge from their tent and make their way to the centre of the arena. They turn to each royal enclosure and bow to the Kings in turn. The crowd welcomes them with polite applause. Indranuj catches his mother's eye. She smiles, and he beams.

For Simha, for Simhasthal, he whispers softly.

The herald introduces their opponents. "And fighting for Princess Idhika, from Vajrapur, Captain Dhananjay, General Rannveer and Prince Biraj."

The crowd roars once more, as the three champions stride into the arena. Indranuj turns to face his opponents. The Vajras assume a defensive stance, sword in one hand, shield in the other. So does Ayushmann. Indranuj, however, fights like his chacha, a sword in each hand, ready to attack.

He finds himself pitted against Biraj, while Rannveer moves against Gautam. As expected, Dhananjay will seek to remove Lord Ayushmann as quickly as possible. If the minister can survive for a few minutes, either Gautam or he is sure to prevail against their opponents.

Kashyap chacha's words play in his mind. *"If your sword were to slip…"*

This is what he has trained for. There will be no second chances. The rules state that one strike to the helm is all he needs to to eliminate an opponent. But he does not plan to aim for the helm. He aims to miss.

Indranuj smiles at his opponent. *Welcome, Prince Biraj. Let us see if you survive this duel.*

The champions wait for the command. Vijendra gestures to Vikrant, bestowing upon him the honour of starting the fight. Vikrant smiles and turns to the contestants.

"Begin."

At once, Dhananjay roars and races across the ground. The man is fast for his size, and pushes his shield in front of him. Ayushmann reacts a fraction too late, and his hesitation proves costly. Before he can firm his stance, he is shoved across the grass and lands on his back. Dhananjay pounces without hesitation with a quick strike to the helm.

The minister is defeated.

The crowd roars its approval as a stunned Ayushmann gets to his feet. He offers his teammates an apologetic look. Only one task was given to him, and he failed miserably. He bows to the Kings, then walks away to the tent, the jeers of the crowd still ringing in his ears.

Indranuj grimaces. Three against two. Biraj and Rannveer still hold their defensive stance, and wait for Dhananjay to return to their line. The Captain prefers to showboat for the crowd, whipping them into a frenzy before rejoining his side. Once he does, they move to attack.

"Quick," Gautam shouts. "Against me."

Indranuj stands back-to-back with his chacha. A good defensive position, allowing them to cover all sides. But the Vajras are prepared, and they quickly split their lines. Biraj moves to engage Indranuj, while Rannveer and Dhananjay attack Gautam.

"Simha, give me strength," Indranuj whispers, then launches into the attack.

It takes him a few seconds to realise the Vajra Prince is prepared for him. He has practiced against two swords, and knows how to counter. From the corner of his eye, he sees his chacha trying to breach the defences of the two soldiers, but the numbers are against him. Indranuj does not care. If he can end Biraj's life, they will win more than just the contest.

Swing. Swing. Thrust.

Swing. Swing. Thrust.

Swing. Swing. Thrust.

Indranuj moves into a routine, knowing that Biraj is content to defend, confident that the numbers will soon be in their favour. When he least expects it, Indranuj switches the move.

Swing. Swing.

Biraj waits for the thrust, his shield instinctively moving to block the move. A smile breaks across Indranuj's face. He switches the grip on his sword. It arcs low through the air and catches Biraj below his thigh. Indranuj yanks the sword towards himself, and the Vajra Prince loses his balance and lands on his back.

Indranuj's heart skips a beat. *This is my chance.*

He thrusts his sword downwards, aiming for Biraj's neck, hoping and praying the steel will slip between shoulder guard and helm. But the Vajra Prince senses the blow coming. He instinctively pushes his shoulders up against his neck, and the Simha blade slides harmlessly across his helm. Biraj stares at him, his eyes betraying his bewilderment.

He knows what I meant to do. Indranuj silently screams his frustration. He thinks about striking again, then decides against it. It would be too obvious. Behind him, his chacha still struggles against the two Vajras.

Indranuj runs to his aid, seeking to surprise Dhananjay. But the man anticipates his strike, and ducks under it. With one sword freed, Gautam cuts through Rannveer's defences and lands a telling blow against his helm.

Unfortunately for him, and for Indranuj, Dhananjay's momentum takes him behind the two Simhasthalis.

To their blind side.

Indranuj turns in time to see the Captain's strike, which lands true and hard on Gautam's helm. The crowd gasps, and many heads shake in disapproval. Though not against the rules, it is considered cowardly for a man to strike from behind. Dhananjay may win the fight, but his victory will be tinged with dishonour.

The man does not seem to care. He smiles at Indranuj as the defeated champions bow to the Kings and make their way to their tents.

"Only you and I remain, Your Highness," he says.

"Not for long," Indranuj says.

"You sound confident, little Prince." Dhananjay scoffs. "Your father was the same. Until he lost his head."

The mention of the late King stirs the anger inside Indranuj. The young Simha struggles to contain his emotions. Yet he must, if he is to win.

Your hubris will defeat you, Gautam chacha's words whisper in his ears.

He takes a deep breath, trying to calm his heart. Once it resumes its normal beat, he focuses on his opponent. For such a large man, Dhananjay's feet move quickly; his arms are stronger than steel. They lock eyes through the narrow slits in their helms. Neither blinks, neither glances away.

Indranuj attacks first. A half-hearted thrust, designed to test the Vajra's defence. Dhananjay brings up his shield, sword at the ready to take advantage of any misstep.

Indranuj makes none, and quickly steps back. They circle one another, observing, analysing. The next move belongs to Dhananjay. His feet step forward, and Indranuj brings his left sword to defend the strike. The Vajra pivots and tries to come at him from the right. Indranuj is quick, and his other sword blocks the move.

Dhananjay laughs. "Good, good. You know, you might be better than your father. The man had little skill, and even less courage."

His taunts finally cut through the Prince's defences. Indranuj roars and attacks, his blades whirling through the air, battering against Dhananjay's shield, gaining momentum with each strike. His fury reaches its peak, and he swings hard, when the unexpected happens. Dhananjay drops to one knee, brings his shield under the Simhasthali Prince and swings him over his head.

Indranuj finds himself flying through the air.

You must react, his mind screams at him. *Now.*

He fights the urge to tighten his muscles. His body resists, but he keeps it loose as gravity drags him to the ground. He falls on his back and uses the momentum to speed up his recovery. Once his buttocks touch the ground, he lifts his head, rolls over till his feet are firmly pressed against solid earth, and pushes himself up.

He stands, and a hush descends upon the crowd. Indranuj feels the sun hot upon his face. He turns to his opponent. On the ground between them, metal glints in the sunlight.

His helm.

He touches his face. The sweat drips down it freely. He wipes it off. It matters little.

Helm or no helm, he promises himself, *this ends now.*

He hears a woman scream from the Simhasthali enclosure. "Please, Your Majesty, stop the fight."

He glances up to see Gayathri plead with Vijendra. He grimaces in disgust. One more of his family grovels before the Vajra King.

"Give up, young Prince," Dhananjay mocks him. "Walk away with your head intact." He laughs. "Did you know that after your brother fled, we played a game of catch with Giridhar's head? The blood made it slippery, yes, but that only made the game more interesting. Remain here, Prince, and we will do the same with you."

Before Indranuj can react, King Vijendra calls out. "Your Highness, I request you to concede."

Indranuj ignores him. He walks up to where his helm lies and kicks it away. He then swings both his swords and firms up his stance.

Mayhem ensues in the arena. In the Simhasthali enclosure, Vikrant jumps to his feet. "Indu, drop your swords at once."

Rannveer joins in, screaming at his junior. "Captain, withdraw from the arena. Now."

Dhananjay turns to his General, and bows his acknowledgement of the order. His lowers his sword, and makes to walk away to the Vajra tent.

Then he attacks.

His target is clear. Indranuj's unprotected head. The Simha Prince is pushed backwards, and deflects most of his blows. He does not make a move to attack, allowing the burly Vajra to charge at him. The man tries every trick in the book, but each time, Indranuj's blade blocks his.

He pays a heavy price for it. Dhananjay's strikes shiver up the Prince's arm and rattle his teeth. The Vajra is strong and relentless. A few more minutes of this, and Indranuj will be unable to grip his sword.

He waits for the next strike. The blade swings, and sunrays dance off its steel. Indranuj does not raise his sword to meet it. He drops his shoulders and twists his head beneath the blade, which nicks his ear as it whistles past.

The cut stings, but the joy of succeeding easily overcomes it. Indranuj moves behind his opponent and stabs his sword downwards. The blade sinks between the armour plates, cutting into the leg. Dhananjay bellows in pain and drops to one knee, as blood gushes out to puddle on the ground.

Shock waves race through the crowd. Accidents occur in a fight, but this was deliberate. Indranuj smiles at the audience, uncaring, unconcerned. He turns to face his opponent.

Dhananjay tosses his sword and shield to the ground. He raises the hood of his helm, and laughs at the Prince as he shouts out, loud enough for everyone to hear. "Your Highness, I concede."

Indranuj laughs as well. "As I knew you would."

"I congratulate you," Dhananjay shouts. His voice drops to a whisper. "Now, be a good boy, and go collect your reward from my King."

The smile broadens on Indranuj's face. "I intend to collect it right now."

He uses his sword to knock the helm off Dhananjay's head. The man's eyes widen. Time slows, as everyone in the arena realises what he means to do. He can hear their cries as his sword cuts through the air.

"Nooooooo," Gautam screams in the tent.

"Induuuuuuu…" his mother shouts from the enclosure.

"Stop him now!" Vijendra barks at his guards.

Too late.

The blade slices through the man's head. It topples to the floor and watches its murderer with stunned eyes. Indranuj smiles.

For Giridhar, for Simhasthal, he whispers, before dropping his swords to the ground.

CHAPTER FIFTY-FIVE

They gather in the throne room. The Simhasthalis, the Vajras, the royal families. Vikrant is offered a seat by the throne, along with Vijendra and Indrani, while the rest of his family remain below with the other ladies and lords.

He glances at them in turn. Gautam looks dejected, as does Kashyap. Gayathri tries to stand strong, though it is evident she fights to hold back tears. His mother shows no signs of weeping. She stands proud, resolute, ready to do battle for Indranuj.

Vikrant turns to his brother, who stands in the centre of the hall, a prisoner surrounded by four guards. His eyes blaze with conviction, and show no sign of repentance.

Indu, he wants to call out, *why did you do it?*

His thoughts are broken by the Rannveer's fury.

"A crime has been committed, My King," the General thunders. "Captain Dhananjay was a good soldier, widely respected by his comrades and people." He stares at Indranuj with accusing eyes. "The Prince murdered him. The Captain was unarmed, on his knees. The match was over. There was no reason for this criminal act." He turns back to Vijendra. "I demand justice."

Vijendra nods in agreement. "Justice will be delivered." His voice is kind. "Prince Indranuj, do you wish to speak in your defence?"

Indranuj chuckles as he shakes his head. "No, King Vijendra, I do not."

The court erupts once more. The boy shows disrespect, and Vikrant knows things will get out of hand if Indranuj does not mend his ways.

Their mother calls out, her voice cutting through the commotion. "Your Majesty."

The people fall silent, and Vijendra turns to her. "Yes, Your Highness?"

"You must forgive my son," Nandini demands. "He is young, and easy to anger. We were all witness to the fight. Captain Dhananjay attacked first, even after General Rannveer ordered him to stand down. Words were exchanged, which may have caused more pain than any of us realise. It does not excuse my son's crime, but it justifies forgiveness."

"Forgiveness?" Rannveer looks astonished. "At least you have the decency to admit his crime. Look at your son, Your Highness. The way he stands, proud of his deed. And this is the defence you offer? Hurtful words?"

Before anyone else can speak, Indranuj calls out. "If ambition can allow for a King's head to be cut off, surely hurtful words can justify lopping off the neck of a common Captain."

You should remain silent, Vikrant mutters under his breath, but it is too late now. The barb has struck its mark. A red-faced Vijendra jumps to his feet, but before he can erupt, his Queen grabs his hand.

"Answer me this, Prince Indranuj," Indrani says, "if a Vajra had committed such a crime in Simhasthal, what would be his punishment?"

Indranuj stays silent.

But Vijendra smiles. "We do not need the boy to answer, My Queen. The King of Simhasthal sits with us." He turns to Vikrant. "Your Majesty, Vajrapur will soon be as much your home as Simhasthal. As its future ruler, I leave this decision to you."

Rannveer shouts out once more. "Your Majesty, there is only one punishment for murder."

Vikrant glares at the General, for he understands the sentence he demands.

Death.

The universe conspires to test his resolve. Nandini and Gayathri turn to Vikrant with fervent hope. He ignores them and studies his younger brother, unrepentant, proud, righteous. From the day he was born, Vikrant has loved him. And now, he must decide whether to send him to the gallows.

He leaves me no choice. "My father taught me two ways to deliver justice," Vikrant says. "By the blade of my sword, and by the conscience of my heart. It does not matter which I choose today." His sadness consumes his soul as he locks eyes with his brother. "Prince Indranuj, you executed an unarmed man in cold blood. Under Simhasthali law, under Vajra law, under the laws of the gods, I hold you guilty of the crime, for which the punishment is death."

The smile vanishes from Indranuj's face. Nandini collapses onto her chair, and Gayathri holds her mother close. Rannveer is surprised as well. Apparently, he did not expect such steadfast devotion to the law from the Simha King.

Vikrant turns to a smiling Vijendra. "Your Majesty, in view of my marriage to Princess Idhika, I request that the sentence not be carried out until the day after the wedding."

A most reasonable request, one which Vijendra is only too pleased to grant. He commands the guards. "Escort Prince Indranuj to the dungeons. See that he has thick bedding and good food. I wish for him to spend his final days in comfort."

The guards grab Indranuj by the arms and lead him away. Dejected, he casts one last look at his King. Vikrant knows the thought which races through his mind. *My older brother, the one who always looked after me, now sends me to my death.*

"Dada," Indranuj calls out plaintively.

Vikrant steels his heart and offers no reply. The deed is done, the punishment passed. He must see this out to its bitter end.

CHAPTER FIFTY-SIX

A half hour later, Nandini storms into Vikrant's room, where he sits in conversation with Atulya. Seeing the two of them together fuels her rage, which already burns as hot as the fires of hell.

"How could you?" she accuses her son.

Vikrant remains silent. He prefers not to offer an explanation.

And if he did, she wonders, *would I accept it?*

She doubts it. *Beware the fury of a wronged woman,* the philosophers say. They should have known better. The fury of a wronged mother is far worse, and she is proving it at this very moment.

Gayathri, Kashyap, and Gautam follow her in, their morose faces adding to the ones already in the room.

"Your Majesty, you can still reverse your decision," Kashyap throws his support behind Nandini. "Vijendra needs our army. He needs *us*. If you meet with him in private, he will surely heed your request."

"And why should the King do such a thing?" asks Atulya, his voice unnaturally calm, given the circumstances.

Nandini glares at him. *I knew we could not trust him.*

Atulya ignores her anger. "I would consider the act immoral. There is no doubt Indranuj killed an unarmed man. It matters little if the man provoked him verbally. He had no cause." He turns to Gautam. "Colonel, he is your student. I ask you; would you condone his actions?"

Nandini turns to Gautam as well, her eyes begging him to speak up for the sake of her son's life. Gautam appears uncomfortable to be put on the spot.

"The provocation does not matter," he says at last. "Prince Indranuj committed murder, plain and simple. And the punishment for that, even in Simhasthal, is death."

Nandini cannot believe her ears. *Does everyone wish to condemn my son?*

"I do not agree," protests Gayathri, belying her mother's thoughts. She glares at Vikrant. "I have always supported you. As a child, as a man, as a King. I even supported your decision to ally with Vijendra and marry Idhika. But this—no, I cannot support you in this. I will not."

"Then you lose the right to say you have always supported me," says Vikrant, with a rueful smile.

"You will not reconsider?" Nandini asks.

Vikrant shakes his head. "No. To do so would only subvert justice. That is not the Simhasthali way."

"Then you are no son of mine," Nandini roars.

"So be it," Vikrant thunders.

Nandini is stunned into silence. Not once in all his years has he spoken this way to her. Or to anyone. He was always her soft-spoken boy, timid, shy. But now, a stranger stands before her, and she wonders where her motherly love was spent.

"I lost all of you on the Laalkhet," Vikrant says. "I lost you the day my father died, and I became King." His tone hardens. "I am no longer your son. No longer a brother, or a nephew. I am the King of Simhasthal. For better or worse, the command is mine. And you will obey."

His words cut deep. She did not believe he had it in him. A long silence follows, before she speaks again. "And what does our King command?"

"Leave Indranuj to his fate," Vikrant says. "Get some rest. And prepare yourselves for my engagement."

Nandini glances at the others in the room. Like her, they are hurt, angry, disappointed. All except Atulya, whose face remains impassive. It appears her son has chosen his future. To rule them all, with only the schoolmaster and Ayushmann for company. *So be it.*

Kashyap is the first to react. Without a word or a bow, he storms out of the room. Gautam, however, bows before he leaves. Gayathri steps forward to face the man who was once her brother. Tears freely escape her eyes, but he remains unmoved. She, too, walks away without bowing.

Nandini stands before him last. She bows low, lower than she has to any King, before looking him in the eye. "We shall do as you command, Your Majesty."

Then she leaves.

CHAPTER FIFTY-SEVEN

The tiny tavern booms with laughter.

Its customers are a raucous bunch, more so when arrack fills their bellies and their wives are absent. A dozen pitchers have made the short trip to their table and back, with the thirteenth on its way.

Chandran sits with the strangers, the coins are piled thick and tall in front of him. A game of dice is in progress. The men call out the numbers they believe will fall. Bets are laid and the cubes are rolled. A four and a six. The losers curse, the winners cheer, and Chandran laughs as he adds to his pile.

They know him well here. He has visited many times, as goodwill ambassador of Simhasthal. Those days and nights in Vajrapur were always his favourite. This is the life he desires, simple, enjoyable, far removed from the politics of the palace.

He grins. *Soon it will be mine.*

There will be a wedding. Then a war. And at its end, his governorship will follow.

The serving girl arrives with another pitcher. She is a pretty girl, with the wide hips and heavy bosom so treasured in establishments such as this. Chandran regards her with lusty eyes, as do the other men, who help themselves to handfuls of her soft flesh as she refills their glasses and leaves without so much as a murmur.

The game resumes. Chandran rolls the dice. A three and a four. He curses good-naturedly. His winnings far outweigh this loss. He rises from the table and collects his coins in a pouch.

"I don't trust you Vajras," he says. "By the time I piss and return, I might end up poorer than a beggar on the street."

His companions roar their laughter, and one of them slaps him on the back. Chandran makes his way to the yard at the back, where the shrubbery is thick, and serves to answer nature's call. Once relieved, he heads back in.

The serving girl from earlier walks down the corridor. A smile breaks across her face, and she looks at him inquisitively. Chandran feels a stirring in his loins. He nods at the girl, and her smile widens. She leads him up a small staircase, to the shabby chambers on the first level, where she chooses a room and holds the door open. Chandran enters, and is surprised to see another woman sitting on the bed. He recognises her at once.

Atishi.

The serving girl closes the door and leaves them.

"It is good to see you again, Your Highness," Atishi says.

"You do not know how good it is to see you," Chandran says.

Atishi's girlish giggles are sweet music to his ears. Of all the wonders he has experienced in Vajrapur, she is the most wonderful.

She had entered his life four years ago, a gift from Vijendra, which he thought to refuse. He still loved his wife back in those days. But Gayathri had taken leave of their marital bed after she became pregnant with the twins, and months had passed since he last felt a woman's touch.

No harm could come from one night's indiscretion, he had thought. She was a whore, and would view him as another man to please and forget.

But he had been wrong. She had gazed deep inside him, secreted out his deepest carnal desires, and satisfied them all.

After that night, he had made his way to her bed at every opportunity. Their relationship transcended whore and master, and he had found it easy to share every secret, even confessing to her that he was Vijendra's spy in Simhasthal. His caution had disappeared easily, once he was between her legs, where it felt warm and empowering, like the world belonged to him.

And now, here she sits, the nymph who haunts his dreams. He takes her in his arms, but she pushes him away.

"What is the matter?" asks Chandran, puzzled.

"You have broken my heart, Your Highness," Atishi pouts.

"And how have I done that?" Chandran asks.

"Four days have passed since you arrived in Vajrapur," she says. "I waited and waited, yet you did not seek me out."

Chandran jumps to her side and takes her in his arms once more. "It is not that I did not want to, my dear. My wife is with me. Besides, would you have had the time? You have spent every night in Vikrant's chambers."

Atishi holds him tight, crying. "I only do so because King Vijendra commands it. If you cared for me even a little, you would have tried to rescue me."

Chandran's focus is distracted by the crush of her soft breasts against his chest. "I will do anything you command."

"Then come see me tonight," Atishi begs him. "King Vikrant does not require my company. He is not in the mood." She pauses for a moment. "I heard his younger brother has been imprisoned."

Her pallu slips, and Chandran loses himself in her ample cleavage. "He has," his lips move of their own accord.

"Then why don't you ask your wife to spend the night with her mother?" Atishi says. "I am certain Ranimaa Nandini will require comfort and support."

Chandran smiles, impressed. "A fabulous idea. My mother-in-law will be pleased to have her company."

"And I will be pleased to have yours," Atishi purrs.

Chandran laughs and squishes her body into his. She lets him paw at her for a while, then breaks away. "Do you remember the way to my cottage?"

Chandran nods his head. "I do."

She leans in and whispers into his ear. "Then I will see you tonight, Your Highness."

She kisses him on the cheek, readjusts her sari, and leaves the room. Chandran remains seated for a while, his heart thumping in his chest.

Tonight cannot arrive soon enough.

CHAPTER FIFTY-EIGHT

"Ladies and lords, Your Royal Highnesses, Your Majesties. Princess Idhika of Vajrapur."

The herald steps aside, as Idhika enters the garden. It arrives at last. The night of her engagement, celebrated beneath a cloud of hurt and animosity.

The day's sordid events had reached her ears. Dhananjay slain; Indranuj imprisoned. A black day, not one she would have chosen.

But the event cannot be postponed, and a nervous energy consumes her as she walks past her guest, anklets thinking, red sari swishing, the thousand crystals sewn into the fabric shimmering in the torch-lights, a dazzling vision to behold.

Curious eyes turn to face her, but she does not meet them. Her focus lies on the royal dais, where Vikrant waits, hand held out for her. She gratefully accepts it.

Idhika had feared he would give the game away. She need not have worried. Vikrant appears awestruck, the way he had been the very first time they met. There is genuine admiration in his eyes, one which she wishes to return. But she cannot. Not as long as he remains servile to her father.

As they take their seats, Idhika mutters softly. "You sentenced your brother to death?"

"I did," Vikrant whispers.

"Why?" Idhika demands to know.

"For you," comes his answer.

They face their guests, and Idhika smiles. It is a brave face she puts on, for she finds being the centre of attention a little disconcerting, and an iron ball takes hold of her chest, growing larger every second. She breathes deeply, begging her nerves to calm themselves. The gifts will now be presented, and the bride-to-be will be welcomed by all.

The herald steps forward and calls out the first name. "Lord Atulya and Lady Akanksha of Simhasthal."

The two ascend to the stage and bow to the King and Princess. They present a gift of books, favourites of the former schoolmaster, one which they hope will add wisdom to their marriage. Idhika and Vikrant thank them, and they move on.

One by one, the other guests make their way to the stage. They offer their congratulations, their blessings and their gifts. The Vajras smile, while the Simhasthalis speak through gritted teeth. Their angst is understandable, and easily forgiven.

After the ladies and lords are done, the royal family takes the stage. Prince Biraj comes first. He offers a diamond encrusted sword to Vikrant and a ruby necklace to Idhika, who thanks him. "I will treasure this gift, chacha. You have been a friend to me all these years, and I hope our friendship will continue even after my marriage."

"I assure you it will, Your Highness," says Biraj, before he leaves.

Lord Ayushmann follows, the grin on his face as wide as ever. Queen Indrani had reluctantly agreed to allow him to be presented as part of the family. He bows and presents a simple basket of fruit. Nectarines from the Andhakaranya, Idhika notes with surprise. *How does he know they are my favourite?*

"I apologise, Your Highness," Ayushmann says. "I am your uncle, yet I have been absent almost all your life. I hope this humble gift goes a little way to mending my mistake."

"Thank you, Lord Ayushmann," Idhika says. "But how—?"

Ayushmann cuts her off, still smiling. "As my King will tell you, I try to know everyone's secrets." He bows once more and proceeds to join the other guests.

Princess Gayathri arrives next, with Lord Chandran and their children in tow. She presents Idhika with a wooden lady warrior. "Many say women aren't brave enough to be soldiers. I say any woman who marries and bears children is braver than all men."

Idhika laughs. "I agree, Your Highness. And I thank you." She looks at the boys and girl clutching their mother's sari. "Your children are beautiful."

"My pride and joy," Gayathri says. "I hope you have many children, and find as much happiness in them as I have."

So do my parents, Idhika thinks.

She does not dwell on it. Instead, she winks. "How many children I have depends on your brother's efforts."

The Princesses laugh, even as Vikrant blushes. Chandran leads his family away as a hesitant Gautam and a sullen Kashyap arrive. Idhika surprises them by bowing before they can.

"Colonel Gautam, General Kashyap," she says, "I feel like I have known you for many years."

"Forgive me, Your Highness," Kashyap says, "I do not understand."

Idhika smiles. "If there is a tale of love as famous as yours, I have yet to hear it. Poets, singers, historians, all have penned your story. Men may revere you for your battle prowess, but we women admire you for your relationship. I pray my marriage sees half as much happiness as yours has."

Gautam bows his head. "I pray for the same, Your Highness."

"As do I," says Kashyap, smiling benevolently, before he exits the dais.

I may have won him over, Idhika thinks, *but I wonder the next will be as easy.*

The herald calls out the name. "Ranimaa Nandini of Simhasthal, wife of King Giridhar, mother of King Vikrant."

Idhika touches the feet of her future mother-in-law. Nandini raises her up. Their eyes meet, and the Princess feels her sadness.

A mother's sadness.

"It is an honour to meet you, Your Highness," Idhika says.

Nandini cups her cheek. "You are beautiful, my child. More beautiful than my son let on. It pleases me to welcome you to our family." She places her palm on Idhika's head. "*Soubhagyavati bhava.*"

May your husband live long. The blessing is usually reserved for married women, but Idhika understands why Nandini offers it early. She blesses me with what she has been denied.

Still, the Princess is a little hurt. *She blesses me with her son's long life, not my own.*

An attendant steps forward with a necklace, thick gold with a large blue diamond at its heart, which Nandini presents to Idhika. "This belonged to my husband's grandmother. My mother-in-law presented it to me at my engagement. I now entrust its care to you."

Another attendant arrives with a firewood box, from which Nandini retrieves a dagger. On its hilt, the great white lion roars.

"My father presented this to yours," she tells her son. "I hope you keep it close, and remember him. If you can."

Her words sting. Still, Vikrant forces himself to smile and touch his mother's feet. She does not bless him, and Idhika does not blame her.

The last announcement of the night is made. "Queen Indrani and King Vijendra of Vajrapur, mother and father of Princess Idhika."

With broad smiles, the King and Queen arrive on the dais. Two attendants trail behind them, pillows in hand, upon which rest two golden crowns.

"My daughter, my son," Vijendra says, "We present these to you, in honour of your union, and our alliance."

The attendants bring the crowns forward. At its centre, the bird-shaped land of Saravat is etched. Idhika assumes this is the new symbol of their empire, which her father presents early. The King and Queen hold it up high for all to see, before placing the crowns upon Idhika and Vikrant, who touch their feet and are blessed in turn.

Now that the gifts have been presented, the time arrives to say the words. They step forward before their guests, who watch on intently. An attendant arrives with two cages, a restless white dove inside each. One male, one female.

Vijendra addresses the guests. "Ladies and lords, I thank you for blessing us with your presence on this auspicious day. Tonight, I ask you to bear witness to my daughter's intention to wed King Vikrant of Simhasthal."

Nandini echoes his words. "And I ask that you bear witness to my son's intention to wed Princess Idhika of Vajrapur."

The attendant steps forward and holds up the cages. Idhika and Vikrant reach in and grab the doves, then face each other and speak in one voice.

"Blessed by the gods and our families, I choose you to be my partner, in this life and for seven births after."

They turn to the guests and release the doves. White wings flutter as the birds make their escape. As expected, they fly together. A good sign, symbolising the future of the marriage.

Muted applause greets their flight. Idhika is not surprised. The wealthy know the trick. The birds will fly as they always have, together, guided by instinct and survival. Maybe we are not so different. For what else is marriage?

She glances at Vikrant. The rituals have been followed, the words have been spoken.

A sad smile crosses her face. *For better or worse, he is now my partner for life.*

CHAPTER FIFTY-NINE

In the cottage, a single lamp is lit, its weak light barely illuminating the room. Atishi sits on her bed, dressed like a noblewoman. No, a Princess. A bride on her wedding night, sitting in nervous anticipation of her lover's arrival.

The silence of the cottage soothes her troubled mind. Alas, it will not be for long. She has work to do. A task sour as lemons, but important.

The coming days will decide the fate of Saravat, and she must play her part well. If not for herself, then for Princess Idhika. The gods know the girl deserves a better life than she has been given. Locked away in a palace, alone, miserable, a bargaining chip for her father's grand ambitions.

Why do I care, she wonders.

Atishi does not belong to this kingdom, nor this land. She is a foreigner here, with no family ties to hold her back.

But what is family?

She never knew her true parents. Not really. Mother for her was the mistress who taught her to spread her legs. Father was the man who hauled away the customers who got too rough. And sisters were the other girls who welcomed a different man in bed every night, sometimes with her help.

The Princess is family as well. Not in the same way, for their stories are different. Yet their cages are the same. Sometimes, Atishi wonders if there isn't any difference between the rich and the poor. Maybe, if you are born a woman.

For us, life never changes much.

She hears a floorboard creak outside. Her guest has arrived. She readies her mind and body as the footsteps approach. The door to her room swings opens, and Lord Chandran walks in. He smiles, pleased by the way she is dressed.

The way his wife dresses.

He sits on the bed and strokes her feet, his palm as smooth as her creamy skin.

"Good evening, My Princess," he says.

"Good evening, Your Highness," she replies.

His smile widens, as she knew it would. She had sensed it the very first time he visited her. His insecurity at being denied the title, at being ruled by his wife's family and her. She had coaxed it out of him, with coy servility, and he had never stopped lusting for her since.

"Have you missed me?" he asks.

"My body longs to feel your touch, Your Highness," she replies. "Without you, I am nothing."

He reaches out, grabs her *pallu*, and yanks it off her. Atishi breathes heavily, as he continues to pull and rip at her clothes until the last piece of fabric is cast away. The sight of her naked body heightens his excitement.

"Undress me," he commands.

She obeys without question. Once he is naked, he pushes her head down between his legs. She knows what she must do.

It is easy enough, since the man is not very large. She pleasures him for a few minutes before he roughly throws her on the bed.

"Do you like that, Princess?"

"Yes, Your Highness," she replies.

Her role is clear. She is a tool, to be used however he likes. He crawls up her body and enters her. She cries out her pleasure, though she can barely feel a thing.

Little does he know she had prepared herself before he arrived, with a cream mixture her old mistress had taught her to make. Unfortunately, the man has staying power. He grunts on top of her for a long while, his violent hands roaming her body, before he finally reaches his climax and rolls over.

Atishi sighs, pretending to be content, as she runs a finger through his hairy chest. "Your Highness, I am so happy you could see me tonight."

"As am I, my dear," Chandran replies. "Your idea was perfect. My wife was only too happy to keep her mother company."

Atishi giggles. "Little does she know what you are up to."

Chandran laughs as well. "She is a foolish girl. Still beautiful, I admit, even after three children. But she cannot compare to you." He grabs her breast. "You are truly desirable."

His touch hurts, but she is used to it. Many men are this way. What pleasure they derive from the pain, she cannot say. Nor does she want to think of it. The girls in her old pleasure house told horrid tales of the men they had been with, and she used to shudder to think of what she would do if that were to ever happen to her.

Chandran still speaks, unaware that she pays no attention. "If only Gayathri was more like you. But no, she likes to keep me under her thumb, the way her family does. But once I receive my governorship, I will show her who is boss. Not her dead father, not her coward brother. *Me.* And she will submit to my command, once and for all."

The thought brings new life within him. He flips her on her stomach and lies above her. She senses his intention and tries to relax. It will be over soon, she whispers to herself, all the time groaning and moaning to make him feel like he pleasures her.

He lasts a little longer, but not much. When he withdraws, she feels a numbness down below. Thankfully, she has ointments to bring relief.

Chandran rolls off the bed and starts to dress. "I will see you again tomorrow," he says. "My wife will spend the night with Idhika, as is the custom."

Atishi knows of the ritual. A female relative of the groom will keep the bride company the night before the wedding, and tell her what to expect in her new household, mostly about the likes and dislikes of her husband, and the customs of her new family.

Sadly, the same is not done for the groom.

"I beg your forgiveness, Your Highness," Atishi says. "The King has me performing other duties tomorrow."

Chandran genuinely looks sad. He leans over and gently caresses her face. "Hmm. It does not matter. By the turn of the year, I will be governor of a kingdom, and maybe the King will see fit to make a gift of you to me." He squishes her cheeks in his palm. "Would you like that?"

She smiles through the pain. "Nothing would bring me more joy, Your Highness."

Her words please him. "Good. I will see to it."

He leaves her lying on the bed. Once the outside door closes, Atishi rolls onto her back. Her body needs medicine. She reaches into her bedside drawer, removes a small green pouch, and lets the contents fall onto the bed. A variety of ointments lie before her. She selects one, squeezes a little cream onto her finger and massages it in.

"Has he always treated you this way?" Gayathri asks.

Atishi does not look up. The Princess had arrived earlier this evening, to watch her husband betray their marriage.

She nods her head. "Always, Your Highness."

Gayathri takes the ointment from her hands and squeezes a little on her finger. She massages it into the flesh her husband violated. "I am sorry. I did not know."

"There is nothing to be sorry for, Your Highness," Atishi says. "There are many kinds of men. It does not matter if they have a lady at home or a monster. They seek the other, if they have the coin."

Gayathri continues to rub in the ointment. "My husband dreams of the day he will be free of my grasp. I will see that it comes sooner than he expects."

Once the medicine is applied, Atishi pulls a robe on, and offers Gayathri a washcloth to wipe her hands.

Gayathri smiles. "Please thank the Princess for helping me see the truth."

Atishi smiles in return. "It wasn't the Princess, Your Highness."

"Then who?" Gayathri asks.

"Your brother," Atishi says bluntly. "King Vikrant."

Shock races through Gayathri's body, and she stands frozen, wide-eyed, with her mouth gaping open.

"M-m-my bro-ther?" she stammers.

Atishi nods her head. “It is he who commanded me to reveal your husband’s infidelity.”

The truth stares Gayathri in the face. “This means… he knows about my husband? About Vijendra?”

He knows everything. “And about you.”

Gayathri does not know how to react. She holds her head in her hands, her body wracked by her sobs. “He must hate me. He must want me dead.”

“He does not,” Atishi assures her. “He seeks to repair relationships. All of them.” She lays a gentle hand on the Princess’ shoulder. “Rest now, Your Highness. Soon, all will be as it should. Your brother promises.”

A confused Gayathri simply nods her head. Atishi pities her, as she sees her out and watches her head back to the palace. It is not easy for someone like her, a born Princess, who has spent a lifetime believing in her own power and cunning, only to have it all shattered in the space of a single night. But Gayathri needed to know the truth. Vikrant had commanded it, and Atishi had obeyed.

She rests for an hour, then heads to the palace to make her report to her new King.

CHAPTER SIXTY

"Good morning, Your Highness," Vikrant calls out cheerily. Idhika's eyes narrow when she spots him. Atishi had informed her that they arrived half an hour earlier, but she expected to find him seated by the pond, wearing that ponderous expression which seems so natural on him.

Yet here he swims, up and down the cool water, at peace with the world. His mother cries in her chambers, his brother rots in prison. But who would think that if they saw him right now?

She stands at the pond's edge. "You arrived early."

"I did," Vikrant says. "For some reason, I could not bear to wait out the time in those stuffy chambers."

"I see," she says. "I guess lack of sleep explains why Atishi does not appear to be herself today."

Vikrant smiles. "That I cannot honestly say. However, I am well rested."

Idhika stares at him, frustrated by her own failings. Four days they have spent together, yet she still has not got the measure of him.

Vikrant senses her annoyance. He stops swimming and looks up at her. "My Queen-to-be, I suspect you have a lot to say, and I am tired of straining my neck. Perhaps you would consider joining me?"

Idhika regards him curiously for a while, then shrugs. There is no point in simply standing here. She sheds her clothes, enters the water and swims to him. "Here I am."

"What do you want to know?" Vikrant asks.

"Why you sentenced your brother to death," she says.

His eyes betray his sorrow. "My mother demanded the same answer. What choice did I have? He committed the crime. And the sentence is clear."

Idhika does not agree. "You could have asked my father for mercy. He does not care for a Captain's life. He would have found a way to grant it."

"Only if I begged," Vikrant replies. "I think I have done enough of that. No more."

Idhika is surprised. Her father has managed to get Vikrant to surrender to a great many things, and she understands his reluctance to contest those commands. But now—

"You place your pride before your brother's life?" she asks.

"Pride?" Vikrant laughs. "I think by now I have shown how little pride I possess. No, sweet Idhika, I do not do so out of pride."

"Then why?" she asks.

"For my kingdom," he says.

Her frustration grows. "I do not understand."

Vikrant smiles. He does look sweet when he smiles, enough to make you forgive him a thousand mistakes. But Idhika is not in a forgiving mood today.

"It was my grandmother who first spoke the words to me," Vikrant says. "You are no longer the son of Giridhar. You are the King of Simhasthal, she said, and the future of my people rests in my hands. My brother's life is willingly given for the cause."

Idhika cannot believe her ears. "Does servility to my father further your people's cause, or your own?"

"I would die for my people," Vikrant declares. "There is no cause greater than their happiness."

Once again, Idhika finds herself vexed. "Your Highness, I believe the time has come to speak plainly. We are to be married tomorrow. For better or worse, my future is now tied to yours. And for the first time in my life, I wish to have some say in what lies ahead."

Vikrant seems amused, and Idhika wonders if this is all a game to him.

"Have you ever been to Shitakul?" he asks.

Idhika shakes her head.

"But you have heard of the white lion?" he asks.

Who hasn't? "It is the emblem of your clan."

"It used to hunt them once," he says, "When they roamed the frozen wastelands. Fifteen feet long, six feet tall, claws as big as daggers, sharp enough to rip a man to shreds."

"Have you ever seen one?" she asks.

Vikrant shakes his head. "I had hoped to, but it was not to be. There is a custom in Simhasthal. At the age of fourteen, boy or girl, you are taken to live in Shitakul for five days. It is our way of staying connected to our Kura heritage. You should never forget where you come from."

The memory builds in his mind. "After my fourteenth name day, Kashyap chacha and Gautam chacha took me there. The first day passed without much incident. They set up camp. Fished through the ice. Told stories from centuries ago when the clan wandered that land. It was cold, but we had carried enough furs to keep an army warm."

"The second day, we explored our surroundings. Kashyap chacha pointed out the trees. I had read about the snow forests, but did not expect them to be that way. Tall, with long needles for branches, and snow clumping everywhere."

"The third day, my uncle took us hunting. Gautam chacha asked me to place my feet only where his landed. Not to step anywhere else. I found that odd, but did as told. The two kept a wary eye out, as did the thirty soldiers who accompanied us."

"The next morning, we set out to hunt the *heeran.* It is similar to the deer in the Mrugaranya, but taller, and a lighter shade of gold. Women lust to cover themselves in its thick coat, which is light as cotton and warm as summer. We spotted it easily, for there were many which wandered the snow lands. The males have antlers as tall as you, and eyes that shine when they caught the sun."

"We returned with two. Their meat was delicious, and the pelts were kept aside for me to present to my mother and sister. We were to leave on the morrow. But I did not want to, for I was yet to see the white lion."

"Gautam chacha laughed at my anxiety. *Many cry at the sight of one,* he said, *and you cry in its absence*. I admitted I would be scared if I saw one, but it is the emblem of my clan. If I do not see it, how can I respect the power it symbolises?"

"A fair point," Idhika says.

"He agreed as well," Vikrant says. "So he told me the secret of the lion. It hunts in the woods, for that is where its prey is most abundant. I was surprised. He would not be invisible there. Gautam chacha laughed at me again. Oh, but he is, he said."

Idhika's curiosity is piqued. "How can he be invisible in the woods?"

She has never seen Vikrant smile this way.

Triumphant. "He hides beneath the snow."

It takes a moment for his words to sink in. She repeats them slowly. "He. Hides. Beneath. The. Snow."

The thought churns in her head. She imagines the white forest. An innocent deer walking through the woods. The snow erupting in a shower of ice. And giant teeth sinking into meaty flesh.

The unseen predator.

She sees Vikrant watching her. For the first time, she thinks him determined. Ambitious. Strong.

"Do not dwell too much on this," he says. "Tomorrow, we are to be wed. And if my sister's wedding is anything to go by, it promises to be a long day."

He holds out his hand, and she takes it. Together, they wade to the shallow end and walk out onto solid ground. Idhika shouts out for her handmaidens. "Ladies."

Her hand remains in Vikrant's. They still have a few moments alone with each other.

"Jayendu has agreed to meet with me," Vikrant says.

"I see," says Idhika, though she clearly does not. "For what purpose?"

"To discuss our futures, and your father's grand plans. It seems even Jayendu is not pleased."

Idhika chuckles. "That old man is never pleased. Things must progress the way he desires, and he will not tolerate Kings or Princes messing with his cause."

"That is what I am counting on," Vikrant says. He squeezes her hand. "Jayendu, my mother, my people, even you. You have all been looking at me as the problem. By tomorrow, I hope you will see that you were wrong."

"If you are not the problem, then what are you?" Idhika asks.

"What I have always been," Vikrant says. "The solution."

Her mind tingles with a million questions, which must now wait to be answered. The handmaidens arrive with Atishi, and busy themselves drying and dressing the couple. Vikrant does not leave her hand, nor does she leave his. For the first time since she laid eyes on him in that peace tent, Idhika believes that he may actually be the husband she has always desired.

She smiles, thinking of her father's reaction when he realises it as well.

CHAPTER SIXTY-ONE

Jayendu holds Datta's hand and shuffles carefully across the jetty. Only a few feet remain, but they may as well have been a thousand, and the loose wooden planks conspire to further slow his progress. It does not matter. The barge belongs to him, and the sailors wait patiently, ready to reach out and help him onto the boat once he arrives.

At long last, he makes it, and sighs with relief. Half the journey accomplished. Now he hopes nature does not ask him to answer its call. A swaying boat is more than enough to test his wobbly body to the limit.

He spots his guests, Atulya and Vikrant, who stand to show their respect. And so they should. The boy may be a King, but in stature, Jayendu towers over him. He signals the captain to cast off, then hobbles over to the Simhasthalis, grimacing as he squints to get a better look at the Simha King.

He is much more impressive from afar. Jayendu shakes his head. Does it matter? He has come to judge the boy's intelligence, not his physique.

He bows and speaks kindly. "King Vikrant, it is a pleasure to meet you at last."

"I thank you, my lord," says Vikrant, bowing even lower. "The pleasure and honour are both mine."

Atulya bows his head. "Lord Jayendu, we appreciate you arranging this meeting. I am certain it wasn't easy."

Jayendu offers him a wry smile. *No, my friend. It was easy enough.*

After the debacle in the arena, followed by an even bigger one in the throne room, he had considered refusing the meeting altogether. The boy King is now little more than Vijendra's puppet, ready to lop off his own brother's head to prove his loyalty. But he had agreed to hear them out, and so he had made arrangements.

He had sent instructions for Atulya to ask Vijendra permission for a barge-ride down the river. The King would not refuse, not after Vikrant sentenced his younger brother to death, and would surely be in desperate need of some peace and quiet.

As expected, Vijendra willingly agreed, and commanded Jayendu to provide the barge. The Parasu accompanied Vikrant, as did the Vajra guards, but their silence is absolute.

Jayendu chuckles. *I pay them far more than the King ever could.*

He guides his guest to the seats in the middle of the barge. "Shall we speak business then?"

A groan escapes his lips once he sits and rests his weary legs. The pain is almost unbearable.

"Are you alright, my lord?" Vikrant asks.

"Old age, my boy," Jayendu says. "Nothing can defeat it." He gestures at the bench in front of him. "Sit, sit. Let us talk. I have waited long to see what prize my kingdom has won."

Vikrant laughs as Atulya and he take their seats. "If you are anything like your countrymen, I fear you will be disappointed."

"Yes, my fellow Vajras take you for a coward," Jayendu says. "Most of them prayed that the wedding would be called off. Or that you would give reason for Vijendra to doubt your usefulness."

"So far that has not happened," Vikrant says.

"It has not," Jayendu agrees. "Quite the opposite. Vijendra appears more and more enamoured by your ingratiating ways."

"As was intended," Atulya says.

Jayendu looks sharply at the schoolmaster, and regards him suspiciously. "What is that supposed to mean?"

Vikrant speaks up instead. "People are far too concerned about my past and present. I keep my eyes focused on the real prize. The future."

"And what might that be?" Jayendu asks.

"Emperor of Saravat," Vikrant says.

Jayendu raises his eyebrows. "You believe that prize to be yours?"

Vikrant's smile is confident. "It will be, as long as Vijendra believes me to be his most loyal supporter."

Jayendu smirks. "Then why did you ask for this meeting? As you say, the prize is yours."

Vikrant leans forward. "When Vijendra chose me as his successor, you were furious, because you did not approve of his choice. I have the same complaint about your choice, my lord."

Jayendu watches him through narrowed eyes. *The boy has been trained well*

Jayendu glances at Atulya. There can be no doubt. The schoolmaster may keep his silence, but the words were written by his hand.

Vikrant continues. "Lord Atulya informs me you have long held to the notion that Saravat needs an Emperor. One ruler, to unite all five kingdoms. A few months ago, I would have disagreed. But now I sit before you, a believer. Our peace is fragile. It needs a strong ruler."

"Vijendra is that strong ruler," says Jayendu, his tone adamant.

"Come now, old friend," Atulya scoffs. "Surely you do not still hold to that." He takes Jayendu's silence as a sign to continue. "I recall those long discussions, sometimes lasting late into the night. Saravat needs an Emperor who would unite the land, keep it safe and serve it faithfully. That is not Vijendra."

"His mistake was choosing me," Vikrant says. "Not exactly what you had in mind for his heir. Naavipur is a small kingdom, and their Princes are traders, not fighters. Your only other choice was Prince Sreedharan." He smiles. "He would not have been my first choice. But I can understand your reasoning."

"Ruthless," Jayendu declares, "That was my criteria. We need a leader who will do what it takes. I had commanded Vijendra to kill your father, then march to Simhasthal and end the royal line. Yet he chose not to." He searches for any sign of anger on Vikrant's face, but finds none. "I am an old man now, Your Majesty. But in my youth, I travelled the world. There are enemies beyond the sea, bloodthirsty barbarians who would destroy our way of life. Saravat itself has seen it twice before. Once, when the Vajras crossed the Dakshinasagara and conquered three-fourths of the continent. And then again, when your ancestors came down the mountains and annexed half of Vajrapur. Their greed was limited, but who is to say the next horde might not want it all?"

"I agree," Vikrant says. "I did not come here to dispute the need for an Emperor. Only the man who must sit on the throne." His voice falters for a moment. "Did you not consider anyone else? Any other King?"

Jayendu recognises the emotion, and smiles. "You speak of your father, of course," he says, and his tone softens. "To be honest, I admired King Giridhar, and I did consider him for Emperor. But yours is a proud clan, and I know he would never have agreed."

"He would not have," Vikrant admits. "Still, he died for your ambition. As have thousands of others. I ask that you do not let their sacrifices go to waste."

"I hope it will not, Your Majesty," Jayendu says. "Still, it does not answer why I should trust you."

Vikrant's smile touches his eyes, which pierce into Jayendu. "You have plotted to kill my family, planned the battle which led to my father's death, schemed to have my betrothed married off to another Prince. And yet, here I sit with you. Scheming against my future father-in-law, marrying the daughter of my father's murderer, and sentencing my brother to death for my cause."

His voice is strong, his gaze intense, and Jayendu can see the determination that lurks behind them.

"If you consider Vijendra ruthless," Vikrant continues, "What am I?"

Jayendu does not know how to react, and a turmoil rages within him. A strange feeling, one which he has never felt before, not even when his wife died.

Vikrant senses his inner conflict, and lays a gentle hand on the old man's shoulder. "You believe Sreedharan to be the heir. I believe it should be me. So let the two of us settle the matter, once and for all." His grasp tightens. "I ask you to forget about the past and the present. Let us think of the future. Leave Vijendra out of this. We do not need him. Not anymore. Allow me to lead our armies in the conquest of Saravat, and challenge the Trilohan Prince. If I win, I promise to unite the five kingdoms under my rule. And if he defeats me, you will have been proved right." He pauses a moment, and when he speaks again, it is with kindness. "Either way, you will leave this world knowing Saravat is in safe hands."

An impressive offer. Jayendu thinks back to all the stories he has heard of the scared little boy, who has turned out far more intelligent than anyone could have guessed.

Still, he finds himself unwilling to agree. "I love Vijendra like a son."

"You love Saravat more," Atulya argues.

Jayendu smiles at him. "Perhaps, but not by too much. I have sacrificed everything for him."

"Is that why you made him King?" Vikrant asks.

Jayendu's body goes rigid. The ache in his knees intensifies, and the throbbing of his heart quickens, sending blood racing to his brain, where a million thoughts gather at once to torment him.

What does the boy know? "Speak plainly, Your Majesty."

"It's something I have heard spoken about you," Vikrant says. "Lord Jayendu is not a man to sit by and let Kings and Princes ruin his plans."

Jayendu smiles. "I am not."

"You only choose certainties," Atulya chimes in. "You chose Vijendra. And we know you chose him when he was yet a boy, with two older brothers in line to the throne before him. We need to know what made you certain he would become King."

Jayendu shakes his head. "My dear friend, if I tell you that, you will be able to secure the loyalty of every Vajra who lives and breathes. Rannveer, Biraj, the army, everyone."

Atulya exchanges a surprised look with his King, then turns to face Jayendu. "If you could manage such a momentous feat, my lord, the gods themselves would be jealous of you."

Jayendu chortles and rubs his knees. "The gods send me pain everyday, only to remind me of how mortal I am. No, my friend, it is no great feat. Only a secret. A dirty lie I have kept to myself for many years."

"What secret, my lord?" Vikrant asks.

Should I tell them, Jayendu wonders. He weighs his options. Even armed with the truth, the boy King may prove no match for Vijendra, who has forged his destiny with a sweet tongue and a cruel mind.

Still, the Simhasthali deserves the chance to try.

Jayendu decides to reveal the truth. Atulya and Vikrant are surprised. No, they are shocked, horrified, and he wonders if they still desire to be his allies.

Vikrant recovers first and clears all doubts. "Perhaps you should have been Emperor, my lord."

Jayendu shakes his head. "It was not my idea, Your Majesty. It was Vijendra's. When he told me his plan, in that moment, I knew he would be the best person for the job. But now—" He sighs. "I do not give you my support. Only the chance to succeed. Ask your Lord Ayushmann to meet with Prince Biraj and General Kashyap. I will give you all the information you need to convince them both."

Atulya nods his head. "We thank you, old friend."

"Keep Saravat safe," Jayendu says. "That is all the thanks I need."

He bows his head. The Simhasthalis walk to the other side of the boat and leave him to mourn.

And so he mourns. The loss of a friend, a son, his partner in crime for so many years. Together, they had pursued this dream. And now, so close to achieving it, all his meticulous planning has come to naught.

He laughs to himself. Despite his failure, it appears Saravat will get the Emperor it truly deserves.

CHAPTER SIXTY-TWO

A grateful Rannveer thanks the gods for the day's break. The frivolous festivities which precede a wedding have always challenged his disciplined mind. Give him a sword and an enemy any day of the week. The thought brings a smile to his face. On the morrow, the wedding will be done with.

And then, they will ride to war.

He has waited twenty-seven years for this moment. A long and distinguished career already, with his greatest battles yet to be fought.

Rannveer knows the war for Saravat will not be easy. Many papers pile on his desk, with disturbing reports from the other kingdoms. The Naaviks have hired the Jahati Brigade to shore up their numbers, and the Trilohans have contracted the Barabos Battalion.

He does not know which one is worse. The thought of mercenaries on Saravati land offends his patriotic nature, yet he cannot deny their value. They are fearsome warriors, who will prove tough to defeat on the battlefield. And if the two kingdoms form an alliance, then…

He sets the thought aside. He will not doubt his King. Not again. He remembers how he had feared going to battle against Simhasthal. But Vijendra's strategy had worked, and his army had prevailed. Once the King reads these reports, Rannveer is certain he will devise a strategy to counter them both.

His men arrive, eager to take advantage of his presence. They occupy his time with reports of bandits in the Andhakaranya, or with requests for leave, or with good tidings in their family. He does not turn away a single man. They are like family, prepared to lay down their lives for him, as he is for them.

Noon passes before he the last of them comes and goes, and he rides back home for a leisurely meal with his wife.

He smiles as she rushes out to greet him. But the smile vanishes, once he sees her face riddled with anxiety.

"What is the matter?" he asks, as he jumps off his horse.

"We have an unexpected guest," Kruttika says.

A guest? "Who?"

The fear grows in her eyes. "Lord Ayushmann."

The Queen's bastard brother.

The General's lips curl into a grimace. He does not like this one bit, but he must remain calm, for Kruttika's sake at least. He gives her a reassuring peck on the forehead, then makes his way to his living room.

Ayushmann lazes on a divan, sipping a lemon sherbet and admiring his surroundings. He stands when he sees Rannveer approach. "General, my sincere apologies to your wife. I fear I startled her with my unexpected arrival."

Rannveer gestures for him to take his seat, then takes a chair facing him. "I confess to being equally surprised, my lord."

"Then my apologies to you as well," says Ayushmann, his ingratiating smile stretched wide across his face. "I come with a message from Lord Jayendu."

The casual mention of Jayendu's name startles Rannveer. *What game is the old man playing?*

If Ayushmann speaks the truth, and his relaxed behaviour strongly suggests he does, then Jayendu has decided to back King Vikrant. This is good news, which should gladden his heart. Vijendra and Jayendu on the same side would only strengthen their cause.

Then why do I feel afraid? "What is the message?" Rannveer asks.

Ayushmann's smile mocks him. "You appear nervous, General."

"I am," Rannveer replies honestly. "Your words and actions do not inspire confidence."

Ayushmann laughs. "Fear not, General. I am on your side, and always have been. You are important to us."

"I am only a soldier," says Rannveer, a bitter edge to his voice.

"But not an ordinary one," says Ayushmann. The laughter subsides, the smile vanishes, and his face turns grim. "You are *the* soldier, General. *The key.* The key to save Saravat."

Understanding dawns at once. They desire control of the Vajra army. *Through me.*

The implication is clear. Jayendu has not just thrown his support behind Vikrant, he now allies with the Simhasthalis and seeks to depose King Vijendra. A treasonous act, which the old man will pay for with his life.

I will see to it myself, Rannveer promises himself.

Ayushmann must have read his thoughts, for he speaks kindly. "General, think long and hard before you act. Lord

Jayendu is not a foolish man, and he must have found good cause to support my King. Believe me, so will you."

Rannveer glares at him. "I find no reason to believe you. As for my loyalty, it is not for sale."

Ayushmann chuckles. "I fear you do have a price. Just like everyone else."

"That may be true in Simhasthal," Rannveer scoffs. "Your gold holds no worth for me."

"I respect you far too much for that, General," Ayushmann says. His voice strengthens with belief. "Instead, I offer to win you over. With the truth."

What truth, Rannveer wonders.

He must have spoken the words out loud, for Ayushmann smiles. A sad smile.

Rannveer senses his pity. *But why?*

"It is a cruel truth," Ayushmann says. "One which I fear will break your heart." He walks over and looks kindly at the General. "The message from Lord Jayendu is this. He begs you to trust him for one more night, and asks you to meet with me on the road to Ilaava. At midnight. You will see what I have to show you, and hear a terrible story. At the end of it, if you remain unconvinced, then you may inform King Vijendra of our activities, and we will gladly confess to the crime."

Rannveer studies him with hateful eyes, his anger not directed at the Simhasthali, but at his own misfortune. So close to the war he desired, and the man who brought them all to its precipice appears to have thrown in the towel.

Still, I will give him tonight. Rannveer owes the old man that much. Jayendu found him when he was a nobody, a lowly captain, and made him the General he is today. He does not know what information Jayendu wishes him to see, but he will hear it, and then present the complete treachery to his King.

Rannveer glares at the Simhasthali and nods his head. "I will see you at midnight."

Ayushmann smiles. "I thank you, General." He makes to leave, then stops and turns around. "I almost forgot. Lord Jayendu also requested the presence of Prince Biraj with us tonight. I fear the truth will be important to him as well."

You did not forget, you only waited for me to agree. "I will send a message. But I do not guarantee His Highness will agree."

"He will," Ayushmann says, "If you word the message correctly."

"If you say so," Rannveer replies gruffly. Then curiosity gets the better of him. "Why do we need the Prince?"

Ayushmann smiles. "The lock we must pick needs two keys. You are one. Biraj is the other."

With those strange words, he leaves. Rannveer heads over to the table to pour himself a cup of madeira. He drains the glass in one go, then pours himself another, and drinks that as well. Frustration continues to build in his mind, and he can hear the gods laughing. Our plans were too well laid for their liking.

He sets the cup down. Time to write the message, and choose a loyal messenger. He heads to his study, when the sudden thought of tomorrow's wedding comes to his mind.

He shakes his head. *I wonder if it will even take place.*

CHAPTER SIXTY-THREE

Nandini gazes out the window, watching nature burst with life in the gardens. The birds are in fine fettle today, and their singsong mischief flutters among the branches.

She shakes her head, and a wry smile crosses her face. *I might have liked the city, if my husband's killer were not its ruler.*

Kashyap intrudes her thoughts. "I wonder what Giridhar would have said about our situation."

She turns to face him. "He would have thrown Vikrant over his lap and given him a few good whacks."

Despite their circumstances, Kashyap laughs loudly, and she finds herself laughing as well. She is grateful for his company in these difficult times. Whom else could she turn to? Her son?

Your King, she reminds herself, her flesh and blood, who means nothing to her now, the way her feelings mean nothing to him.

"Did I fail as a mother?" she asks.

Kashyap shakes his head. "You were a good mother to your children. And Giridhar was a good father. How they turned out is not your fault."

Nandini wants to believe him. But how can she? Two of her three children remain devoted to the land that made them. And the third—

"I tried to love my children the same," she says. "But I seem to have gone wrong with Vikrant."

"You may have loved them the same," Kashyap says, "But life tasks them with different roles. Gayathri, a mother and wife. Indranuj, a soldier and a follower. Vikrant, a King. That is what shapes them." He sighs wistfully. "It was the same for Giridhar and I. Our mother loved us equally, but he was always meant to be King, and I the soldier."

"You speak the truth," Nandini says. "But I still wonder how my son could prove so selfish and ambitious."

"I do not think that of Vikrant," Kashyap says. "I cannot."

The poor man, Nandini thinks. *This must as hard for him as it is for me.*

Vikrant and Indranuj were the sons Kashyap never had, and they grew up in his arms, just as they did in Giridhar's. Her mind wanders back to those good old days. Giridhar and Kashyap taking the boys to the festival games. Kashyap teaching first Vikrant, then Indranuj how to wield a sword. All of them swimming in the river.

Simpler times, to which she longs to return. But they will never return. Her son has seen to it, by breaking her heart, turning it to stone, and crumbling it to pieces for all time to come. Indranuj's sentence will be carried out in a few days. A part of her flesh, gone from this world forever.

Will I ever recover, Nandini wonders. "When Atulya arrived with the news of Giridhar's death, I went to your mother's room. She is the strongest woman I have ever known. But in that moment, her world collapsed." The memory causes her to shiver. "Soon, that will be my fate."

"It will not," Kashyap says.

"My son commands it," Nandini scoffs. "Who can stop him?"

Kashyap's voice chokes. "I may have to agree with my King's decision," he says, "But I will not see it carried out."

Nandini's heart jumps within her breast. *Do I hear correctly?* "What do you mean?"

Kashyap shifts uncomfortably, knowing he spoke out of turn. "Do not concern yourself with such matters, Your Highness."

Nandini does not let him off so easily. "Have you planned something? What is it? I beg you, do not hide this from me."

Kashyap regards her warily. His mind appears in turmoil, unable to reveal the truth.

At long last, he sighs. "Tonight, while the kingdom sleeps, five of my most trusted men will sneak into the prison and break Indranuj out. I have given them detailed instructions. They will see him safely returned to Simhasthal, and hide him there. Do not worry. Your son will live."

Hope springs once more within Nandini's heart, but fear quickly returns to consume it. "Kashyap, if you do this, Vikrant will have your head."

"It will not come to that," Kashyap says. "Do not worry, Your Highness. My men will not fail." He lowers his eyes. "And I have to do this. This is all my fault. I seeded the idea in Indranuj's head to seek revenge in the arena."

Nandini glares at him, stunned. She cannot believe her ears.

"What do you mean?" she demands to know.

Kashyap looks up, and she can see the shame in his eyes. "I only meant for him to make it look like an accident, one easily dismissed in the heat of the contest. I did not expect him to take it this far."

Nandini acts out of instinct. *A mother's instinct. A mother's fury.*

Her right hand arcs through the air and cracks against Kashyap's cheek with all its might. He grimaces, but the sting he feels is nothing compared to the pain in her heart.

Everyone plays their own game; everyone seeks their own vengeance. They do not care about her children. Not Atulya, who twists the mind of her older son. Nor Kashyap, who put her younger son at death's door.

"How could you, Kashyap?" she accuses him. "The boy has a temper, and you stoked it to the point where he could not see reason."

Kashyap hangs his head in shame. "The blame lies with me, and I will willingly give my life for it. But Indranuj will live. I promise you that."

And my cup of sorrow overflows. Nandini weeps, for he does not understand. Kashyap will return her son to her, and in the bargain, cost her a brother. A rock, who has always stood by me and mine. *How will life ever be the same?*

"I would see you both live," Nandini says. She grabs him by the shoulders. "Promise me, you will flee with Indranuj, and return to Simhasthal. Hide where you must, and stay alive."

Kashyap does not reply. He remains still, his face a mask of stone.

"Promise me," she commands.

Reluctantly, Kashyap nods his head, and she holds him close. Her tears flow freely as she prays to the gods, begging them with all her heart to keep him safe. And in their kindness, if they could find a way, she asks them to return her sons as well.

Her youngest, who faces the hangman's noose. And her oldest, who has lost his way.

CHAPTER SIXTY-FOUR

"How did my father and you meet?" Vikrant asks.

What prompts the question, Atulya wonders.

He sits in the King's chambers, watching the man who once bounced on his lap as a boy. Anxiety is writ large on both their faces. If all goes as planned, it promises to be a long day, and an even longer night, and of all the questions which will be answered, this seems the most irrelevant.

He smiles at Vikrant. "Why do you ask, Your Majesty?"

"I do not believe I have ever heard the story." Vikrant says.

Atulya understands his intention. Ayushmann has yet to arrive with Rannveer's reply. The wait might run long, and the King seeks to make the time pass faster. He nods his head. Maybe the story of Giridhar and his first meeting might just do the trick.

"We first met thirty-seven years ago," he says. "I was thirteen then, a student at my father's school. You never met him, but he was a famous teacher and philosopher, one of the very best, and people, rich and poor, came to meet him from all over Saravat."

"Then, one day, King Hridhyanshu arrived at our town. A rare privilege, for the townsfolk, and for the administrator of the city, Lord Dilip. But the King did not grace the Governor's home. No, he rode across town to the tiny school on its outskirts, where he stopped to meet my father, who was once his classmate."

"My father rushed out and bowed to the King. 'Your Majesty,' he said, 'It is an honour to receive you.' King Hridhyanshu laughed in return and embraced baba. 'Ani, you fool,' he shouted, 'Is this any way to greet an old friend?' My father could only laugh and return his affection. Then, your grandfather beckoned Giridhar over.'

A smile crosses his face. "I still remember the first time I saw Giridhar. Only seven years of age, already as tall as me, and strong as well. Yet the smile on his face was gentle, and so was his voice. King Hridhyanshu introduced him in the funniest way possible. 'Ani,' he said, 'This is my son, Crown Prince Giridhar. Future King of Simhasthal, and the biggest idiot in my family.'"

Vikrant smiles. "Sounds like *dadaji*. How did my father react?"

"The way he always did," Atulya says. "With cheek. And wit. He stepped forward and bowed to my father, then said, 'I am honoured to make your acquaintance, masterji. My father has informed me your school turns idiots into geniuses. I hope I will not prove too hard a challenge.'"

Vikrant chuckles. "Baba always had a comeback ready."

Atulya laughs as well. "He always did. My baba called me over and introduced us." He leans back in his chair and his eyes water. "I did not know it at the time, but your father and I were to become thick friends over the years. He was closer in age to my brothers. Shubham, who became your teacher, and Priyanshu. But our minds were of the same bent, and it was hard to separate us."

"Did you not feel the same about Kashyap chacha?" Vikrant asks.

A smile crosses Atulya's face as he remembers Kashyap. "By the time he arrived, Akanksha and I were to be wed. I was to be a family man, and a teacher soon, and both occupied my time."

"It had nothing to do with him liking boys?" Vikrant asks.

Atulya chuckles. "No, Your Majesty. I admit it was tougher for him in those days. But Giridhar and I never cared. Love is love. And to be honest, even if people thought it an issue, none would dare tell Kashyap to his face. The man could strangle a lion with his bare hands."

The image of his chacha wrestling a lion brings a smile to Vikrant's face. Atulya is pleased. His King puts on a brave face, but the stress must be eating him up inside.

As it does me. Atulya regards him curiously. "Why did you ask about your father?"

Vikrant blinks furiously, struggling to hold back his tears. "I think of him a lot these days. There have been only two people in my life who have never tried to change me. Him, and you. The two of you have given me strength, courage, wisdom. But not once did you think me less of a Simhasthali because of my nature."

Atulya shakes his head. "Most men are scared to think beyond what they believe. Your father was not like most men. Thankfully, neither was I. All metal is forged in the fire, yet all are not the same. Some are gold, some steel. And a wise man knows to tell which is which."

"Which am I?" Vikrant asks. "Steel? Or gold?"

Atulya smiles. "It depends, Your Majesty, on whether you look within or without."

Vikrant returns his smile. A soft knock sounds on the door, then it opens and an attendant walks in. "Your Majesty, Lord Ayushmann requests an audience."

"Show him in," says Vikrant, his voice betraying his eagerness.

The attendant bows and withdraws. A couple of seconds later, Ayushmann strides through the door and closes it behind him. He bows to the King, before walking over to the cabinet to pour himself a cup of madeira. Once the spirit is within him, he takes a chair.

"What news?" Vikrant asks.

Ayushmann looks pleased with himself. "I have delivered the message to the General. And if I say so myself, I believe I have convinced him. Of course, we will only know at the midnight hour."

His happiness fails to dispel the gloom.

"I wish we did not have to wait so long," Vikrant says. "What about Prince Biraj? Has the General agreed to bring him along?"

Ayushmann nods his head. "Yes, Your Majesty. He will send a message. But I cannot say if the Prince will agree."

"Well, at least the message will be sent," says Vikrant, before turning his attention to the gardens outside.

Does he feel as tired as I do, Atulya wonders. Surely, he must. These past few days and nights have tested their resolve, and now they must have patience. Plenty of it. If the night goes as planned, then the dawn will herald a new beginning.

For them.

And for Saravat.

CHAPTER SIXTY-FIVE

My last night as a Princess.

Idhika wonders how she feels about it. Nervous? Excited? Sad? She cannot say. After all, which Princess has ever been married under such circumstances?

She turns to Gayathri, who spends the night in her chambers, to teach Idhika the ways of Simhasthal and its royal family. But they have spoken little of it, opting instead to drink and talk and pass the time till sleep arrives.

"Were you this nervous before your wedding?" Idhika asks.

Gayathri smiles and shakes her head. "I fear Chandran was more nervous."

Idhika nods her head. "I guess he would have been. Marrying a Princess. Moving into a palace. His life was about to change forever."

"So is yours," Gayathri says.

Idhika does not reply. In a way, their lives are so different, yet so similar. Gayathri's father had commanded Chandran to live in the palace after her wedding. Her father commands Vikrant to do the same.

Yet, the Simha Princess had found peace within her marriage. A husband to support her in every decision. Vikrant, on the other hand—

What were his words? *I am the solution.*

To what problem, she wonders.

Gayathri interrupts her thoughts. "What troubles your mind?"

"Your brother," Idhika replies without hesitation.

Gayathri raises her cup. "To King Vikrant, heir to the imaginary throne of Saravat."

Idhika giggles. Come dawn, she will have a new family. Strangers, one and all. Except for the Princess. She believes the two of them will get along well enough. They have lived similar lives, dreamed similar hopes, and had those hopes burned to ash.

Maybe all women have, and society simply refuses to let them admit it.

"He is a strange man," Idhika says.

"He always has been, from the day he was born," Gayathri says. "He looked like my mother, but it was my father who loved him more."

That's odd. Idhika believed Ranimaa Nandini to be a loving mother. Doting, caring, affectionate, her oldest son the apple of her eye. Then again, she had only met her once. A short meeting, barely a minute long.

"Do not get me wrong," Gayathri continues. "My mother loved him, but she loved Indu and me more. I was her firstborn, he was her last, with Vikrant forever caught in the middle." She drains her cup, then refills it. "But for my father, he was the heir, the chosen one, and he had to be taught. More than others, for he was weak and timid."

"But not stupid?" Idhika asks.

"Never stupid, no," Gayathri admits. "He has always been intelligent. A thinker, not a doer. *An odd Simhasthali,* my chacha used to call him. Unfortunately for me, he was born with a knob of meat between his legs, and I was not." Her face roils in disgust. "Not that I would want one. Such a weird thing to have, dangling all the time. But I do like the power that comes with it."

"We have better powers," Idhika says.

"Like what?" Gayathri asks.

Idhika smiles mischievously. "The power to drain the blood from their brains, and whisper our commands in its absence."

Gayathri laughs heartily, wine spurting from her nose. She wipes her face and continues to chuckle as she raises her cup. "To the greatest power in the world."

Idhika raises her cup as well, and they empty its contents. She refills both their drinks.

"Do you think your mother will change her view of me?" she asks.

Gayathri regards her curiously. "How does she view you now?"

"The daughter of the man who killed her husband," Idhika says.

Gayathri tries to set her mind at ease. "Fear not, Idhika. My mother will not blame you for your father's sins."

"But if Indranuj loses his head," says Idhika, her voice betraying her anxiety, "I will also be the wife of the man who executed her son."

The words hang heavy in the air.

She did not wish to speak it, but it came out nevertheless. How could it not? It has been on her mind since the judgement was pronounced. On the morrow, her new life will begin. But in its aftermath, another's will end.

"When we were growing up," Gayathri says, "Both my brothers treated me like a second mother. I used to feed them, play with them, sing them songs and tell them stories. Even when my children were born, I felt more love for my brothers than I did my flesh and blood."

"Yet you betrayed Vikrant," Idhika says.

"Did I?" asks Gayathri, her voice devoid of guilt. "I betrayed my father, dear Idhika, and I do not regret it. Your father had informed Chandran of his plans for my brother, and the promised reward was greater than anyone could offer. Vikrant would marry a brilliant and beautiful Princess, and would one day be Emperor of Saravat." She sips her madeira and smiles. "I ask you, which mother would not do what I did?"

"What of Indranuj?" Idhika counters. "He faces the hangman's noose."

"I have faith in Vikrant," Gayathri declares. "He will not let anything happen to Indu."

Idhika's regards the Princess curiously. She seems remarkably sure of her brother. "How can you be certain?"

Gayathri smiles. "Set your mind at ease, dear Idhika. Enjoy your last night as a Princess. By noon tomorrow, your life will change forever."

She sets her cup aside, then does the same with Idhika's. The two walk to their respective beds, bid each other a good night's sleep, and get comfortable under the covers. A short while later, Idhika hears the soft snores of Gayathri.

Like a mother to Indranuj and Vikrant, she had said. If she can sleep this comfortably, maybe there is conviction in her faith.

The coming day will reveal the truth of it. For now, she must get some rest. Tomorrow, her life will change forever.

For better or worse, only the future can say.

CHAPTER SIXTY-SIX

Atishi returns to the kitchen to refill the pitcher. She does not rush, for there isn't any need to. She glances at the nightcandle. Midnight is over an hour away.

Carrying the pitcher, she returns to the porch, where Ayushmann stares at the woods, lost in silent contemplation. Atishi smiles. She understands the need for solitude, especially at the end of a stressful day.

The night promises no relief. Ayushmann must ride to Ilaava, in the hope that Rannveer and Biraj will join him. And she must visit King Vikrant's chambers, to wait with him until the minister returns. Their plan is in motion, and the results will be known only once dawn arrives.

Her thoughts turn to her mistress, who spends the night in her chambers with Princess Gayathri. This will be Idhika's last night as a girl, as a Princess.

Tomorrow, she will be a woman. *A Queen.*

Atishi refills their cups and takes her seat. "Do you think Rannveer will come?"

Ayushmann looks at her with tired eyes. "A man arrives at your doorstep. By all appearances, your enemy. Yet he comes carrying information, which he then refuses to reveal, only offering hints as to its importance. At the very least, wouldn't you be curious?"

"I would," Atishi admits. "Yet the General is a committed soldier. And loyal to Vijendra. He might ignore you."

Ayushmann smiles, and even that seems an effort. "Rannveer believes Jayendu to be the source of my information. The secret keeper of Vajrapur himself."

Atishi grimaces. "A most necessary evil."

It saddens her to say it. Worse, it saddens her to believe it. All the ills that have plagued Vajrapur, and now Saravat, can be traced back to one man.

Jayendu.

If not for him, Idhika would have led a Princess' life, free to roam and study and have friends. But Atishi cannot deny he changed her life. When Queen Indrani commanded, it had been Jayendu who had found her out and bought her freedom. Once, before him, her destiny was to remain a whore, to spread her legs for traders and mercenaries. But now, here she sits, plotting to change the destiny of a continent.

They sip their drinks in silence, happy to listen to sounds of the forest. Atishi wonders if this is the life she should aspire for. A house in the woods, a man to keep her company. Simple, sweet, comfortable.

She laughs in her mind. *A bastard and a whore. A good combination.*

"What do you think of?" Ayushmann asks.

"Tomorrow," Atishi replies.

"Do not do that, my dear," he says.

"Why?" she asks.

Ayushmann pours himself some more madeira and sips it slowly, then looks at her and smiles. "Tomorrow is an illusion. Those who do, make it happen. Those who think, it passes by."

"Clever words from a clever man," says Atishi, her voice neither mocking nor cold. "Yet a woman knows better. We always have one eye on tomorrow."

"Even after I have asked you not to?" asks Ayushmann, his eyes teasing.

"Precisely for that reason, my lord," says Atishi, serious. "Women know their tomorrows are decided by men. Sometimes they command, sometimes they ask. But the result is the same."

Ayushmann bows his head. "Then I apologise, and promise never to ask or command." He looks her in the eyes. "And I mean that."

Atishi smiles, knowing that he truly does. The man stands apart from the rest of his sex. If there were thousands like him, perhaps the face of Saravat would change. And it would not take a Vijendra or Jayendu to make it happen.

She places her cup down. "You must head out. Better to arrive early and get the lay of the land."

Ayushmann nods his head. He drains his cup, takes her hand in his and gently kisses the back of her palm. Atishi feels his moustache tickle her skin.

"We shall meet later tonight, my lady," he says, "And together discover what fate has in store for us."

She watches him go. A small part of her wishes to call him back, to hold him in her arms, even if only for a few minutes. But she cannot. There is much for her to do as well.

She sips her madeira in silence and waits for midnight to arrive.

CHAPTER SIXTY-SEVEN

Biraj tosses and turns in his bed, cursing the heat. The covers have been thrown off, as have his clothes, until he sleeps only in his *langot*. But even that doesn't help much.

He turns to glance at the branches outside his window. The leaves do not stir.

It is not the weather, a voice whispers, *it is your mind.*

The past five days have tested them all, especially the 'First Fight', which ended with the head of Captain Dhananjay rolling on the ground. Biraj did not care much for the man, but he was a Vajra, who was murdered in cold blood, and Prince Indranuj's sentence was just.

Biraj feels no pity for the boy. He remembers the Simhasthali's sword stabbing down towards his neck, and how his quick reactions had saved him that day. The boy had come baying for Vajra blood. His wish had been granted, and he must pay its price with his own life.

The death sentence remains a much-discussed topic, which many consider an ill omen for the marriage. Biraj wonders if his brother will pardon the Simha Prince, but so far, Vijendra has given no inclination to do so. Nor has Vikrant requested mercy, which many expected him to do.

Maybe he will tomorrow. And though Biraj wouldn't like it, maybe the King should, if only for Idhika's sake. No Princess… indeed, no woman should be married under such dark clouds.

A year separates them, and Biraj considers himself less of an uncle and more of an older brother. He has always been fond of her, especially during her childhood, when he was among the few permitted to speak to her. She would drown him in questions, questions about the other kingdoms. How they live. What they eat. What they wear.

Maybe this war will last a year. A couple at the most. And then she will be wedded to the heir of Saravat, free to roam wherever and whenever she wants.

He hopes so, for her sake. Not for his own though, for a cruel fate lies in store for him after the war. Vijendra had discussed it with him only a week past. Marriage, which he has been dreading ever since he came of age. He does not wish it. A simple life, that is all he craves. To follow and to obey. Who knows? His wish might be granted. The war might last for years, or the enemy might get lucky, and end his life.

A knock intrudes his thoughts. Biraj turns to the sound, puzzled. *Who could it be at this hour?* He jumps out of bed and opens the door.

An attendant stands outside, a scroll in his hand. He bows, then hands it over. "Apologies, Your Highness. A message from General Rannveer."

Biraj accepts the scroll, thanks the attendant and closes the door. He lights the lamp on his dresser and reads the message.

At midnight, meet me on the road
to Ilaava. Alone.

A strange message at a strange hour. And on the eve of the wedding, no less. After all they have been through this week, he had hoped for a good night's sleep, not a midnight meeting cloaked in mystery.

But it comes from the General, who must have his reasons. Biraj glances at the nightcandle. Midnight is a couple of hours away. Plenty of time to get ready and leave.

He retires to bed, more uncomfortable than before, and tosses and turns as his mind continues to be plagued with uncomfortable thoughts. At the appointed time, he dresses and leaves for the stables. There, he wakes up a drowsy attendant, who runs to fetch the Prince's horse.

Biraj arrives at the outskirts of Ilaava to find the General waiting for him, along with two other men. Datta, the household head who has served Jayendu for almost thirty-five years.

And Lord Ayushmann.

"What is the meaning of this?" asks Biraj, confused by the Simhasthali's presence.

Rannveer's reply only adds to it. "Lord Jayendu has sent them," he says. "They mean to show us something."

"Show us what?" Biraj asks.

Rannveer shrugs. "I do not know. But once we have seen it, we shall speak to the King, inform him of Jayendu's treacherous activities, and see what he commands."

None of this makes sense. "What treacherous activities?"

"Allow me to remove the confusion," Ayushmann speaks up. "Your Highness, the General is trying to inform you is that Lord Jayendu has thrown his support behind King Vikrant in the war for Saravat."

Biraj does not know how to react. *Jayendu? With Vikrant?* The old man has always been one of Vijendra's staunchest supporters. *Was,* if what Ayushmann says is true, which it surely is. The presence of Datta, riding alongside the Simhasthali, provides indisputable confirmation.

Biraj cannot deny his curiosity is piqued, but not enough to commit treason against his King.

Against my brother. "If Lord Jayendu and King Vikrant conspire against my King, I wish them luck." He turns to Rannveer. "And you as well, General, if you do not have the good sense to return with me this very moment."

Rannveer stares at him, his mind in turmoil. Biraj understands. He wants to unearth what plans the old man has hatched with Vikrant, and bring it to Vijendra's attention.

So be it. Biraj will inform his brother of the General's intentions. He turns his horse around and makes to leave, when Ayushmann calls out.

"I beg you to stay, Your Highness," says the Simhasthali, with genuine concern. "The truth I seek to reveal concerns you directly."

The man pricks at my curiosity again. Biraj reins his horse in and looks behind. "In what way?"

Ayushmann smiles, knowing he has hooked his fish. "It's the reason you were born. And the reason your mother died."

He wins my curiosity over. Biraj finds himself unable to come to a decision. Stay, and he proves to Ayushmann that he can be turned against his brother and his kingdom. Leave, and the alliance will come to an end this very instant.

Maybe it already has.

Biraj decides Rannveer has the right of it. It is better that he sees the information, and then returns to the palace. He turns his horse back around.

"I will accompany you," he says to Ayushmann. "And I will listen to what you have to say. Then I will see you to prison."

Ayushmann bows his head. "If it comes to that, Your Highness, I promise, I will resist."

He nods his head at Datta, who leads the way. They ride in silence through the sleeping village, each lost to their own thoughts. Once they pass its end, they come across a path which cuts through the fields on the right. They take it, riding for half a mile until they reach a fork in the road. They turn left here, ride another mile, reach another fork, and cut to the right.

After two hundred metres on this narrow track, they arrive at a farm, which consists of two small cottages of equal size adjoining each other. A dead place, with lamps and torches unlit. Datta dismounts and the others follow his lead. They hobble their horses, then make their way to cottage on the right.

Datta knocks on the door. There is no answer. He knocks again, loudly, and shouts out as well.

"Shaukat!" his voice booms in the silent night, drowning the chirps of the crickets and the bats.

A noise sounds within, and a man's feeble voice calls out. "Coming, coming."

Through the stained-glass window, they see a light flicker. The door opens, and an old man stands before them, his wrinkled hands straining to hold the lamp up.

"Who is it?" Shaukat brings the light closer, and his cataracted eyes widen. "General Rannveer, Prince Biraj." His gaze turns to Ayushmann. "And... forgive me, my lord. I do not recognise you."

Ayushmann smiles. "I am Lord Ayushmann. Of Simhasthal."

Shaukat chuckles. "Are you now? I heard you are the Queen's brother, the one whom she prayed was dead."

Biraj bristles at the disrespectful mention of his sister-in-law, but Ayushmann laughs. "I am indeed, my friend. And I do not blame her. If you knew me, you too would wish I were dead."

Shaukat laughs heartily, then waves them in. "Come, come. I am afraid my home is not worthy of receiving such distinguished guests as yourselves. But it will have to do."

Datta remains with the horses, while the others follow him to a small living room, where he gestures for them to take a divan. He then heads to the kitchen, returning a minute later with cups and a pitcher of arrack. He pours a cup for each of them, then himself, before sitting on the only chair in the room.

"I hoped the gods would bring you to my doorstep before I died," he says to Biraj and Rannveer. "And now, here you sit." He senses their hesitation. "Drink, drink. It is not as good as the madeira in the palace, but it is good arrack."

Ayushmann and Biraj take small sips, but Rannveer leaves his drink untouched. "The most influential man I know said you have important information of some kind. Information that concerns Prince Biraj and me."

"I do," the old man says.

"Would you care to share it with us?" Biraj asks.

Shaukat fixes his gaze on the Prince. "Your Highness, do you know what I am?"

"I do not," Biraj admits.

"I am a potion master," Shaukat declares. "The very best in the land."

What secrets can a potion master reveal? Biraj does not attempt to hide his confusion. "You mean you make medicines?'

Shaukat smiles, his shrivelled lips cold and cruel. "I also made poisons."

Poison? Biraj exchanges a quick glance with Rannveer, then glances at Ayushmann. The Simhasthali sits relaxed, as if this conversation is proceeding exactly as he planned.

Biraj turns to Shaukat. "How does that concern me? Or the General?"

Shaukat chuckles. "I will tell you, if you promise not to kill me where I sit."

An exasperated Biraj nods his head, and Rannveer does the same. This seems to satisfy Shaukat, who gulps the remainder of his arrack and stands. He holds the lamp up, his pale face almost ghost-like in the light.

"You have to understand," he says. "I did the deed because the Prince—" He corrects himself, "no, he is the King now. I did what King Vijendra commanded me to." He gestures for them to follow him. "Come, it is better if I show you."

He leads them outside the house, then crosses across to the other cottage. He unlatches the door and lets them in.

What a strange room, Biraj thinks to himself.

It is filled with shelf after shelf of colourful liquids—green, yellow, blue, red, purple, white—which glow in the light of the lamp as the men walk by. Shaukat sets the lamp down and lights a couple others. He then heads to a shelf and picks up two vials.

He sets one down on the table. The liquid within shines a bright green. Biraj wonders what kind of poison it is, and what connection it has with him. Shaukat removes another vial, this one with a white liquid, and sets it down beside the first. Rannveer's eyes widen with recognition.

Biraj is surprised by the look on the General's face. *He has seen this medicine before.*

Shaukat points to the green one. "This one is a poison, which I created myself." He holds up the white. "And like all good potion masters, I also made an antidote."

The impatience in Biraj's voice wears thin. "I am sure you are good at your job. However, if you could tell us what this poison does, it would be helpful."

Fear clouds the old man's eyes, and his voice trembles as he speaks. "It causes the fever." *The fever.*

For a few seconds, Biraj does not understand. Then he does, and he wishes the earth would open up and swallow him whole. The implications of what the old man says races through his mind. If Vijendra ordered this, then he has the blood of thousands of innocents on his hands. Not Simhasthalis, not Trilohans, nor Naaviks, nor Saptas.

Vajra blood.

He can feel a similar anger in Rannveer, who stands by his side, fists clenched and tremors coursing through his body. Biraj knows of whom he thinks. His father, whom the fever took before old age could. And his son, the little boy who never faced this cruel and unforgiving world.

Biraj looks at the two vials which rest before Shaukat. Innocent looking pieces of clear crystal glass, holding life and death inside. The green caused the deaths of his mother and brothers. The white gave him life.

And saved Vijendra as well.

Biraj shakes his head, trying to banish the thought. "I cannot believe it."

"It is hard to believe," Shaukat admits.

"Yet you claim it to be the truth," Biraj accuses him.

"Sadly, Your Highness," Shaukat says, "I do not have to claim it. I know it to be true. I am as guilty as your brother in this matter. Thankfully, I will face the gods soon enough, and hear their judgement." He smiles wryly. "I think we all know what that judgement will be."

"Indeed we do," says Ayushmann, speaking for the first time since they entered the room. His voice is kind. "You only followed orders, my dear Shaukat, and I hope the gods will show you some mercy."

Shaukat smiles at him gratefully, but Ayushmann already turns to face Biraj and Rannveer, and his voice hardens as he presses the issue. "But now, Your Highness, General, you have a decision to make. My King requests your support. Will you give it?"

Rannveer is the first to react, and Biraj could swear he has never seen the General so despondent. He does not reply, nor does he acknowledge the Simhasthali's request with a gesture of any sort. Instead, he storms out of the room, and a few seconds later, they hear the sound of hoofbeats racing away.

Biraj turns to face Ayushmann, who looks at him with fervent hope.

My decision will turn the tide. "What does King Vikrant ask of me?"

Ayushmann tells him.

Biraj is surprised. "Is that all?"

Ayushmann smiles and nods his head. "For now, yes."

Biraj thinks the request over in his mind. After a long deliberation, he gives his answer. "It will be done."

Ayushmann beams. He bows to the Prince. "On behalf of my King, on behalf of Simhasthal, and on behalf of Saravat, I thank you, Your Highness."

Biraj bows his head, then returns to his horse and rides back to Dhaningarh.

CHAPTER SIXTY-EIGHT

Vikrant makes his way down the heavy stone steps. Dawn is a few hours away. With it, will come a new morning. And his wedding. He casts the thought aside. He has more important business to attend to.

He passes through the entrance of the prison and sees his brother.

The cell is small, but as Vijendra promised, it has been made comfortable. A thick mattress has been provided, and on it, Indranuj rests. He must have heard the soft footsteps, and his red, watery eyes glare back at Vikrant.

He was not expecting me. "Hello, little brother."

Indranuj's lips curl in disgust. "Did you beg Vijendra's permission to come see me?"

The barb doesn't sting. Quite the opposite. Vikrant smiles. "Vijendra is not aware of my visit. Prince Biraj arranged it."

Indranuj laughs. "So, now you grovel before the Prince? Isn't that beneath you, Your Majesty?"

Vikrant's smile remains. "To see my brother? No. But I did not have to grovel. He was only too happy to see to my request."

His easy demeanour unnerves Indranuj. "You are to be wed in the morning."

"I am," Vikrant says.

"Shouldn't you be resting?" Indranuj taunts him.

Vikrant pulls a chair from the corner and brings it closer to the bars. "I thought I could spend a few minutes with my brother. Maybe he would like to congratulate me on my upcoming nuptials."

Indranuj watches him from his cell. Their eyes lock, and neither blinks. Vikrant resists the urge to smile. Their actions are childish, yet they feel so good.

When they were children, they would settle arguments this way. First, they would fight, then spend hours staring at one another until one of them gave in. It never occurred to them to storm off to separate rooms.

Brothers can fight, but brothers cannot part ways.

Vikrant knows he must now be the mature one. After all, he is King, and also four years older than Indranuj. Yet he cannot give in. *I must have the upper hand in our discussion.*

The minutes tick away, and Vikrant is impressed. He did not expect Indranuj to hold back his rage this long. Just as the thought crosses his mind, his brother caves.

"I cannot believe you are still going to marry her," Indranuj shouts in frustration. "Why, dada? Why are you doing this?"

How do I make him understand, Vikrant wonders. He knows there is little he can say to convince his brother. Their father never spent time teaching him the value of thinking ahead, which is what Vikrant does at the moment. Plan for the future. Not just for himself, but for their kingdom.

"Indu, I know you are upset," he says. "But you have to trust me. Everything I do, bitter though it may taste right now, is for the betterment of our family and our kingdom."

"I am trying to trust you, dada," Indranuj says. "But you have to make me understand."

"I cannot," Vikrant says. "I cannot, because I was given an impossible choice."

"If you had to marry anyone, you could have married Princess Jyothika," Indranuj insists.

"I could have," Vikrant says. "But then, I would be allied with Prince Sreedharan. King Theeran may be just as bad as Vijendra, but his son is another level of cruel."

"How bad can he be?" Indranuj asks.

Worse than you can imagine. "Sreedharan has a bloodlust all of Saravat cannot sate. Even his own father keeps him away from their capital so that death does not wander its streets. I decided it would be better to ally with the man who killed our father than be seen in the same camp as that monster."

Indranuj does not pass any comment. Instead, he resumes his silent treatment from earlier.

Vikrant sighs in exasperation. "Do you remember the time I taught you to swim?"

He had been nine years old then. Indranuj had been five, and terrified of the water. But Vikrant had loved nothing more than to head to the river and swim the afternoons away.

The river flowed down the mountains and into the valley a few miles from the fortress. In the winters, which lasted six months of the year, it would turn to ice. But in the summer, the water ran warm enough for a dip.

Indranuj had hated the water. Still, he would love going there with his dada. He would sit on the river bank and watch as Vikrant did somersaults, or dove under and re-emerged fifty metres away. He would then clap and cheer, and ask his brother to do it once more.

"I remember you tiring of my excuses," Indranuj says. "You demanded I learn to swim."

When Indranuj had refused to learn, Vikrant had dragged him into the water.

"Hold my hand, Indu," Vikrant had said, "And trust me. I will not let you go."

Indranuj had reluctantly obeyed. He had tightened his grip on Vikrant's hand and let his brother lead him in until the water lapped his chin.

Vikrant had placed a hand on the back of his head. "Now I need you to relax, and let your feet float."

Indranuj had done as he was told, and his feet had risen in the water. For a moment, panic had gripped him, but then he had felt his brother's reassuring hand on his back, and he came to lie upon the water.

They had floated the rest of the afternoon, and not once did they let go of each other's hand. The following day, Vikrant had taught him the basic strokes and breathing techniques. Within a month, Indranuj was able to swim on his own, and soon came to love the water as much as his dada.

"Those were happier times," Indranuj says.

"Maybe it can be so again," Vikrant says.

Indranuj looks at him, curious. Vikrant falls silent. He does not speak for a long while, and fixes his gaze at the entrance. A few minutes later, footsteps sound on the stairs outside, running towards them, and his face breaks into a smile.

"Finally," Vikrant declares. He turns to Indranuj. "I was beginning to believe they would never arrive."

Indranuj has no clue what he speaks of. He stands and holds the bars of his cell.

A few seconds later, Captain Dushyant bursts through the entrance with four Simhasthali soldiers. They freeze when they spot their King sitting before them. They first look surprised, then afraid.

"Captain Dushyant," Vikrant greets them warmly. "I trust your break in was easy?"

"It was, Your Majesty," Dushyant replies instinctively, though he remains puzzled by his King's casual demeanour. Surprise appears on his face, as he suddenly realises. "There were no guards outside."

"I know," Vikrant says. "I had asked for them to be removed."

"You asked—?" Dushyant does not understand.

"Do not let this concern you," Vikrant says. "Please return to General Kashyap and Colonel Gautam. Inform them that I have taken the matter of Prince Indranuj's well-being in my own hands. If they would be so kind as to visit me an hour after dawn, I will fill them in on the details."

Dushyant stands rooted to the spot, as do his men, unsure of what to do next.

Vikrant walks up to him and his voice turns cold as ice. "Are you refusing my command, Captain?"

Dushyant jumps out of his stupor and bows his head. "No, Your Majesty. I will follow it to the letter."

He orders his men to fall out. Once their footsteps have faded, Vikrant turns to Indranuj. His brother is as confused as his soldiers, but now is not the time to explain.

"You remember when I taught you how to swim?" Vikrant asks. "You trusted me that day. I ask that you do the same now."

Indranuj nods. Vikrant reaches through the bars and pulls him close. He gently kisses his forehead.

"I must leave you now, little brother," he says, then pretends to be serious. "The time has come for me to face the dreaded spectre of marriage."

"You still intend to marry her?" Indranuj asks.

Vikrant smiles and nods. "Believe me when I say this, little brother. Idhika will be the greatest Queen Simhasthal has ever had."

His brother remains silent. Vikrant does not bother convincing him. He knows it in his heart that his words will be proven true. Idhika will be a great Queen.

And a great Empress.

CHAPTER SIXTY-NINE

Is this really happening to me?

Indrani did not believe it could. Yet she feels it. A mother's anxiety. When was the last time she had felt this way? A lifetime ago, when her first son was about to be delivered. It had lasted a week then, and ended when he was born, dead, a lump of flesh and bone in her arms.

She had cried then, the way she feels like doing now.

Her daughter will soon leave her. It matters little that she will remain in her kingdom. Indrani will give her away, to be a wife and a mother, and live a life apart.

Carrying this unexpected ache in her heart, she enters her daughter's chambers, where Gayathri and a few handmaidens fuss over Idhika, perfecting her make up and jewellery. The two Princesses stand when Indrani walks in.

The Queen cannot take her eyes off Idhika. A vision in red, an ethereal beauty. She surprises Idhika by taking her face in her hands and laying a gentle kiss on her forehead.

Idhika wonders what has come over her mother. "Maa?"

"You look beautiful, my child," says Indrani, emotion welling in her eyes.

"A reflection of her mother, Your Majesty," Gayathri comments.

Indrani turns to face her. "You are kind to say so, Your Highness. But I believe I stand but a pale shadow of my daughter's brilliance."

Idhika has never heard her speak this way. "Are you okay, maa?"

Indrani smiles, and forces her tears to retreat. "Never better. Are you ready?"

Idhika nods her head.

"Then come," Indrani says. "Let us not keep your King waiting."

She draws the pallu over her daughter's head, takes her hand, and they leave together for the wedding *mandap*, while Gayathri returns to join the guests.

They pass through the corridors, perfumed by the sweet scent of marigolds which deck the walls. In the gardens outside, the guests are seated, and their chatter passes through the archways and into the palace. Indrani cannot make out what they say, but she feels their excitement.

This is the wedding they have been waiting for. The wedding which will change the fate of Saravat.

She halts under an arch and turns to her daughter. "I know I have treated your cruelly. But I hope one day you will see that I had to. For this moment. We have trained you for it all your life." She squeezes Idhika's hand. "You are my daughter. You have my beauty and my intelligence. Make them your strengths, and all that we have promised will be yours."

Indrani can feel Idhika's fingers tense, and for a moment, she wonders if a barb might come flying her way. Then, the fingers relax, and Idhika smiles. She nods her head, and Indrani kisses her forehead once more.

She turns to a herald, who stands twenty feet away, and nods at him. The man nods his acknowledgement, then turns to the other side and gestures to the herald on the far side. Indrani knows who stands there.

Ranimaa Nandini. And King Vikrant.

The herald turns once more to her and nods his head.

The moment arrives.

Still holding her daughter's hand, Indrani leads her through the arch. All eyes turn towards them. Few, if any, will watch Vikrant and Nandini. No, they will look at Idhika, and Indrani, for they are the true power in this alliance.

Two aisles have been cut through the seating arrangements, a 'v-shape' that meets at the mandap. Indrani leads her daughter down one, Nandini brings her son down the other. This is their motherly right, to give away the children they bore for nine months and fed life from their own bodies. Now, they will finally break the umbilical cord, and their children will move on with new partners.

The thought brings tears to her eyes. Genuine tears of sorrow, for she never intended to fake them. Indrani hates the idea that her subjects will see her this way, an ordinary woman and mother, saddened at the thought of her child departing for another home.

This is the only time she will allow it.

They arrive at the mandap, in step with Nandini and Vikrant. The priests rhythmically pour ghee into the fire, which burns hot and high. A good omen, one which signifies the blessings of the gods for this union.

The mothers turn to face one another, and Indrani is not surprised to see the grief in Nandini's face.

One son gets married. Another waits for the hangman's noose.

No mother's heart is large enough to deal with such conflict. Indrani feels a drop of pity for her, but not more. If Vijendra had fallen on the Laalkhet, she doubts Nandini would have shown her much sympathy.

She holds out Idhika's hand, which Nandini accepts and places in Vikrant's. A sad smile crosses their faces, as the same thought runs through their minds. *My flesh and blood, I now hand you to another.*

Idhika and Vikrant step onto the mandap. Vijendra is already seated, which Kashyap takes the seat where Giridhar would have sat. The priests chant louder as the bride and groom take their seats, and horns blow to honour their arrival.

Nandini sits to her son's right, and Indrani takes her place to Idhika's left. She glances at the guests, who have turned up in their finest garments, and gold and diamonds and rubies and sapphires all glitter in the warm morning sun.

They had dressed the same at her wedding, which had taken place in Naavipur. Her father, Lord Satwik, had invited all the noble families from the five kingdoms to attend. Gifts had been presented, and she had known her worth to them then. She may have become a Princess, but they saw her for what she was. An upstart marrying above her station.

Now they sit and watch and smile, as her daughter marries a King. How she wishes she could laugh at their fawning faces, but she resists the urge, for such pettiness would be beneath her. There is one face that she would have liked to smirk back at, though, but the man is missing.

Lord Jayendu.

He had written last night, begging the King's leave to skip the event. His spirit was willing, but his body was not, and he meant to return to the comforts of his home in Krasheerpur.

The old man does not wish to witness the failure of his scheming, and Indrani was glad to hear it. She did not want to see his ugly face on such an auspicious day.

I am being unfair. If not for Jayendu, none of this would have been possible. Yet she cannot help herself. The idea may have been his, but it took Vijendra's and her brilliance to see it to fruition.

Her thoughts return to the present. To her daughter, and her son-in-law. Vikrant adores Idhika. She can see it in the way he looks at her, the way he holds her hand. Strangers they are, yet they appear as if they have known each other for many years.

The sight gladdens her. Idhika has not had much joy in her life. But if Vikrant can give her that happiness, along with a few children, then she will consider her daughter's life blessed.

The priests ask them to rise. The guests stand as well, as the garlands are brought out. The frivolity of the occasion is missing. In usual circumstances, the groom's brothers and cousins would come and lift him up and prevent the bride from placing the garland around his neck.

But his brother is in jail, which turns this exchange into a sombre affair. Once they are garlanded, the priests tie the end of Idhika's sari to Vikrant's angavastram. Seven times they will walk around the fire. He will lead the way the first four times, she will lead the way the last three.

Saat pheras, to bind them together for life.

Idhika waits for Vikrant to starts the first phera, but he takes her hand and brings her in step with him. Then they walk.

Together.

Equal.

An audible gasp runs through the guests. No man has ever done this. Not even Vijendra, and he is the only man Indrani knows who would treat his wife as an equal.

Hand in hand, they complete seven circles of the sacred fire. Then, they turn to face the guests. Flowers shower upon them from all sides. Indrani tosses the petals with unbridled glee.

The wedding is over.

Now, the war begins.

CHAPTER SEVENTY

'The Great Battles of Vajrapur.'

Rannveer had first read the book at the age of seven, and it had changed his life forever. A voluminous tome, which recounted every significant war the kingdom had ever fought, and the names and deeds of its brave warriors. General Sudhakar, who defeated King Harish of Triloha in single combat. Prince Suman, who lost his life saving his brother in the Eleven Year War against Naavipur.

But Rannveer's favourite was King Anjuman. From all accounts, a kind and brave man, who was treacherously murdered by Simha and his barbarian horde. His death led to the first of many battles between the two kingdoms, and laid the foundations for the birth of Simhasthal.

One day, we will avenge our murdered King, young Rannveer used to say before he slept each night. The promise grew stronger, as did the boy, who joined the army at the age of sixteen, a tradition his family had kept alive for eleven generations.

Army life offered him contentment, and a sense of duty. I am the protector of my kingdom; he would often say to himself. Not that there were many enemies to protect against. Peace reigned in Saravat, and the only battles they fought were with forest bandits and nomad tribes from distant lands.

He was seventeen when he married his childhood sweetheart, Kruttika, the neighbour's daughter. He had been in love with her from a very young age, and was overjoyed when her father agreed to their match.

Whether the marriage brought him good luck, or if his talent played a part, he could not say. But he rose to the post of Captain very quickly, the youngest ever. Soon, he was twenty-five years of age, respected by his colleagues and his kingdom, happily married, and father to two sons and a daughter, with another child on the way.

Despite all of this, Rannveer could not claim to be content. He longed for the excitement of war, to quench his childish thirst for revenge against the other kingdoms, and he waited for the day when his desire would be realised.

One evening, a messenger arrived with a summons from Lord Jayendu. Rannveer could not refuse. Jayendu was the richest man in the continent, and a close confidante of the King.

He arrived at the palatial mansion at a ghostly hour, and though Jayendu had never met him before, he greeted Rannveer as he would an old friend. There was one other man in the room, and Rannveer bowed to the scion of the house he serves. *Crown Prince Vijendra.*

Rannveer had lost a father to the fever, and had been saddened to learn the Prince's older brothers had been taken as well. But his sorrow had soon turned to joy, when he discovered the character of the man who took their place. Little was known about the young Prince at the time, other than he was a quiet man, strong-willed, father to two sons, babes who never once drew breath.

Fate had dealt Vijendra an unkind hand, but the man was not one to complain. He threw himself into his work, especially when it came to the army. Rannveer was pleased by his revolutionary ideas and strong ideals. "Be ready for battle," he would often say, even though the last major battle in Saravat had taken place five decades ago.

This mattered little to Rannveer. The Prince's words were music to his ears, and he longed for the day when the man would be King.

The three sat to drink.

"What do you make of your duties?" Jayendu asked.

"It is a good life, my lord," Rannveer said. A smile crossed his lips. "And not a very dangerous one."

"You find that boring, don't you?" Vijendra asked.

Did I speak out of turn? "No, My Prince. I did not mean—"

"Captain." Jayendu laid a reassuring hand on his shoulder. "You may speak freely here. Your words will never be repeated outside these walls."

Rannveer looked at the two powerful men. *What do they want from me?* He opted for the safest course.

To speak the truth.

"I do not find it boring, Your Highness," he said. "But I do hope to see real battle in my lifetime."

"Why?" Vijendra asked.

"To right past wrongs," Rannveer said. "My children have been born in peaceful times. But the blood of our ancestors bought that peace. Not blood paid willingly, but spilled by the blades of our enemies. We did not avenge them, and have grown lesser for it."

"I could not have put it better," Jayendu agreed.

"But more importantly," continued Rannveer, his courage overcoming good sense, "I seek it for my children's future. My father was born poorer than his, and my children are likely to end up poorer than I." He addressed Vijendra. "I mean no disrespect to your father, King Dhirendra, or your ancestors. But they have lost us our land, our wealth, and our dignity. And now, things get worse after the fever. The other kingdoms shun us. Trade has disappeared, and poverty grows in its absence. If we do not act soon, Vajrapur will crumble."

A smile broke across Vijendra's face. The Prince did not seem offended. Far from it. He appeared genuinely happy. "You speak the truth, Captain. Colonel Prateek was correct in his assessment of you."

Rannveer's eyes widened. So, his commanding officer had recommended him.

But for what purpose, he wonders.

"You wish to know why you are here," Jayendu said.

"I do," Rannveer admitted.

Jayendu smiled. "Let me put you out of your misery. There will come a time— maybe not for a few years, maybe decades— but there will come a time when Vajrapur will march to war. And when that day comes, we will need loyal men such as yourself to be ready."

Rannveer felt renewed hope beat in his chest. "I am at your service, my lord."

Jayendu rose to his feet. "Then go home with the knowledge that you are not alone. We will remain in touch."

Rannveer stood and bowed to the Prince, then to Jayendu, and took his leave. He rode back to Vajrapur, elated.

For many months after, he met with Vijendra and Jayendu, and with other men dedicated to the cause. Rannveer was surprised by how many answered Jayendu's call. And not just from Vajrapur.

In the meantime, life continued the way it always did, and changed the fortunes of all involved. The King married another noblewoman, Queen Susheela, who soon gave birth to a son, Biraj. A spare, in case anything ever happened to the Crown Prince.

Rannveer had a son as well. Sanket, his third, who quickly become the apple of his eye. Thoughts of war disappeared from his mind when he held his child. He remembered the still births of Vijendra's sons, and knew he could not bear the loss of his own. *You shall grow up in peace*, he would often tell him, *and live a long life*.

Then, the fever returned.

It turned his world upside down. Lord Jayendu lost his wife, and Vijendra his stepmother. The Prince almost died as well, as did his half-brother, with both surviving at the very end.

But Rannveer's son did not. His Sanket, his sweet innocent child, snatched away so soon. The loss was too much to bear. He withdrew from the world, from the army, from the grandiose plans of Vijendra and Jayendu, and disappeared into the Andhakaranya.

Three years he lived there, alone, battling bandits and beasts. Three miserable years tortured by his loss and his anger. Life was cruel, and he longed for it to end.

But it did not, and one fine day, in a moment of madness, he journeyed to Krasheerpur.

To the home of Lord Jayendu.

"Take me back," he said.

Jayendu readily agreed.

And now, here he stands, on the precipice of the war he always desired.

General Rannveer wears his armour and watches his reflection in his bedroom mirror. A tired man stares back at him. Since the day he returned, he has been a loyal soldier, through and through. And look what it has bought him.

A Simhasthali General, to give him commands and lead him in battle.

And a dead son, who unknowingly died for the cause.

He glances at his reflection once more, then leaves his home and rides to the palace. The hour creeps past one in the night, and the road is empty, as he had expected it to be. The city had feasted in celebration of the Princess' wedding, and the madeira had flowed freely all day. Most of them would have retired to bed, either too drunk or too tired.

Perfect.

Rannveer arrives at the palace to find Captain Sambhit waiting with a hundred Vajra soldiers and a hundred Simhasthali soldiers. The poor man looks confused as he awaits the General's orders.

Let me put him out of his misery. "Follow me, Captain," Rannveer commands, then enters the palace.

The guards on duty are surprised to see him walk in, and even more shocked to see him followed by soldiers, half of them Simhasthali. They jump to attention nevertheless. Rannveer calls out to the commander, who runs over

"By order of the King," Rannveer tells him, "The guard is being changed."

A hesitant soldier looks back at him, unsure of what to do.

"Now!" Rannveer hisses with the full force of his authority.

This time, the obedience is immediate. The commander gathers his guards and leads them out of the palace. In silence, Rannveer is pleased to note. Captain Sambhit's men and the Simhasthalis settle into their place. The procedure is repeated on each of the five levels, until the new guards have the run of the palace.

Once he is satisfied, Rannveer returns to the lowest level to find Prince Biraj and King Vikrant waiting for him.

"Is it done?" the Simhasthali asks.

"It is done, Your Majesty," Rannveer says.

"Then I will see to my wife," Vikrant says. A pleased smile breaks across his face. "By now, I am certain she has become the most anxious bride in the history of the world."

Biraj and Rannveer offer him weak smiles, and he walks up the corridors to celebrate his wedding night.

The General watches him go, and shakes his head.

What a wedding night it will be.

CHAPTER SEVENTY-ONE

Has my husband abandoned me?

Idhika glances at the nightcandle. Three hours have passed since her handmaidens had walked her to her new bedchamber. They had giggled and laughed, and passed lewd comments on what awaited her.

But Idhika had not laughed. She had barely smiled. Though she knew what to expect in theory, putting her knowledge to practice seemed daunting, and her heart had beaten faster with each step.

They had helped her onto the bed, draped her pallu over her head, and bowed while still giggling.

"We bid you a good night, Your Majesty," they had said, before leaving Idhika alone to contemplate her new title.

Queen of Simhasthal.

At long last, Vikrant and she are wed, only five days since they first spoke at the pond, two months since they met in the peace tent. So much had happened since, so much had changed. Yet, one thing has not.

She will remain in Vajrapur, a prisoner to her father's ambitions.

She does not dwell on it too much. Far weightier topics consumer her mind. Death, which had preceded this union, and will soon follow it.

A Prince, and a hangman's noose.

She thinks of Indranuj, her brother-in-law now, rotting in a cell somewhere beneath the palace. Did someone have the decency to bring him a plate from the wedding feast? Or would that have rubbed further salt in his wounds?

He must hate her, her family, and she cannot blame him. She wishes none of it had happened. Not King Giridhar's death, nor Captain Dhananjay's, nor the Prince's imprisonment. Still, she is glad for one thing. *Vikrant is my husband.*

She hates him for the decisions he has made, yet she cannot deny his place in her heart. His servility to her father is only matched by his affection for her. Maybe time will prove his actions right. A few years, a decade.

But by then, they will have lost their youth, to children, to the five kingdoms. To duty. Who can say if these feelings will survive?

She chuckles. She cannot say if they will survive the night.

Four hours have passed, yet there has been no sign of him. Idhika tires of the long wait. If only Atishi were here, to keep her company. The last she had seen of her friend was the morning of the wedding, when she had come to convey her best wishes for Idhika's future.

Atishi had looked tired then, and Idhika feels that way now. A noise outside the room distracts her. She wonders if Vikrant has arrived. But the door remains shut, and Idhika remains alone.

She glances at the nightcandle. Only five hours till dawn. Time enough for them to consummate the marriage. Surely, Vikrant does not plan to keep her waiting much longer. It would prove a tough task to achieve on her own.

A few minutes later, the door opens, and Vikrant walks in, dressed in the sherwani he had worn at the feast, with his crown still on his head. Not the one his ancestors wore. No, a new crown, forged by her father, with the bird-shaped continent on its crest. He does not greet her, or even glance in her direction. Instead, he walks right across to the dressing screen at the far corner of the room.

Two people arrive with him. The first is a Simhasthali attendant, one of the many who follow Vikrant around and cater to his every need. The man races behind his King, carrying clothes in his hands.

The second person is someone Idhika knows only too well.

Atishi.

Her friend walks into the room as if she always meant to be there. Idhika is glad to see her. And confused as well.

A smile crosses Atishi's face as she bows. "Your Majesty."

Idhika cannot hold back her curiosity anymore. "What is going on?"

Vikrant's head stares at her from above the screen. Even as he gets changed, he smiles at her. "You might want to change into something more comfortable, Your Majesty. We have somewhere to be, and it will be cumbersome for you to attend in those heavy clothes and jewellery."

Somewhere to be? It is our wedding night. The only place we should be is here, in our bed, naked in one another's arms, she wonders.

"Where do you mean to take me?" she asks.

Vikrant looks at her with kind eyes. "You will know soon enough. For now, I ask only that you trust me." He turns to Atishi. "Help my Queen get dressed."

Atishi opens the dresser, from which she retrieves a simpler sari and blouse. Idhika walks over to the other dressing divider, and remains silent as her friend dresses her.

Once she is ready, she walks out to find Vikrant waiting for her, dressed in everyday clothes. He holds out his hand. "Come with me."

She takes the proffered hand and follows him out of the room, wondering where he plans to lead her. Outside, the Parasu stand guard, along with some Simhasthali soldiers, and their presence surprises her.

Where are the palace guards, she wonders.

The soldiers go down on one knee and clasp their fists against their chests. They salute their King. And Queen. She finds herself getting used to her new title.

Atishi leads the way down many corridors. The Vajra guards are here now, but if they are surprised to see their former Princess out and about on her wedding night, they do not show it. They join the Simhasthalis by going down on one knee and clasping their fists against their chests.

At long last, they arrive at their destination. Atishi holds the door open for them. Idhika hesitates and looks at Vikrant. "Why are we here?"

Vikrant smiles. "To build the future you desired."

Still uncertain, Idhika walks past Atishi. Inside, her confusion grows by leaps and bounds. In the room, comfortably seated and sipping madeira, nine people sit. Ranimaa Nandini, General

Kashyap, Colonel Gautam, Princess Gayathri, Lord Atulya, Lord Ayushmann, General Rannveer, and two Princes.

Prince Biraj. *My chacha, who is her father's most devoted soldier.*

And Prince Indranuj. *My brother-in-law, who should be in prison.*

Vikrant offers her a cup of madeira. She does not accept it. "What is going on here?" she demands to know.

Vikrant starts to answer, but Biraj stops him. "Please, My King, allow me to answer."

My King? Idhika cannot believe her ears.

Biraj offers her a chair. "Your Majesty," he says formally, "Please sit and listen. All will be revealed."

Idhika finds herself taking the chair, and accepting the cup Vikrant had offered. Biraj sits by her side, and tells her a story she can scarcely believe.

Once he is done, she turns to Vikrant.

Still dazed and unable to come to grips with this new reality, she asks him, "What do you mean to do now?"

"With your permission," he says, "I mean to confront your father."

"And then?" she asks.

His voice echoes his steely resolve. "And then, end his reign."

She blinks, and wonders as to her heart's feelings. It feels numb within her chest, and she cannot say if it turns this way with grief or indifference. She searches her mind, and its answer is clear.

He stole your life. She nods her head. "Let me know when it is done."

CHAPTER SEVENTY-TWO

The leaves do not stir.

It's the kind of weather that has always bothered Vijendra. He stands in the balcony outside his bedchamber, praying for a breeze to blow. It does not. He sighs. All the power in the world, yet this is something he cannot command.

Nature has always been the only thing to make him feel small. From a very young age, Vijendra knew his life would be greater than what the gods had written for him. There was a time when he was only a thirdborn son, forever under the rule of two older brothers, his destiny to be the Prince forgotten by the ages.

Until he seized it for himself.

He turns his thoughts away from his destiny, towards more pleasant times, when life was simple and his hands were not stained with blood.

The only times he can remember were the ones in Simhasthal. With Giridhar and Kashyap, playing in the orchards, fighting in the courtyard, swimming in the river. He misses Giridhar. An older brother, he had called himself on the Laalkhet, minutes before Vijendra took his life. He had been right. He was the brother who had taught Vijendra more than anyone else.

Well, almost anyone else.

Try as he might, his mind keeps returning to Jayendu. The old man who had spotted his potential when he was only seven.

"One day, you will be more than a king," he had told him. "You will be an emperor."

Prophetic words, which had pleased the young boy, as Jayendu had known it would. For a seven-year-old, the fanciful dream of becoming an emperor was all too powerful.

But it had not remained a dream. It had grown in his mind, larger and larger, until Vijendra found he had no choice but to fulfil it.

But now, at the end, he wonders if it had all been worth it.

Thousands have died, and thousands more will die.

He glances at the nightcandle. Only a few hours remain till dawn, and sleep still does not arrive. Maybe it won't tonight. The prospect of the coming war excites him more than he could imagine.

A gasp sounds inside his bedchamber. *Strange.* Vijendra had thought Indrani to be asleep. He enters their bedchambers, and his eyes blaze with anger. *What is he doing here?*

Ayushmann stands with a broad smile across his face, and a sword at Indrani's neck. Vijendra moves to fetch his sword, but Ayushmann's voice calls out to him.

"I would not bother, Your Majesty," he says. "The General has your sword."

Vijendra whips around, and his anger disappears. The Simhasthali did not lie, but he had failed to mention which General. Vijendra expected to find Kashyap standing behind him. Instead, Rannveer stands there, the King's sword in one hand, his own blade in the other. The implication of his presence and his actions can mean only one thing. *Jayendu has switched sides.*

Alarm bells ring in Vijendra's mind. Does the old man mean to support Theeran and Sreedharan over him? Impossible. Jayendu's fondness for Sreedharan as heir to Saravat is only matched by his dislike of Theeran's indiscernible qualities.

Vijendra's first thought is for his wife, whose faith in him keeps her calm, even with a sword at her neck. His second thought is for his daughter, who might not see the dawn after her wedding night. He then thinks of Vikrant, who at his moment must lie beside Idhika, content and peaceful that their future is bright.

And finally, he thinks of the sons the two of them might have had, the sons who would take the place of the ones he and Indrani could never have. The sons who would one day rule Saravat.

Maybe they still will.

I am not dead yet. He smirks. "So, my dear General, it appears you have played the game better than I expected. Tell me, how much gold did Jayendu offer you to betray me for the Trilohans?"

A third voice calls out, one he does not expect.

"He does not betray you for gold, Your Majesty," Vikrant says. "In fact, some might say it is you who betrayed him."

Vijendra turns to see the Simhasthali step out of the shadows. The man he had sat with on the mandap this morning. The man who married his daughter.

The man who would have been his heir.

Vijendra questions himself for the first time in his life. Jayendu has thrown his support behind the boy, that much is clear. But against him? *Why?*

"What is the meaning of this?" Vijendra thunders.

"Forgive the intrusion, Your Majesty," Vikrant says, "But I believe the time has come for us to lay all our cards on the table."

"What cards?" asks Vijendra, trying to sound aloof.

Vikrant smiles. He reaches into his tunic, retrieves a small vial and places it on the table. The liquid inside glows an eerie green.

Vijendra's face turns pale. *They know.*

His mind returns to the twelve-year-old boy who had sat in Jayendu's study and spoken of the future.

"There are two types of people in the world," Jayendu had said. "The dreamers who believe in the impossible, and the realists who know it can never be."

"Which one must I be?" Vijendra had asked.

"You must be the unknown third," Jayendu had replied. "The one who makes the impossible possible."

Vijendra had done so, and he had sacrificed everything for it. His mind, his body, and in the end, his soul as well. At the age of seventeen, he had come up with a plan. *So simple. So effective.*

At first, Jayendu had balked at the idea. *It was necessary,* Vijendra had argued, *if they were to succeed.* Jayendu had eventually come around to his way of thinking. The old man had found the potion master and tasked him with creating the perfect poison. And once it had been made, they had put the plan in motion. *Dark was our sacrifice. Great were its rewards.*

Rannveer confronts his King, and death dances in his eyes. "You killed my son."

Vijendra does not reply.

The calm deserts Indrani, and confusion arises in its place. "My love," she says, "What does he speak of?"

Vijendra turns to his wife. His love, his life, from whom he never kept any secret. Except this. Even she would have said he went too far. How could she understand? None of them can. In the pursuit of greatness, there is no sacrifice too great.

Vijendra looks away from Indrani and back at Rannveer. "I ordered his death. But it was a necessary sacrifice."

"No, Your Majesty," Rannveer thunders. "You did not just sacrifice my son's life. You sacrificed the life of my wife, who weeps for him to this day. You sacrificed my peace of mind, my soul, which was ripped from me as I lit his pyre. Not a day goes by that I do not see his face. Pale, grey, the life sucked out of him. On your command."

Vijendra ignores him. Indrani looks afraid. He must see to her. He walks over and takes her in his arms. Ayushmann withdraws, but keeps his sword at the ready.

"Are you okay, my love?" Vijendra asks.

Indrani nods. "I do not understand what is going on."

Is she brave enough to live with my sins? "The General speaks of his son, whom I had poisoned when he was only three months old."

Indrani is horrified. "Why would you command such an act?" *Why indeed?*

Vikrant answers for him. "The fever."

Vijendra nods his head. "The fever."

It had not been difficult to achieve. Armed with the poison from the potion master, his loyal followers had spread it throughout Dhaningarh, and a few neighbouring villages and towns. A few drops in a cup, a few drops in a soup, a few bottles laced with death. The fever spread like wildfire.

Ten died the first week. Thirty the next. Within a month, three hundred were dead. The time came to put their plan in action.

"Once enough people had died," Vijendra says, "We spread the poison in my brothers' families. The results were guaranteed."

They perished within a week. His brothers, their wives, three sons and two daughters. His father had been distraught, as had his mother. Yet for Vijendra, it had been a triumphant moment.

"The children?" asks Indrani, still in the thrall of her initial shock. "You killed them as well?"

"The line of succession had to be clear," says Vijendra, without a hint of remorse. "I had to be the Crown Prince. And there could be no suspicion of my ascent. People had to believe it was my destiny. And they did, especially after I survived the fever myself. All of them, including my father, believed fortune favoured me."

"But my love, the children were—" Indrani starts.

Vijendra stops her. "Greatness requires sacrifice."

"What sacrifice have you made, Your Majesty?" Ayushmann scoffs. "You have demanded blood, yet never shed it yourself."

A sad smile breaks across Vijendra's face. "I sacrificed my daughter. Her childhood, her innocence, her hopes and dreams. I cut them out from her heart when she was a child, and tossed them to the flames."

"And you call that your sacrifice?" Vikrant asks.

Vijendra nods his head. "One day, you will be a father. Ask me then if it was not my sacrifice."

"I doubt you will see that day, Your Majesty," Vikrant says.

"I doubt that as well," Vijendra agrees.

He kisses his wife, knowing he feels the touch of her lips for the very last time. She looks at him, uncomprehending, as he leaves her side and walks over to Vikrant.

"Take care of my daughter," he says. "Treat her well, better than I did."

"I will, Your Majesty," Vikrant says. "Do not worry yourself on that account."

"Good, good," Vijendra mutters. "I suppose you will consider your father's death avenged now, and return to Simhasthal."

Vikrant shakes his head and smiles. "No, Your Majesty. I have promised Lord Jayendu that I would take over your mantle. Saravat needs an Emperor."

Not for the first time that night, Vijendra is surprised. "How did you convince the old man?"

"I showed him I could be even more ruthless than you," Vikrant says. "It wasn't easy, but he now knows it to be true."

"I see." Vijendra smiles and clasps him on the shoulder. "I chose you for the wrong reasons, but in the end, my choice was right."

"It was," Vikrant agrees.

"One last favour, Your Majesty," Vijendra says. "I beg you to treat my wife with the honour she deserves."

Vikrant nods his head in agreement. "She will remain Ranimaa of Vajrapur, comfortable and respected till the end of her days."

Vijendra bows his head in gratitude, then turns to Rannveer. "I am ready, General."

"No," Indrani shouts. She jumps off the bed and grabs his hand before anyone else can react.

"My love—" Vijendra starts to say.

She does not let him finish. "In life and death."

Her grip is strong, her eyes unwavering. He knows she means it, and no words will dissuade her. He squeezes her hand, and nods his head. "In life and death."

Rannveer turns to look at Vikrant, sees him assent, then returns to Vijendra and Indrani. "This way, Your Majesties."

He leads them through the palace. Vijendra notes the presence of Simhasthali guards among his own. Rannveer must have placed his loyal men everywhere, and Vikrant's men add to his numbers.

A bloodless coup.

Well, not entirely.

They enter the prison to discover Lord Chandran's body hanging from the ceiling. The Simhasthali's eyes pop out from their sockets, and his tongue hangs limp and blue. The smell of shit and piss stains the air, and Indrani wrinkles her nose.

Rannveer leads them to their cell, thankfully far from the sight of Chandran's body. They enter and take their seats on the cold hard floor. The steel gate clangs shut behind them, and Rannveer turns the key in the lock.

"You were a faithful companion, General," Vijendra says to him. "I thank you for your service."

Rannveer bows. "Goodbye, Your Majesties. I pray the gods have mercy on your souls."

He leaves, and they sit in the loneliness, each to their thoughts. Vijendra wonders what manner of execution they face. An axe to chop off their heads, a noose to snap their necks, or an assassin, to sneak into their cells under the darkness of night and slit their throats.

He does not have to think for long. Footsteps approach, and the man he had hoped not to see peers at them through the bars.

"Hello Biraj," Vijendra greets his brother.

Sad eyes stare back at him. "You killed my mother."

"I killed thousands," Vijendra admits. "Your mother was one of them."

"But you let me live," Biraj says.

"I let you live," Vijendra nods his head. "It was Jayendu who convinced me. Your death was unnecessary, your mother's was. She would have always eyed the throne for you, and we could not have that."

Biraj nods his understanding. "You were like a father to me. Queen Indrani like a mother. I loved you more than anything in this world."

"And we loved you," Indrani says. "You were to be our heir, the man who would rule the land. But you turned out to be a soldier, a man who obeyed." Hurt tinges her voice. "If you had grown up different, none of this would need to happen. But still, we loved you, more than we cared to admit. You were the son we never had."

A lonely tear rolls down Biraj's cheek. "I will always be the son you never had." He bows low to Vijendra. "Goodbye, dada." He bows to Indrani. "Goodbye, maa."

"Live long, my son," Indrani blesses him.

He leaves them alone in the dank cell. Vijendra holds the bars and watches him go. Biraj disappears around the corner and his footsteps soon fade away. New footsteps arrive, growing louder by the second, until the reach the end of the stairs. *The Parasu.*

Two masked soldiers walk with purpose towards the royals and enter the cell. Vijendra backs away and looks at his wife.

Indrani shows no sign of fear. In fact, he has never seen her look braver. She takes his hand and kneels on the floor.

The Parasu draw their swords, and their dark eyes stare at Vijendra from behind their masks. For some strange reason, the first line of their oath rushes into his mind.

Dead we are now, death to our enemy.

Prophetic words, soon to be fulfilled. They will now get their vengeance, for the death of their fallen comrades, and of their beloved King Giridhar.

A smile breaks across Vijendra's face. *Soon, I will be with my old friend.*

He turns to Indrani for the last time in his life. "Forgive me, my love," he says. "I failed you."

He kisses her softly, and she kisses him back, her tears flowing freely. She does not seek to deny his guilt, nor assuage it.

It would serve no purpose.

The Parasu raise their swords. Vijendra closes his eyes and bows his head, ready for the cold kiss of steel. He feels it upon his neck, and a final thought enters his mind before the light dies out from his life.

His end heralds the dawn of a new promise. A new oath, to be taken up by the Parasu, and the peoples of Vajrapur and Simhasthal.

For Vikrant, for Saravat.

CHAPTER SEVENTY-THREE

Divesh feels his stomach churn as he rides to the palace. The day had not begun well for the Vajra messenger. At dawn, he had answered a knock on his door, to find a soldier carrying a summons.

From General Rannveer.

What could he want this early in the morning, Divesh had wondered, and so he had asked. The soldier could only share rumours, which Divesh could scarcely believe. A coup at midnight. King Vijendra, deposed. Queen Indrani, imprisoned. Their daughter—now wife to King Vikrant—a prisoner in her marital bedchamber.

Worried, he had quickly set out, and now arrives at the palace to find the guards have changed. New faces stand watch, half of them Simhasthali. The Parasu are there as well, observing him behind black masks as he makes his way to the General's office.

He knocks on the door, which is almost immediately opened by Rannveer. Divesh is surprised to see the General's eyes are red and puffy. Clearly, the man has not slept all night.

Rannveer hands over a scroll, with the seal of a roaring lion. *The Simhasthali seal.* He issues a simple instruction. "Deliver this to Lord Jayendu. No one else."

This worries Divesh more than the lion seal. Up until now, messages were always handed over to the staff, never to the lords. But he does not comment. He bows and leaves.

He usually allows himself time on the road to Krasheerpur, to take in the scenery and enjoy the country air. But fear grips him today, and he rides hard for the village. He arrives in a little under an hour, and is greeted by smiling faces of dairy farmers moving about their morning's work. He does not return their smiles, as he rides all the way across town and passes through the gates of Lord Jayendu's house.

Datta walks out to greet him. "Welcome, Divesh. It is good to see you after so many weeks. How are you?"

"I am good, saheb," he replies, a nervous edge to his voice. "By your kindness, and Lord Jayendu's."

Datta smiles, and holds out a hand for the message. Divesh swallows hard. *This is too important for the likes of you or me.*

"Forgive me, saheb," says Divesh, with as much servility as he can muster. "General Rannveer commanded me to deliver this personally to Lord Jayendu. No one else."

Datta regards him suspiciously, and Divesh wonders if he has taken offence. He is pleased when the reply remains friendly.

"I see," Datta says. "Come with me."

Divesh is led into the house. He has never been inside, and finds it less lavish than the palace, but more tastefully decorated. At least, the gold lightning bolts are missing. Datta leaves him in the study, then goes to fetch his master. Divesh remains standing, uncomfortable and nervous.

Lord Jayendu arrives a few minutes later, holding Datta's arm for support. He plops himself into an armchair before turning his attention to Divesh.

"What is the message?" he asks.

With trembling hands, Divesh hands over the scroll. Jayendu breaks the seal, then unrolls the paper. A few seconds later, tears roll down his eyes.

A stunned Divesh cannot believe what he sees. The richest man in the land, openly weeping. A moment later, the realisation hits him.

The rumours are true. *The King is dead.*

EPILOGUE

A dejected Kartik makes the long, lonely walk from his chambers to his father's office. He does not wish to be the bearer of bad news, but his spy had not given him much choice.

The man had left only a few minutes ago, after delivering his report to the Prince.

'King Vijendra is dead.

King Vikrant takes his place.

The war for Saravat continues.'

This is not what he had hoped for. Still, the death of Vijendra brings him some joy. The world is better off without him.

He arrives at his father's office, hesitant to enter. King Theeran will not be pleased. When there were two Kings in the enemy camp, there was always a chance that they would tussle for power. In war, a confused army is easier prey.

But now, Vikrant has united two kingdoms under his rule. Kartik would love to find out how he did it. He knows the Simhasthali King well, and did not think him capable.

None did.

He can dither no longer, and knocks on the door. A gruff voice answers. "Enter."

He opens the door and walks through. King Theeran sits

at his desk, quill in hand, a sheaf of paper in front of him. He looks up at his son.

"What is it?" He demands to know.

"A message from Vajrapur," replies Kartik, refusing to meet his father's eyes.

Theeran is alert at once. "Is Vijendra on the march?"

Kartik shakes his head. "Vijendra is dead."

The smile on Theeran's face is the happiest Kartik has ever seen. Unfortunately, he knows it won't remain long.

"This is great news," an overjoyed Theeran declares.

No, it is not. "Baba, there is more. King Vikrant takes his place. Our spy reports that he plotted the death of Vijendra, and now seeks to crown himself Emperor of Saravat."

A stunned Theeran grips the arms of his chair. A few seconds pass, as he tries to recover and gather his thoughts. "So, there will be war?"

"There will be war," Kartik says.

Theeran's fury rages like a storm. "So be it. We will ready our forces. When will the Barabos Battalion be here?"

"In a month," Kartik replies.

Theeran nods his head and looks away. Kartik understands it to be a dismissal. He turns to leave, when the door bursts open, and a chill runs down his spine.

A tall man walks in, dressed in a red dhoti with a white angavastram loosely thrown across his naked torso. His jaw is off-putting, set in a permanent half-smile, half-scowl, yet his eyes are mesmerising, light brown with flecks of green.

Prince Sreedharan strides in purposefully and towers over his younger brother.

"So, what have I missed?"

Glossary

1. ***Aarti thali:*** A plate containing vermillion, a few grains of rice, and a lit wick-lamp, typically used in a ceremony to welcome a guest.
2. ***Angavastram:*** A cloth that hangs from the shoulder of the man, or is draped around the torso.
3. ***Arrack:*** An alcoholic drink made from palm, rice, or sugarcane.
4. ***Asana:*** A pose or posture in yoga practice.
5. ***Ayuralaya:*** An ayurvedic infirmary.
6. ***Ayushman bhav:*** A traditional blessing which means "May you live long".
7. ***Baarat:*** A procession of guests who accompany the groom to the wedding.
8. ***Beta:*** A word used to address one's son.
9. ***Chacha:*** A word used to address father's brother.
10. ***Dada:*** A word used to address the older brother.
11. ***Dadi:*** A word used to address the paternal grandmother.
12. ***Dhol:*** A native Indian percussion instrument.

13. ***Didi:*** A word used to address the older sister.
14. ***Ghee:*** Clarified butter.
15. ***Kabaddi:*** A game of Indian origin where players raid the enemy territory.
16. ***Kukri:*** A short knife with a curved blade.
17. ***Langot:*** A loin cloth styled as underwear and primarily worn by men.
18. ***Madeira:*** Alcohol.
19. ***Mandap:*** The decorated canopy under which wedding ceremonies take place.
20. ***Myna:*** A small bird found in South Asia.
21. ***Pallu:*** The loose end of the sari that hangs from the shoulder.
22. ***Paratha:*** A stuffed flatbread made of wheat.
23. ***Rakshasa:*** Demon.
24. ***Sari:*** An unstitched garment worn by Indian women.
25. ***Sherwani:*** A knee-length, long-sleeved coat buttoned up to the neck, worn by royalty.
26. ***Vaidyas:*** Physicians who have studied ayurveda.
27. ***Veerbhadrasana & Ardhachandrasana:*** The warrior pose and the half-moon pose, respectively, in yoga.

ACKNOWLEDGEMENTS

I would like to express my gratitude to the people who helped me create this book.

To *the amazing team at Nu Voice Press & Hubhawks,* I want to thank you for the release and promotions. A special thanks to *Vedika Paliwal* for her superb editing, and to *Tarun Singh Negi* for outstanding cover and map design.

To *Priyank Bengali,* a big thank you for designing the sigils for the different kingdoms. You can check out Priyank's work on his Instagram pages *@friyank* and *@boldinc703.*

To *Ketul Patel,* I will forever be grateful for your creation of the first map of Saravat. To view Ketul's insane portfolio, visit his Instagram handle *@limnoland.*

To *Madhavi Kalra,* thanks for all the help in getting the nuances right. For those who love learning about culture, you can follow her Instagram handle *@culture.collage.*

To *my friends and family,* thanks for the tremendous support and love.

To *my cousin Anup,* a big thank you for the guidance, and above all, for pushing me to set all other worries aside and focus on getting this book out.

To *my niece Avni,* a big sorry that I did not write a book for your age group. I promise, it is on my list.

To *my mother,* the biggest thank you for four decades of your patience with my nonsense. Seriously, you deserve an award for this singular achievement.

And to *Mira,* my partner-in-crime, whom I probably owe a million dinners and vacations for ignoring her as much as I did while I completed this book. I will make up for it.

And then, it's on to Book Two.

ABOUT THE AUTHOR

Manoj was born and raised in Mumbai. After graduating from St. Xavier's with a degree in Statistics, he switched paths and joined an advertising agency instead. Over the next twenty years, he worked at some of the biggest agencies in the country and created memorable campaigns for major companies.

But the storytelling bug was something that he couldn't shake off. He quit advertising to pursue his passion full time, and the result is *The Crown of Blood*, the first book of The Saravat Chronicles.

When he is not writing, Manoj loves to travel and discover new cuisines. He is also an ardent supporter of Arsenal FC.